East of Nowhere

East of Nowhere

ROBERT CHALMERS

Atlantic Books
London

First published in Great Britain in 2004 by Atlantic Books,
an imprint of Grove Atlantic Ltd.

Copyright © Robert Chalmers 2004

The moral right of Robert Chalmers to be identified as the author of this work has been asserted in accordance with the Copyright, Designs and Patents Act of 1988.

This novel is entirely a work of fiction. The names, characters and incidents portrayed in it are the work of the author's imagination. Any resemblance to actual persons, living or dead, events or localities, is entirely coincidental.

Every effort has been made to trace or contact all copyright holders. The publishers will be pleased to make good any omissions or rectify any mistakes brought to their attention at the earliest opportunity.

All rights reserved. No part of this publication may be reproduced, stored in a retrieval system, or transmitted in any form or by any means, electronic, mechanical, photocopying, recording, or otherwise, without the prior permission of both the copyright owner and the above publisher of this book.

The author and publisher wish to thank the following for permission to quote from copyrighted material: A.P.Watt on behalf of The National Trust for Places of Historic Interest or Natural Beauty for 'The Ballad of East and West' (Kipling); Doug Smith for 'Home With Me' (Chumbawamba) © Chumbawamba; Disney Publishing Worldwide for 'You Can Fly! You Can Fly! You Can Fly!' (Cahn/Fain) © Walt Disney Music Company, 1951; Butch Hancock, administered by Bug Music for 'She Never Spoke Spanish to Me' (Hancock); Sony/ATV Music Publishing Limited for 'Yesterday' (Lennon/McCartney) ©1965 Northern Songs. All right reserved; Warner Bros. Publications U.S. Inc. for 'Rednecks' (Newman) © 1974, 1975 WB Music Corp. (Renewed) All rights reserved; Warren Zevon Living Trust for 'My Ride's Here' (Zevon) © 2002 Zevon Music, Fled Is That Music. All rights reserved.

ISBN 1 84354 297 8

Printed in Great Britain by William Clowes Ltd., Beccles, Suffolk

Atlantic Books
An imprint of Grove Atlantic Ltd
Ormond House
26–27 Boswell Street
London WC1N 3JZ

'Today we were unlucky, but remember we only have to be lucky once. You have to be lucky always.'
Provisional IRA message to Margaret Thatcher, 13 October 1984

'Lost: Tom Cat. One eye, one ear, no tail, recently neutered. Answers to the name of Lucky.'
Ken Dodd and others

'Behind the moon, beyond the rain... many, many miles east of nowhere.'
Trailer for *The Wizard of Oz*

East of Nowhere

When he looked back on that morning, as he did, time after time, he could never understand how he'd forgotten to be discreet. Adultery had become a discipline to Miller, in the pursuit of which he'd learned – like a seasoned assassin, or a bomb disposal expert – that brief moments of precious intensity were best secured through scrupulous attention to detail and diligent forward planning, and that impulse was his enemy.

That Wednesday, though, some new instinct settled on him. It happened abruptly, in the way that a man might walk along the same clifftop path every morning for twenty years then, one day, for no reason, glance down into the void and step off.

It happened – every time he thought of it, the memory horrified him more – in the office. And not just in the office, but in Bowker's Cupboard. He'd worked with Charlotte, his temporary assistant, for two weeks without really noticing her at all. But that morning, just before seven, as he settled behind his desk, sifting through a pile of irregular expenses claims, she was stretching up to reach some box files on the far side of the room, with her back to him. He watched her. It was the first of May, and she was wearing a beige cotton jacket and a cornflower-blue skirt that finished just above her knee.

He stopped scrutinizing journalists' invoices for first class flights, luxury hotels and other privileges he had prohibited on the morning he took over as editor, and instead found himself staring absent-mindedly at her calves. He thought about the time, during the war, when British women used to paint a false seam on the back of their legs, to simulate the nylon stockings they didn't have. When the weather was warm and overcast, like today, he wondered, did they go out unpainted, on the grounds that it was too hot to wear real stockings? Could a woman paint those lines herself? If she was left-handed, would the left leg be harder to do than the other? Would she use a mirror? If she didn't paint her legs herself, then who did? And if you were painting seams for someone else, would you use some sort of flexible straight edge, or draw the line freehand? And what with? Eyeliner? Ink?

He noticed that she'd stopped what she was doing and she'd turned round to face him, as if waiting for a response. He was staring fixedly at her kneecaps. His eyes rose, and met hers.

'I'm sorry,' he said. 'I was miles away.'

He rubbed his eyes, pressing into them with the index finger and thumb of his left hand. Even with his eyelids closed, her knees were still there, like twin circles burned on to a sunbather's retinas.

'Oh really?' she said.

She walked out of the room and, as she passed him, she squeezed the top of his arm. He watched her cross the editorial floor and open the door to Bowker's Cupboard. She switched on the light, which was on the outside, and went in. After a couple of moments, she closed the door behind her.

Charlotte didn't know she was in Bowker's Cupboard. She was new. She called it the Stationery Room. Bowker had left the paper two years earlier and the storeroom had been his preferred venue for seducing vulnerable young women employees when the building was quiet. He'd had a lock fitted on the inside of the door. It was a small sliding chrome bar, which had been fixed so low, just a few inches from the ground, that the general run of visitors – the kind who came to the stationery cupboard for stationery – wouldn't ever have noticed it was there. Bowker had found the lock in France, where it had been electrically wired to switch on the light in a public toilet, once a customer drew it across into the closed position. The difference with Bowker's lock was that, once you were in the cupboard, sliding it into the locked position turned the light not on, but off.

For all his resourcefulness, Bowker, like most philanderers, had become careless. For months before he was dismissed, his cupboard had become a standing joke. Even now, among staff of longer standing, any reference to fetching stationery or stamps had become tainted by crude innuendo.

Miller got up and walked out of his glass-walled office. The editor was always in the building by seven and it was generally half an hour before any of his journalists were at their desks. If he'd met anyone as he crossed the main floor he would have turned back but, as luck would have it, every desk was empty.

He reached the door of Bowker's Cupboard and stood facing it. The fire doors leading to the main staircase were just a couple of yards away, to his left. Realizing they might open at any moment, he tried to think of some plausible reason as to why he might have been there, and couldn't. He heard what sounded like footsteps coming up the stairs. Flustered, he opened the cupboard door without knocking, then closed it behind him. She turned to face him. She was startled, and put her hand on her collarbone, like an actress in a silent film. 'You made me jump,' she said.

He put his hand on her right shoulder. She turned her head to look at his hand and he saw her notice the jagged scar running along the inside edge of his slightly deformed first finger. He felt suddenly uneasy and, without thinking – to distract her, as much as anything – put his left hand on her other shoulder. She leaned forward and put her arms loosely around his hips. 'What's happening here?' she said. Then, to his surprise and relief, she kissed him.

He took off her jacket. They lay down with an awkward urgency, like strangers paired in a three-legged race. She was almost six foot, three inches taller than he was. Bowker's Cupboard was eight foot square, with shelves covering every area of wall except the door. There were boxes below the bottom shelf, which was no more than a foot off the ground. She couldn't lie down until he'd pulled a battered old box of air-mail stickers out from under the shelf on the far wall. That gave her the room to stretch her feet out. He lay down next to her, on his back, staring at the boxes of envelopes, Sellotape and printer cartridges. She took his left hand. With his right, he felt for Bowker's switch. When he drew the bolt across, the light went off and the only illumination was from the skylight in the room's high ceiling. Through it came a dim shaft of blue light. It felt like night.

'You've been here before then,' she said.

'No,' he told her.

He took off her skirt. In a matter-of-fact way, as if for a medical examination, she slipped off her pants.

He stared at the barely discernible line of fine blonde hair that ran down her abdomen and noticed that, unlike most women he'd known – women like his wife, who spent most weekdays in health clubs in the Home Counties – she didn't have what he'd learned to call a bikini line. Any object, it occurred to him, becomes even more intensely itself when placed in an unfamiliar setting. In this cupboard – far more than would have been possible in any masseuse's bedroom furnished with satin sheets, low lights and essential oils – his temporary assistant radiated an unimaginable level of erotic charge. He gazed down, motionless, at this conspicuous woman's thighs, and said nothing. He was interrupted by her undoing his belt and pulling down his trousers and shorts.

'Hey,' she said.

She pulled him on to her, and took him by the hips, and held him still. She twisted under him.

'There,' she said. 'Morning Mr Miller.'

Thirty seconds later he was lying in her arms, panting, exhausted, and already overtaken by shame and foreboding. Her breathing was steady and unaltered. She was still wearing her blouse. He was still wearing his jacket.

'Hey,' she said again, noticing his appalled expression. 'It wasn't that terrible for you was it?'

'I'm sorry,' he said.

'It's OK.'

'I'm really, really sorry. I've never done anything like this before.'

She said nothing.

'I haven't,' he repeated.

In another place he would have seduced her again – if seduce was a verb that had any meaning in Bowker's Cupboard – with gentleness, affection, and a sort of fleeting sincerity. But now, as he inhaled through his mouth to quieten his deep breathing, he could hear the creak of shoe-leather less than a foot from his ear, and the squeak of the fire door. Though they were locked in, if anybody so much as tried the cupboard door, he was finished.

He lay there, next to her, on his back, staring up at the skylight, paralysed by a creeping awareness of his situation. He began to imagine a face appearing through the glass above him, and felt a surge of panic. He tried to concentrate on the writing on the cardboard boxes: Self-Adhesive. Urgent. Fragile. Do Not Bend. Important.

He tried to think. It was still early. Bowker's Cupboard was very near the fire door. With luck they should be able to dart through it, and into the stairwell, unnoticed. But there was no way of knowing who they might meet once they were on the stairs.

They got to their feet and dressed, face to face. As she put her jacket back on, he could feel himself starting to sweat with fear. When he looked down to do up his belt, he was still breathing heavily. Something about the action made him feel like a rapist.

Charlotte took charge of him like a mother. She straightened his tie which, like his jacket, he had not thought to remove. She adjusted his lapels. He made a half-hearted attempt to reciprocate, and touched her breast by accident. She gripped him by the wrist.

'Listen,' she said. 'I'll go out first, on to the stairs. If it's OK, I'll cough.'

He bent down to open the bottom lock but, before he could reach it, she'd slid it open, deftly, with her foot. The room was flooded with unforgiving fluorescent light, like a pub at closing time. She listened at the door. 'Right,' she said, and slipped out.

What if it's not OK? Miller thought. He was silently promising the same God he hadn't implored since he was eight that he would never, never be unfaithful again, if only he could exit Bowker's Cupboard undetected, when he heard a theatrical cough. He burst through the fire doors wearing the look of a hedgehog going through the sound barrier, and met her on the stairs. They were alone. There were no footsteps. 'We'll go up to the canteen,' she said, 'and we'll get some coffee. Then we'll get the lift down. It's over. Relax.'

The canteen, which was on the next floor, was full of staff having breakfast before settling down at their desks for the day. Coming in, he sensed a familiar, reassuring deference. Conversations became hushed. People who had documents on their table started to look at them. The drinks counter was at the far end of the room. He followed Charlotte as she picked her way through the tables. They queued, collected the drinks, which she paid for, then sat at a table.

'Can I ask you something?' she said.

Miller started to squirm.

'The thing is,' she went on. 'I've forgotten what I went in there for. Do you know?'

'No.'

'Do you think my memory's going?' She laughed, awkwardly.

'No,' he said, wishing that it was. 'Don't get paranoid.'

He followed her out.

'See?' she said, once they were in the lift, with the doors closed, alone again. 'Easy.'

'Didn't you notice anything when we were coming out of the canteen?' he asked her.

'No.'

'They were giving me weird looks.'

'Now who's paranoid?' she said.

Walking back across the editorial floor, he saw there were two people on the foreign desk, next to his office: Simon Feasey, the foreign editor, and his deputy, Catherine Davies. As they greeted him, Miller kept his eyes on them, looking for any sign of an unusual reaction, and found none.

They turned back to their work. The editor leaned over them as they examined a possible headline for the Overseas News in Brief column.

'Lagos: Hertfordshire mother of three assaulted by corrupt African police.' There was a picture of the victim, a white woman in her thirties.

'It's a few letters over,' said Feasey. 'What could we cut?'

'African,' said Davies. 'Where the hell do you think corrupt police would come from in Nigeria – Wolverhampton?'

Feasey turned back to his screen and began to make the alteration.

'No Simon,' Miller said. 'Leave African. Cut "of three". '

'Why?' said Davies, with a rising inflexion that bordered on insolence.

'I don't know,' Miller said. 'It just has a nicer ring to it.'

'Even if,' he heard Davies mutter, 'it is fucking tautologous.'
'What?' he asked her.
'It repeats the obvious,' she said.
'I know what tautology is, love,' he told her. 'Come and have a chat to me some time. You tell me about your first-class English degree and I'll tell you about mine.'

He went back into his office and sat down at his desk. He was comfortable here. Ten years ago Miller had been a news reporter who drank too much; he'd reinvented himself, under his wife's steadying influence, as an editorial executive. The paper's main enemies – paedophiles, suicide bombers, rapists, crack dealers, socialists and asylum seekers, bogus or otherwise – had coalesced, in his mind, into a coherent unit of evil, whose members worked together and shared information; a coalition it had become his mission to defeat by whatever means was required. On the wall above his head was a framed cartoon he'd brought with him from his last office. It showed a gladiator standing over the body of his terrified rival, his foot on his windpipe. The caption read: *Numquam calcite hominem humi casum; quid melius tempus?* 'Find out,' Miller would say, when anybody asked him what it meant. Nobody had.

On top of the pile of papers on his desk was a resubmitted expenses invoice from a golfing correspondent, Peter Axon. It came to three hundred and thirty one pounds and nineteen pence and he'd rejected it first time round on the grounds that fifteen pounds of the money had been spent on an umbrella and, as Miller had pointed out in his memo, 'you should have your own wet weather equipment – adjust accordingly'. Miller checked Axon's revised claim and noted that the item had been removed. He was about to pass the new version when he noticed that the invoice total had remained unaltered – three hundred and thirty one pounds and nineteen pence. He added up the figures again, checking with the supplied receipts: the total tallied. Turning over the page, he found a postcard from Axon, with the scrawled message: 'PS: Find the umbrella.'

He showed it to Charlotte. 'If they used half this creativity in their writing,' he said, 'we'd have a fuck of a lot better newspaper.'

'You know what?' said Charlotte, who seemed, unlike Miller, to have left the cupboard far more assertive than she went in. 'I really don't think you should be getting involved at this level. You're the editor for God's sake, not the accounts clerk.'

'But that's just it,' he said. 'It's at every level. From freelance photographers fiddling their petrol money to the managing editor billing us for his first-class upgrades, and the five-figure sweeteners to get in new writers.' He picked up the next document in the file. 'Look at this.'

It was a two hundred and forty pound lunch bill from the news editor, Ian Garfitt. 'Send it back to him,' he told Charlotte, 'with forty quid and a memo. If he wants to spend two hundred pounds on his lunch, that's his business, not mine.'

'Send it back?' she said. 'To Garfitt? He'll go mad.'

'You've met him then,' Miller replied. 'Anyway, that's his problem. We can't go on like this.'

'There's a note with it: "Please settle promptly." '

'That's what I like best about my job,' he said.

'What?'

'Never having to say "please".'

'What's next?' he asked Charlotte.

She stood behind him and lifted the small pile of invoices he'd discarded, revealing his desk diary.

'You've got a breakfast,' she said. 'With Linda Mealing.'

Miller winced. Mealing was a merciless gossip columnist who'd left the paper two years earlier for a rival tabloid. Miller was set on hiring her back.

'When?'

'Now.'

'Come with me,' he said. 'Bring your notebook and get me a contract form.'

They left their coffee untouched. She handed him the form, which he folded and put in his inside pocket. On their way out, Charlotte left the memo and the invoice on Garfitt's desk: the news editor, to Miller's great relief, wasn't there. He'd arranged to meet Mealing in a café outside the building, so as not to alert her current employers, or alarm his current gossip writer.

'What's she like?' Charlotte asked him, as they left the building.

'She... you see my hand?' he said. He held out his first finger and showed her the scar running down its length. The whole finger was bent over at a slight angle where it met the knuckle. 'When I was a boy,' he told her, 'I used to have a paper round. My father had the paper shop. I've always loved papers. Dogs,' he added, 'were the main problem. When I go back to that road, I can still remember the houses that had them. The worst one was this Alsatian at number thirty-one. They had this heavily sprung letterbox; you had to hold it open to get the paper in. The dog used to fling itself at your hand as you pushed the paper through. Then one day I went up the path with the paper, and there was no noise from the hall. I thought – OK, great, it's died. Then I put my hand through: it had managed to train itself to stifle its barking. It was waiting there, totally silent. It nearly tore my hand off.'

'And?' she said.

'Linda's vicious,' he said. 'She's deceitful. She's completely without principle. But not so as you'd notice.' He paused, then added, with no sense of irony: 'I've got to get her back.' Charlotte laughed.

'Didn't you have a dog?' she asked him.

'Yes.'

'What was he called?'

'Heathcliff.'

'Heathcliff? Very literary.'

'Well, Heathcliff was a smart dog. He bit me too.'

They walked on together, side by side, Charlotte slightly ahead of him, on his right. Noticing how her left hand swung back, as she walked, Miller thought about taking it in his right, then didn't. The pavement narrowed as they approached the entrance to the café. It was obstructed on Miller's side by an elderly black man who was sitting in a wheelchair, a blanket over his knees. The editor ignored the man's mumbled request for change and then – rather than slowing down and walking round him, behind his secretary – stepped over the beggar's feet so as to keep pace with her.

'That'll cost you,' the man shouted.

'How much?' Miller replied, sarcastically.

'A day's bad luck.'

As Miller walked away the man spat at him, and missed.

Mealing was late, as he knew she would be. Miller sat down at a table for four, facing away from the entrance, with Charlotte opposite him. She slipped her jacket off and over the back of her chair, in one easy movement; as she did it, his eyes met hers for a moment, then she looked away.

'Why did he say that, do you think?' she asked him.

'Who?' he asked.

'That man in the wheelchair. Because you didn't give him any money?'

Miller laughed. 'No,' he said. 'I pass him every day. I never give him any money.'

'Why then?'

He looked up. 'I think it was because I stepped over him,' he said. 'Stepping over a beggar: one day. I get off pretty lightly, compared to breaking a mirror.'

'That would all depend what your bad luck is,' she said.

The editor smiled. He felt someone place a hand on each of his shoulders. He looked round, and Mealing was there.

She sat down at his side.

'Coffee,' the writer said. It was a command, not a request.

Miller's assistant started to get up.

'Sit down Charlotte,' Miller said. 'I'll get them.'

He left the two women together.

As he turned away, he felt like ordering champagne. Some force must have been protecting him as he left Bowker's Cupboard. That weekend, he thought, his earlier repentance forgotten, he'd take Charlotte to Edinburgh, or Paris, or Geneva, and make it up to her. Then he'd hire her permanently.

'You really are very beautiful dear,' Mealing was saying to Charlotte as he returned with a small plastic tray on which he'd

placed the coffee, some individual cartons of milk, and his VAT receipt. 'What on earth are you doing with him?'
Charlotte smiled.
'How much?' Mealing asked Miller. He picked up the receipt.
'I don't mean the fucking coffee,' she said.
'We'll pay you what you get now,' he said. 'Plus twenty.'
She looked at him and said nothing. When her silence didn't provoke the blurted improvement she'd hoped for, she allowed a look of faint disappointment to cross her face.
'I've heard,' she said, 'that's it's usual to make some sort of payment; I believe it's called *ex gratia*...'
'My accountant,' Miller said, 'once told me: "if people ever start talking Latin to you, give me a ring".'
Mealing smiled.
'Charlotte dear,' she said, 'would you mind going to fetch me some sugar? You're closer to it than I am. It's just there darling,' she said, pointing. 'Behind you.'
Charlotte got up and walked over to the sugar counter.
Miller looked in his inside pocket for the contract form.
'One or two?' he heard Charlotte call.
'Two,' said Mealing, cheerfully.
'When you ring your accountant,' the columnist told Miller, 'tell him sixty thousand up front. For the *ex gratia*.'
'There's a board meeting next week,' he said. 'I'll try. We've put a ban on one-off payments. I can't promise.'
'I'm afraid it's a... what's the word... a pre-requisite. It's what I need.'
Need, thought Miller, with a twinge of fury. It was the first time he'd been angry that day: he must be feeling better.
'Are there any questions,' he asked her, seeking a formal conclusion to the meeting, 'that you'd like to ask me?'
'Yes,' she said. 'Just one.'
'OK,' he said.
'Why is it,' she asked him, 'that the back of your jacket, and the back of her blouse, are both covered in air-mail stickers?'
She noticed Miller's expression go from false amiability, to

bemusement, to mortification.

'And bits of dust,' Mealing added.

'What?' he said.

'Why is it,' she repeated, 'that the...'

He got up and, trying not to run, headed for the gents, where he shut himself in a cubicle. He took his jacket off and stretched it out by the shoulders. He found five of the blue, self-adhesive stickers. He pulled them off, screwed them up in the palm of his hand, and dusted the back of his jacket down. He was about to put it back on when he had a shudder of horror as he found another of the stickers, hidden under the left arm. It reminded him of a sequence he'd seen in which Humphrey Bogart emerged from an equatorial river, covered with leeches. Mealing had worked with Bowker for years. She knew all about his cupboard. He dropped the ball of stickers in the pan and flushed the toilet. They floated. He left them there and went back into the café, wearing an expression of transparent guilt.

Mealing was still there, at the table. She'd finished her coffee. Charlotte was sitting across from her, in silence. In the ashtray, he noticed, there were three more air-mail stickers and a sliver of brown parcel tape. 'You forgot your sugar', he said to Mealing, noticing the two unopened packets on the table.

'I don't take sugar,' she told him. 'I never have. Sugar disagrees with me. Talking of which,' she added, 'how are you? Feeling better now Edward?'

He glared at her.

'Can I have another one dear?' she asked him.

'Another?'

'Another question.'

She looked at him with a mixture of pity and triumph, as if she was a poker player whose royal flush was about to cost Miller his house.

'Whatever happened,' she continued, 'to Paul Bowker?'

'He's in New Zealand,' he told her.

'About the pre-requisite,' she added. 'Can you manage eighty thousand?'

'Yes,' he said.

From the moment Miller and Charlotte entered the newspaper's ground-floor reception, he could tell from the security guard's face that details of his appearance in the canteen had got around. They entered the empty lift. The doors closed.

'Did you take off your jacket,' he asked her, 'in the canteen?'

'Yes,' she said. 'I think so. When we were sitting down.'

'Shit.'

'My dad,' Charlotte told him, 'is a joiner.'

'Oh,' he said. There was a sign behind her head: 'Do Not Use Lift in Conditions of Emergency.'

'You know what he says?'

'Who?' Miller's mind was wandering; he was unsure of how to torment himself first – by remembering that security man's sneering look, or anticipating the reception he was about to get when he stepped out of the lift into the office.

'My dad.'

'No.'

'My dad says: "Most things are fixable, at a price. Other things pass."'

He turned to face her. 'I know there's nothing I can say...'

Before he could finish the thought, the lift doors opened.

They'd not taken ten steps across the floor when Garfitt saw them, and leapt out from his desk a few yards away. He took Miller by the lapels and forced him up against a pillar. Even in a suit, with his dark features, muscular build, and deep red veins in his face, Garfitt looked like a village blacksmith in a bad melodrama.

'You got my memo then,' said Miller.

Charlotte turned on her heel and disappeared down the stairs.

Garfitt tightened his grip on Miller's jacket. He pressed inwards, hard, with his fists clenched, so that his knuckles were bruising the editor's collarbone.

'The thing is, Edward – I mean – how can I put this: you may not have noticed, but I'm not really a memo kind of a guy.'

Miller shut his eyes and breathed in deeply through his nose, like a meditator seeking a place of transcendental calm, and not finding it.

A small crowd had gathered, but did not intervene.

'I know you're new,' Garfitt continued. 'And that you're trying to make a name for yourself…'

Miller stared past him at the far wall, and said nothing.

'But that name,' Garfitt continued, 'is cunt.'

He could feel the eyes of his staff on him. Garfitt let go and stood back, one eyebrow raised, waiting for the puny lunge from Miller that would allow him to knock the editor out. When it didn't come, he took hold of him again. Garfitt arched his shoulders back at an angle which suggested to Miller that he should prepare himself for a head butt.

The lift doors opened again. Charlotte ran out, followed by Thomas, Miller's driver. Thomas was from Ghana and he had served four years in the paratroop regiment. He was four inches taller than Garfitt, and forty pounds heavier. The news editor straightened his torso and nodded to the chauffeur. With a sarcastic smile to Miller, he released his lapels.

'It's the same for everybody,' the editor said. 'That means you don't fly first class any more. You go economy. If at all possible, you don't fly at all. You catch the train. And you don't run up two hundred and forty pound bills at The Portofino every day. You have to think about eating somewhere else. Somewhere just a little bit more reasonable. Like that high class Chinese. You know – the one where the owner's handwriting looks just like yours.'

'OK,' said Garfitt. A worrying new note – one of calm – had entered his voice.

'What?'

'OK. I mean… I can't help but admire the way that you're leading by example.'

'What do you mean?'

'How can we possibly fly business,' Garfitt asked, waving at Charlotte, 'when you two send yourselves freight?'

There was a strangled snort from the news desk, as Claudia, Garfitt's assistant, struggled to suppress a laugh.

'Get out,' Miller told him. 'Clear your desk. Now. You're fired.'

'Are you sure Edward?' Garfitt said. 'What for?'

'For assault,' Miller said.

'Delighted,' he replied. 'I'll see you at the tribunal.'

He walked out, whistling a tune Miller couldn't quite place. The editor retreated into his office, where he picked up his appointments diary. He sat behind his desk looking down at it, unopened.

Claudia came in without knocking, something she never did, and showed him a possible story for the next day's front page: a story about a British lorry driver in Dover who was trying to sue his French employer for racial discrimination. Miller glanced at it.

'It's fine,' he said, without thinking. 'Carry on working on that.' He was struggling to gauge the gravity of what was happening to him. Garfitt's whistling was going round in his head. He needed to get out; he needed to think. Claudia left without speaking. He hummed a few bars of Garfitt's tune to himself, then stopped when he realized that it was 'Leaving on a Jet Plane'.

'What else,' he asked Charlotte, 'do I have today?'

She walked over, took the appointments book, and opened it.

'Mauldeth Hall called again,' she said, 'to confirm that you're going there on Friday morning. They said you need to arrive by eight thirty. I've booked you into the Intercontinental in Manchester.' Mauldeth Hall was his old school; he'd agreed to speak to the boys at assembly. His heart sank further. He was about to postpone the engagement when he remembered that it would get him out of London for a day.

'Tell them it's OK,' he said.

'And today you've got lunch,' she said, 'with your father-in-law. At his club.'

'Cancel him.'

'You cancelled him last Friday,' she said. For the second time. 'Where does he live?'

'Brighton.'

'He'll already have left.'

She closed the diary. 'And this evening,' she said, 'it's your wedding anniversary.'

He looked over at her, but she was gazing into the distance, out of the window. He put his head in his hands.

'You're having dinner,' she said. 'At Cardamom in Oxted.' There was no trace of emotion in her voice. 'With your wife.'

'Charlotte?'

'What?'

'Can I see you again?'

'Again?'

'Somewhere else?'

'What for?'

'Pardon?'

'With a view,' she asked him, 'to what?'

He pointed at the brass plaque on his wall. 'Do you know what that says?'

She shook her head.

'It means: Never Kick a Man When He's Down? Name Me a Better Time.'

He looked at his watch; it was almost twelve. He ventured across the floor. As he walked, heads went down, about ten yards ahead of him, as people sensed his approach.

Thomas met him downstairs, at the main entrance. Miller got into the front seat of the car, as he usually did on shorter journeys. They set off, and the editor stared straight ahead of him. He reached in his inside pocket for his mobile. It wasn't there. The day seemed to have acquired its own horrible dynamic; he felt like someone carrying a fridge tray full of water across the kitchen, who receives one small jolt which sets up peculiar and unexpected aftershocks, which any attempt at correction only intensifies. He asked Thomas if he could borrow his phone for the day. The driver handed it to him. Miller put it on the dashboard in front of him.

They drew up outside his father-in-law's club. Edward could see Charles Portal already, an overweight, grey-haired figure in an expensive navy blazer, at a table by the window. Walking in, Miller felt immediately soothed by the low, soporific hum of hushed male voices, the waiters in black tie and white cotton gloves; the haze of Havana smoke, and the crimson velvet curtains.

He arrived at the table just as Charles was taking delivery of an aperitif.

'You don't drink any more Edward, do you?' his father-in-law said.

'I do,' he said. 'I mean – I am. Today.'

Portal looked at him.

'It's my wedding anniversary,' he said.

'I know.'

'I'll have one,' Miller called out to the waiter.

'One of what, sir?' the man asked, in a heavy Polish accent.

'One of those, er...' He pointed at his father-in-law's glass. 'Drinks.'

'What is it?' he asked Charles, as the waiter left.

'It's a dry martini,' his father-in-law said. 'Are you all right?'

'Yes,' said Miller. He wondered if, by some sort of osmosis, Charles had found out about Bowker's Cupboard. When the waiter returned, he took his drink from the man's gloved hand before he'd had chance to put it down on the table.

'Cheers,' said Charles. 'How's Ellie?'

Miller took a long draught of the dry martini. It was very cold, and it tasted like pure gin.

'She's fine,' he said.

He had no idea how his daughter was. He left most days at six, and wasn't back until ten. If his eight-year-old daughter existed for him in any meaningful way, he reflected, as the drink's forgotten perfume began to course around his system, it was as a series of entries on his credit card bill. The Pony Club. The Skiing Holidays. The Winter Clothes. The Summer Clothes.

'How many years is it now?'

'How many years is what?'

'That you've been married to my daughter.'

'Ten,' he said.

'Nine,' Charles corrected.

There was a pause.

'I knew Elizabeth would be a woman of spirit,' Portal continued, 'from the day she was born. When she was seventeen, the day after

I'd taken her up to the crammer at Cambridge, she phoned to tell me that this grubby Pakistani had followed her home and offered her a hundred pounds to go to bed with him. She said…'

Charles put back his head and roared.

Hearing his wife's name, Miller, who had started to rally slightly, relapsed. He tried not to show it, but managed only a grin like an embalmed corpse.

'She said…' his father-in-law repeated. 'Why don't you go home, and spend it on a washing machine for your wife.'

He laughed again, but then his expression became suddenly serious, and he leaned forward.

'You are treating Elizabeth well, I hope?' he said.

'What? Yes. Why?'

'Because the last couple of times I've seen her she's been looking distracted; a little weary. Which is not like her,' Portal added, 'is it?'

'She's fine.'

Charles had made his money running a consultancy that briefed companies, including Miller's, on the allegiances of its workers, especially where human rights organizations and protest groups were concerned. He was a senior freemason, and it had been his contacts within the Lodge who had rescued him when he was threatened with court action over what had been termed 'inappropriate' telephone surveillance. Even now, semi-retired, he boasted, he could get anybody's line tapped.

'If you ever need anybody checking out,' he told Miller, 'or – how should I put this – dealing with, give me a call. You and I understand how these things work.'

Charles had become accustomed to a certain style of living. He ordered lobster, which he ate noisily, using an array of steel utensils which were delivered on a metal plate, as to a dentist. He had a half bottle of Sauvignon; Miller chose a rare steak and a bottle of Bordeaux. They'd just started the main course when Thomas arrived with his mobile, which Miller had borrowed, then left in the car. He placed it on the table, gave a slight nod of acknowledgement, then left.

'If you don't mind me asking,' Charles said, 'on what criteria did you choose your driver?'

'On the criterion,' Miller said, 'that he drives like a saint.'

His father-in-law stared out of the window and watched Thomas getting back into the car. 'When he's with you,' he said.

Miller didn't reply.

'Does he take the car home after work?' he asked.

'Yes.'

'I expect he gets pulled over a lot,' he said, 'where he must live.'

'I don't know where he lives,' said Miller. 'He's never said.'

Charles took him lightly by the wrist. 'Don't get me wrong,' he said. 'I'm used to working – if you can call it that – with our tinted friends. It's the Eastern Europeans I really hate. The way they've latched on to our softness when it comes to the victim culture. I see modern England,' he added, 'if I can borrow a phrase from your own fine newspaper, as "Toad Hall Under The Weasels" .'

Miller nodded.

'And I'm fed up of being gypped,' Charles said, raising his voice slightly, 'by gyppos.' He glanced defiantly at the waiting staff, hoping for signs of annoyance, and found none.

'I worked for twenty years in Nig-Nog land,' he said. 'And I always promised myself that one day I'd go back. I never have. But now I don't need to. Now, it's come to me.'

He roared with laughter.

'I had one of them in my house last week,' he added. 'Did Elizabeth tell you?'

'What? No,' Miller said. 'In your house?'

'He was burgling it. Or rather trying to. I came downstairs and surprised him; I saw him legging it down to the beach.'

'What did you do then?'

'I called the police. I said "There is a large black man..." '

Miller gave him a doubting look.

'No, I did. A "large black man". I dine with the chief constable at the Lodge every month. He's taught me to be careful. "A large black man, and he's just broken into my house." They said: "Is he still there, committing the offence?" I said "No". They said "Well we regret that we don't have a unit free for up to an hour." I told them: "That's OK – take your time. I've shot him." I had a squad car at the door in two minutes.'

Miller looked at him. In his own mind, the dislike of black immigration – though strong – was essentially generic, and didn't prevent him forming a relationship with an individual. His father-in-law was one of the very few men in Britain who made him feel like a liberal.

'How many men have you shot?' he asked Portal.

'Only one. In the Kabaw Valley, in Burma, when we were trying to drive back the Japanese. It was very hard, you know in that jungle terrain, at the end of the war.'

'Apparently some of them,' Miller said, 'preferred death to surrender.'

'That's right,' Charles replied. 'But you're talking about the Japanese. The man I shot wasn't from Japan. He was from Didcot.'

'What?'

'He was from Didcot,' Portal continued, 'and he was a deserter. Actually that's flattering him – he didn't even have the courage to desert. He broke cover when he saw a Japanese patrol passing by and ran away, exposing his position, an act of cowardice that cost the lives of eight of his comrades. We were burying the bodies after nightfall when he came back, whimpering like a dog.'

'So you shot him.'

'What? Yes.'

'In the back? Like a deserter?'

Portal looked offended.

'Between the eyes.'

'What did your commanding officer say?'

'Randolph?' He laughed. 'Randolph gave the command.'

Portal asked for the bill.

'You will – I hate to press this point – but you will take good care of my daughter, won't you, Edward?'

'Yes,' said Miller.

'Good. I'm so glad. Because I can't stand a deserter.'

They left the club and went into a pub across the road. It was old-fashioned, very expensive, and empty. They'd been there for half an hour when a young vagrant in torn jeans came in. He didn't buy a drink. He sat down at the next table, staring at them, and eavesdropping.

Charles turned to face him.

'I won't beat about the bush,' he told the stranger. 'How much do you want to go away?'

The man looked taken aback.

'Five pounds,' he said, in a Belfast accent.

'Oh, come on,' said his father-in-law. 'You're worth more than that.'

He pushed a ten-pound note into the stranger's shirt pocket. The man got up and left.

When they came out of the bar it was half past five. It was almost six years since Miller had stopped drinking and smoking. His energy had gone into his work. It had given him an edge. Now, after four hours of mixing his drinks, he felt pleasantly heartened but a little unsteady on his feet. Heavy cloud was gathering. The day had turned humid, and oppressive. He got in the car next to Thomas, and wound down his passenger window.

'Oxted?' his driver asked.

Miller nodded. He dialled Statham, his managing editor, on the mobile.

'I saw Mealing this morning,' Miller told him.

'Oh yes.'

'She wants a hundred and fifty.'

'You realize,' said the voice at the other end of the line, 'that is five proper jobs. Five real people.'

'Real people,' said Miller, 'don't bring in readers.'

'You're the boss,' said Statham. There was an unpleasant, jocular tone in his voice.

'Oh,' said Miller, 'and she wants eighty as a signing-on fee.'

'We don't do that any more,' said Statham. 'On your orders.'

'I'm changing my fucking orders,' Miller shouted.

'We can't do it.'

Statham had never spoken to him like this before.

'Hide it in the accounts.'

'How do you think we can hide eighty grand?'

The car drew up at a red light.

Pedestrians traipsed across in front of them.

'I'm telling you,' Miller said, through his teeth, 'that we have to.'

'And I'm telling you,' Statham replied, 'that we can't.' Then the managing editor hung up.

'Cunt,' shouted Miller. He slammed the mobile against the dashboard with all his force, and it shattered into pieces.

An Asian woman and a girl of five or six, who was eating an ice-cream, were on the pavement, level with the open passenger window. Hearing Miller, the girl closed her hand involuntarily, crushing the cornet, so that the ice-cream fell off and rolled under the car. The little girl bent down and looked for the ice-cream then, realizing she couldn't retrieve it, rested her sticky fingers on the lower rim of his open window, and stared at Miller, apparently in shock.

'Can't you keep your brat under control?' he shouted at the mother.

The girl stayed where she was. Miller put his face very close to hers.

'Get your filthy little hands off my car,' he told her.

The girl's bottom lip began to tremble. Then her whole face corrugated, and she burst into tears, but didn't move.

The light was still on red. Miller pressed the button to close the electric window. He kept his finger on it, pushing hard, as though this would accelerate its movement. The girl's hands rose with the top of the glass, till her arms were almost fully extended, and her small fingers were about to be trapped in the top of the door. Miller picked up a copy of a street atlas and rapped her firmly on the knuckles. Her fingers disappeared and the window closed, muffling the sound of her sobbing.

The lights changed. As they pulled away, the mother was gesturing at the car. Miller half-turned and gave her an ironic wave. He took an unused white handkerchief out of his pocket, and wiped a smudge off the inside of the glass.

He became aware of the sound of an indicator, which clicked back into place automatically as they completed a left-hand turn into Park Lane, restoring the silence.

'Mr Miller.' He looked across. It was the first time that Thomas had ever instigated a conversation.

'What the fuck do you want?'

'I'm sorry Mr Miller,' he said, 'but that was my phone.'

The editor said nothing.

'I need it,' Thomas added.

'Why?' Miller snapped.

'I need it tonight,' he said, 'because I am going to propose to my girlfriend.'

He put the accent on the second syllable of that last word. Miller had noticed before how the Ghanaian accent, though he could hardly take it seriously as a form of English, seemed to have an intrinsic gentility. Still the remark horrified him. Thomas would never have dared say this unless he knew.

'You've decided to propose on your mobile?' Miller asked him.

'No sir,' said Thomas. 'But I think she may want to call somebody afterwards. She doesn't have a phone at her flat.'

Miller inhaled deeply, out of irritation. He breathed out through clenched teeth. He opened the passenger window again, and stared out. 'Pull over,' he said, a few moments later. He went into a mobile phone shop and bought two new telephones; a top-of-the-range model for himself and a cheaper one for his driver. He rang each with the other, to leave their respective numbers in their memory.

'You tell me that,' he said. 'About proposing to your girlfriend. And I don't even know where you live.'

The driver said nothing.

'Where do you live?'

'Tooting Bec,' said Thomas.

He started to wonder if his driver's girlfriend was white or black.

'Your fiancée,' he said, '... is she...'

'Marie,' he interrupted, 'is from Sri Lanka. Sir.'

As they came into Croydon, the weather broke. Miller stared

ahead of him as the driving rain beat down on, but did not dislodge, the grime encrusted on the mud-flaps of a lorry in front of them. Miller looked at the name on its tailgate – Allinson: Flour and Bread. It was an honest name, like his own. 'Miller' had come to serve him as Christian name and surname. 'Edward' was too formal when long, too casual when shortened. 'Miller'. An honest name for an honest trade. Which of his ancestors had been a miller? All of them? Or perhaps there'd been a time in England when people abandoned their given surname and called themselves after the trade they followed, whatever it was. Probably that name was given to a man by others. Under that system, he wondered, what name would he bequeath to his children? His thoughts went back to Garfitt, when he had him pinned against the column. 'I know you're trying to make a name for yourself...'

At Purley, he pondered the consequences of his situation. He began with the first, catastrophic certainty: that everybody in the company, from the tea-boy to his driver, to the board of directors, now had an ideal opportunity for blackmail. The next few days would see every grudge surface; every demand articulated. And then he'd had unprotected sex with a woman he hardly knew. He rehearsed the possible consequences, building from gonorrhoea, through hepatitis C to Aids. What else might she have? What else might she do? That curious phrase she'd used – 'fixable, at a price' – kept coming back to him.

'Thomas,' he said.

'Yes?'

'Do you have any music?'

He'd anticipated reggae or soul, but the driver put on some piece of classical music – Miller knew nothing about classical music – whose haunting, desolate mood captured his own, and intensified it.

'What the hell is this?' he asked.

'It is "The Song of the Earth,"' said Thomas. 'By Mahler.'

Miller looked at his watch; it was almost six-thirty. He'd intended to go home first, to change, but now realized he'd have to go straight to the restaurant. He couldn't face the thought of ringing to tell his wife. He could hardly ask Charlotte to do it. He called his home number and, to his great relief, got the answering service. He left a message telling Elizabeth he'd see her at Cardamom.

Thomas drove into the village, through the pouring rain. They passed The Green Man, the local pub, then Miller's own house, Everdene – a detached property, with gables and twin garages – on the left. Directly opposite, he saw Mr Illingworth sprinting from his large off-road vehicle into the porch of his house, Glastonbury, a newspaper over his head. Miller gave him a look of scorn. Illingworth took the 6.08 into London every morning. He used his black Mercedes four by four to drive two miles to the supermarket once a week. He jogged. He lived alone. Behind his back, Miller called him 'the faggot'.

Cardamom was at the far end of the High Street. It was owned by the only Asian in the immediate area, who lived in a large house just outside the village. People came from London specially to eat there. It had stars. It was expensive. It had pretensions. You could never get a table. Not that that bothered Miller. Miller loathed it.

They arrived there at seven fifteen. He was about to get out when Thomas opened the glove compartment and, without speaking, handed him a small gift bag from a department store. He glanced inside and saw a package wrapped in gold paper. It was Elizabeth's anniversary present – an eternity ring, which he'd paid for, but not wrapped, or set eyes on. He'd left the instruction to buy one, at five hundred pounds, with his previous secretary, on her last morning. He'd forgotten all about it. He didn't even know who'd bought it for him. Probably Charlotte.

He walked up the steps; a waiter in dinner dress held the glass door open for him. He caught sight of himself in a mirror as he went through the entrance hall: his face was flushed, and he had the beginnings of a hangover. He felt tired. He would have liked a shower.

The head waiter pointed out his table. It was empty, and in the centre of the room. Miller decided to wait for his wife on a stool at the bar which ran down one side of the restaurant.

'Give me a whisky,' he said to the barman. The man was bald, Indian, and wore glasses. There was some kind of religious book behind him, on the counter by the sink. Miller felt so swiftly superior to him that he almost sensed the beginnings of pity. 'On ice,' he added.

Miller noticed that his shoelace was undone; when he kneeled down to tie it, a couple of credit cards fell out of his top pocket on to the carpet. He bent down to pick them up. When he stood up again, the barman hadn't moved.

'What kind, sir?'

'Scotch,' he said. 'You know what fucking Scotch is don't you? Or are you fucking deaf?'

'I meant a blend, sir,' the barman said, 'or a single malt.' He took a step back so that Miller could see the couple of dozen varieties of Scotch whisky on the shelf behind him. He climbed back on the stool.

'Glenmorangie,' he said. 'A double.'

He drank half of it. In the large mirror behind the bar, he saw his wife arrive. He didn't turn round. She hadn't seen him. He watched her, in reflection, give her coat to the doorman, then make her way to the table. Observing her from a distance, Miller noticed that she still turned heads. She looked radiant: tall, her blonde hair pulled back severely from her forehead. She was wearing a scarlet dress which he'd never seen before – though God knows he'd know all about it when the bill arrived.

He swivelled on his seat, and got down awkwardly. He approached her table, carrying his drink. She looked up and smiled. She was wearing a black chiffon necktie, but no jewellery.

'Evening darling,' she said. She got up and kissed him on the cheek, then sat down again. She didn't mention the whisky. She didn't appear to have noticed.

'How was your day?' she asked him.

'The usual,' he said, remembering to keep stock still at the moment of the lie.

Then she was off, with the usual litany: the house, Ellie's pony, Ellie's school, the fitness club, the tennis... he found himself brooding on his own problems again, half listening, a skill he'd perfected when he'd been on the news desk, keeping half an eye on the news agency feed, half on the computer screen.

The waiter arrived. He had a supercilious look that made Miller hate him on sight. He handed them menus. Miller didn't look at his. While Elizabeth ordered an elaborate lamb kebab, he tried to think of something plain and unpretentious that they might not have.

'I'd like... fish curry,' he said.

'Fish,' the man said, with a forgiving smile, as if talking to a child, 'is essentially a Bangladeshi dish.'

'Then I'll have what she's having,' he said, pointing at his wife. 'And some Bamboo Olay.'

'He means Bombay Aloo,' said his wife.

'Not Bamboo au lait,' said the waiter. 'I believe that's a soup dish. Popular with French pandas.'

He felt himself sinking into a cold fury.

'How was Ellie today?' he asked, keen to change the subject.

'Still staying at my sister's,' she said. 'Like she has been for the past week. As you know.'

'Oh,' he said. 'Yes.'

'You've never quite connected, have you', she said, 'with Ellie.'

He said nothing. He finished the whisky and ordered another.

'You're drinking, dear,' she said.

'Yes.'

'Why?'

'To celebrate.'

Over coffee, he handed her the package.

'Happy anniversary,' he said. 'Darling.'

He watched her unwrap it, realizing that, so far as he knew, there could be absolutely any object in that box, from a baby tarantula to a kidney bean.

She looked inside.

'You're sweet,' she said. She turned the box round so that he could see the ring, but did not put it on.

She leaned down, reached into her handbag and produced a small package, in scarlet crêpe paper with a white satin bow. She called over the waiter and ordered champagne.

'Which kind?' he said. He gave a sneering look at Miller. 'French?'

'Your best,' she said.

He opened the package carefully. Under the outer wrapping he could feel another layer of coarser paper. He lifted it out and turned it over: it was an envelope; sky blue, with a broken red border. In the top corner, he saw the printed motif: Air Mail.

'You know you told me darling,' she said, 'you were so sweet – you told me that if ever I met somebody I really, really liked…'

He looked up at her.

'Oh no – do open it, dear,' she said. 'Do. I chose it myself,' she said, 'just for you.'

He pulled at the seal on the envelope. There was something heavy, of irregular shape, inside it.

'It was after you were – excuse my directness, dear – shagging that girl from France who was working for us,' she said. 'You remember – the one with the nice eyes who liked horses – what was her name…'

'Odile', he said. He put the envelope down.

'That's right, dear. After I found out you were shagging Odile. You told me that if ever I met anybody I really, really liked, that I would be free to go.'

He said nothing.

'You do remember that dear, don't you?'

'Yes,' he said.

'Oh good,' she said. 'I'm so pleased.' She paused. 'Because I have.'

'What?'

'Because I have,' she said. 'Met somebody.'

'Who?'

The waiter arrived with the champagne and an ice bucket.

Standing at Elizabeth's shoulder, he began to open the bottle.

'It's Mr Illingworth,' she said.

'Illingworth?' he repeated. 'In Glastonbury? The faggot?'

'How many women has it been dear?' she asked him.

The waiter was still at her side, toiling over the normally swift business of untwining the protective wire cap.

'How many women what?'
'That you've slept with – that you've shagged.' She paused. 'Since me.'
'Six,' he said.
His reply was followed by a resonant pop.
'How many really?' she repeated. 'Thirty?'
'Eighteen', he said, in a tone of defeat.
'And how many men do you think I've slept with? In that time?'
He said nothing.
'Have a guess,' she said.
The waiter poured a little of the vintage champagne into her glass.
Miller stared down at the eternity ring, still in its box, and the unopened blue envelope, and the bubbles rising in the half inch of wine in Elizabeth's crystal goblet.
'No,' he said.
The wine waiter rested the bottle in the ice bucket and started to back away. Elizabeth beckoned to him. He came back.
'What would you say your job is?' she asked him.
'I'm sorry madam... I...'
'You're a waiter aren't you?' she said. Her voice had her father's commanding tone. 'Aren't you?'
The man nodded.
'Well wait.' She smiled. 'I haven't tasted the wine yet.'
He remained by the table, staring at the far wall, his hands clasped behind his back. She turned back to Miller.
'Go on dear, please. Do try. Just for me.'
'Well I'll tell you anyway,' she said. 'It's one.'
Silence.
'Illingworth,' he said.
'Oh no,' she said. 'I haven't slept with him yet. I mean he's been asking me to for weeks – absolutely pleading actually – but I haven't. I'm sleeping with him tonight. He's waiting for me now,' she said. 'In Glastonbury. Naked. Between sheets of pure Egyptian cotton. In his bed.'
'How do you know?'

'I made him promise.'
'Who then?'
'Who what?' she said. 'Oh – the other one. Yes.'
'Mr Dhorajiwala,' she said.
She tasted the wine.
'That's lovely darling,' she said to the waiter. 'He won't be needing the ice bucket.'

The waiter put the champagne bottle on the table and retreated, joining the rest of the staff who, Miller noticed, had gathered at the end of the bar, at a discreet distance, but within earshot.

'Who,' Miller asked, 'is he?'

'He's the owner of this restaurant, dear,' she said. 'Mr Dhorajiwala is a marvellous, generous, inventive…' She gave a vaudeville wink towards the lurking staff '… cook. And he's absolutely tremendous in bed. I slept with him last year,' she said. 'Twice. Well,' she added, 'twice at the one – you know – go. To spite you.'

She poured him a glass of champagne. He swallowed it, in shock.

The waiter returned and left them the bill.

'Open your present dear,' she said.

There was silence in the room. He might as well have been on a stage.

He tore open the envelope, clumsily. Inside was her set of house keys.

'I had a telephone call this morning,' she said, 'from a Mr Garfitt. He told me that you had been – excuse me again dear but I'll quote him directly – fucking your secretary in the stock cupboard.'

He listened hard for some ambient noise to cling on to, but even the reassuring sound of cutlery had died away. He thought about berating the watching diners but decided against it.

'Ask me what I did then dear.'

Miller said nothing.

'What I did then, I called your secretary. He looked up in disbelief. 'I called your Charlotte. And I asked her if it was true.'

She poured herself more wine.

'And do you know what she said?'

She took a sip and let out a loud, vulgar laugh, very like her father's. 'I'm sorry. You must forgive me.'

'What did she say?' Miller hissed.

'She said... no. I'm not going to tell you. Ask her yourself,' she added, 'when you see her at work, tomorrow.'

He filled his water glass with champagne, and drained it.

The waiter arrived with the bill, and waited.

'The thing is,' she said, while Miller fumbled for his credit card, 'that with the others, it was – it was still sort of intimate. It was just between the three of us. I've grown used to being betrayed. I don't – I didn't – mind being betrayed. But I will not be humiliated. I know what it feels like, and I don't like it. And you,' she added, 'won't like it either.'

'Don't go,' he asked her. And then, more quietly, 'Stay.'

'Stay?' she repeated, at volume. She gave the word a rising inflection, like a ham actress playing Lady Bracknell. And then – in the same declamatory tone of voice, her eyes on the back wall: 'With *you?*'

She emptied her glass and stood up. A waiter arrived with the receipt and his wife's coat. She walked towards the door. Miller picked up the ring box and followed her. Outside, she put up her umbrella, but did not offer to share it, and they set off in silence. He kept pace with her as they walked side by side, along the High Street in the driving rain. Then, still without speaking or making any gesture of farewell, she turned and walked up the gravel path to Glastonbury, opened the door with a key and went in. Miller stood in the road and watched as the hall light went out. The bedroom light was on, he noticed. To judge by the shadows on the curtains it was not a strong overhead light, but a more subtle source of illumination – small spotlights perhaps, or two bedside lamps.

He turned and let himself into Everdene, which was in darkness.

He switched on the light in the living room and sat down on the sofa. Various photographs, mainly of their daughter, were missing. The frames were still there, but they were empty. A couple of pictures of Elizabeth herself had been left undisturbed. Also intact, and promoted to a central position on the mantelpiece, was a wedding portrait of the two of them. He got up and stared at it. He looked at her eyes, full of expectancy, and love. He heard the rain lash against the window.

He looked at his watch: it was quarter to eleven. He pulled out his new mobile. When the call was answered, he could hear the sound of cutlery, and violin music.

'Thomas?'

A pause.

'Yes.'

'Get over here.'

There was no reply.

'Get over here now,' Miller said, 'or you're fired.'

Half an hour later the doorbell rang. Miller looked through the bull's eye in his door and at first didn't recognize his driver, who was wearing baggy canvas trousers and a T-shirt.

They walked to the car. Miller got in the back. Thomas set off, back to London.

'Stop,' Miller shouted, as they passed The Green Man. 'Wait.'

He went in and bought two packets of cigarettes and a lighter. The Green Man, sensitive to the tastes of its wealthy clientele, kept a wide range of tobacco including unfiltered Gitanes, the cigarettes he'd smoked before Elizabeth had made him give up. As the car moved off again, he opened the packet. He removed the top piece of silver paper, brought the cigarettes up to his nostrils and breathed in, deeply. How could he ever have stopped smoking, he asked himself as he lit one: the captivating process of ignition; the first, glorious hit of nicotine. The deep, scouring sensation as the unfiltered smoke hit your lungs. He stared admiringly at the clouds on the packet.

'Where to?' said Thomas.

'What?'

'Where to?' He looked in the rear-view mirror.

'Take me to Larkin's,' Miller said. It was a media club in the West End, which he didn't care for, but which he knew would be open till four. They arrived just before half midnight.

'Now wait here,' he told Thomas, as he got out.

'How long...'

'Until,' he snapped, as if to a child.

He walked in and noticed, to his relief, that there seemed to be none of his enemies there. He sat at the counter and ordered a beer, and a large whisky on ice.

He looked to his right; there, on the next stool, he saw Gerald Staley, his restaurant critic. He was wearing a polo shirt, and he had a boarding card and passport sticking out of the breast pocket. He looked drunk. He was opening small greaseproof packets containing what looked like elastic bands, and chewing them loudly at the bar. Staley, a widower, had resigned as travel editor and gone back to writing, in order to spend more time caring for his only son, who had been born deaf.

Miller loathed his writing; Staley used a limited range of adjectives, often diminutives, some of his own invention, which were intended to bring out the sensual quality of food, but which left Miller feeling physically sick. 'Chocolatey... moist... flavoursome... tangy.' He watched Staley eat with a mixture of fascination and disgust. He could have punched him.

'It's breakfast time for me,' Staley said. 'I'm starving.'

He opened another packet.

'Eighteen hours ago,' he added, 'I was in Singapore.'

'Oh?' said Miller, with an intonation suggestive of boredom. 'Press trip?'

The food writer nodded.

'I still love to do a bit of travel writing, when I can get away, you know. It's just so exhilarating – that feeling of setting out in the morning, looking for something, and not knowing what you'll find – or whether you'll find anything at all.'

'Really,' said Miller. 'And you like that, do you?'

'I love it.' Staley licked his fingers noisily. 'Have you been to Singapore?'

'No.'

The writer tore into another greaseproof packet. 'It's dried squid,' he said, 'in chilli. Try one. It's chewy...'

'No,' said Miller.

'And spicy,' Staley said. He talked with his mouth open. 'And even though it's salty, it's succulent. And very delicious.'

Miller ignored him.

'What were you doing eighteen hours ago?' Staley asked him.

'I don't know,' said Miller. 'What time was it?'

Staley stared at his watch. 'That would have been... seven fifteen.'

'At seven fifteen,' the editor said, 'I was committing suicide.'

'You didn't manage it, then,' said Staley.

'On the contrary, Gerald,' he told him. 'I did.'

Miller slid off his stool without excusing himself, and set off for the gents. He recognized a distant memory from his drinking days – the way that, late at night, licensed premises sometimes acquired the character of a labyrinth so complex that even the shortest of journeys to the toilet was marred by a fear that he would never find his way back. In this respect Larkin's, which Miller visited only occasionally, was especially daunting. The gents – which was behind an unmarked door, to confuse and intimidate non-members – was upstairs, at the end of a series of narrow passageways. As he made his way out of the bar he passed a disabled facility. Eager to avoid further conversation with strangers – or, worse, acquaintances – in the distant main toilets, he went in. The overhead light had been left on. He was looking up at it as he stepped through the door and fell over a body. Picking himself up, Miller saw it was Simon Feasey, his foreign editor. Feasey stayed where he was, kneeling by the toilet, fully dressed. The seat was down.

'What are you doing here?' Miller asked him.

'Didn't you lock the door, you wanker?'

It was a new voice, a woman's, coming from behind Miller's back.

He looked round and saw Feasey's deputy, Catherine Davies. She drew the bolt across. She was looking at Feasey with fury. There was a credit card in her hand.

Miller got to his feet. Feasey stayed on the floor. He clasped his arms round his knees and drew them up to his chin. He had the impression of having caught two of his employees *in flagrante*, but couldn't understand how they could look quite so guilty when they were both fully dressed. Then he saw two lines of powder laid out on the sink.

'What are you doing?' he asked them.

'Nothing,' said Feasey. 'We were about to… it's…'

'It's cocaine,' said Davies.

She had the expression of a woman who was staring defiantly at the ruins of her career. It was like looking in a mirror. She bent over and snorted one of the lines, with a rolled twenty-pound note. Miller steadied himself against the sink. He drew on his cigarette.

'What does it… how does it make you feel?' he asked.

Feasey glanced up at him as though he thought the question was a lure into some further disgrace. Davies took a step closer to Miller. She noticed his disordered state and the cigarette in his hand.

'Better,' she said. 'It makes you feel better.'

Davies rolled the banknote again and handed it to him. Miller bent down and took the second line. When he raised his head again, he saw that Feasey was still hunched over, with his chin pressed against his kneecaps: pondering, no doubt, the anti-drugs stories that had run most days since Miller arrived, and the paper's tireless campaign to restore the death penalty for dealers.

'Shall we have another?' Miller asked Davies.

She shook her head. 'You need to wait a while,' she told him. 'Go and have a drink.'

'Are you coming?'

'No,' she said. 'We were just leaving.'

She opened her wallet and produced a large wrap of the drug, in silver paper. She handed it to Miller. He started to fumble around for money. 'No,' she said. 'It's OK. Keep it. It's a present.'

'Thank you,' he said. He put the small package in his inside pocket.

He looked at Feasey. 'Tell him not to worry,' he said to Davies. 'What the fuck does he think I'm going to say? Who to?'

Back at the bar, Staley was waiting for him, with his dried cuttlefish. Miller felt an unpleasant acrid drip from the back of his sinuses to his throat.

'This one's the most expensive,' Staley said, handing him one of the small packets. 'But I don't think it smells very nice.'

'No,' said Miller. He put it in his pocket, unopened. 'But what does?'

Staley began fumbling in his holdall. He pulled out a few sheets of paper and handed them to Miller. The editor glanced at the first page. He could make out the odd word in the pale electric light: 'tangy', 'more-ish' and 'squid'.

'Don't read it now,' said Staley.

'I won't,' said Miller.

The food writer was still looking at him, expectantly.

'I'll give you an honest opinion on it tomorrow,' the editor told him.

Staley seemed about to make a remark, then didn't.

'What were you going to say?' Miller asked.

'Nothing.'

'No – go on.'

'I was going to say…' Staley hesitated. 'What other kinds of opinion do you have?'

'None, Gerald,' said Miller, seething at the impudence of this last remark. 'By the way, you know you were saying how much you love setting out in the morning, and looking for something, and not knowing if you'll find it?'

'Yes.'

'Do you feel up to doing that for me tomorrow?'

Staley looked doubtful.

'I suppose I could,' he said.

'Good.'

A pause.

'But go where? Look for what?'

'A job,' said the editor. 'You're fucking sacked.'

Miller went back to the disabled toilet, where he clumsily dispensed another line, using a twenty-pound note and his fingers. It was longer and thicker than Davies's had been. He snorted it, then filled the washbasin with cold water and put his face into it. It felt tremendous. Catherine was right, he thought. He felt – just a little – better.

He knelt by the toilet fully dressed, as Feasey had. He took the ring box out of his jacket pocket and, leaving the ring in its place, emptied the rest of the cocaine into it, then put it back in his inside pocket. There was a distant roll of thunder. He took out his mobile and dialled his driver's number.

'Thomas,' he said.
'Yes.'
'What day is it?'
'What?'
'Just fucking tell me,' he said.
'It's Wednesday,' Thomas said. 'No. It's Thursday. Morning.'
'Go and get Sarah,' Miller said.
'Sarah.'
'Sarah Webb.'
'The agony aunt,' said the driver, with a neutral expression.
'I've not got her number,' said Miller. 'But she lives in Gerrard Street. Number 18.'
'I know where she lives,' said Thomas. 'But it's two o'clock in the morning.'
'Just fucking get her,' said Miller. 'Tell her it's a matter of life and death.'

He went back to the bar. Staley was standing in the doorway of the club, staring out into the street. Miller ordered another whisky; he'd just finished it when Webb arrived, looking flustered. She was a woman of about forty, a little older than him, maternal-looking, with broad shoulders, straight brown hair and glasses. They'd had a short-lived affair before he married. Sarah, he thought, was the one person who might help him. She was often consulted by people at the paper, from the canteen staff to the editors. Agony aunt didn't do her justice. She was single and dependable. She had a psychology degree. She was sober. She was only in the office on a Friday. News of his embarrassment wouldn't have reached her yet. He didn't want to confide in anyone who knew.

'I passed Gerald Staley on the way in,' she said. 'He pushed past me.'

'Really?'

'He seemed to be crying.'

'I just sacked him.'

'What for?'

'For being a prat.'

Sarah sat down on the next stool. She'd pulled on a T-shirt and jeans; the clothes were slightly wet and clinging to her. Raindrops were running down her forehead. He lent her his handkerchief; Sarah took it and spread it out on the bar. Apart from a slight smear of ice-cream, it was just as it had been when he'd set out that morning: white, starched and perfect.

'You don't cry yourself, then?' she said.

'No,' Miller told her.

Sarah pressed the handkerchief against her face, then gave it back to him. She was strong and handsome, Miller thought, if not conventionally alluring. Even so, how different his life might had been if...'

'This had better be good,' she said. 'I went to bed at eleven.'

'It is,' he said. 'Don't worry. It is good. It's very good. It's the best.'

'God Almighty,' she said, 'you're drinking.' She took hold of his chin and turned his face towards hers. 'You look terrible.'

He got her a drink. 'Let's not sit here,' she said. 'This place is crawling with hacks.' She steered him away from the bar; they sat down on a leather sofa in a quiet corner of the large room. He told her about the cupboard, and the Indian restaurant, and the air-mail envelope.

'Jesus Christ.' She laughed.

'I'm glad you think it's funny.'

'OK,' she said. 'But come on – it was hardly Romeo and Juliet, was it, you and Elizabeth.'

'What do I do now?' he asked her.

'Go away,' she said.

'Where to?'

'Abroad,' she said.
'How long for?'
'A fortnight. At least.'
'Where to?' he repeated.
'You tell me,' she said.
'What do I say to the paper?'
'I'll talk to them.'
'What about Linda Mealing?'
'Hire her.'
'She's blackmailing me.'
'I think that bomb has been kind of defused, don't you,' said Sarah, 'since everybody in the building knows already.'
'They'll fire me,' he said.
'I doubt it,' she said. 'They like you. Circulation's up. Advertising's up. This is not a sacking offence. Go away. And when you come back, don't look at the papers. Then it'll all be rumour. But what are you going to do about Charlotte?'
'Sack her.'
'You don't have too much trouble firing people do you?'
'I quite like it,' Miller replied. 'It's like clearing out an old sock drawer.'
She went to the bar and came back with a gin for herself, another whisky, and a large bottle of mineral water. 'Try and drink some of this,' she said. He noticed another rumble of thunder, louder than the first. Miller sniffed. His thoughts were coming very rapidly, and on an unusually diverse range of topics.
'Have you ever had the feeling,' he asked her, 'of totally losing control?'
Sarah raised her eyebrows, but said nothing.
'I remember when I was a boy,' he said, 'I had a book that had a chapter in it about that Russian space dog; the one they sent on the first manned space flight.'
'Manned?'
'Well – you know – dogged. They poisoned its last dinner and, er…' He sniffed heavily, and swallowed. 'I can't remember where I was.'

'The dog.'

'Who, Heathcliff?' Miller asked.

'What?' she said. 'No. The dog. The space dog.'

'Right. She had her breakfast, and they strapped her into this rocket and three minutes later she was in orbit. I mean – what must that feel like, Sarah?'

'What do you think it feels like?'

'This,' he said.

'Are you all right?'

'I'm perfect.' He swallowed again; the bitterness was still in his throat. 'Never better.'

He turned to face her. 'Will you come home with me?'

'Why?'

'So that I won't be alone,' he replied.

'No,' she said. Then: 'How are you going to get home?'

'Thomas,' he said. 'He's waiting outside.'

A look of disgust passed over her face.

'It's three o'clock,' she said. 'I have to go. Call me.'

When she'd gone Miller finished her drink and went outside to find his driver. The street was empty; thunder was still rolling in the distance. He called Thomas's new mobile, and got the answering service. He went back into the club, and sat at the bar; he ordered another whisky. He told the barman to call him a cab and asked for the bill. Miller paid it and was putting his wallet back in his pocket when he felt the eternity-ring case and the twenty-pound note. It was still rolled, though more loosely. He thought about going back to the disabled toilet, but he felt unsteady on his feet. In the end, after a furtive glance around the bar, he turned away from the main room towards the pillar next to him, put the banknote into the ring box and, pressing against one nostril, inhaled hard. As he did so, he was dimly aware of a flash of lightning, and some kind of scuffle by the exit.

With some difficulty, he slipped the box and the money back into his inside pocket. He reached out for his glass, but it had gone. The manager was at his side. 'Out Mr Miller,' he said. 'Now.'

He was taken firmly by the arm and pushed into the driving rain. He walked on to Charing Cross Road and tried to get a cab; the one or two he saw with their For Hire signs lit didn't stop for him. In Denmark Street he found an unlicensed Nigerian operator who asked for a hundred pounds up front, then began the long journey to the editor's Surrey home.

Miller got in just before four thirty. He went into the living room and sat on the sofa, from where he could see the road. He looked across at Glastonbury. Illingworth's dim bedroom lights were still on. The curtains were still drawn.

He looked around for his wedding picture. It was where Miller had left it, in the middle of the mantelpiece. He stumbled through to the kitchen – where, he noticed, the work surfaces were piled with unwashed plates and dishes – and rummaged under the sink, in a cupboard full of DIY materials. He returned to the living room carrying an aerosol can of silver paint. He sat down again, put the wedding photograph on his knees, and sprayed over it until nothing of the picture, or the wooden frame, was visible.

His eyes went up to Illingworth's house again. Miller opened the front door. He draped the doormat across the threshold, in case the door slammed shut, locking him out. The rain had eased to a gentle drizzle and the storm was over. His silver aerosol still in his hand, he walked unsteadily towards Illingworth's large black Mercedes.

Mindful of his condition, he took particular care to keep the first letter legible. When he'd finished, he stood back, wiped the rain out of his eyes, and examined it. Unmistakably a W, it was two foot high; a little too wide perhaps, covering half of the passenger door. He made the A narrower. He'd completed the N, half-way along the side of the car, when he remembered that he'd not brought his cigarettes with him.

He went back in the house, where he lit a Gitane. Outside again, with his can in his hand, he kept the cigarette dangling from his mouth, like a French artist, as he completed his work. The final R, he noticed with satisfaction, was in a position which allowed him to extend its last, descending stroke into an elegant curve, following the line of the rear-wheel arch.

He closed the front door behind him and sat on the sofa again. He put the aerosol on the mantelpiece and watched as trickles of paint ran down the side of the can. There was paint on his shirt and hands too; on his trousers, a large patch of silver which, when he put his legs together, had a neat rectangular space in the middle, where the material been protected by the wedding photograph. He stared at the oblong for a few moments, then got to his feet. He was sweating, and the strength seemed to have gone from his legs. He staggered towards the stairs, and the quiet of his deserted room.

He woke at eleven. His bedroom curtains were open and he was lying in bed, naked except for the white shirt he'd put on for work the previous day. Glancing down, he noticed that he still had on his tie, which was hanging loosely around his chest. He had a headache. It was only when he squinted into the sunlight and noticed the outline of Glastonbury, opposite, that he remembered she had gone. A feeling of nausea came over him and he lay back down, flat on his back, and stared at the ceiling.

There was an insistent pain in his bladder. Still on his back, he half-raised himself by taking his weight on his elbows, but even this movement seemed to drain him of energy. He wasn't sure if he could sit up, let alone stand. He lay back down again and then, with his hands clasped behind his head, urinated where he was. For a moment he felt gloriously liberated. He felt the warmth flood over his lower abdomen and the pure cotton front tails of his shirt. It was comforting, and briefly he was a child again, with his needs in someone else's hands.

Then he noticed another, less attractive feeling – a cold, clinging effect from his shirt and sheets. If he moved, even slightly, it was far worse. He was lying stock still, wondering what to do about it, when the doorbell rang.

Then, in a second, he saw the truth of it. It had been a sick joke on the part of his wife – a crude ploy intended to turn him, for the next ten years, into the husband he ought to have been for the last nine. And now, after a night in a suite at the Marriott, she was back. The doorbell rang again. This wasn't the time to test her patience. Miller pulled himself from the bed, vaguely aware of an unpleasant note in the air. He picked up a large towel that was lying on the floor, and wrapped it round his waist. It was blue, and faded, and it was decorated with a map of the Côte d'Azur. But the towel trapped the shirt's sodden flaps against his upper thigh and held them there, cold and repulsive. He pulled the amber-stained shirt-tails out so they hung down over the towel. The bell rang for a third time.

He made his way slowly downstairs: the towel was so tight that it made every step difficult. He looked down at the discoloured shirt and decided to put the door on the chain. He opened it and squinted through the gap. His nose almost touched the forehead of a woman, who was peering through the crack from the other side. Moving back a couple of inches and closing one eye, he saw that it was not his wife. She was smaller than his wife. She had dark hair and she was formally dressed, in a navy blue suit and black shoes.

'Mr Miller?'

Her voice had an urgent, commanding tone.

'Yes.'

'Let me in please.'

'Is it something serious?' he said.

'I'm afraid so Mr Miller.'

'Is it a matter…' he added, looking down at his shirt, 'of life and death?'

'I'm sorry,' she said. 'Please let me in.'

He opened the door. Next to her, on her right, he noticed a small man, holding a large black case of the kind used by lawyers to transport box files to court. Miller turned round and the two followed him as he began to shuffle awkwardly down the hall into the kitchen. They waited as he bent down to pick up a small pile of credit cards and banknotes, then the set of keys he'd thrown down on his return the previous evening. He saw, but ignored, the air-mail envelope and Staley's packet of squid. A little further down the hall, he stooped to collect a packet of Gitanes, a disposable lighter and his ring box. He carried the objects clasped to his chest with his left hand: the act of kneeling had loosed his towel a little, and he walked more freely into the kitchen, holding it in place with his right.

He sat down at the table, lit a cigarette and inhaled deeply.

His visitors were still standing.

'Has there been an accident?' he asked them. The smoke hit his stomach, and he felt suddenly faint. He got up, steadied himself with both hands against the sink, and vomited over the washing up. His towel fell to the floor. He thought about trying to retrieve it, then vomited again. Gasping for air just before he retched for a third time, he was vaguely aware of the man taking something out of his bag. The girl had picked his lighted cigarette off the floor; she extinguished it in a saucer, then went to the sink and turned on the cold tap. She handed him a glass of water. He rinsed his mouth out and spat into the sink. He found a cloth and wiped his eyes, which were streaming. As he bent to pick up the beach towel, he saw that the man was squatting at his level six feet away, holding a camera. He started firing off frames, using flash and a motor drive.

'What speed film are you using?' Miller asked, trying to bring some small element of normality to the bizarre scene unfolding in front of him.

'Four hundred,' said the photographer.

'You could have done it without flash,' Miller said, 'using sixteen hundred.' His towel back in place, now wrapped too tightly again, he advanced towards the photographer, taking absurd small, twine-toed steps, like a model in a figure-hugging ball gown. The man picked up his bag and backed off down the hall. Miller turned and let him go. The front door slammed. He heard a car start, then pull away.

When he came back into the kitchen, the woman was at the table, emptying a sachet of a hangover cure into a fresh glass of water. He sat down on a chair opposite her and kept his eyes on the granules as they dissolved.

'Where did you find that?' he asked her.

'I brought it,' she said. She handed him her press ID and a business card which carried the name of a liberal broadsheet.

'Ah,' he said. 'I see. Morning, Miss Ellis.'

She reached into her shoulder bag and produced two miniatures: one of brandy, one of port. She poured them together into another glass. She set both glasses, the medicine and the alcohol, in front of him.

'Go on,' she said. 'Drink them. That's the best cure there is.'

He swallowed the first, but left the alcohol untouched.

'The thing is,' he told her, 'I'm not really a drinker.'

She offered him one of his own cigarettes, which he accepted, and inhaled a little more cautiously than the last. His heart was racing.

'What's your name again?' he asked her.

'Rebecca,' she said.

'Who's he?' he asked, gesturing towards her absent colleague.

'Rod,' she said.

'Don't I know him?'

'You might do,' she said. 'He's a freelance.'

'You'll excuse me asking you this…' he began. 'But what the hell…'

'The thing is,' she told him, 'you were in Larkin's last night.'

He nodded.

'Well so was Rod.'

'Oh,' he replied. 'I didn't see him.'

'No,' she said. 'But he saw you.'

She handed him a photograph. It was over-exposed, probably taken in haste with a compact, and the candles and spotlights in the background were showing the signs of camera shake. But the image in the foreground was all too clear. It was Miller himself, sitting at the bar, holding a rolled twenty-pound note, his unscarred left index finger pressed to close his left nostril.

He picked up the brandy and port, and tasted a little of it. It was sweet, cloying, and reassuring. It reminded him of some cough mixture he'd had as a boy. He started to feel a little better.

'This picture,' he said. 'Are you giving it to me?'

'Yes,' she said. 'If you'd like to keep it.'

'Thank you,' he said. 'I would.'

'But then we do have the originals.'

He drained the glass.

'Coffee?' she asked.

'No,' he said. 'Thank you.'

He got up and turned his back on her, and began rinsing vomit off a plate.

'What do you want?' he asked her. 'Money?'

'No.'

He turned the tap off and sat down again.

'You see…' For the first time, he noticed, his visitor was starting to look a little flustered. 'We're aware that your newspaper has taken quite a firm line on the question of, er, drugs... I mean quite rightly, quite correctly. I mean none of us... and so I – just – we wanted to give you a chance to put your side of the story.'

It was when he heard this last cliché – widely parodied in the business as the inevitable prelude to a merciless hatchet job – that Miller's mood, which had ricocheted between bewilderment, resignation and despair, finally settled on rage. He looked at the girl. If she'd been working for him, he'd have sacked her on the spot for that last imbecility. For a moment, his unease was overcome by anger and contempt.

'You'd like to hear my side of the story?' he said, pointing at the photograph. She nodded.

'Why?' he asked her.

There was a silence.

'Because...' she began. 'I think... the thing about this is...'

'Why?' he asked again. 'Why? When I'm already fucked?'

He looked at her. She said nothing. She stared at her shoes.

'How old are you?' he asked her.

'Twenty-four.'

'I guess you don't usually dress like this Rebecca, do you, at your paper,' he said. 'Not at your office. Unless it's one of your dress-up Fridays.'

She didn't reply, but he saw her glance down at his stained shirt and his beach towel – arranged unfortunately, as if on purpose, so that his knees neatly displayed the outline of Cap d'Antibes – struggling to stifle her disgust. He felt an impulse to strike her across the face with the back of his hand and she seemed to sense it. And then – perhaps it was a legacy from his days as a young reporter in Oldham, when he'd had the job of rifling through bereaved parents' wardrobes, looking for pictures of their murdered child while an older colleague detained them with a shorthand pad downstairs – some perverse part of him put himself in her position.

'I will have a coffee,' he said. 'Please.'

'You can take your jacket off,' he added. After a moment, with a kind of furtive reluctance, she did. She was wearing a man's white shirt, with button-down breast pockets. She put on the kettle, then went to the sink and, as the electric element creaked into life, began rinsing more vomit off plates. 'Leave it,' he shouted at her. She looked up at him. There was a suggestion of fear in her eyes. 'Leave it,' he said more quietly. 'We'll go next door. To the front room.'

On the kitchen table in front of him there was a cassette recorder that he hadn't noticed earlier. It was a black model, about the size of a thick paperback, of a kind that most journalists had abandoned in favour of less cumbersome digital machines. Its small red lights were flashing. The tape was rolling. He left it on. The microphone was propped up in the fruit bowl. Next to it he saw the pile of notes and the small jewellery box. He opened it, to see if the ring was still in it, and found that the box was still half-full of cocaine. He tipped the powder out on to the wooden table, lifted the ring out, held it up to the light, and looked at the small sapphire stones. He put it back in the box. Using his guest's business card, he coaxed the powder into a six-inch line. Rebecca was staring at him from across the room, the kettle in her hand. Her mouth was slightly open. He rolled one of the twenty-pound notes and snorted what was left of the drug.

'I've never had this before last night,' he told her. She didn't reply.

'May as well be hanged,' he added, 'for a sheep as a lamb.'

He got up and shuffled into the next room. She followed him, with two mugs of coffee.

'My mother told me never to say front room,' he told her.

'Why?'

'Because it made people think you only had two rooms.'

'Why did that bother her?'

'Because we did.'

She sat down on the sofa next to him and picked up her coffee. He left his untouched.

Her eyes went to the mantelpiece: the obliterated wedding photograph, and the silver aerosol next to it.

'What does your father do Rebecca?' he asked her.

'He's a judge.'

'You've forgotten your tape machine,' he said.

She looked at him, hesitant and guilty.

'Go on,' he said. 'Remember what you came for.'

'What?'

'My side of the story.'

She returned with the cassette recorder which she switched back on and left on the table in front of them.

'What did your father do?' she asked.

'He was a newsagent.'

'News runs in your family,' she said, with a nervous laugh.

'That's right,' he told her. 'Like judging does in yours.'

They sat together on the sofa, facing the window, side by side. If someone had looked in from the road, he thought, they might have been taken for two people watching a bad disaster film.

He stared silently ahead of him, at Glastonbury.

'What...' she began. 'Is there anything I can...'

'What time is it?' he asked her.

'Half eleven,' she said.

He could feel tears in his eyes.

'What is it?'

He kept staring straight ahead of him.

'Look over there,' he said.

'Where?'

'There,' he said. 'At Glastonbury.'

'Glastonbury?'

'It's the house,' he said. 'Over there.' He pointed. 'Look at the upstairs curtains,' he said. 'Do you notice anything?'

'They're closed,' she said. Then: 'Has somebody died?'

'They're closed,' he said, 'out of respect for my wife.'

The girl looked puzzled.

'My wife,' he said, 'has never been more alive. My wife is in the bedroom. Having sexual intercourse.'

'Having...' she began.

'Or recovering,' he added, 'from having sexual intercourse.'

'Is that – is Glastonbury – your house too?' she asked.

'No,' he said.

'Who...'

'It belongs to Simon Illingworth,' he told her. 'He's a barrister. He's in the bedroom as well. He lives there. He's normally up at five thirty. But he's not normally making love to my wife. My wife left me,' he said. 'Last night.'

'I'm sorry,' she said. 'Did you love her?'

'What?'

'Did you love her?'

He looked down at the urine-soaked shirt, then at the tape recorder. 'I think I might have,' he said. 'Once.'

She placed her hand on his forearm for a moment, then took it away.

He paused. He felt the beginning of a rush from the drug. Nothing, it occurred to him, could make this situation any better, or any worse. He was on board the express now, and he was going all the way.

'She left me,' he added, 'because I slept... because I... had sex with... my secretary. In a store cupboard.'

'I see,' she said. 'That would do it.'

'It would,' he said. 'It did.'

His mind started to wander.

'I always thought,' he added, 'that he was gay.'

'Who?'

'Illingworth.'

'Why?'

'Because he looked it.'

'Did that bother you?'

He looked at her. 'What?'

'Your newspaper,' she added, 'might give people the idea that you don't like homosexuals.'

'I don't,' he said.

'Or black people.'

'I don't like them either,' he said. He noticed her check the level on her tape machine. She saw him catch her at it.

'When I used to find myself doing that,' he said, 'I knew it was going well. I knew it was rolling.'

'Why don't you like them?' she said.

'Who?' he asked. He felt another flash of rage at her moral superiority. 'The niggers or the queers?'

He breathed in deeply, through irritation.

'You know...,' he said, 'when I have – when I had – a quiet evening at home... I used to watch the old Ealing comedies. They're so restful. So calm. Why do you think that is?'

She didn't reply.

'I'll tell you why it is,' he said. 'It's because they have country lanes with birds, and horses, and not many cars,' he said. 'And cities with large Gothic town halls, and a main square with four straight roads leading off it, called Market Street, High Street, Corporation Street and Queen's Street. It's because there are red buses with conductors, who look after their passengers. Who pay their fares in old coppers. Who tell the time by public clocks. Who visit tiled public conveniences named Ladies and Gentlemen. Who *are* ladies and gentlemen. It's because there are young people who say please and thank you. Who are not illiterate. Who do not spray graffiti on other people's property, and fill the air with vile oaths. There are steam trains which leave on time. There are firemen who shovel coal into their boilers, who take pride in their job. There are no menacing yobs on street corners. No old ladies being mugged for their fish and chips,' he added. 'And no black people.'

She was looking at him as if he was insane.

'Or people,' she added, 'like Hassan Ignatovich.'

Miller glared at her. Shortly after he'd taken over the paper, the news pages had run a picture of a paedophile's house on a council estate in Malden, Essex. The photographer, who had been sent to photograph number 83, came back with a shot of the wrong house, as a result of which Mr Ignatovich, who lived at 38, had been burned alive, by vigilantes.

'That wasn't my fault,' he said.

'Oh really?'

'Anyhow he was...'

'Yes?' Rebecca interrupted. 'What shall I put there? Bosnian? Islamic? An asylum seeker?'

'Put what you like,' said Miller.

He took a deep breath, and closed his eyes.

'Have you got any more port?'

'No.'

'Can I have some water?'

While she was gone, he stared at the curtains opposite. They hadn't moved.

She handed him the glass and sat down again.

'Is that her?' she said. She pointed to one of the photographs over the mantelpiece.

'Yes,' he said.

'What's her name?'

'Elizabeth.'

'She's beautiful,' she said.

'You know – I noticed that again last night,' he said. 'My wife is a very beautiful woman. She had beautiful arms.'

He shut his eyes. He started to shiver. He felt the girl put an arm round his shoulders. He could feel her small right breast as it pressed against his ribs. She held him firmly, as if she was trying to stop him from disintegrating. Her skirt must be touching his urine-soaked shirt, it occurred to him, but she seemed oblivious or indifferent to it, like a nurse.

'Your heart,' she said.

'My heart?'

'It's racing.'

'Yes. Sorry.'

'What did she think about the other women?'

'Which other women?'

'The other women,' she added, 'that you've slept with since you were married.'

'Oh,' he said. 'Them.'

'You slept with a lot of them.'

'Yes,' he said. 'How did you know?'

'I didn't,' she said. 'How many?'

Some last instinct of modesty flickered in him.

'No,' he said. 'I don't...'
She leaned forward and switched off her tape recorder. She unplugged the microphone.

'About eight.'

She kept her arm round him, and rested her head on his shoulder.

'How many really?'

'Eighteen.'

'Did you ever fall in love with them?'

'Always.'

She laughed.

'No. I did.'

He was breathing irregularly and in unusually deep gulps. He wondered if he was going to have a heart attack.

'Try to breathe more gently,' she said.

'What's happening to me?'

'It's a panic attack,' she said. 'I used to get them.'

'Is that what this is?'

'Yes.'

'You know,' she said, 'you can get black people that say please and thank you, and white people that spray graffiti.'

'I've heard that,' he said. 'Yes.'

Miller got to his feet abruptly. He went to the window and looked out. Now he was standing he could see Illingworth's car, in its bold new livery.

'Oh shit,' he said.

She came and stood next to him.

'Oh dear,' she said. 'That is a mess.' She turned around and picked up the spray can. 'I guess you don't need to be Sherlock Holmes to work out who did that.'

'No,' he told her. 'You don't even have to be Watson.'

'If I'd been with you,' she began, 'I'd...'

'Go on,' he said. 'You'd have stopped me. Like hell you would.'

'I'd have told you,' she went on, 'that there's only one N in wanker.'

He went back to the window and looked again at the graffiti, unmistakable in all of its seven letters.

'Oh fuck,' he said. 'I think I stopped in the middle for a smoke.'

He sank back into the sofa. She sat down next to him and put her arm back on his shoulder. He didn't resist. It seemed to be doing him good.

There was a silence. 'And black people,' she said, 'can shovel coal into steam locomotives.'

'Black *people*,' he repeated. He laughed, for the first time that day. 'I love your newspaper.'

'At least we're not racists,' she said. She drew away from him.

He got up again.

'In our country,' he said, 'if you don't mind me calling it that, blacks are over-represented in statistics of crime.'

'In certain categories of crime,' she said. 'White people,' she added, 'are over-represented in certain categories of crime.'

'What – fraud you mean? Well you need intelligence to do that.'

'Are you saying,' she asked him, 'that you believe white people to be more intelligent than black people?'

'I don't know. But I'd like the freedom to debate it.'

'Well debate it,' she said. 'We're debating it now. Who's stopping you?'

'On the front page of my newspaper.'

'Why?' she said.

He felt dizzy and sat down again. He held out his left arm and extended his fingers. They were trembling alarmingly. He felt her arm round him again and he was grateful, even though he knew this gesture, just like the last time she did it, was anything but sincere.

'When I... when I was with my secretary in the stock cupboard,' he said, 'I showed absolutely no regard for her...' He stopped.

'Go on,' she said, softly.

'For her... physical, or emotional... experience. For the first time ever, in my life.'

'Oh yeah?' she said, playfully. It was possibly the first genuine remark she'd made all day.

'Yes,' he said. 'When I was nine, at primary school,' he said, 'I put my hand up Linda Reece's dress, in assembly. An hour later I was stood in Miss Sykes's room, with my parents, and her parents. I remember – you know how you blush, and it might be bad, but it's short? I remember blushing and it didn't stop; I remember thinking, thank God there isn't a mirror in here, because I don't ever want to see this colour. If I see it, I'll remember it.'

'What happened?' she asked.

'Miss Sykes told my parents – why were they both there?' he asked. 'She told them what I'd done, and I was sick on my shoes,' he said. 'I remember they brought me these rough tissues out of the toilets. I remember there was a map on the wall and I was staring at it, to block out what was happening to me. I just picked out this one town, and I thought if I ever get out of here, and live my life, I could move there, perhaps to a monastery, and nobody would know me, or know what I'd done.'

'Where was it?' she asked.

'Vilnius,' he said.

'Where?'

'Vilnius. It's in Lithuania.'

She laughed.

'I think it's since then,' he said, 'that when I've been with women, I've always tried to be...' He paused. How had he got himself into this? 'I've always tried to be considerate to...'

'I think I see what you're saying,' she said. 'Do you think that you've been over-sensitive?'

He said nothing.

'When I met my wife,' he said, 'she was sitting on the terrace at a hotel in France, and the sun was going down. I remember she was wearing this green floral dress, showing her arms... and then the sun set and it was getting cold. I told her, isn't it funny how, when you're cold – say when you're in the shower, there's a point at the back of your neck where, if you keep it warm, then you feel warm all over. I think it must be some neurological thing or something...'

'And?' she asked him.

'And she said "where?" and I just put the base of my thumb, here, against her neck.'

'What did she say?'

'She said hey, you know what? I'm still cold. And I went to take my hand away and she said no – leave it there. I like it.'

He was shivering, and his heart was racing faster. His breathing seemed no longer to be automatic; at times he seemed to have lost the need to breathe. Then, after thirty seconds or so, he felt faint and took a large, involuntary gulp of air. He stared at Glastonbury and began to imagine that Illingworth was pulling his clothes on, about to come out and see the damage to his car, a prospect that worried Miller more over his spelling than his crime.

'Are you cold?' she said. She rested the inside of her forearm against the nape of his neck.

'Rebecca?' he said.

'Yes?'

'Call me a doctor now please.'

'Shall I drive you to Casualty?' she asked.

'The National Health?' he asked her. 'After what I've been taking? Do you think I'm fucking mad?'

He handed her his address book.

'Dr Norman,' he said. 'Tell him I think – no – tell him *you* think I'm having a heart attack.'

He went upstairs to take a shower. Taking off his shirt and seeing his chest seemed to make the possibility of sudden death imminent. He stepped into the shower cubicle. He washed the cigarette smoke out of his hair, and opened his mouth and let the water rinse the bitter flavours of vomit and cocaine out of his mouth. Even in the shower, he noticed, his thoughts were ranging wildly, and out of his control. He looked down at his penis. How much more of a gentleman, he thought, he might have been without it.

Miller stepped out of the shower and found a dressing gown. He carried the old towel and his sodden shirt up to the bedroom. The smell, now he was clean, was unmistakable: urine, sweat and stale whisky.

Just for a moment he'd forgotten the young woman downstairs. He contemplated going down and asking her for mercy, or offering her money. It was a brief thought, and not one on which he wasted much time. It didn't work like that.

He found a pale blue shirt that was too big for him. He put it on and felt more comfortable. If it had been tight it would have reminded him of his heartbeat. He pulled on a pair of blue jeans and black suede shoes with no socks.

He came down. 'He's coming straight round,' Rebecca said, brightly. She stood very close to him, and took both his wrists. She looked into his eyes.

'Don't worry,' she said, almost as if she meant it. 'You'll survive.' She kept close to him and tilted her face at a slight upward angle, as though inviting a kiss.

He stepped back from her. A car drew up outside. Andrew Norman, wearing a pinstripe suit, as he always did, came in with his bag.

'Morning,' he said to Rebecca.

He turned to Miller. 'Wife away?' he asked, loudly and cheerfully.

He noticed his patient's expression.

'Christ,' Dr Norman said. 'I've seen you look better. What is it this time – another brain tumour? The liver cancer? Oh no, right, you're having a coronary... Mind if I make myself a coffee first?' He set off for the kitchen.

Miller showed the journalist out.

She was half-way down the garden path when he called her name.

'Yes?' she came back and stood facing him in the doorway.

'You forgot your jacket.'

'Oh – right.'

She went to step past him, but he took her by the arm.

'Can I ask you something?'

'Yes.'

'Do you know how long I've been a journalist?'

'Ten years?'

'Fifteen.'

He put one hand on her shoulder and the other on the left breast pocket of her shirt. The doctor reappeared at the end of the corridor then, seeing them in this position, turned on his heel and went back into the kitchen. With his right hand, Miller undid the button that fastened her pocket.

'May I?' he asked. He pulled out a digital tape recorder, no bigger than a matchbox.

'One hour thirty two minutes,' he said, reading the display. 'How long do these things do?'

'Two and a half hours.'

'Where's the microphone?'

'It's built in.'

'I should get one,' he said. He switched the machine off, opened it and took out the disk. He held it up to inspect it for a moment, before replacing it.

'Except that I'll have no cause to use one now, will I, not in my new profession. Whatever that is.'

She looked down again.

He handed the machine, and the disk, back to her.

'Crucify me Rebecca,' he said. 'It's all you can do.'

He watched her walk over to examine Illingworth's car. She was dialling a number on her mobile as she stepped into the road, which she crossed without looking. It was only fortune, Miller found himself thinking, that prevented her from being knocked down and killed.

He closed the front door and walked through to the kitchen, where he found Dr Norman making himself coffee. Miller sat down at the kitchen table. The doctor stood over the kettle, his back to the editor. Miller closed his eyes, wondering how to explain his condition. It didn't help that he knew Norman socially; he played golf with him most weekends, listening as the doctor enthused over classical music, fine art and other things that Miller pretended to know about, but didn't.

With his eyes shut, he thought, it might be easier, just as some things are more easily said on the telephone.

'In the past twenty-four hours,' Miller said, his eyes screwed up tightly, to the point that he was seeing strange luminous shapes, and in pain; 'my life has collapsed around me, at every level. I used to think I knew the meaning of the word catastrophe. I didn't.'

Hearing no response from the doctor, he opened his eyes again. Norman was still facing away from him. He turned around to face his host.

'Miller,' he said.

'Yes?'

'Have you got any biscuits?'

The editor took a cigarette from his packet and, holding it like a pencil, drove the end against the table-top several times, to remove any loose flakes of tobacco.

'No,' he said.

Norman turned away from him once more to pick up his coffee, had a final glance in the cupboard, then came and sat down opposite Miller.

'Now,' he said. 'What can I do for you?'

'Did you hear what I just said?'

'I... no. I've just come from a bad case. And I was out on a call at six this morning. Forgive me.'

Miller lit his cigarette. 'Do you hate me or something?'

'Hate you?' the doctor replied. He laughed. 'On the contrary. All doctors love hypochondriacs.'

'Why?'

'Because hypochondriacs, generally speaking, are people of imagination. They are, by definition, in good – usually excellent – health. They brighten up our day. They break up the procession of the...'

'Of the what?'

'I was going to say: of the sane people dying.'

Norman sipped his coffee. 'If that grotesque physical parade could be called a carnival,' he said, 'when one of you comes to the surgery, you're like the clowns coming on.'

A pause. 'I have just come from the house of a man of thirty-two,' he said. 'His girlfriend died of cancer. They have a two-year-old son. Now he – the father – has a terminal disease.'

'Even hypochondriacs can die,' said Miller. 'Even hypochondriacs get terminal disease.'

'Yes,' said Norman. 'But when that happens, they're not hypochondriacs. When that happens, they're patients.'

'Are you a good doctor?' Miller asked him.

'I am a very good doctor,' he replied. 'Very good – not brilliant. But there is one skill I have never mastered.'

'What?'

'I have never mastered the art of breaking bad news.'

'What do you mean?'

'First I try to pretend it hasn't happened...'

'To the patient?'

'Often. Then...' Norman sighed. 'Then, since you ask, I try to give them a more comforting diagnosis, which invariably turns into a strange downward spiral, over the next couple of sentences, through more and more serious conditions... at the end of which I usually blurt it out.'

There was another silence, during which Miller noticed he seemed to have stopped needing to breathe again, and so didn't. Then, after fifteen seconds or so, he gasped for air as if he'd just surfaced after being trapped under water. He exhaled, felt he was going to pass out, and gasped again, too fast and too hard. He gripped the edge of the wooden table with both hands; as he did so, he dropped the lighted cigarette which rolled towards Norman, who picked it up and tossed it over his shoulder into the sink.

The doctor took Miller's left wrist in his right hand, and held it firmly. With his free hand, Norman reached out to pick up his coffee, then didn't. His eye met Miller's, then he looked away again. They remained silent there, in the same position, for thirty seconds. Miller's breath was still coming in deep, irregular gasps.

'Have you got a paper bag?' the doctor asked Miller.

'What?'

'A paper bag.'

Norman saw one, on top of the bread bin. He picked it up, and emptied its contents on to the table: four large chocolate-chip cookies from the local bakery.

'There you go,' said Miller, between gasps.

The doctor ignored him.

'Get up,' he said, 'and come through to the living room.'

'I can't.'

'You can.'

'I'll faint.'

'You won't.'

Miller got to his feet and walked through to the living room. Norman followed him, carrying his medical bag.

'Lie on there,' he said, indicating the sofa. Miller collapsed on to it. He was sitting on something hard: he got up and pulled out his mobile phone, the one he'd forgotten to take to work with him the previous day. Norman took the paper bag, parted the top and blew gently into it. 'Now breathe into this.'

Miller managed a mutinous look. 'Are you taking the piss? I didn't know,' he added, 'that I had biscuits.'

'No,' said Norman.

Miller took the bag, breathed into it, and handed it back to the doctor.

'Now,' said Norman. 'Keep that over your face. Breathe in and out. Slowly. Until I tell you to stop.'

The doctor opened his leather case and took out a stethoscope. He undid Miller's shirt, and put it to his chest.

'Am I having a heart attack?' Miller asked, through the bag.

'No.'

'Are you about to go into your strange downward spiral?' Miller asked.

'No.'

'You would tell me if…'

'Yes. Just keep breathing slowly.'

He felt Norman undo his left cuff, and there was a tightening around his upper arm. The doctor looked at the blood pressure gauge, said nothing, removed the device, then went back to his bag. He produced a flat piece of white triangular plastic, tipped some round white tablets into it, and began channelling them into a small brown bottle.

'How's the breathing?' he asked.

'Better,' said Miller. He put the paper bag down.

'Good,' said Norman. 'Now. What the hell have you been doing?'

'I had quite a bit to drink yesterday.'

'Really?' the doctor replied. 'I'd never have guessed. How many units?'

'What's a unit again?'

'A bottle of wine – ten. A large whisky, four.'

'I don't know,' said Miller. 'Forty?'

Norman was giving him a forbidding look which Miller, who was used to reprimands for partial disclosure, took as a signal of doubt at his estimate.

'OK,' he said, 'maybe fifty.'

'And a night of passion.'

'No,' said Miller.

'Anything else?'

'I had a bit of cocaine.'

The doctor picked up the paper bag and placed it on Miller's chest. 'Use it again,' he said, 'if you need to.'

'What's wrong with me?'

'You were hyperventilating.'

The doctor disappeared into the kitchen and came back with a glass of water. He was balancing it on a saucer. There were a few pills next to it.

'I was what?'

'You were taking in too much oxygen.'

'Why?'

Norman turned away from him, facing the road. 'Because you're a...' He stepped closer to the window.

'Good God,' he said. 'There's a photographer taking pictures of Illingworth's car.'

Miller picked up his biscuit bag, and raised it to his face again.

'Jesus,' Norman said. 'He's got on the wrong side of somebody. They've written...'

'I know,' said Miller.

He kept the bag to his face for a minute or so and his breathing returned to normal.

'How does this work?' he asked.

'If you gasp for air,' the doctor said, turning towards his patient, 'you're taking in more carbon dioxide. Less oxygen. It's very simple.'

He turned back and looked out of the window again.

'So you knew about Illingworth's car.'

'Yes,' said Miller. 'It was me.'

'Why the bloody hell did you do that?'

The editor put his paper bag down. 'Because I was too paralytic to think of making a petrol bomb.'

'Oh,' said the doctor. 'But why...'

'Because Elizabeth is up there,' said Miller, indicating the bedroom curtains, still closed. 'In Glastonbury.'

'Where's Illingworth?'

'He's in there too.'

'In there? Why? Oh.'

He picked up the saucer holding the water and the pills, and started walking towards his patient, then stopped half-way.

'*Illingworth?*'

Miller shrugged.

'Take these,' Norman said. There were two pink capsules and two of the round white tablets. Miller swallowed them. His sleeve was still rolled up. Without asking his permission, the doctor took a blood sample.

'Keep your feet up. Then – can you do me a favour?' He reached into his bag and took out a pen and a newspaper. He folded it over to reveal the cryptic crossword. 'Finish this.'

'Why?'

'Because I bet someone I would. I've been struggling with nine across.'

The doctor started to leave the room.

'Where are you going?'

'I'm going for the biscuits.'

Norman disappeared. Miller looked down at nine across. The clue had been circled in black ink: 'Toasting Lucan or – "Cheers!" (15)' He hadn't done a crossword for ten years. He shut his eyes and pondered it. He could hear Norman in the kitchen, making phone calls. He started to feel very slightly better.

The doctor came back, and took his pulse again.

'Done the crossword?' he asked.

'No,' said Miller. 'I didn't know you liked the crossword.'

'I don't,' said Norman. 'But it's very therapeutic. Have you never read *The Crack-Up?*'

'No.'

'A crossword distracts you. Language, not drugs, is the best analgesic.'

'My father...' Miller began.

'Yes?'

'My father used to be in the air force,' he said. 'He told me once that they had this exercise where they were put in a tank, to simulate conditions of altitude, and the oxygen was gradually reduced in it, until they lost consciousness. He told me that to take their minds off what was happening, they told them to calculate the numerical value of the letters in their name...'

'That's the idea,' said Norman. 'But the crossword is the best. The crossword takes you somewhere else.'

Miller looked around the room.

'I want to be somewhere else.'

'Good,' Norman said. 'I've booked you into the Northgate.' It was a private clinic popular with celebrities. Miller often bought stories from disloyal staff there. A reporter posing as a nursing auxiliary had returned with a picture of a once-ebullient chat-show host attempting to mutilate himself with a table knife.

'What?' Miller asked him. 'Why?'

'Because your pulse was running at between 160 and 180, with slight arrhythmia.'

'Is that bad?'

'It's not good.'

'Blood pressure?'

'Slightly raised. Not bad.'

'What's my heartbeat now?'

'It's ninety,' said Norman. 'And slowing.'

'Is that OK?'

'It's better.'

'It won't get any slower in the Northgate,' said Miller.

'Why?'

'Because they hate me there.'

'Who?'

'What do you mean, who?'

'The patients,' Norman said, 'or the staff?'

'Oh,' Miller replied. 'I see. Both.'

'You need to go to bed,' said the doctor. 'And rest.'

'The thing is,' said Miller, 'that I have to get away.'

His visitor stood up, and looked over at Glastonbury. 'I can see that.'

'No,' Miller said. 'I mean away. Out of London.'

'Why?'

'That woman who left just now… she knows about the drugs.'

'And?'

'And she's a journalist.'

The doctor sat down. 'One of yours?'

'No.'

'Oh dear. And do you think she's going to, er…'

Miller pressed his lips together tightly, and nodded.

'When?'

Miller looked at his watch. 'It's half one now… she'll have to go through the tape… get it lawyered… nobody else has the story… there's no way they'll rush it in today. It'll be out on Saturday morning.'

'Well get your driver to take you to Wales…'

'*Wales?*'

'All right, Scotland,' said Norman, irritated. 'The Lake District. Check into a comfortable hotel, as Mr Smith, and go to bed, and stay there. Then call me.'

'But I feel better,' said Miller.

'You feel better,' said Norman, 'because you have had 180 milligrammes of beta blockers and ten milligrammes of diazepam chasing each other round your system. Of course you feel better. That would make anyone feel better. But you aren't better. Being well, and believing you're well, are not the same thing. Remember your brain tumour? And the rabies, and the anthrax? You of all people should know that.'

Norman handed him two small pill bottles. 'One of each,' he said, 'morning and night. Don't drink any more alcohol. And don't for Christ's sake take any more drugs. Or stimulants. No tea. No coffee. No Coca-Cola. You can have water and a little fruit juice. Or herbal tea.'

'Herbal tea?' Miller sneered.

'When you eat,' Norman added, 'eat a little. Don't go mad.' He shut his bag. 'Talking of which,' he said, 'how long have you been smoking again for?'

Miller was about to correct his grammar, then thought better of it.

'Well? How long?'

The patient looked at his watch.

'I see. Well stop.'

With that, he left him there, on the sofa. The front door slammed. A minute later, the doorbell rang.

Miller got to his feet. When he opened the door, Norman was back again. His black Saab was outside, the driver's door open and the engine running. The doctor was smiling.

'Congratulations!' he said.

'What?'

'Congratulations!' Norman said again. He went back to his car, got in and closed the door. 'Nine across,' he shouted through the open window, as he pulled away.

'Oh,' said Miller. 'Yes. Right.'

Miller paced from room to room, wondering what to take with him when he left. All of his possessions – his clothes, his books, and the handful of vinyl records and CDs in the living room – suddenly looked worthless. He couldn't imagine what had made him buy them, still less see what sense there'd been in keeping them. He saw the futility of his belongings for the first time, as if he was returning from some other, more objective, place.

Miller picked up one book – a life of Baden-Powell that his father had given him as a boy – and dropped it into a small canvas holdall he took from a cupboard in the bedroom. He packed a new white shirt, still in its plastic and card, boxer shorts, a pair of formal black shoes, a tie and his best black suit. To these he added his new mobile, his address book, Swiss army knife, and the small monogrammed wallet that contained his passport, driving licence, a credit card and two hundred and fifty pounds in cash. He found a clean white handkerchief and a roll of gaffer tape: 'The two things,' his father had told him, 'that you must never forget, on any journey. They always come in useful.'

Miller walked out of the bedroom, across the landing and into his study. He opened a desk drawer and removed the cheque books and cards for his five joint bank accounts. He put all the books, cards and financial documents in a large white envelope on which he wrote, in large capitals, 'TAKE EVERYTHING'. He left it on the desk in front of him. Leaning down, he pulled the bottom right-hand desk drawer out as far as it would go, then felt for the hidden catch that allowed it to open a further six inches, revealing a compartment from which he retrieved a pile of letters from other women, his secret mobile phone and charger, together with the account book, and debit card, for the building society account he concealed from his wife. He put the account book and the card in his pocket, and dropped the letters and the mobile into a carrier bag.

He looked back into the bedroom to see if he'd forgotten anything, and noticed the state of the bed. Keeping the carrier bag looped over his wrist, in case he put it down and forgot it, he pulled off the soiled sheets and carried them downstairs. He approached the washing machine, then saw that it was full of damp clothes. He had no idea, in any case, how it worked. The four large chocolate biscuits, he noticed, were still on the table, untouched.

He walked into the living room and thought about leaving the sheets in the laundry basket in the kitchen, but didn't, because that way they'd be discovered. Instead he piled them on to the large freestanding grate in the open fireplace. He pushed the carrier bag full of letters under them, and set fire to it with his lighter. The paper began to burn but was soon overpowered by the damp cotton, which smouldered disappointingly. Miller went back to the DIY cupboard in the kitchen and found a bottle of turpentine. He scattered a little on the sheets, which flared up cheerfully, then began to burn. He was standing back to admire his work when there were several pops followed by a satisfying bang – the death throes, he realized, of the secret mobile which he'd left in the bag with the letters.

As the flames began to die down again, he looked around the room. His eye fell on his wife's small record collection. Sorting quickly through the vinyl albums, he chose a compilation of Neil Diamond and a collection of Percy Grainger's arrangements of English folk songs. The nights she'd made him spend in concert halls listening to men in evening dress extolling the joys of ploughing. He took the records out of their cardboard sleeves and placed them on the fire, with another small dash of turps. Then he added his old work mobile, which was still lying on the sofa. It expired in a series of crackles.

He turned his attention back to Elizabeth's music library. He fanned out a dozen albums on the carpet in front of him like playing cards: Art Garfunkel, Bread, Phil Collins. In the end he put them all on, in their sleeves this time. He stood them up on the grate, propped against the back of the chimney. The fire had subsided to a sullen red glow and one feeble flame which the weight of the new records instantly extinguished. He stood back again and watched as a sullen wisp of smoke rose around the smiling face of Chris de Burgh.

Over at Glastonbury, he noticed, a gap of a few inches had appeared between the bedroom curtains: allowing in enough light, he guessed, for a modest lover to get dressed by. He took the paper bag off the sofa, put it in his holdall, then set off towards the village. To his great relief, he met nobody he knew, and so walked unnoticed into the station.

He took a black cab from Victoria to Euston, where he boarded the Manchester train. Settling back in his first-class seat, he examined the faces of his fellow travellers for signs of recognition, found none, and thanked heaven that he had restricted his occasional broadcast appearances to the radio. Outside the newspaper industry, his face was barely known. When the train pulled out he experienced a sense of relief verging on euphoria. As it picked up speed, on the outskirts of London, he fell asleep.

He woke with a start. The guard, an elderly West Indian, was tapping his metal punch against the side of Miller's seat. The editor, who hadn't bothered to buy a ticket, reached into his shirt pocket, took out his credit card and handed it to the man.

'Manchester,' he said.

The guard thanked him. Miller didn't reply.

The man swiped the card in the ticket machine, then disappeared down the train. A few minutes later, he came back.

'I'm sorry sir,' he said. 'It's been declined.'

'It's what?'

'Your card,' he said, 'has been declined.'

'Ring them,' Miller snapped.

'I have done.'

He looked at the guard, who met his stare and held it. Miller inhaled deeply and breathed out slowly through his nose. He found his wallet and pulled out his banknotes.

'How much?'

'One hundred and ninety-five pounds, sir.'

'Bloody hell.'

Miller gave him two hundred. The guard handed him five pounds and his ticket.

'Thank you sir.'

He glared after the man. Miller paid his credit card bill automatically, every month, by direct debit. It was never declined. The train headed north. He looked out at the terraced houses, with greying whites hanging on their lines, like tattered signs of surrender. The more he thought about it, the less he felt like going to the Intercontinental, where Charlotte, or anyone else at the paper, could reach him at any moment. He thought about checking into another hotel, but with so little cash on him he felt uneasy at the prospect of a second misunderstanding over his credit rating.

He tried to think who he still knew in the north of England: the answer was almost nobody. He opened his address book. By the time he'd got to G, he'd counted a dozen former friends who had disappeared from his life, in most cases out of disaffection with his politics. As a young man Miller, like most of his contemporaries, had flirted with Communism, though his true instincts, the ones he expressed every day in his paper, had never altered.

As the son of a newsagent, Miller had gone to Mauldeth Hall – an exclusive secondary school at Alderley Edge, in Cheshire – on a poor boy's scholarship. This was an academic distinction which – in a school overwhelmingly populated by wealthy fee-paying students who had performed less well in the entrance exam – made him the victim of a curious combination of envy and derision.

Not that his fellow pupils had remained any truer to their egalitarian principles, he reflected, as he began to glance at random through the rest of the book. Peter Lawrence, the cannabis dealer and hard-line Marxist, was now accountant for a golf club outside Knutsford. Daniel Furini – whose father had owned a string of ice-cream parlours in the north-west, and had brought instant pleasure to millions of children – was wreaking slow misery of the most adult kind, in his capacity as the nation's most feared divorce lawyer. Furini was the only one of his contemporaries to have been in touch recently: he'd sent Miller a card to say he considered his newspaper "contemptible shit".

Leigh Tebbutt...

Tebbutt. He was another bursary boy, and the last school friend he'd been in contact with, though he hadn't seen him for five years. Leigh, who had always been in trouble at school, had done a research degree, then become a teacher at a state secondary school in Wilmslow, a Manchester suburb that was like a little piece of Surrey. He was unusual in that his view of the world was cynical and marginalized to the point that he saw the various shades of party politics as alternative forms of surrender, and as a result had always been less horrified by Miller than others were. Tebbutt was one of the people Miller had lost touch with after Elizabeth reinvented him. He closed the book.

The feeling of release he'd experienced on leaving London had faded. In its place was another emotion, one that he vaguely recognized but hadn't experienced for years. It was only when the train stopped at Stafford and he saw a middle-aged woman sitting alone on a bench, her eyes fixed on the sun which was going down behind the Universal Grinding Wheel Company, an empty dog-lead clutched tightly in her hands, that he finally put a name to it – loneliness.

Miller tried to list what friends he had outside of business, and could think of none. He took out his mobile and dialled.

'Come over,' Leigh said, as if they'd last spoken the day before. 'Kate's away.'

Miller left the train at Macclesfield and took a cab. He arrived at Wilmslow just before seven. Leigh opened the door of his ground-floor flat. He was as Miller remembered him – a bear of a man, with unfashionably long, dark brown hair, a broad, generous face and a moustache. But one thing was different – he looked more relaxed. He was very tanned. Behind him in the hallway there was a fridge freezer, almost blocking the passage; there was just room to squeeze past it. Leigh did.

'Been away?' Miller asked, following him, then pulling his bag after him, through the narrow gap between fridge and wall.

'Yes,' Leigh said. 'Come in. I'm *de Rodriguez*.'

'You're what?'

'I'm *de Rodriguez*. It's a Spanish expression. It means: I am in the condition of Mr Rodriguez. It means that your wife has gone away, and left you in the house alone.'

'You wonder,' said Miller, trying to sound light-hearted, 'what Mr Rodriguez did, to pass into the language like that.'

'You do.'

Leigh led him into the kitchen. It smelt damp. Half the floor was covered with carpet tiles, the rest with bare floorboards. From habit, Miller began casting a surreptitious eye round the room. There was a full-sized, bright red aluminium dustbin in one corner. On the window sill, he noticed a couple of party invitations. One was from Andrew Maxwell, who they'd both been at school with.

They went through to the large living room, where the main wall was filled with Tebbutt's extensive collection of rock and roll music.

Leigh opened a bottle of red wine and poured himself a glass.

'No thanks,' said Miller.

'Still off it?'

'I'll have one later.'

'Good,' said his host. 'I've got a few friends coming over.'

'I don't want to come to a party.' As he said this, Miller realized how used he had become to doing nothing he didn't want to do, and how on this occasion he had no choice.

'It's just a few friends from Barcelona; my mate Patrick and...' He paused. 'Don't laugh.'

'I wasn't.'

'And five – no six – Iberia air hostesses.'

'Who's Patrick?'

'He's their English teacher.'

'Are you still teaching at Wilmslow Comprehensive?'

'No. I left.'

'Why?'

'I was in the playground one morning,' Leigh said, 'and I found myself telling off this eleven year old for bouncing a football while he was waiting in line to go into assembly. He burst into tears. I just turned round and walked out of the front gates. I never went back.'

'Why?'

'I got tired of acting like a bastard. Some of us don't enjoy it, you know.'

'What are you doing now?'

'EFL.'

'What?'

'English as a foreign language. I did that for two years in Spain. Now I recruit the teachers.'

'Who for?'

Leigh laughed. 'They're called Oxbridge House.' He caught Miller's look. 'Correct,' he said. 'They're dodgy as fuck. Talking of which,' he added, 'are you still running that pathetic rag?'

'No,' said Miller. 'I've resigned.'

'Well if you ever want to work in the sun for eight-fifty an hour…'

'I'll get back to you on that one. How do you persuade them to work for that?'

'Because they're all desperate, or hiding from something. It's the middle-class version of minicabbing.' Leigh looked at Miller, who had never shown any real interest in his teaching work before.

'What are you doing up here anyway?'

'I've come up to speak at the Hall.'

'You're joking. Is Stiffo Woodmason still there?'

'Yes.'

'Well just remember he's only after your money. They're totally loaded already. Make sure you give him some shit. You know Ingham's still there.'

'Ingham? Oh. Yes. Didn't he try to get you to, er…'

'Yes,' Leigh said. 'Did he you?'

'Yes.'

'Can I come?'

'No.'

Leigh showed him his room. It was empty except for a narrow single bed with no headboard and a white chest of drawers made from chipboard. There was a mirror and a cheap alarm clock. There were no curtains.

'Look,' Miller said, 'I've got to eat. Have you got any food?'

Leigh stepped into the hall and opened the door of the fridge. The main compartment was crammed with bottled lager. In the door, there were a couple of pints of milk.

'No,' he said.

'Why's the fridge here?'

'I accidentally turned its socket off last night,' said Tebbutt. 'It soaked the kitchen floor.'

The doorbell rang.

Patrick – a well-built, fair-haired man of about thirty, wearing a new Hawaiian shirt decorated with Cadillacs and palm trees – led in his women students. Two were still wearing their uniforms and had to go and change.

'This is Sylvia,' Leigh said, introducing Miller to a thin, dark woman in her late twenties.

'Hallo,' said Miller. He shook the girl's hand, a formality that seemed to amuse her. He felt faint, and distracted, and old. 'Look, Leigh, I've not eaten all day. I'm just going out for a bit.' He walked down the road and went into a brightly lit Chinese. He sat at a table, alone, with a beef and spring onion, and egg fried rice, listening to 'Things We Said Today' in Mandarin. When he'd paid the bill, Miller had four pounds left in his pocket. He considered various possibilities – of not going back to Leigh's house; of not turning up at the school the next day. He gave up when he couldn't think where to go if he didn't make the speech. At least Mauldeth Hall was a plan.

As Miller turned back into Tebbutt's road, he could hear the Beach Boys. The music got louder as he approached Leigh's house, and very loud once one of the young women arrived at the front door to let him in. He edged past the fridge and went into the living room. In the middle of an improvised dance floor, Sylvia was dancing with Tebbutt to 'Barbara Ann', her arms around his neck. Miller tapped him on the shoulder – then, when he didn't respond, led him away by the arm.

'When's Kate back?'

Leigh ignored him. 'That's a very strange line to write,' he said.

'What?'

'I mean – do you think any man ever went to a dance *not* looking for romance?'

'Yes,' Miller replied.

'Who?'

'Me.'
'Really? When?'
'When do you think? Now.'
'Now? Are you mad?'
'Listen,' Miller said. 'When's Kate back?'
Leigh swayed slightly. 'I think she said Thursday – what day is it today?'
'Thursday.'
'Oh no – then it's tomorrow.'
'What,' Miller asked him, 'if she comes back today?'
'What?'
He took Tebbutt by the shoulders.
'What if Kate comes back today?'
Leigh broke away from him. He pushed through the dancers and turned off the music. He switched the overhead light on.
'In the unlikely event of an emergency evacuation,' he said, 'your nearest exits are…' He pointed his outstretched arms in front of him, to the side, and to the rear. 'Please remain calm and leave in an orderly manner. And ladies, please remove high-heeled shoes.'
He switched off the light again. The Beach Boys returned, this time much louder.
Miller went into the kitchen alone and poured a small glass of white wine. He carried it to his room, where he slipped his bare feet out of his shoes. He took his two pills, lay back on the bed, and closed his eyes.
He slept fitfully, half-woken throughout the night by music, laughter, and raucous exchanges in a language he didn't understand. At three, with events still in full swing, he thought about getting up and moving to a hotel. He was sitting with his feet on the floor, before he realized he had nowhere to go. He fell asleep for another couple of hours, then woke at the climax of a dream about an air crash. His nightmare was enhanced by what sounded like real sounds of splintering wood and glass.
He was woken again, this time for good, by the slamming of a car door. He sat up and looked at the clock; it was ten past six. He picked

up his bag, went into the bathroom, took a shower and shaved. He put on his new shirt, his tie and his suit, and slipped his medication and mobile phone in his trouser pocket. He was going to put his shoes on when he realized that he didn't have any socks, or any money.

Barefoot in his formal outfit, he walked into the living room. There were air hostesses asleep on sofas and cushions, among the dirty ashtrays and empty wine bottles. He went down the corridor and peered into Leigh's room. Through the crack in the door he could see him asleep, under the covers. Miller had crept into the room by the time he saw Sylvia, naked and lying on her back, next to Leigh. Holding his breath, he covered her gently with the light bedspread, and shook his host awake.

Leigh groaned. 'What is it?'

'I've got a problem,' Miller whispered. 'Get up.'

Leigh pulled on a robe and followed him into the kitchen.

'Make us some coffee,' Leigh said.

'I've got no socks,' Miller told his host. 'And no money.'

Miller boiled the kettle and poured two instant coffees. On the remaining carpet tiles, he noticed large footprints left by somebody who had apparently stepped in a can of matt emulsion. Looking more closely, he saw the marks had been made not with paint, but blood.

Leigh opened a drawer, took out fifty pounds and gave it to Miller. On the sink, there was a pair of soiled white socks. He handed them to his guest, then sat down and put his head in his hands.

Miller handed Leigh the black coffee, and went round the corner, into the corridor, for the milk. He came back a moment later, empty-handed.

'Where's the fridge?' he asked.

'It's in the cellar,' Leigh said. 'Patrick sort of... surfed on it, down the stairs. He took his shoes and socks off, to get more – what do you call it – purchase, on the metal.'

'Did it work?' asked Miller.

'Yes. It's just that he went through the door at the foot of the stairs and then he landed on this pile of empty lager bottles.'

Miller took a few paces down the hall. He could see the fridge lying at the bottom of the flight of steps, at an ugly angle. The cellar door had splintered like matchwood. He noticed patches of congealed blood on the red hall carpet. He came back.

'Why did he do that?'

'He's a bit wild,' Leigh said. 'And he'd had a lot to drink. And some sulphate and a couple of Es.'

Miller – who only a few days earlier would have considered reporting Tebbutt to the police – said nothing. He looked at the socks, still on the table in front of him. He could see the imprint of feet much larger than his, their individual toes marked out in sweat and grime. Next to the socks were several sheets of paper with phrases written on them in felt marker: 'Broke Fridge.' 'Flooded Kitchen.' 'Smashed Door.'

'Are these socks Patrick's?'

'Yes. Look, just take them.'

Miller picked up one of the sheets of paper.

'When did you write this?'

'Oh.' Leigh looked a little embarrassed. 'Last night.'

'What is it?'

'It's something called Nine... for God's sake Miller it's six in the morning. Leave me alone.'

'Where's Patrick?'

'Where do you think he is? He's in fucking Casualty.'

He'd hoped to have ample time to make notes for his speech, but he had to wait half an hour for the taxi, and the traffic round Alderley Edge was far worse than he'd expected. When he finally got to the school gates it was eight thirty-five.

Places from his childhood generally appeared to have physically shrunk when he went back to them. But Mauldeth Hall – its stern redbrick towers flanked by generous expanses of well-tended playing fields – actually seemed to have got bigger.

As Miller walked up the drive, surrounded by small groups of boys in the familiar uniform of blue and old gold, resentment at the injustices he'd suffered as a boy began to rise in him. His anxiety began to return. He was breathing too deeply. He felt he would pass out. He looked around him, wondering where he might find a paper bag.

At the end of the drive he turned right, away from the main stream of youths, and made his way into a small, side quadrangle. He retreated into a corner of the cloisters, turned his back on the empty courtyard and lit a cigarette. He took out his mobile and called Norman.

'How are you?' said the doctor. 'I was hoping you'd ring. Are you in bed?'

'No,' said Miller. 'Listen. I'm feeling weird again.'

'You're what?' said the doctor. 'You're breaking up.'

'I'm feeling weird again,' Miller shouted, articulating carefully, 'and in half an hour I have to speak to thirteen hundred bloody schoolboys and I haven't got a clue what I'm going to say. I think I'm fucked.'

He heard a noise behind him, and turned round. A group of about a dozen boys had gathered, eavesdropping, no more than three yards away from him.

'Fuck *off*,' Miller shouted at them. They retreated.

'Sorry?' asked Norman.

'Nothing.'

'Are you hyperventilating?'

Miller looked behind him again. The quadrangle was empty.

'Not yet,' he said.

'Have you taken the medication I gave you?'

'Yes. No. Not today.'

'Well take it.'

'OK – right.'

'Then talk to them about newspapers. You must do that every week for God's sake.'

'OK.'

'But listen – when you've finished – call me back.'

'OK,' said Miller.

'It's important.'

'Right.'

He took out the bottle of diazepam and, his cigarette between his lips, twisted off the cap. The rising smoke made his eyes water. In his haste, he tipped half of the contents of the bottle into his palm. He was going to put them back but decided to count them first. There were eight. The ancient school bell began to toll, painfully close to him, summoning the boys for assembly. Miller hesitated, then put all eight pills into his mouth. When he swallowed them, they stuck in his throat, which was dry with anxiety. He saw a drinking fountain. It was very low. He bent down over it. At first he pressed the metal lever too hard, so that water spurted into his eyes and over his nose. He put his mouth directly over the nozzle, pressed and swallowed the water and pills.

'Hey!' The voice came from behind him, authoritative and angry. 'What the hell do you think you're doing?'

Miller looked up.

It was a man in his mid-twenties, wearing a black gown.

'I'm your... I've come to do the speech,' he said. He wiped the water off his face, using the back of his sleeve.

'The what?' The younger man had his eye on the cigarette and was covering Miller's exit, like a defending rugby player. He glanced behind him in search of assistance in case he needed it.

'The speech,' he repeated. 'In assembly. I am Edward Miller.'

'Oh.' The man's expression softened a little.

'Well put that out. Then follow me.'

Miller crushed the Gitane under his heel. The teacher picked it up with a look of disdain and carried it to a nearby waste bin.

It was a ten-minute walk round the grounds to the staff common room. On the way, they passed the main assembly hall, which was hung with paintings by Burne-Jones, Rossetti and other Pre-Raphaelite painters.

'You're the newspaper editor?' the teacher asked.

'Yes. Do you read our paper?'

'No.'

By the time Miller was sitting in the common room with Woodmason, holding a cup of tea, listening to the head teacher drone on about restoration funds and investment deficit (it was his true reason for inviting the editor, as Leigh had said; Woodmason hated his paper, they all did) – a kind of transcendental calm was settling on him. He could feel the muscles at the back of his neck relaxing, like taut guy ropes being slackened to face a storm. His fear had gone: not only was he not afraid, he could hardly imagine under what circumstances he would ever be afraid again.

His beatific mood was spoiled only by the sight, across the room, of two of the teachers he had most detested. Like Woodmason they were old men now, but still unmistakable: Mr Moore, the French teacher, who was famous for seducing the Parisian schoolgirls he used to bring over to his family home on cultural exchanges, and Father McWhirter, the divinity master, who Miller loathed. He felt pleasantly unsteady on his feet. A forgetfulness was creeping over him. For a moment he couldn't recall McWhirter's name, or why any of them should have been there at all. He looked further round the room, in search of familiar faces, but found only Mr Ingham.

'Isn't it a bit risky,' he asked Woodmason, 'having those Rossettis up in the hall?'

'It would be,' he said. 'Between you and me, the real ones are all in a bank vault in London. Those are all copies. Don't put that in your paper.'

'No,' said Miller.

They made their way out of the common room; Woodmason led him down a corridor to a heavy oak door, where they waited. Miller could feel the vibration of the organ, whose note of resonant doom served only as a reminder of his impending public disgrace. Behind the door, he remembered, there was a passageway that ran under the choir stalls and up to the stage.

'Don't forget – you don't have to preach,' said the headmaster. 'They like something with a bit of zip in it, you know.'

Woodmason waited for the sound of the organ to die away, then led them through the door, up a flight of steps and on to the stage. There were three lecterns in front of them. Woodmason took the central position and waved Miller to the one on his right. On the left was a senior prefect, who began to read a lesson. Miller looked ahead of him. He could see the faces of a thousand boys on the floor, eight feet below him, divided by a central aisle. There were three hundred more up in the gallery at the far end of the room. He felt tremendous. He felt as if he was floating.

Woodmason introduced Miller.

'When I was a boy here,' the editor said, 'back in the 1970s...' Already, he sensed his audience retreat into its familiar torpor, the boys' faces rigid with boredom. 'I remember how I used to sit – very much as each of you is sitting now, on those oak chairs – listening to the words of the guest speaker.'

He could pick out the faces of the individual teachers, sitting at the end of their classes, on the aisle. He looked at McWhirter and remembered how the vicar had sent him home from a school camp, for drinking beer, and made him hitchhike back through the night, on a Sunday, from Carmarthen to Oldham. He was fifteen. His fury at the memory fused with his frustration at the recent, catastrophic sequence of events for which, he began to convince himself, Father McWhirter might, in some indirect way, be personally responsible. Then he was struck by another thought: that he had nothing left to lose.

There was a restlessness in the hall; boys were fidgeting, some even muttering. He'd paused too long.

'Here, when I was a boy,' he went on, 'I can remember Stiffo' – the sudden and complete silence in the hall at these last two syllables proved beyond doubt that Woodmason's soubriquet had survived unaltered – 'explaining that, in the same way as a builder has an artist's impression of the completed edifice on his wall, so your visiting speakers serve to represent the perfect fulfilment of the plans you boys nurture for your own lives. You are the work in progress,' Miller added, 'I am the finished article.'

'Of course,' he continued, 'I cannot speak in detail of your individual ambitions – though if any of you wish to pursue a career in print journalism, I suggest you begin taking notes now. But I can tell you a little about my own condition. At the time of speaking,' he added, 'I am the editor of a national newspaper. Last night,' he added, 'I slept in my clothes in a Wilmslow maisonette in the company of six air hostesses from Iberian Airlines and a man from Dorset who surfed down the stairs on a fridge freezer under the influence of ecstasy and is currently, so far as I know, still waiting for treatment in Accident and Emergency.' He paused. There was absolute stillness in the hall. 'I am in his socks.'

His audience had gone from languid indifference to galvanized attentiveness. 'Professionally speaking,' Miller went on, 'I owe this school everything. It was here, for instance, that I first observed the power of journalism, when Nigel Parker, then sixteen' – out of the corner of his eye, he saw the seated figure of the headmaster tense up – 'was caught red-handed selling amphetamine sulphate to three eleven-year-olds inside the school grounds. When summoned for the announcement of his son's expulsion,' he added, 'Parker's father pointed out that he was the news editor of the northern edition of a national newspaper and that he would ensure that the incident received the publicity it deserved.' He paused. 'In the end,' he said, 'Mr Woodmason decided that confiscation of the drugs was sufficient punishment.'

There was a movement half-way down the aisle: he saw Father McWhirter, on his feet, trying to usher his boys out, and none obeying.

'This was an expensive school in those days, as it is now,' he went on. 'I know that because I watched as the burden of the fees broke one father, then killed him, as it has killed other fathers and will kill more, some of them yours.' He leaned forward towards the microphone, with the confiding look of a politician. 'But what do they buy with their money?'

Silence. 'I'll tell you,' he said. 'They buy an education. It was here that I learned to drink to excess and to write – two accomplishments that, in my early days in newspapers, became dangerously intertwined.' He turned to Woodmason. 'It's true Stiffo,' he said. 'I couldn't pick up a pen unless I was ripped.'

The headmaster gave him an imploring look, which Miller ignored. 'The other thing he bought,' he continued, 'was privilege. Mr Woodmason used to tell us, as he no doubt still tells you, that privilege brings with it certain responsibilities. We each of us hear that phrase and fulfil our responsibilities in our own way. Speaking personally, I have recently deserted my wife and daughter. Since I was married nine years ago,' he added, 'I have slept with eighteen women, including three...' he paused. 'I'm not sure,' he said, 'whether you pronounce the s in au pairs. Perhaps Mr Moore can help you with that later. In the past forty-eight hours alone,' Miller added, 'I have committed adultery, taken a Class A drug and caused criminal damage.'

Prefects, on the whispered instruction of teachers, had opened the six large doors that led out of the hall into the corridor, but still not one of his audience had moved.

'You may argue,' he said, 'that I am unusual; that I am the exception that proves the rule. I disagree. As an Old Mauldethian, I would say I am fairly typical. As regards the living, who come to address you from time to time, I would guess that their speeches are masterclasses in hypocrisy and concealment. As for the dead...' He gestured to his left, at the great wall covered with oak panels inscribed, in gold leaf, with the names of old boys who had fallen for their country.

'I remember how I would sit and memorize those names – Adams, Alderton, Ambrose and the others – and imagine their heroism in battle, and the nature of the wounds that finally brought them to glory. To me, they were heroes. Now, I realize that, in their day as in ours, the ranks would have been dominated by cowards and drunks, of whom one in eight would have been mentally ill, and one in five a sodomite. They are united not by courage, but by the fact that they are all dead and, like you, all male.'

'And that,' he added, 'is an aspect of Mauldeth Hall which has not altered. Who, of my age, can forget that day in the seventies when Mr Woodmason went on national television and explained that 'Mauldeth Hall will never go bi-sexual. That said,' he went on, 'the school can never be accused of intolerance, or lack of sexual diversity, so long as it continues to employ Mr Ingham.'

'I would like to thank you for listening to me today,' he said, 'and to express the hope that each of you will go out into the world and strive to distinguish this school as something other than a breeding ground for tap-dancing civil-rights barristers, homosexual theatre producers, and the home for a few cheap reproductions of old paintings by...' he looked across at the pictures by Burne-Jones and Rossetti, and his mind went blank. 'By the, er... the Pre... The Pre... The Pre-Requisites.'

He sat down to complete silence. A burst of ecstatic applause from a section of the gallery was quelled by members of staff. A short, ginger-haired boy seated at the organ produced a tremendous blast from the instrument that made Miller's ribcage vibrate. He got up and, without looking behind him, left the stage, through the door he'd come in by, and took a side passage that led past the bins by the chemistry block. As he made his way out, by the tradesmen's entrance, a small group of boys ran up to the railings and gave him the thumbs up. Miller waved back, gaily.

He walked back down the winding lane into the village of Alderley Edge. On the High Street, he looked among the estate agents and French restaurants for a minicab company but couldn't find one. The once attractive Cheshire village was choked with expensive cars and lorries carrying limestone north from Derbyshire. Mock Tudor pubs and coffee houses had been given names commemorating King Arthur, whose army was believed by some to be sleeping beneath the Cheshire plain: The Wizard; The Quest; The Lancelot Arms. Set back from the main road, on the hill above the village, he could see a hotel called Camelot Court.

Miller felt in his pocket and could find only a couple of pounds. For a while he waited at a bus stop marked 'Wilmslow'. He wasn't used to waiting. After ten minutes, when the service arrived, it was a yellow minibus already packed with standing passengers. When it set off after collecting only two people from the queue, Miller began walking. The road twisted and rose as it left the town, and there was no footpath. The heavy lorries thundered past, inches away from him. He felt the sweat rise under his armpits and collar. All of his clothes were beginning to acquire the unpleasant adhesive quality of his borrowed socks.

He came to a small junction where he pressed the button to operate the pedestrian crossing. While he was waiting, he took off his tie and undid his top button. He looked back at the road and noticed that a car had stopped. It was a Daimler, driven by a businessman who was looking at him strangely. Glancing up, Miller realized the driver was annoyed because the pedestrian light was green, and yet he wasn't crossing. As he stepped on to the road, his tie in his hand, the light began flashing amber and the car set off at speed, almost knocking him over. Miller jumped back, caught his heel on the kerb, and fell backwards on to the pavement. His tie landed in the gutter, where he left it.

It took him an hour and a half to reach Leigh Tebbutt's house. There was a utility truck outside it, with the battered fridge in the back. The front door was open. Miller went in without knocking. He glanced into the living room, where the only signs of the previous night's festivities were a vacuum cleaner and open windows. At the foot of the cellar steps, two workmen were fitting a new door.

He found Leigh sitting at the table in the kitchen, the sheets of paper, inscribed with details of damage, in front of him. The missing floor tiles had been cleaned and replaced.

'Who did all this?' Miller asked.

'The girls,' said Leigh. 'You should have seen them. They're absolutely amazing. Sylvia said they can turn round a Boeing 767 in forty minutes. When you think how big one of those aircraft is, I mean when you see it on the ground it's absolutely massive; it's the size of a small...'

'Yes,' said Miller. 'I know.'

He sat down. He was sweating heavily. There was a kitchen roll on the work surface next to him. He tore off a handful without asking and wiped his face with it.

'Are you all right?'

'People have been asking me that a lot lately,' Miller replied.

He pointed at the pieces of paper.

'So what are these?'

'I have this game with Kate,' Leigh said. 'Called Nine Lives. When I was teaching, if one of the kids had done something they couldn't own up to, I used to say to them well tell me as much as you want to in nine syllables. Nine noises, I used to say. They didn't know what a syllable was. I'd tell them listen – you know you can't do yourself much damage with nine noises.'

'Did it work?'

'Often. What usually happened, they'd start to think how they could fit it all into that number of sounds and once they'd done that they were generally so proud that they'd tell you – they couldn't resist it.'

Miller looked at the phrases scattered on the sheets of paper.

'So these are for Kate are they?'

'Yes,' said Tebbutt. Well – when I've finished, yes.'

'How about: "Spanish air hostess has slept in your bed"?'

'No,' said Tebbutt. 'That doesn't work.'

'What?'

'That doesn't work. That's ten.'

Miller looked out at the newly replaced carpet tiles and the space where the fridge freezer had been.

'You're going to struggle to fit the air hostesses into this at all aren't you?'

'That's my feeling,' Leigh said, 'yes.' He paused. 'Did you do the speech?'

'Yes.'

'How did it go?'

'Terrible.'

'What did you...'

'I can't. I'll tell you one day. Not now. I just can't.' He looked down at his socks. 'I'm totally in the shit.'

'How can you be?'

'What do you mean how can I be? I am.'

'How? Tell me.'

'Why?'

'Because there's always something you can do to redeem a situation.'

'So I've heard.'

Miller cast his mind over the wreckage of the past couple of days, looking for some area of possible salvage.

'I got drunk the night before last,' he said, finally. 'I sprayed my neighbour's car with an aerosol.'

'Does he know it was you?'

'Yes.'

'That's criminal damage.'

'Yes.'

'Unless you can persuade him not to press charges. Has he told the police?'

'I don't know.'

'Do you know anybody who's in touch with him?'

Miller gave a hollow laugh. 'Sort of.'

'How many people?'

'Two.'

'Well ring one of them.'

Miller took out his mobile.

'Use the land line.' Leigh waved towards the phone.

'No.'

He called Dr Norman.

'How did it go?' asked the doctor.

'What?'

'The speech.'

'Oh – perfect. Except I called the Pre-Raphaelites the Pre-Requisites.'

'Ah,' said Norman, 'the Pre-Requisites. I know them well. They painted that one still life over and over again – Passport, Tickets, Money.'

'Listen,' said Miller. 'You remember the car – Illingworth's car.'

'I do,' said the doctor, 'yes.'

'Well could you talk to him? Could you ask him not to press...'

'I have.'

'What?'

'I already have.'

'Oh,' said Miller, 'and was he OK about that?'

'Yes,' said Norman. 'Well, more or less. Now listen – there's something else I need to talk to you about. Are you sitting down?'

Miller remembered the blood sample. 'Is it something in the test results?'

'No,' said Norman.

'Not the results?'

'No.'

'Really?'

'No. Stop it.'

'What then?'

'It's not your test results. Your test results are fine. It's more to do with... Oxted.'

'Oxted.'

'It's... It's your house. There was a bit of a fire.'

'What?'

'It's a bit... burned. A bit burned out.'

'Burned out?'

'Well – just the ground floor. And some of the first. And then…'

'The roof?' Miller interrupted.

'The roof…' Norman repeated. 'The roof's… gone.'

'What?'

'Your house… it's not so much burned out, really; it's more sort of… burned down. Yes,' he said. 'That's it. Your house…' He pronounced the next phrase slowly, and with exaggerated clarity and pride, like a spy who, after a moment of forgetfulness, has just remembered a vital password: 'Your house… has burned down. That's it.'

Miller said nothing.

'The police,' the doctor continued, 'are there.'

'Did you tell them where I am?'

'No. I don't know where you are. Where are you?'

'Are they with you now?'

'Who?'

'The police.'

'No. I told them I'd speak to you, and that when I did you'd come back and talk to them.'

'Why didn't you tell me this morning?'

'Because you sounded on the edge of collapse.'

'Oh,' Miller replied. 'Yes.'

'They think,' Norman said, 'that you did it deliberately. Did you?'

'No.'

'Anyway,' said the doctor, 'you have to come and see them.'

'How?' Miller asked. 'My credit card won't work.'

'Elizabeth stopped it,' said the doctor.

'How do you know?'

'She called me last night. She's been quite – well, very – distressed. It's a terrible sight, when a house burns down, even when, as in this case, there are no victims. And when there *is* a body – as a doctor, let me tell you, I have had to enter premises…'

'Right,' Miller said. 'OK. Never mind that now.'

'And your father-in-law – he's not taken it so well either – actually he's taken it much worse than her…'

'Worse?' asked Miller. 'Why?'

'Well the thing is that Elizabeth – she was very distressed, as I told you, and so she implied – well to be more accurate, she told her father that she didn't leave you so much as, er…'

'Yes?'

'You left her.'

'Oh dear,' said Miller.

'Tell me where you are,' he added, 'and I'll send a car. Or I'll come and get you myself. If you're in England.'

'I am,' said Miller.

'In that case…' The doctor's voice assumed a graver tone. 'They also asked me to tell you that you can report to your nearest police station.'

'Has Illingworth made a complaint about the car?' he asked.

'He has done,' said Norman, 'yes.'

A flicker of efficiency from his old life, the one where he had control, rose in Miller.

'Is there a warrant?' he asked.

'No,' said the doctor. 'Not yet. I believe they're waiting for results from forensic.'

'Forensic,' Miller repeated. 'Right. I'll call you back.'

He switched the phone off.

He could feel Tebbutt's eyes on him.

'What is it?' his host asked.

'I can't.'

'You can,' the teacher said. Then: 'What about Nine Lives?'

'Oh for God's sake, Leigh,' said Miller. 'Grow up.'

'Please yourself.'

He looked at Tebbutt, and realized that, for the moment at least, he was his only possible source of help.

'Wife gone,' Miller said.

'Good. I mean… right. That's two.'

'House burned down.' He paused, and counted on his fingers. 'She thinks, by me.'

'Ah. Is she right?'

'No. Well… not on purpose. I did make a fire as I was leaving.' He lit a cigarette. The smoke rose in shafts of sunlight and particles of dust raised by the workmen below.

'You lit a fire?'

'Yes.'

'It's May.'

'I know.'

'What with?'

'Sorry?'

'What did you make the fire with?'

'Sheets,' he said. 'Letters. Mobile phones. Some albums.'

'Photograph albums?'

'Records.'

'Records?'

Miller nodded. For the first time, Tebbutt looked shocked.

'Whose?'

'Elizabeth's.'

'No, I mean who made them?'

'Phil Collins. Sting. Chris de Burgh.'

'Oh,' said Leigh. 'I see. OK, fair enough.'

'Where did you make it?'

'In the fireplace, where the fuck do you think I usually make the fire?'

'Except that usually,' Leigh said, 'your house doesn't burn down.'

'I leaned the records against the back of the chimney. I thought it had gone out. I suppose they must have fallen forward on to the carpet.'

'What did you start it with?'

'Turpentine.'

'Oh, shit.'

Two workmen were standing in the hall with their tools; Leigh gave one of the one-hundred-pounds cash, then showed the pair out.

'What do I do now?' Miller asked his host.

'Go back.'

'Why?'

'The thing is,' Leigh said, 'I don't see you have any choice.'

'I can't go back.'

'Why not?'

'I just can't. She'll get me arrested. And that's just her. Then there's my father-in-law...'

Miller remembered his secret building society account. He went into the room where he'd slept and picked up his travelling bag. Back in the kitchen, he opened the holdall and found the account book.

'I've got one thousand three hundred and fifty pounds,' he said. 'If I can get it out.'

'How long will that last you,' Leigh asked, 'at your usual rate of spend? A week? No. Less. That's the thing with the rich. You know a lot, but you don't have the faintest idea of how much money you need to live.'

Miller found a half-pint tankard. He filled it with water from the tap, swallowed it, then poured another one. The glass was decorated with a picture of a beefeater and the words: 'A Souvenir from the Tower of London'.

He drank half of it, then stopped.

'Eight-fifty an hour?' he said.

'What?'

'Can I go to Spain?'

'No.'

'You said...'

'Never mind.'

'You said that everyone out there was hiding from something.'

'They are.'

'Well, then.'

He looked down at his clothes – the filthy borrowed socks, the sweat-soaked white shirt, the thousand-pound black suit with a slight bulge in the right breast, caused by the pill bottles in his inside pocket. He closed his eyes. They prickled and stung from fatigue.

'Please.'

'I can't...'

'*Please.*'

'They did call yesterday,' Leigh said, 'to say they needed someone.'

He took out a business card from his wallet, but didn't give it to his guest. Miller could read it though, and his old instincts began working to commit the details to memory: Christopher Devlin, director. There was a line drawing of an ivy-covered tower, and quadrangle. And, in cod Elizabethan lettering: 'Oxbridge House, Barcelona'. He couldn't make out the full address.

'How much money have you got?' Leigh asked, 'when you've paid me back?'

'Thirteen hundred.'

'Can you get it in cash?'

'I'll try.'

'Well you'll have to. The flight could be a couple of hundred at this notice – then there's your food and board until you get paid... that'll leave you about six hundred. He'll have most of that off you once you arrive.'

'What?'

'Christopher's OK,' Leigh said. 'He'll look after you, once you're there.'

'He sounds like Fagin,' said Miller.

'That's how it works. You've got an English degree, haven't you?' asked Leigh.

Miller nodded.

'Where was it you went – Sussex?'

Miller nodded.

'That'll do.'

Miller drank the rest of his water and sat down at the table.

'Who do you teach?'

'What?'

'Out there. Who are the students?'

Leigh shrugged. 'Businessmen. Secretaries. Anyone who can pay.'

'Where from?'

'Mostly multinationals.'

'No I mean – where from – which countries?'

'Oh – they're nearly all Spanish. Catalan. You get the odd North African.'

Miller raised one eyebrow, a trick his father had taught him.

'Let me ask you something,' Leigh said. 'Do you ever wonder why nobody you used to know ever keeps in touch with you?'

'Because I don't keep in touch with them.'

'But do you ever get invitations? Even to bin, or ignore?'

'No.'

'Well I'll tell you why that is,' Leigh said. 'It's because you're such a bigot. They don't ask you,' he added, 'because they despise you.'

Miller lit another cigarette.

'You haven't mellowed, have you?'

'No,' Leigh grinned. 'I've got worse.'

'What's your excuse?' Miller asked.

'Wilmslow. What's yours?'

'Do you despise me?'

'You know what I think about you?' Leigh said. 'There's a poem by Walt Whitman where he says that most of us are a mystery to ourselves; that we get only fleeting hints and tiny inklings of what we are.'

'Oh,' said Miller. 'Really. And?'

'And I don't think you're like that. I think that on the whole you know yourself pretty well. You've had to, to succeed. And – since you ask – there are parts of you that I quite like. I remember you in your Trotsky T-shirt. But there's another part of you that I don't think you know at all. It's about 20 per cent. And it's pure racist tosser. How in God's name,' Leigh continued, 'did you get like this?'

Miller hadn't been talked to in this way since he left school.

'I...'

'What did your dad think of West Indians?'

'He...' He tried to think of a clever reply and couldn't. 'He hated them,' he replied, defiantly.

'Was your mother the same?'

'No.'

'Did you respect him?'

'My dad? Yes, I suppose so.'

'Why?'

'Why not?'

'Because nobody of any intelligence has ever held views of that kind.'

Miller looked at the floor. In his open bag, he could see his father's *Life of Baden Powell*. He took it out, opened it, and searched through it for a few moments.

'The stupid inertness of the puzzled Negro,' he read, 'is duller than that of the ox. A dog would grasp your meaning in half the time. "Men and brothers". They may be brothers, but they are certainly not men.'

Leigh took the book out of his hands. Miller's father had wrapped it in brown paper to protect the original hard cover. Tebbutt looked at the inside front page, where the name Clive Miller was written in blue-black ink. It had been crossed out in red biro and Edward Miller written below, in an unsteady childish hand.

'How old were you,' Leigh asked him, 'when he first read you that?'

'I'm not sure. I remember that I had to ask him what an ox was.'

'What else did he bring you up on?'

'I don't know… Rudyard Kipling…'

Leigh went over to the red dustbin, put the book in, and closed the lid. Angry and confused, Miller drew breath to retaliate, then, wary of alienating his sole ally, said nothing.

'Go on,' Leigh said. 'What were you going to say?'

'Walt Whitman,' Miller said. 'He fucked boys didn't he?'

'Yes,' said Tebbutt. 'Just like your man with the ox.'

'He didn't,' Miller replied, with the calm of full certainty.

'You know I have a doctorate?' Leigh asked.

'Yes.'

'Do you know what it's in?'

'No.'

'It's in "Images of Empire in Late Victorian Literature",' Leigh said. 'We know now. Trust me. He did.'

He was still holding the business card.

'I'll make you a deal,' he said. 'I'll help you on two conditions. First that you never – if you do go out there – talk any of this shit to the people you work with. In or out of school. The one thing the director there can't stand is racism. OK?'

Some residual sense of his old authority flickered in Miller, who contemplated a sarcastic response, then resisted it.

'OK?' Leigh repeated.

'OK.'

Leigh handed him the card. Miller put it in his inside pocket, with the pills, without looking at it.

'And the other?' he asked, unable to resist a hint of mock-deference.

'That you don't tell Christopher I sent you. You can tell him you know me but if he asks if I'm a close friend, you say no. And if he asks if I sent you for a job, you say no.'

'Why?'

'Because that's how it works. And because I know these people. This is my living.'

'OK. Leigh...'

'Yes?'

'What about my name?'

'What?'

'I'd like to use another name.'

'You'll be freelance,' Leigh said. 'Which in this case means that you are paid in cash and, if the revenue call, you hide in the toilets. You can call yourself what you like.'

He looked at his watch. 'I've got to have a shower and get in to work,' he said. He shook Miller's hand. As he was leaving the room, he turned back.

'By the way,' he said. 'If you're really worried about someone coming after you, don't fly to Barcelona.'

'Why not?'

'Because flight lists are very easy to check. Fly to France. Then go overland. See you.'

Miller remained at the table. He heard the bathroom door close, and the hiss of the shower. He waited a few moments, then went over to the dustbin and opened the lid. The old book was half-submerged in a mess of baked beans and broken glass. He lifted it out. It was the only thing left to him of his father's. Beans and shreds of bloodstained kitchen roll were stuck to the brown paper cover. He tried to sweep them off with the back of his hand, but the paper tore, staining the faded hard cover with streaks of tomato sauce and blood. He wondered if he could have the book restored, and take it away, and cherish it. The shower stopped; there were footsteps in the bathroom. Miller let the book fall back into the bin. He rinsed his hands, picked up his holdall and went out the front door without saying goodbye.

He walked into Wilmslow, past the black-and-white road sign bearing the small town's name. Wilmslow. Its most refined residents, in common with strangers, pronounced the first 'l', which was traditionally silent. But it was impossible, however you said it, to pronounce the word with a rising inflection, or in any other way that would convey a sense of hope, vitality or joy. There was nothing on earth that could fit the name better than this aloof and disheartening suburb, with the possible exception of a treacherous prefect in some drama set at a minor public school. When he was eleven or so, Miller remembered, his rich aunt had boasted that she was driving out to Wilmslow to see if she could find coriander and how he'd thought she was looking for a play by Shakespeare.

On the main street, he found a branch of his building society. As he waited in line, he looked up and saw a black-and-white image of himself on the overhead monitor. It reminded him of scenes from crime programmes on television. Here in the queue, yards from a cashier, he already looked guilty. His unkempt hair lent him an air of desperation. He was looking in his bag to see if he'd brought a comb, and finding he hadn't, when the woman pressed the synthesized chime to call him over to her counter. It took him a moment to respond.

He handed her the account book and his passport and asked to draw out thirteen hundred pounds.

'I'm sorry, sir,' she said. 'We can only do two hundred in cash. For that much, you need to give forty-eight hours' notice. Can you come back on Monday?'

'No,' he said.

She handed back the documents. Then he remembered that he kept a few business cards wedged in the back of his passport. He found one and passed it to her. He'd entirely forgotten they were there. It was as though Miller, struggling in this traffic-clogged heartland of Arthurian legend, had discovered some ancient magic charm that he was entitled to use one last time. The effect was dramatic and immediate. The cashier looked up at him again, this time with respect.

'I'll see what I can do.'

She disappeared into the back room. He began to be troubled by the thought that Elizabeth might have somehow found out about the secret account, and alerted the building society. He looked behind him and noticed that the exit door was locked; there was a green button that customers had to press before they could leave. His heart was beating faster. But when she came back, she was smiling, and she was holding the money. She counted it out, in twenty-pound notes. She had nothing larger. She was sorry.

'You're lucky,' she said. 'The courier's not been today.'

Miller put the money in his bag and walked down to the railway station, where he took a black cab to Manchester airport.

In the main terminal, he bought two white T-shirts, three pairs of socks and an alarm clock. He went into the bookshop and he looked at, but did not buy, maps of Spain and France. Miller had been to Paris on his honeymoon. France reminded him of Elizabeth. Her French was immaculate. He decided to fly as close as he could to the Spanish border.

He looked across the terminal. It was some time since he'd bought a ticket for himself, and he wasn't sure where to start. He went to the information point to ask about flights to Perpignan. The man there directed him to the sales desk of a budget airline, where he queued for half an hour.

'I want to go today,' he told the young woman.

'I'm afraid not sir,' she said. 'The flight's already left. There's another tomorrow.'

'I need to go today.'

'It's a morning flight. We only fly once a day.' She pressed a button on her keyboard and looked at the screen. 'We have availability tomorrow.'

Miller could sense irritation in the long line behind him.

'What time does it leave?'

'Five minutes past six,' she said. 'Check in ninety minutes beforehand.'

'What? Half four?'

'That's how they keep the price down.'

He opened his packet of Gitanes and took one out. He tapped it against the desk absent-mindedly, out of habit. The movement seemed to irritate the sales woman. She began drumming her long fingernails, which were maroon, against the beech veneer of her desk. Miller looked down at her hands, and she stopped.

'Do you want it or not?'

'I want it.'

'Return date?'

'Single.'

'That's a hundred and fifty-five pounds.'

She held out her right hand, leaving a space between her thumb and index finger, just wide enough to take a credit card.

He pulled the thick roll of cash out of his pocket, and counted out eight notes. The woman looked at him with undisguised suspicion. She handed him five pounds change.

'Name?'

'Edward Miller.'

'Address?'

'What?'

'Address.'

 Why?'

'We need your address Mr Miller.'

'In London?'

'Where you are staying tonight.'

'Oh.'

'Well?'

She began drumming again and this time, when he looked at her fingers, then met her eyes, she continued.

'Camelot Court,' he said. 'Alderley Edge.'

He took a train from the airport to the Cheshire village. He found the post office, where he mailed fifty pounds to Leigh. Walking from the station towards the hotel, he caught sight of himself in the window of

'Raoul's', a barber's shop on the High Street. Two steps led from the pavement up to the glass door. He climbed them, and went in.

There was no queue, but a young man with shoulder-length dark hair and wearing a motorcycle jacket, was just settling in the chair. The hairdresser was a mean-faced man of fifty or so, with small eyes and tight, yellowed skin. He looked as though he might have embarked on, then abandoned, a course of cosmetic surgery. He put a green cape over the customer's shoulders.

'I'll have a zero,' the young man said.

'Down to the wood?' said Raoul, who had a strong Manchester accent.

'Yes.'

The man took out his electric clippers and put them to the stranger's head. Miller watched the thick locks of black hair as they fell to the floor. For the first time since his difficulties had begun, he was completely distracted. He couldn't believe so much hair could be cut off with a razor without being trimmed first, so that it didn't snag up the mechanism. It was like watching some sort of purification; a casting-off of vanity.

'There,' said the barber. 'Handsome again.'

Miller got up and took his place. He'd forgotten what it felt like in a barber's chair – the smell of other men's scalps, cheap hair oils and the feeling of the leather on the seat, so slippery that you were forced to sit up straight for fear of sliding out.

'What can I do for you?' the man asked.

He wasn't sure what to ask for – his own hairdresser, George, came to his house every Sunday, in Oxted, and had no need of instructions. Here, the walls were covered with large pictures of what looked like Mediterranean porn actors wearing the kind of cantilevered bouffants that might have been imposed on them by a cruel enemy, as a forfeit. Miller looked from one picture to the other, trying to decide which would be least humiliating.

'I'll have a zero,' he said, on impulse.

Raoul didn't reply. He put the green cape around him. Miller felt the warm vibration of the electric clippers against his scalp. The barber began telling him how he'd once cut the hair of an international footballer who lived in the area, and then seen his haircut triumph over Munich, on television. He pointed to a small framed picture of the star, on a ledge behind the sink. The player – whose first marriage ended the day after Miller serialized the candid recollections of a Marseille chambermaid – gazed up at him with what looked like an accusing expression. Miller shut his eyes. When he opened them again, he glanced in the mirror, then immediately looked away.

'There,' said the barber. 'Handsome again.'

Miller turned back to the mirror. He looked very different, but not in a way that was attractive or interesting. He looked grotesque. Until now he'd viewed baldness as a minor yet distasteful handicap – brought on, no doubt, by some sordid vice practised secretly by its victims who, now he came to think about it, were distinguished in his mind from the blind and the lame principally on the grounds that they did not beg. Now he was one of them, he feared he would alarm passers-by. When Miller descended from Raoul's into the High Street – tentatively and backwards, like a coward entering an unheated lido – he was surprised and relieved not to attract immediate mockery. Avoiding eye contact with passers-by, he walked as fast as he could up the hill to Camelot Court. There were two silver four by fours parked in front of its main entrance. In the lobby, there was a round coffee table and a suit of armour.

He asked the middle-aged woman receptionist for a room.

'And you're sure it's just the one night, sir?'

'Yes,' he said. 'Is that a problem?'

'No.'

She drew the word out; she had a peculiar, improved accent which meant that, the way she said it, 'no' rhymed with 'blue'.

'Will that be an executive room?'

'What,' Miller asked politely, 'is an executive room?'

'It's…' she hesitated. 'It's a room that's… better.'

'Better than what?'

'Better than…' She stopped herself. 'It's English,' she said, 'for deluxe.' This last word rhymed with dukes.

'I'll have one,' said Miller, with a note of contempt that she didn't catch.

'Smoking or non-smoking?'

His attention was caught by a group of men in their thirties – sales or advertising managers, he guessed – who'd arrived, carrying golf clubs, getting ready for an evening of pitch and putt and heavy drinking. Miller seemed to have lost interest in golf. It was strange how quickly he'd managed to regress from the world of corporate privilege, now he was no longer part of it. He felt more like he had when he'd been a writer, in the days when he needed six vodkas just to get to the keyboard. Hair had fallen inside his shirt. His neck itched.

'Smoking,' the woman repeated – her accent had reverted to her native St Helens – 'or non-smoking?'

'Smoking,' he said.

Miller took a shower, changed into one of his new T-shirts and lay down on the bed. The ceiling was low, and covered with polystyrene tiles. The curtainss and bed covers were in an imitation Liberty pattern. On the wall to his right was a black-and-white photograph of a young couple kissing on a bench near the Brooklyn Bridge. To his left, just above the digital clock showing 18.05, there was a picture of Sir Bedivere. Miller set his own alarm for four a.m., turned away from the lovers to face the knight, and fell asleep.

He arrived at the airport just before five a.m. and sat on a row of seats facing the bookshop he'd visited the day before. It was closed. He tried to persuade himself not to look, but he couldn't. He could see them there, dumped in front of the metal shutters protecting the shop's entrance. They were stacked and tightly bound with translucent plastic tapes, a printed delivery sheet on the top. When he was a boy, he remembered, the newspapers would be dropped like this, outside his father's shop door in the early hours, but tied up with thick cord, not plastic. He went over to the shop and read the sign on the door: Open 6 a.m.

He glanced around and, finding himself unobserved, knelt down and took out his Swiss army knife. He slid the blade into the end of the bundle nearest to him, close to the top of the pile, and began to cut through the taut plastic. The knife was three-quarters through when the tape broke with a noise like a pistol shot, stinging his left hand as it flew back. He looked down; his thumb was bleeding slightly. He worked a copy out from the pile, and stood up. A security guard had appeared, twenty yards away, watching him. Miller walked over to the shop's honesty box – a dustbin-sized receptacle with a thin slot which was designed for use during opening hours by people too busy to queue at the till and, despite its name, had been riveted to the marble floor. With a deliberately exaggerated gesture, he dropped in a five-pound note. The guard gave him a conspiratorial nod, and retreated.

Miller returned to his seat, holding the paper on his knees, folded in two so that the front page was hidden. He remained in this position for a few moments, during which time his thumbprint appeared, in blood, on the back page. He opened the paper with a quick, decisive movement, like a man swiftly tearing a large plaster from his skin in the hope of minimizing the discomfort. A picture of him naked, bending over to retrieve the beach towel in his kitchen, was on the masthead of the paper. His genitals had been blacked out. The headline on the front page read: 'Portrait of a Racist'. Below it was a digitally enhanced picture of Miller taking cocaine at Larkin's. The piece continued over the whole of page three, where there was a photograph of Illingworth's car, and a picture of Miller 'in happier days' as the caption put it, launching a Drugs Alert initiative with the lord chief justice.

'Who do you mean?' a splash headline on this page said, 'The Niggers or the Queers?' The article was punctuated by pull-quotes in bold type, in the style of his own newspaper. 'Use the NHS?' one said. 'Do you think I'm fucking mad?'

He read paragraphs at random, not feeling able to go through the whole piece sequentially.

'Soaked in vomit and urine,' he read, 'his shaking hand clutching his morning glass of brandy, Edward Miller boasted of having begun the previous day by having sex with his secretary, Charlotte Turner, 22, in a stationery cupboard.'

He glanced across at the next column. 'Once out of the stock room, Miller – who believes that many of Britain's problems are down to "semi-literate immigrants spraying graffiti on respectable people's property" – embarked on a drunken, drug-fuelled binge in the course of which he spray-painted the word "Wannker" on his neighbour's Mercedes. "I know how to spell it," protested the editor, who appeared for the interview chain-smoking and wearing only a bath-towel decorated with a map of the Côte d'Azur. "But I stopped in the middle for a smoke." '

There was a verbatim account of his humiliation in the Oxted restaurant, which he guessed had come from the staff rather than Elizabeth, but nothing about the fire at his house, perhaps because the news had reached them too late for the first edition. It would make an interesting follow-up story, he supposed, for the Sunday papers, no doubt accompanied by his wife's reminiscences of their years together.

'Miller, whose newspaper has stridently advocated harsher penalties for drug users and called for the death penalty for dealers,' he read, 'snorted cocaine off his kitchen table before explaining that he seduced

Turner "with no regard for her physical or emotional satisfaction".'

'A self-confessed sexual compulsive,' the paragraph continued, 'Miller, 38, who describes himself as "over-sensitive" in his sexual liaisons with women, recalled having indecently assaulted a fellow pupil while still at primary school. He claimed that his secretary is the nineteenth woman he has seduced since marrying Elizabeth Portal nine years ago. Portal, 32, was unavailable for comment yesterday, though friends say she has already instigated divorce proceedings.'

Miller folded the paper up again and dropped it in a waste bin. He sat down, trying to find some source of consolation. For the moment, he could think of only two. None of the photographs of him – even the one that showed him naked – contained a large, well-defined shot of his head and shoulders; certainly not one that would allow a stranger to recognize him with his unpleasant new haircut. It seemed inconsistent, given the content of the accompanying text, to black out his sexual organs. He thought of an old joke he'd heard about a group of nudists in a park, surprised by passers-by. 'I don't know about you,' one man says, covering his head with his hands while his friends are concealing their privates, 'but I'm known by my face in this town.'

By the time people started to read the paper, Miller reasoned, he would be airborne, so long as there was no delay to his flight. He exchanged his British money for 1,500 euros, then checked in, registering no hold luggage, and went through to the departure gate. The immigration officer let him pass without a second glance. The flight boarded on time. It had all gone too smoothly. Even as he walked up the steps to the aircraft, Miller sensed he was about to be challenged.

As he entered the aircraft, his right arm was wrenched roughly from behind, by a steward. He'd turned left in the cabin, out of habit, and was about to enter the flight deck, whose door had been left open. 'There's no first class on this airline sir,' the young man said, relaxing his hold but not troubling to conceal a smirk. Miller turned round, and took a seat at the rear of the plane, on the left-hand side by a window.

If Miller had no illusions about his powerlessness in the face of his predicament, certain small habits stayed with him. Stepping into the arrivals hall in Perpignan, he felt an irrational surge of anger when he saw there was no driver there, holding his name up on a card. Even after he'd remembered there would be no chauffeur, here or anywhere else, Miller found himself glancing around again, just in case someone he knew was there. A seven-year-old girl ran straight at him, full of joyous anticipation. She was shouting to her father, who was a few yards behind the editor. All around him heads turned back, smiling, to watch the reunion. But Miller kept his eyes fixed on the sign for the train station, straight ahead, and walked on towards it, alone.

At Sants station in Barcelona, he joined the short queue for a line of cabs that stretched a hundred yards to his left, then disappeared around a corner. The vehicles were black and yellow; on its roof, each had a tariff numbered one and two. Just after a taxi had collected its passenger and moved off, Miller noticed, the number two on this display would light up. He was staring back along the line of cabs, wondering what these peculiar indicators were for, when his thoughts began to drift. For the first time in his life, he sensed the onset of real despair. His mood wasn't brought on by the traumatic memory of recent events, or even their speed, so much as where they had left him. He was alone; he was almost destitute and, worst of all, he was abroad.

And abroad – with the exception of a couple of holiday destinations, was never a place Miller had chosen to be. Even when he was in one of the places he could tolerate – Switzerland, or English-speaking areas of Canada, a country he'd come to think of as a more hygienic version of the UK – Edward Miller was a man who loved to come home. In a foreign hotel, he would never put his clothes in the wardrobe, or drawers. Unpacking would have been a kind of surrender. Abroad, to Miller's mind, was the breeding ground of everything he was least eager to encounter: asylum seekers, cannabis cafés, cholera, gay pornography masquerading as art, extreme heat and sedition; intellectual buffoons; terrorists, Aids, and gypsies; communists and blacks. Cynical and knowing in so many other ways, he wore his limited experience of the world like a plume. He had never set foot in Spain.

The first rule he'd imposed as editor was that any foreign story – apart from a natural disaster so colossal that to ignore it would look stupid – must have what he called 'a British dimension'. He loved that phrase. It may be that – as the incumbent foreign editor said when he was resigning, five minutes after Miller had announced his new brief – it was 'a fucking weird principle for a foreign desk'. Once introduced, though, it neatly legitimized a sort of reflex xenophobia that pervaded every area of the newspaper. He retained, on the masthead, the paper's original motif – a sailor raising an eyeglass pointed at the globe. In his own mind though, Miller's vision of the paper was of a man looking down the wrong end of a telescope trained on a Union Jack.

It was only ten thirty in the morning but he could feel the beginnings of discomfort as the sun beat down on his shaven head. The queue moved on. Like a sinner at the gates of purgatory, Miller shuffled forward. There were only half a dozen people in front of him now and he could see the faces of the cab drivers.

If England was Toad Hall under the stoats and weasels, Abroad was the Wild Wood. If its residents had a single shared trait, in his experience, it was dishonesty. And of all the characters he'd met on his few expeditions overseas, none were more nakedly duplicitous than its taxi drivers – and, of these, none more venal than those who queued for hours at International Arrivals. Like the smiling holidaymakers around him, Miller reflected, he was not so much a passenger, as prey. To judge by the length of this line of cars, he thought, Barcelona cab drivers must be rogues to a man.

When he reached the front of the queue, he saw his own driver, a young man of Moroccan appearance. He was unshaven, and he had an ominously servile look. Miller tried to retreat, but stumbled against the luggage trolley of an English family behind him. Rather than turn to apologize, he got into the car and showed the man the card from Oxbridge House. The driver said something he didn't understand; Miller ignored him.

He looked at the taxi meter, which to his surprise was turned on. It had three buttons, identical to the ones he'd seen on the roof; number two was illuminated. The overhead lights were there, Miller realized, to display to police the tariff the driver had selected, to ensure he was not charging a night rate in the morning, or a holiday fare on a working day. Miller looked at the meter in disbelief. What did such an arrangement say about the business ethics of the locals? And yet how invaluable it might be, he thought, to have some variation of this device wired to the heads of other notable swindlers of the innocent, such as barristers, dentists, or estate agents. After a half-hour journey, during which Miller had the definite sense of having seen one building twice, the driver pulled up on a main road in the centre of town and indicated a skyscraper with black-tinted windows.

'No,' snapped Miller. 'Oxbridge House'. He pronounced the name slowly and deliberately, accentuating the final 'se' so heavily that the second word, like the first, had two syllables. With a sigh he got out the business card again, and jabbed his finger at the drawing of the cloisters and the ivy-covered medieval tower.

The driver took the card for a moment, re-read the address, then waved back at the skyscraper. Following his finger, Miller saw that the glass door on the ground floor was inscribed with the school's name, in the same mock-Elizabethan lettering.

'Oxbridge House,' the driver read, from the door not the card, in his best approximation of an English accent, putting the same unorthodox stress on the 'se' that his passenger had.

Miller looked at the meter, which was showing seventeen euros. He handed the man ten, on the assumption that he'd already doubled the legal fare and, ignoring the driver's protestations, walked away towards the tower block.

He was dazzled by the midday sun. When he opened the door that led directly into the school's ground-floor reception area – which was air conditioned and lit by wall lamps because of the limited light allowed in by the dark windows – it felt like entering a refrigerated cinema. For a few moments he had difficulty making out anything at all. Squinting, he saw a large, semicircular reception desk, which was unoccupied. There was a switchboard attached to two old Bakelite telephones. One was ringing, but remained unanswered. Around the walls there were cheap armchairs, two of which were occupied by middle-aged Spanish businessmen. They were wearing short-sleeved shirts and ties, a combination that Miller had always found preposterous. He lit a cigarette.

As his eyes became accustomed to the light, he saw several doors leading off the reception area. Each had a plastic nameplate, with lettering in the same style as the school sign. The nearest room to the reception desk was 'Byron'. From where he was sitting he could also see

'De Quincey', 'Milton' and 'Swinburne'. The walls of reception were hung with posters, each advertising a British region. One, for the East Midlands, showed a milkmaid, a canal barge and, puzzlingly, a space rocket. Another, behind the reception desk, advertising 'Manchester – Gateway to the North' had a picture of Lake Windermere and a Manchester United footballer from the eighties, whose name Miller couldn't quite bring to mind.

The receptionist appeared, out of 'Byron'. A short woman in her early thirties, she was heavily made up and wearing a black, low-cut dress that revealed a figure of such ample voluptuousness that Miller, had he seen it in silhouette, would have dismissed it as a physical impossibility. But he paid no attention to her appearance; he seemed to have lost interest in sex.

She sat down behind the desk. The phone was still ringing. The woman, ignoring it, fumbled in a handbag and produced a packet of cigarettes. She searched around for a lighter. Miller, irritated, got up and lit her cigarette for her.

'*Gracias*,' she said.

She drew on the cigarette, and put the packet back in her handbag before picking up the receiver. It was the second guiding rule of Abroad, after chicanery, Miller thought – *Manyana*. He waited while she had a conversation in Spanish, punctuated by laughter. When she put the phone down, he got up and walked over to her.

'*Diga*.'

'I've come to see Christopher Devlin,' he said.

'Do you have an appointment?'

At the sound of his mother tongue, Miller relaxed slightly.

'Yes,' he lied. 'Tell him I'm a friend of Leigh Tebbutt's.'

The woman laughed. 'Aha,' she said, and winked at him. 'You know the padre.'

Miller took out the visiting card Tebbutt had given him.

'Where,' he asked her, 'is Oxbridge House?'

The woman looked confused. 'You're in it,' she said.

He pointed at the picture of the cloisters, and the ivy. 'What,' he asked, 'is this?'

She took her cigarette out of her mouth and placed it in the ashtray. Miller noticed a thick ring of fire-engine red lipstick round the filter.

'This,' she said, 'is the picture on the card.'

'I see,' said Miller, not expecting her to understand. 'Oh dear.'

'*Si señor*,' the woman smiled.

A fax was coming through on a machine at her left elbow; she turned away from him to read it.

'What's your name?' she asked, without looking up.

Miller's impatience turned to anxiety.

'My name?'

'Your name.'

Flustered, Miller looked around him. His eye fell on a door to his left: 'Wordsworth'.

'William,' he said.

'William what?'

She was looking straight at him now. His mind went blank.

The only image in his line of vision was the poster of the Manchester United player.

'William...' He stared over her shoulder, at the footballer in the scarlet shirt, praying for the name to come.

'Whiteside,' he said suddenly. Because he'd remembered it at the last moment, there was a note of triumph in his voice that she seemed to take for impatience.

'OK, OK,' she said. '*Una momentita*, Mr Whiteside.'

Miller sat down, cursing his ludicrous pseudonym.

She went back into Byron, which he guessed was Christopher Devlin's office. He heard a short exchange with a male voice, in Spanish, during which he recognized Tebbutt's name, mention of which precipitated a burst of laughter. She came out, smiling, and showed him in.

Devlin got to his feet and shook his hand. He was older than Miller had expected – forty-five perhaps – and wore the same uniform of short-sleeved shirt and tie as his students. He had a high forehead, dark brown hair and a moustache; his accent, which was upper class, and a sort of manic geniality, reminded Miller of the English actor Terry-Thomas.

'Is it Will?' he asked, waving Miller to a chair. 'Or William?'
Devlin sat back down behind his desk. It was made of dark oak, very British looking, and had seen some wear: the phrase 'is a Twat' had been carved into the wooden leg closest to Miller's chair. To the left of this inscription, another word had been clumsily gouged out, though at the start of it Miller was almost sure he could make out a 'D'.

'Will,' he said, seeking to distance himself as far as possible from the Lakeland poet.

On the wall behind the school's founder was a framed black-and-white photograph of a steam engine arriving at its destination, and a display of degree certificates belonging to his staff, almost all of whom appeared to have attended Pembroke College Oxford. The wall on Devlin's right, opposite the window, was taken up with bookshelves, stacked with Victorian novels.

'What can I do for you Will?'

'I want a job.'

'Did Leigh send you for work?'

Miller hesitated. 'No,' he said. 'He said I should just tell you I was his friend.'

At this, Devlin relaxed, and became instantly less suspicious.

'Have you taught before?'

'No.'

'Got a degree?'

'Yes. But I haven't got the certificate.'

'Never mind. What's it in?'

'English,' said Miller. 'Is that enough?'

'My own background,' Devlin said, 'is in science. Can I ask you something?'

Miller nodded.

Christopher pointed to a poem called 'The Seafarer', hanging on his wall.

'I was looking at this just now,' he said. 'It's about a sparrow flying on a winter night, and passing through a mead hall. It flies in and settles there for a moment, then sets off on its journey again.'

'Yes,' said Miller, 'thinking this must be a test. 'It's Anglo-Saxon.'

'I know,' said Devlin. 'It says that here. But do you understand what it means?'

'No,' said Miller. 'I mean… perhaps. I'm not sure.'

'How's Leigh?'

'He's fine. I saw him last night.'

'And Kate?'

'Kate,' Miller said, 'is away.'

'Oh,' said Devlin. 'Oh dear.'

'Yes.'

'Do you have anywhere to stay?'

Miller shook his head. 'I just got in this morning. How much,' he asked, 'should it cost for a cab from Sants station?'

'This time of day? I'd say twentyish.'

The school director turned away from his guest and looked through the tinted window. Byron, like all the classrooms in the school, had a window that ran from floor to ceiling, and extended across the full width of the room. The view was of a savings bank, at the base of the next tower, twenty yards away, across an immaculate stretch of lawn. Immediately outside the principal's office was a concrete path, four feet wide, that ran right around the building, and separated the base of the skyscraper from the grass.

'How much money,' Devlin asked, in a casual sort of a way, scrutinizing the façade of the bank, 'do you have?'

'Fifteen hundred euros.'

The principal allowed a look of vague concern to cross his face but said nothing.

'Credit card?'

'No,' said Miller, deciding to keep his secret card for use as a last resort.

'Luggage?'

'This,' he said, pointing to his canvas bag, 'is my luggage.'

Their eyes met for a moment, before the school director looked away.

'Where's Leigh now?'

'At home,' said Miller. 'Call him if you like.'

His host picked up a gilt-edged invitation that was lying on his desk.

'Are you an honest man, Will?'

'Honest?' Miller repeated. 'I'd say so.'

'Let me ask you something; what do you say if you have a meeting you don't want to go to? What's your best white lie?'

'I don't need white lies,' said Miller, forgetting that he had surrendered the privileges of his old life.

'Lucky man,' said Devlin. 'I, however, am not so fortunate.'

'What do you say, then?'

'When I lived in England, I would always say the same thing: "I'm terribly sorry, but I have a prior engagement, in Hull." '

'Oh really?' said Miller. Devlin was the kind of man who, a week ago, he would have got Charlotte to fire by email.

'Hull?'

'The beauty of Hull,' Devlin continued, 'is that they never question it. I learned to say "Hull" immediately, and with great conviction, so they realized I hadn't been casting around for an excuse.'

'You could say any town.'

'Ah, but if you said Brighton, or Harrogate, or Leamington Spa, they'd start asking why. But they know, deep in their hearts, that nobody would ever go to Hull of their own accord. They understand,' Devlin continued, 'that this matter has to be serious. They say nothing because they tell themselves that it must be a funeral. And they know instinctively that it can't be a friend. It has to be a blood relative. Who would go to Hull,' he added, 'out of friendship?'

'So,' Miller said, 'your problem is...'

'I'm invited to the British consulate tonight. Look at this.'

He showed Miller the invitation, and its envelope marked 'Urgent.' Devlin circled this last word, in red felt marker.

'Urgent. That's a word I have almost never used – ever – in my life.'

'Why?'

'Because so little is. I am careful with words. Urgent? Why? Bloody civil servants. Bloody canapés. Bloody British Council.'

'What you need...'

'Bloody real ale.'

'What you need,' Miller began again, 'is the Spanish equivalent of Hull.'

'But that's just my problem,' he replied. 'Compared to Hull, everywhere here sounds good.'

'These people at the consulate,' Miller asked. 'Are they from Spain?'

Devlin shook his head.

'Bloody Whitehall.'

'Well, then. It's simple.'

'What?'

'Stick to Hull.'

'But the distance… the short notice…'

'Merely emphasize the critical nature of your business on Humberside.'

Devlin looked at him with respect.

'Right,' he said. 'We have a week-long training course for teachers. It costs 1,200 euros.' He shrugged. 'Give me 600.'

'Euros?'

'Pounds.'

Miller waited for Devlin to say something else. He didn't.

'Oh,' said Miller. 'I see. Right.'

He counted out 900 euros, which Devlin put straight into his trouser pocket.

'What's the train?' asked Miller, pointing at the black-and-white photograph. It was beautifully composed, like a fine canvas.

'It's by the photographer Colin Jones,' said the director. 'Have you heard of him?'

'No,' Miller lied.

'It's the last steam train ever to arrive at King's Cross. When I have a new student in, I tell them that every learning process is like a railway journey…'

He pressed an intercom on his desk.

'Sonia.'

The receptionist returned.

'I'm taking Mr, er…'

'Whiteside,' said Miller. 'Will.'

'I'm taking Will to Pascual's for an hour.'

'What about Señor Lopez?' she asked.

'What?'
'You're supposed to be taking Lopez.'
'Get Concha to teach him.'
Sonia raised her eyebrows and said something in Spanish.
'In the same class?' Devlin asked her, in English.
Sonia shook her head.
'In the same year?'
'No.'
'Well then,' said Devlin. 'No *pasa nada*. Give him to Concha. I'll be back at four.'
Devlin led the way out of the school, across a piece of waste land and down a small side street. A fire engine passed them, its siren blaring. The vehicle was inscribed, Miller noticed, with the word *Bombers*.
'Bombers?'
'It's Catalan.'
'What for?'
'Express Dairies,' said Devlin, indicating smoke pouring from a building further down the road. 'What the bloody hell do you think it's for?'
They approached a whitewashed, single-storey building with a hand-painted sign that read Café Pascual.
'What was all that about Lopez?' Miller asked, as they approached the bar.
'The thing is...' Devlin said. 'Look Will, if we're short of English teachers and we have a beginner like Mr Lopez, then we use one of the Spanish teachers.'
'To teach him English?'
Devlin nodded.
'Won't he notice?'
'There are a lot of redheads in Catalunya,' the school director said. 'Concha's one of them. She could easily be from, er, Dundee.'
'Except there's not that many Conchas in Dundee,' said Miller.
'What does she call herself when she's teaching Mr Lopez?'
'She, er... look – you go in first, we're here now,' said Devlin.

Miller walked into the bar. It was dimly lit, with a long oak counter and a dozen small tables covered with gingham cloths. A couple of these were occupied; two customers were sitting on stools at the bar. Miller sat down at a table by the window. His shirt and trousers were soaked through with sweat.

Devlin went to talk to the owner, a genteel-looking Spaniard of about fifty, who was playing dice with a black man at the far end of the bar. Next to them, on the counter, was a wind-up gramophone with a faded brass horn. The school principal returned with two beers.

'What are they playing?' Miller asked.

'*Dados*,' said Devlin. 'Poker dice. They'll bet on anything: dominoes, cards; the colour of the next car that goes past.'

He pushed a bottle of Estrella towards his guest.

'So – you were telling me,' said Miller, 'what does Concha call herself when she's teaching English?'

'Sharon,' said Devlin. 'Cheers.'

'Cheers,' said Miller, who drained his glass.

'Bloody hell,' said Devlin, 'you look as if you needed that.'

'I did.'

'Another?'

'No,' said Miller. 'How good is Concha's English?'

Devlin looked uncomfortable.

'Well it's – you know – it's adequate for the job. It's – how would you say – at the required level.'

'Which is?'

'One lesson better than Mr Lopez.'

'Who is wordless.'

'Well... yes.'

'What,' Miller went on, feeling a little restored, 'did Sonia say to you in Spanish?'

'She, er... she pointed out that we had just the hint of a snag on this occasion,' said Devlin. 'Look, all this really isn't important.'

He ordered two more beers anyway. Miller left his untouched.

'When you say snag...'

'Well it's just that they both… it's just that Mr Lopez went to the same, how should I put it…'

'School?' Miller ventured. 'The same school as Sharon?'

'Well, yes; they went to the same primary school up the coast in Badalona. But he's quite a bit older than her. It'll be fine.'

The barman put a seventy-eight on his gramophone and the room was filled with the smooth, mannered tones of a British crooner singing 'Marrying for Love'.

'Who's that?' Miller asked.

'It's George Sanders,' said Devlin.

'How do you know?'

'I gave Pascual the record. Now listen,' he added, 'we don't have a lot of time.'

He placed an ashtray, a wine glass, a knife and fork and a box of matches in the middle of the table.

'In the next hour,' said the school principal, 'I'm going to show you how to teach English.'

'I can't speak Spanish.'

'Doesn't matter.'

Devlin picked up the fork, and held it up.

'It's a fork,' he said.

Miller said nothing.

'It's a fork,' the principal repeated.

'OK,' said Miller.

'OK what?'

'OK, it's a fork.'

'Again?'

'It's a fork.'

Devlin smiled. He got Miller to repeat the construction with each of the objects, one by one – 'It's an ashtray; it's a glass…' After a while he reversed the exercise so that Miller was instigating the statement, and he was repeating it. Then he went through each object again, prompting for the same phrase with the question: 'Is it a fork?', avoiding anything so challenging as a negative response. Finally, using a wider range of items including a bowl of peanuts, an olive, a vase, and a make-up mirror he'd borrowed from Pascual's wife, he drilled Miller for ten minutes with the question 'What is it?'

It was interminable. Miller grew sullen and frustrated, especially as he sensed that the two customers at the bar – an insolent-looking girl with hair cropped almost as closely as his own, and a gangling, sallow-skinned young man with a very large nose and long dark hair – were staring at him. In the man's case it was hard to be sure – his eyes seemed to look in different directions.

'OK,' said Devlin. 'That was twenty minutes. How did that feel – easy?'

'It felt as if you're treating me like an idiot.'

'You think so?'

'Yes. Who are they?' Miller asked, nodding towards the couple at the bar.

'Now they…' said the principal, sipping his beer, 'they are idiots. Real ones. In Spain, unlike in England, we care properly for the insane within the community. They're mental patients from the asylum in Sarria; the local barkeepers take turns to give them lunch, so long as they behave. Ignore them. You are thinking, perhaps,' Devlin added, 'that even a cretin on a lunch break can learn faster than this.'

'Well…' said Miller. 'Maybe a budgerigar.'

'A budgerigar. Right. Let's see how well you take off in Spanish. We'll try ten objects, since you're so cocky.'

He repeated the exercise in Spanish; after half an hour Miller felt mentally exhausted, and was starting to forget words entirely.

'How did I do?' he asked.

'Reasonable,' said the teacher.

'I mean at the end you mistook your peanuts for your mirror, but even a budgerigar might do that I suppose. Oh no hang on,' he added. 'Probably not.'

Miller reached for the beer he'd declined earlier.

'I normally do that part in Japanese,' said Devlin.

'Why?'

'Because the sounds are harder to retain. I never met a new teacher who went too slowly. You need to know how it feels when you don't speak a word. But I thought the Spanish might come in handy, where you're staying.'

'Where am I staying?'

'Oh I forgot – you don't have anywhere, do you? You could try the Britannia. It's close, and it's not too expensive.'

He scrawled the address, and a crude map, on a paper napkin.

'I'll call them,' he said, 'and say that you're on your way.'

'They're still staring,' Miller said, indicating the figures at the bar. The man, in particular, was beginning to unnerve him. Devlin picked up a bottle of beer. He waved it in the air and tapped it with a spoon, like a cat owner with a feeding bowl.

'Don't,' said Miller.

But the man was already on his feet. He collided with a seated diner as he approached, carrying a glass, and glared at the customer when he looked up for an apology. He spilled what was left of his own beer on Devlin's table as he sat down. Miller, apprehensive, moved his bag off the table and put it on the floor between his feet. The woman sat opposite him and rested her chin in her cupped hands, her elbows on the table, staring intently at him and taking up more room than would normally have been socially acceptable. She was wearing a sleeveless T-shirt that revealed her muscular upper arms. There was a tattoo of a red star on her right bicep. Miller sat back in his chair, away from her.

'You in this afternoon Nick?' Devlin asked her companion.

'No, thank Christ,' he replied, in a London accent. 'Tomorrow.'

His divergent gaze allowed him, unnervingly, to look at Miller and Devlin at once.

'Thank God for that,' said Devlin, 'the state you're in.'

'Jordan,' the school director said, turning to the woman, 'this is Will Whiteside.'

The girl gave him a hard look, then a perfunctory nod. The man leaned across and shook his hand.

'Nick Gannon,' he said. 'Excuse her; she's from Leeds.'

'Where are you from?' asked Jordan.

'Oldham.'

'Are you OK?' Nick asked Miller.

'I told Mr Whiteside,' Devlin explained, 'that you were…'
'Don't,' said Miller.
'Fugitive lunatics.'
Nick laughed; the woman didn't.
'But as you see,' Devlin continued, 'they are sane and at liberty; their time is their own, owing to the generous breaks our timetabling allows. These,' he added, 'are your colleagues.'
'What time tomorrow?' Miller asked, tired and exasperated.
'You start at eight,' said Devlin. 'With Mr Maragall.'
'Is there a book?' Miller asked.
'You don't need a book. He's a complete beginner. Just do with him what I did with you. Eighty minutes; if you use more than ten words of vocabulary you're going too fast.'
'Who's teaching Lopez?' Nick asked Devlin.
'Sharon,' said the principal.
'Sharon?' said Nick. 'Oh my God.'
'It'll be OK,' said Devlin. He turned to Miller. 'Things usually do turn out OK – don't you find that Will?'
Miller looked out of the window, up the street, to where an ambulance had joined the fire engine outside the burning building, and said nothing.

On his way to the hotel he stopped at the Corte Ingles, a department store, where he bought a phrase book, a baseball hat, a pair of cheap sunglasses and, with some reluctance, two short-sleeved shirts and a pair of fawn cotton trousers, like Devlin's.
Everything in the Britannia – a small hotel near the Barcelona football ground, was in a different shade of brown. In the lobby there was a tattered Union Jack, a small plaster model of a black cab and a framed print of Kipling's poem 'If'. The receptionist spoke only Spanish. Miller wrote 'Whiteside' on a piece of paper, and they handed him a key, without asking for payment, or for his passport. He let himself into the room, which was tiny and looked out on to the central well of the building. He ran a glass of water from the tap, recoiled at its swimming-pool bouquet, then drank it anyway. He picked up the phone in his room

and tried to order something to eat, but nobody at the Britannia seemed to speak English. He put the receiver down, and fell asleep.

He woke at six the next morning, and began to dwell on some precious things he'd lost. His sense of melancholy centred – a little to his surprise – not so much on his cremated possessions, or even his estranged family. He remembered the remark Elizabeth had made in the restaurant: 'You've never quite connected with Ellie, have you?'

'No,' Miller said, out loud. 'Because she's a part of you.'

When he thought of Elizabeth's new life across the road in Glastonbury, his anger and his wounded pride were accompanied by another, unexpected emotion: just the beginnings of empathy for Illingworth. No doubt his neighbour, too, had been impressed by her self-possession, her caustic wit, and her superior class, just as Miller had been, until she turned all those things on him.

He found himself mourning other, less tangible assets that he no longer had: control, mainly, and a sense of purpose and direction. He took a cold shower and put on his new trousers, his short-sleeved shirt and his English tie. He slipped his phrase book in his pocket, and went down to reception. Before he went out, he stopped to look at the Rudyard Kipling poem, though he knew it by heart. Perhaps it was a lucky omen; a sign that things could only improve. If Kipling, like Baden-Powell, had demonstrated anything, it was that a man could dominate his surroundings anywhere – even if he didn't speak the language. His blood rose at the playful humiliation he'd suffered at the hands of Devlin and his two punks in the bar. But that, Miller reflected, was yesterday. Things would be different, he told himself, today.

Today. He said the word to himself, out loud, and then looked it up in the basic glossary at the back of his phrase book. '*Hoy*'. He wrote it in large letters on his left palm, in biro, and repeated it to himself. '*Hoy*'. The way Miller pronounced it, sounding the 'h', it sounded rousing, like a mariner's call to arms. Encouraged, he left the hotel, and set off for the school.

His route took him past Pascual's bar; he was approaching the entrance, at seven fifteen, when his resolve failed him. He was very hungry. He stopped in a shop doorway and, from the sample menu in chapter seven of his phrase book – 'At the Restaurant' – rehearsed his order for the coffee and pastry he'd chosen as a substitute for the Cumberland sausage, egg, bacon and toast he would really have liked. '*Un café con leche,*' he repeated to himself as he approached the café entrance, like a child reciting a shopping list, '*y un croissant*'.

He stepped into the bar, still practising the order under his breath, hoping it would be comprehensible. The booklet's phonetic guide to pronunciation of the phrase had looked more bewildering than the Spanish. The black man was there again, at the end of the bar, talking to the owner. As Miller was approaching the counter, preparing to deliver his one line, the African walked over to him and asked him something in Spanish. Miller shrugged and shook his head. The man returned to his stool. Miller turned to face the barman, but the phrase had gone out of his head. He could see the toilet door, half-open, to his left. Miller walked in, and drew the bolt behind him. He took the phrase book out and rehearsed the words again. For appearance's sake, he flushed the toilet.

'*Un café con leche,*' he told the owner when he came out, '*y un croissant.*'

As he examined the barman's face, Miller's own features betrayed hope and expectation: it was the kind of look you might see on the face of a bombardier, seconds after launching an artillery shell, as he scanned a distant enemy village for traces of smoke.

'*Si señor,*' said Pascual.

Miller sat on a stool at the bar. There was a newspaper, *La Vanguardia*, in front of him. He picked it up, and examined it. The design was old-fashioned, he thought, and the colour reproduction was poor. When he looked up, the barman was back. He handed him a steaming plate of what looked like stewed squid, and a large glass of red wine.

'*Servidor,*' said Pascual.

Miller took out his phrase book again but as he opened it he saw that the eyes of the owner and the black man were on him. He put it back in his pocket. He'd never had, or needed, a talent for language. His eyes went down to the squid again. Any attempt to amend his order, he reasoned, might make things worse. At least this was food. He took a sip of the wine. The two men to his right went back to their game of dice.

He tried the squid. It was very hot, steeped in garlic, and highly spiced. For all that, Miller, not having eaten for a day, felt better when he'd finished it.

Pascual approached him, and took the plate away.

'*Algo mas?*' he asked.

Miller gave him a vacant look.

'*Gracias,*' he said, hopefully. He pulled out a ten-euro note and handed it to the barman who, to his surprise, returned it.

'It's OK,' Pascual said, 'it's on me.'

'*Que?*' said Miller. 'What?'

'Your order was terrific,' said the barman, in perfect, if heavily accented, English. 'You asked for it beautifully. It's just that I bet Andres…' he indicated the black man at the far end of the bar, who waved, cheerfully. 'I bet Andres fifty euros that if I gave you squid, you'd eat it.'

'You fucking bastard,' said Miller. 'Does everybody in here speak English?'

'Pascual,' said the barman. He held out his hand. Miller, defeated, shook it.

'Will,' he said.

'What's that on your hand?' Pascual asked.

'What?' said Miller, trying to hide his left palm.

'What,' the café owner continued, 'have you written on your hand?'

Miller showed him.

'*Hoy,*' said Pascual.

'It's there because I, er…' Miller stopped.

'No need to explain,' said Pascual. 'You're quite right. One can't be too careful.'

'Because,' Miller went on, 'I wanted today to be better…'

'Better? Better than what?'

'Better than yesterday.'

'I see,' said the barman. 'How's it going so far?'

Miller walked over to the school, where Sonia was sitting alone in reception. She was as heavily made up as she'd been the day before, smoking, and reading a paperback whose bright yellow cover showed a wild-eyed man in a surgeon's gown bending over a corpse, and removing its brain with what looked like spaghetti tongs.

He took the lesson in Milton, with Mr Maragall, a sales manager with a computer firm. He followed Devlin's method and, to his surprise, it seemed to work. At the end Maragall delivered a stream of incomprehensible Spanish, but it was clear from his expression that he left feeling happy – even grateful.

When Miller came out, Devlin was waiting. The director beckoned him into Byron, next door.

'Not bad,' he said. 'Good, almost.'

'Were you listening in?'

'No need.' Devlin tapped on the cheap plasterboard. 'You can hear everything through these walls.'

'I bet that's led to trouble,' Miller said.

'Since you mention it, it has.'

'What now?'

'You're working till nine this evening.'

'What?'

'With breaks.'

He pointed to the planning board in his office, where the name of Whiteside was down for that day, as for the whole week, to teach roughly ninety minutes on, ninety minutes off, over thirteen hours each day. The names of teachers ran in a vertical column down the left of the board. The hours of the working day, eight a.m. to nine p.m., were set out on a strip running left to right across the top of the display. The students, marked on light or dark blue tickets, were placed in line, horizontally, with the name of their teacher. Miller, examining Whiteside's schedule, noticed the ominous number of long gaps between lessons.

'Do you pay me during the breaks?'

'No.'

'So what am I supposed to do for an hour and a half?'

Devlin handed him a green paperback book: Thomson and Martinet: *A Practical English Grammar*.

Miller took it and walked out, back to the bar, where he ordered, and this time got, a coffee. Nick Gannon, the tall Londoner, was sitting at the counter. Miller joined him without asking. Nick had a sheaf of lottery tickets on the bar in front of him and, next to them, a newspaper open at the small ads. He looked at the entries that his new colleague had circled, in a section headed 'Duplex'.

'Are you looking for a flat?' Miller asked him.

Nick laughed.

'Duplex,' he translated. 'Five hundred euros... Mother and daughter duplex, eight-hundred euros.' 'Twin sister duplex...'

'What,' Miller interrupted, 'is a duplex?'

'These are... look. Did they teach you nothing in the monastery?'

'They're prostitutes,' said Miller.

'Sex workers.'

While the teacher kept his left eye on the newspaper, Miller noticed, his right was on the lottery tickets.

'Can you read two things at once?'

'Yes. Good isn't it. I can commit two sins at the same time.'

'Isn't the duplex and the lottery the same sin?' Miller asked. 'Greed?'

'And lust,' Nick said. 'And envy. And afterwards, profanity. Bloody hell, I'm worse than I thought.'

'How much can you win on the lottery?' Miller asked.

'With this draw, about a million euros. I mean... If I won, I'd give most of it to charity.'

'No you wouldn't.'

'OK, I wouldn't.' Nick laughed.

It was curious, Miller thought, how every English accent brought with it some implied attribute of character. Liverpool – sardonic resignation; Manchester – childhood suffering. London – meanness with money.

Miller's eyes went back to the small ads.

'Can you help me find a flat?' he asked, suddenly.

'Where are you staying?'

'It's a place called the Britannia.'
'Oh, shit.'
'What?'
'No, don't panic – the Britannia's fine. I mean, well – it's not actually, but – it's just that... how much are you paying?'
'I don't know.'
'We've got to get you out of there.'
'It doesn't look expensive.'
'No. It's not. Not... normally.'
'Normally?'
'Who sent you there?'
'Christopher.'
'Well that's it, you see.'
'That's what?'
'He always needs his 30 per cent.'
'Thirty?'
Gannon laughed.
'If you're lucky.'
'What?'
'Look,' Nick said. 'What you need to understand is, this business has been taken over by the big players: companies with dozens of schools in different countries. Christopher is really the last one in this town that operates like this.'
'Like what?'
'This is his only school; he has a few legal teachers, on contracts...'
'You?' Miller asked.
'Are you joking? Jordan's legal,' he said.
'So why aren't you?'
'Because when you're legal you earn less. You pay tax. You're in the system. You need papers. You have to study for certificates nobody in their right mind would waste their time on... you're... you're bloody... legal.'
'And when you're not?'
'When you're not legal,' Nick said, 'you get cash in hand and there's no questions asked. There's two ways of doing most things and each

of them has its price. Like at the Hotel Britannia.'

'Where can I go?'

'Give me 400 euros a month,' said Gannon, 'and you can stay with me. For a bit.'

The following evening Miller went with Nick to his flat in the Calle Vic and moved in to – or rather put his holdall on the stone floor of – the spare bedroom. It overlooked a side street in an area called Gràcia. With its narrow roads and small cafés, it was like a smaller, less self-satisfied version of Soho. Miller's room was twelve foot by twelve; there was a metal-framed single bed and a small bookcase that contained two volumes – *Journey to the Centre of the Earth* and *Ivanhoe* – both filched, Miller guessed, from Devlin's library. He used his Swiss army knife to make an incision in the side of the thin mattress, slipped his passport and secret credit card inside, then repaired the cut with gaffer tape. 'You never know,' he remembered his father saying, 'when you'll need it.'

After settling his bill at the Britannia, Miller had only 300 euros left; Nick agreed to be paid by the week.

Miller, as a consequence of his timetable, was almost never there in daylight. He found himself carrying around the green grammar book Devlin had given him. He steeped himself in it, during his lengthy breaks. He learned to identify, and define, tenses he'd never given a thought to: present perfect; present continuous, present perfect continuous. It stopped him having to think or, worse, to remember. He lost himself in it. Language, not medication, he remembered Norman saying, was the best sedative.

Miller's panic attacks subsided, in frequency and intensity, though he still went out with a paper bag, and learned of situations to avoid. One evening on a bench in Diagonal Metro station, in rush hour, he found himself sweating and hyperventilating, breathing from a Corte Ingles carrier bag which an old lady – believing he was attempting to kill himself by suffocation – kept trying to snatch out of his hand. When he turned his back and tried to carry on, she rapped him on the head with her fan. In the end Miller, still breathing from his bag, ran off the platform, up the escalator and back to street level, where his anxiety eased.

For the first week he was with complete beginners, and advanced students who came for conversation. The training course he'd paid for never materialized, but the pay, which Devlin delivered in cash, every Friday, easily covered his expenses, so long as he attempted nothing more extravagant than eating out in cheap cafés. During some breaks, the director would give him classes in teaching different tenses and points of grammar, though the essential technique of what the director called 'the Method' never varied.

'That's the beauty of it,' Devlin said. 'It's simple. A fool could do it, and many do. In the same way that a spacecraft's computer finally comes down to noughts and ones, the Method is never more complicated than 'Is it an ashtray?'

'Even when it's present perfect continuous,' said Miller, glancing down at his green book, 'used as future with a time clause?'

'Yes,' said Devlin. 'The drill is exactly the same. And never, never, name the tense to them. They don't need to know. Though you of course,' he added, 'need to know them all. Do you?'

'Yes,' said Miller.

'Present continuous?'

'What verb?'

'Any verb.'

A child rushed in, past their table, and dashed behind the counter.

'I am running.'

'Simple past.'

'I ran.'

'Present perfect.'

'I have run'

'Present perfect continuous as future,' he added. 'With a time clause.'

'Tomorrow I will have been running,' Miller said, 'since...'

'Yes?' Devlin said. He looked him straight in the eye. 'Since?'

'Since the second of May,' said Miller.

'OK,' said Devlin. 'When you're in the classroom, use things that happen. Make them tell you what people are doing outside your window. Get them to talk about their kids and their animals. What you must never do,' he said, 'is laugh at them. Even a dog doesn't like to be laughed at.'

'Why would you?' Miller asked.

'Well, when they tell you, as one will sooner or later, that on his way to his lesson, he put his dinner in the bank.'

'His dinner?'

'*Dinero*,' said Devlin. 'Means money.'

'Don't worry,' said Miller. 'I'm not going to laugh. I haven't laughed,' he added, 'since the second of May.'

'OK, OK,' said Devlin. 'Laughing isn't a sacking offence.'

'What is?'

The principal didn't reply.

'Have you sacked people?'

'No,' said Devlin. 'Well. Yes. Only one.'

He felt least at ease in the small staff room, where the teachers congregated immediately after lessons. Students' files were kept in a tall grey cabinet, on top of which was a row of champagne glasses, covered in a thick layer of dust. A poster on the wall listed 'The Six Forms of the Future'. Ten minutes were set aside for 'pedagogical reports' at the end of each class, though most teachers spent the time smoking and exchanging news from home, or demeaning anecdotes about their students.

Though the school theoretically taught business English, most of its staff were drifters. Miller kept his distance from them, apart from Nick. Their preoccupations, whatever their age, were the same: food, tobacco, drink, periodically sex or drugs and – above all on the low wages they earned – survival. Observing his new colleagues, after years in the newspaper industry, he was struck by their almost total lack of ambition. Status and power had no meaning for them. And yet they were swiftly energized, sometimes to the point of hysteria, by certain subjects. These included Conservatism, organo-phosphates, fox-hunting and racial prejudice. When the conversation turned to such issues, he kept his eyes forward and stifled his instincts, like a guide dog.

There was a contingent, led by Gannon, who would use the ten-minute 'pedagogical' break to sprint up to the Paris Crêperie on the second floor of the adjacent tower block. Its name was spelled out in neon bulbs on a large sign visible from the school's reception area. It flashed on and off every couple of seconds, in a poor imitation of Pigalle. There, they would drink one, sometimes two, Estrellas, before tearing back for the next lesson.

Miller rarely joined them. He disliked the Paris: air conditioned and soulless, it contained a small drugstore and – the thing he liked about it least – three computer consoles, each isolated in a Perspex booth. The machines offered public access to the internet, which he saw as a threatening fault line which, at the touch of a button, could offer him a glimpse of his old life, and fresh news of his ruin.

So he spent his breaks in the staff room, often with Jordan, the young contract teacher from Leeds, who – despite her appearance – took her work more seriously than some of her colleagues. She exuded a kind of muted antagonism, as if she'd somehow sensed that Miller was everything she despised.

Miller found himself adjusting to the rhythm of life in the city. He got used to having dinner at ten in the evening; he developed a tolerance, if not quite a taste, for the poisonous dark charm of Ducados, the country's most affordable cigarette.

If the abruptness of recent events had made him feel like a mongrel blasted into orbit, Miller's initial reactions – alarm, consternation and disbelief – had faded, leaving him to contemplate, and try to adapt to, his new and alien environment.

It occurred to him that many of the attributes he had come to regard as inborn – things like poise, confidence and authority – had actually been connected with his executive status. The ability to instil deference and fear with a look, or a single word, which he'd assumed to be innate to his character, seemed entirely to have deserted him. At the same time, he was reluctantly rediscovering qualities he couldn't ever remember possessing – patience, thrift, and just the beginnings of curiosity for another culture. It was enough, for the moment, that the panic attacks hadn't come back, and that he was in a place where he couldn't be further humiliated by Elizabeth, either face to face in a courtroom, or in the press.

On the Friday of Miller's second week, Nick left to spend the weekend in Andorra. When Miller, alone in the flat, found himself dwelling on his anxieties – his great fear was that someone would notice his name in an English broadsheet – and his pulse began to quicken, he took to wandering the streets of Barcelona. Wordless as he was, this proved to be a comfort, like walking through a silent film where he had no capacity to influence the plot. Nothing was quite real. He might as well have been a ghost.

He kept his head shaved, using a razor, and – when outdoors – his baseball cap, and his sunglasses, on. As he approached the tower block, at seven thirty on the Monday morning of his third week in Spain, he sensed that he was beginning to adjust to his new surroundings. Then he walked across reception, opened the door of the staff room, and heard Jordan's voice exclaim: 'Edward fucking Miller'.

He froze in the doorway, like a man playing grandmother's footsteps for his life. Sonia, who'd been close on his heels, walked into the back of him and together they half-fell into the room.

Miller attempted to keep his composure. He started looking through the filing cabinet for his class notes. This kept his back to Jordan, who he hadn't seen as he entered the room, because her chair was behind the open door. Nick was lounging across two seats to Miller's right, by the window, reading a crime thriller.

'Edward and Elizabeth,' Jordan sneered. Miller glanced over his shoulder and saw that she was reading to Nick, from an article. There was a new masthead – the globe and the telescope had gone – but he had no difficulty in recognizing the paper he used to edit.

'They sound like members of the fucking royal family,' she complained to Gannon. 'What kind of a man calls himself Edward?'

Nick shrugged.

'Do you know anyone who calls himself Edward?' Jordan asked Miller.

'No,' he said.

'"Edward". I mean he's got to be...'

'What?' Nick asked her.

'I don't know. Fucking anal.'

Miller turned round, as casually as he could manage, and looked at the page. To his great relief, the photograph of him was small, and very poor. The piece was in a News in Brief column and from its length – twenty lines or so – he gathered it must be an update on his continued absence. It was ominous, though, that the basic details of his disappearance seemed to be common knowledge. What he couldn't understand was why his own newspaper – the one publication that might have spared him – was giving his disgrace any coverage. He turned to the leader page. 'Editor,' he read, 'I. Garfitt.'

'That miserable fucking coke-snorting hypocrite,' Jordan said. 'I hope he's fucking dead.'

'Why?' Miller asked.

'Why?' She turned on him. 'Have you never seen this newspaper?'

'Well...'

'Well, have you?'

'Once or twice.'

'Well, then.'

'If you don't like it,' he asked her, trying to sound supportive rather than indignant, 'why do you buy it?'

'I don't buy it. One of those morons – she motioned towards the clients waiting in reception – brought it in. I'm always amazed when I see it in a shop.'

'Why?' He kept the irritation out of his voice.

'Because fascist propaganda isn't sold, is it? It's dropped, on the enemy, like bombs.'

'So when do you see it?'

'When I lived in London,' she said, 'if someone left that evil rag on the Tube, I'd read it, just like I did now, to see if it had changed – which it never had, except to be more full of hate and fucking racism – and then I'd take it home, like I'm going to now, and set fire to it.'

'Why not drop it in a waste bin?'

'Because then someone might pull it out and read it,' she said. 'And believe it.'

'Do you think all people are that stupid?' Miller asked.

'No Will,' she said. 'Not all people.'

'Who, then?' asked Sonia, who was still standing in the doorway.

'I don't know... you could start with the two million assholes that buy it. You know why I really hate these fuckers?' she said, pointing at one of the columnists. He was a former neighbour of Miller's, a fat Catholic moralist who – as he could have informed Jordan, had the circumstances been different – had survived a heart attack sustained while having sex with his assistant in a seaside hotel during a Conservative Party conference.

'Because they blab.'

'They blub?' Sonia asked.

'Blab,' Nick said, without looking up from his paperback. 'Regular verb. Random and profuse disclosure, by cowards.'

'They blab,' Jordan went on. 'This is written by people who blab, about people who blab, for people who blab. And I,' she added, sounding more Yorkshire than ever, now that she was angry. 'Don't blab.'

'You've got me interested now,' Nick said. 'Chuck it over.'

Jordan threw the paper in his face. He reassembled it.

'Hey Will,' he called out, 'he looks a bit like you.'

The young woman leaned over Gannon's shoulder.

'Hey, he does,' Jordan said. Then she laughed. 'Only joking.'

Miller went back into reception, still early for his morning appointment with Mr Maragall. Through the tinted windows, he could see an elderly window-cleaner, standing on the path outside. He was holding a rubber scraper, half a metre wide, which he applied half-heartedly to one of the tinted panes. The man, Miller noticed, wasn't even looking at what he was doing: his eyes were on a young woman coming out of the bank behind him. A cigarette dangled from the workman's lips.

Miller identified countless examples of inefficiency at the school. True, Christopher kept the Bakelite phones locked when he wasn't around; but there was pilfering of stationery, abuse of the photocopier and abysmal timekeeping; the window-cleaner was just the latest example. He watched as the ash from the man's cigarette fell, unnoticed by the smoker. The huge single panes of each of the ground-floor windows were set at a slight angle, slanting outwards as they neared the ground; the ash began to run down the incline then lodged in a smear of grime half-way down the glass, where it stayed.

Restless, Miller reached for his packet of Ducados, which turned out to be empty. Then he began scrutinizing the pack, memorizing the tar level, nicotine content and weight when packed.

In his old life, it had been during his rare moments of inactivity that Miller was at his most acutely focused – brooding on recent triumphs or disasters; devising his strategy for the days ahead. Now, what alarmed him more than anything was a period of idleness, which would give him the chance to contemplate the past or – worse – ponder his future. That way, he knew, lay torment, and a fresh collapse.

Miller screwed the empty cigarette packet into a tight ball and kept it clenched in his left fist. He looked up at Sonia, behind the reception desk. She was reading the final pages of a paperback whose cover was decorated with a human skull; an adder was threading itself through the left eye-socket. The title was in English: *The Eighth Pan Book of Horror*, edited by Herbert Van Thal. The receptionist was utterly gripped, like a relative scanning a newly posted list of war wounded. She finished the last page, closed it, and glanced over to her left, where the window-cleaner had stopped scraping altogether and was gazing at her through one eyeball-sized section of perfectly clean glass. Seeing himself observed, he resumed his task with feeble, perfunctory strokes.

Miller walked over to Sonia's desk.

'Can I borrow this?' he asked her, pointing to the book.

'Sure,' she said.

He was about to sit down, when he noticed her packet of Fortuna, open on the desk.

'Can I have a cigarette?'

'No.'

He assumed she must be joking, and reached out his hand.

'I said no,' she told him. 'We buy our own here, like in prison.'

He picked up the book and went into Christopher's office.

'Do you ever have work,' he asked him, 'at the weekend?'

'No. Well...'

He indicated the planning board. There was a session from nine till one on Saturday morning, with Gannon's name against it. In the place where the blue student name-tags should have been, there was a large plastic cutout of a death's head.

'We have the Saturday Group,' Christopher said, 'in the morning. And they're Nick's.'

'Do they know,' Miller asked Devlin, 'that their marker is a death's head?'

'They do.'

'And they don't mind?'

'The Saturday Group are remarkable in many ways,' said Devlin. 'Not least because they have an honest acknowledgement of their own limitations, and they have set themselves an attainable goal.'

'Which is?'

Devlin sighed, deeply.

'Their job,' he said, 'is to refuel airliners at Barcelona airport. This requires them to liaise with English-speaking air crew. The only elements of the language they require to master are: how much, how many, and the numbers up to a thousand. Each of these accomplishments has so far eluded them.'

'How many of them are there?'

'Three. Paco Calamita – if ever a man deserved his name, it's him; that's the one word of English he's grasped, actually, calamity – and Jordi and Luis, the Lesseps brothers: two men whose brains, I truly believe, will find their final resting place not in a churchyard, but a science museum.'

'How long have they been coming?'

'Two – no, three – years.'

'*Years?*'

'There are some skills,' Christopher said, 'that certain individuals will never master. It could be whistling, or spin bowling, or the art of love. For Paco and the Lesseps brothers, it is speaking basic English.'

'All of them?'

'Sadly yes,' said Devlin. 'I was trained, as I told you, as a scientist,' he added. 'I am genuinely convinced that the Saturday Group constitute, in their own way, as remarkable a phenomenon as photosynthesis, alchemy, or ball lightning. Except that those phenomena imply a degree of wonderment, and illumination. The Saturday Group are more, er…'

His voice trailed off. He pointed up to the photograph of the train at King's Cross.

'Odd, isn't it,' he went on, 'how even today, in the nuclear age, engine capacity is commonly assessed in horse power.'

'What?' said Miller.

'In the same way,' Christopher continued, 'I still tend to think of human intelligence as being measured in candles. A man can be bright, or brilliant, or have a dazzling intellect. Other men fail – quite literally – to hold a candle to him. Now with the Saturday group...' He sighed, deeply, and gazed out of the window, towards the bank, as if for consolation. 'We are at the other end of the spectrum, so to speak. They are, er...'

'Dim?' said Miller.

'Not exactly,' Devlin said. 'I would say it's more a case of their flame having gone out altogether.'

'Have you taught them?'

'Yes. All the regular teachers have. And they've all been broken, eventually. Nick's the last. Though God knows, the others tried. It's double time,' he said. 'But double isn't enough. Is it Nick?' he called out to the teacher, who had just come in to reception. He came into Devlin's office.

'What?'

'Double pay – not enough for the Saturday Group.'

'No,' Nick said.

'Why do you do it?' Miller asked him.

Nick gave him an irritated look. 'Habit.'

'What do you do afterwards?' Miller asked.

'I go to the beach,'

'What then?'

'What do you mean what then? I go to the beach, like everybody else does, and then...'

'Yes?'

'I sit on it.'

'Then what?'

'Then I, er...' Nick looked at Christopher for help.

There was an uncomfortable silence.

'Then I... come back.'

'Can I come with you this weekend?' Miller asked.

'If you like,' said Nick. 'Be here at one, on Saturday.'

Walking up to the school at twelve thirty on Saturday, Miller was surprised to see that the window-cleaner was back, standing on the concrete path that ran round the base of the tower. He was at work on the tinted front of Milton. On the other side of the glass, Miller could make out three Spaniards. One – a small, bald man – was on his feet and gesticulating angrily at Nick. The other two, who were seated, were clearly the Lesseps brothers; their faces shared a bizarre, asymmetrical quality. One of them was leaning forward, counting on his fingers; the other appeared to be asleep.

But it was the window-cleaner who caught Miller's attention. He was working on the massive pane with a rubber scraper that was hardly wider than a safety razor, even though his full range of much larger implements was in the bucket next to him, and he was attending to every fleck and blemish on the glass with the scrupulousness of a surgeon preparing his own operating table.

Miller let himself in through the main door and went to sit in the staff room. He'd just had time to light a Ducados and put his feet up on a chair when the door was flung open and Nick burst in. He was carrying the green folder that contained the Saturday Group's notes. He walked past his colleague as if he wasn't there. There was an alarming look in his eye; distant yet purposeful. It was the sort of expression Miller had seen on the faces of 1930s B-movie actors in the moments after they were recruited to the ranks of the living dead.

Nick stood in front of the tall filing cabinets, then slammed his forehead into the doors, so hard that the toughened steel was dented. A couple of champagne glasses fell off the top of the cabinet and smashed on the floor.

'Morning,' said Miller. 'What's up?'

'What's up?' Nick sighed. 'What's up…' There was a vengeful calm in his voice that, combined with the violence of his last gesture, Miller found unnerving.

'What's up is that I hate them.'

'You what?'

'I hate them,' Nick said, 'because they are fucking stupid. No.' He paused. 'I don't hate them because they are fucking stupid. Hamsters,' he added, 'are fucking stupid. But you can't hate a hamster. A hamster tries its hardest. A hamster puts its best foot forward. Nobody would want to strangle a hamster. Hamsters,' he said, 'are OK.'

'Sit down,' said Miller.

'I hate them,' Nick went on,' because they are fucking stupid, and they fucking argue. Paco – that fucking bald cunt – sorry Will; he's like... he's like Jesus Christ, or Charles Manson.'

'Pardon?'

'Because if you met him, you'd think – yes – this man is certainly unique. This is a man who stands out. There is nobody like him, anywhere in the world. But that's not what's really remarkable.' Nick gave Miller a sort of imploring look. He seemed on the verge of tears.

'What's really remarkable,' he continued, 'is – *where did he find the others?*'

He sat down.

'You know what he said to me just now? He said – you know when he signs them up Devlin shows them his railway engine and gives them all that shit about learning English being like a journey?'

Miller nodded.

'Paco said: "Today, we stop at wrong station."'

'What did you say?'

'I said – in Spanish – "Paco, when you're on the wrong train, every station is the wrong station."'

Miller peered out across the reception area. The door of Milton was open but no sound was coming out.

'Haven't you got twenty minutes left?'

Nick shook his head.

'Like all hostages,' he said, 'we have developed certain rituals, in order to survive.'

'Such as?'

'Such as, I keep an ashtray on the table with five euros in it – my chair always has its back to the window – and the first one to spot that

Juan, the window-cleaner, is here, and say so in English, gets the money.'

'Why?'

'It makes them feel there's at least something they can achieve. And for the last half-hour of every lesson, I leave them with a pen in their hands and I get them to describe what the window-cleaner is doing, as he's doing it; what he's wearing, whether he's smoking; whether he looks happy.'

'Does a window-cleaner,' Miller asked, 'ever look happy?'

'This one does,' Nick said. 'I give Juan ten euros to take half an hour over it.'

'Good God,' said Miller, 'that must make for interesting reading.'

'Oh you'd be surprised.' Nick opened the green folder and handed Miller three pieces of paper.

'This is last week.'

Miller looked at the first page. It read like the wilder moments of a dead stream-of-consciousness poet, spiritually channelled by a lunatic.

'Calamita?' said Miller.

Nick nodded. 'But the Lesseps brothers are no better. I mean – let me ask you something. If you instructed three men, who have been learning English for three hours a week every week for three years, to describe a window-cleaner at work, there are certain nouns you'd expect to occur. Is that fair?'

'Yes.'

'Not every week maybe – but from time to time.'

Miller nodded.

'Such as "window", ' Gannon said.

'Right.'

'Wrong.'

Miller looked at the other two sheets of paper.

'See any windows at all?'

'No.'

'And yet look more closely,' Gannon said, 'and you will notice one word that occurs in all three answers.'

'Bloody hell,' said Miller. 'Torque?'

He drew breath.

'Don't ask,' Nick said. 'All they really need to understand is "litre" and "how many".'

'I know,' said Miller. 'That should be fairly...'

'It should be,' Nick interrupted. 'It would be. Except for one thing. They can't fucking count.'

'In English?'

'In any language.'

Miller gave him a look of disbelief.

'Listen,' the Londoner said. 'When you came in, we were practising "how much" and "how many" with shopping lists. As Christopher once told me,' Gannon went into an excellent impression of Devlin's upper-class accent – ' "One cannot practise those structures using aviation fuel all morning. Even in the language of Dickens and Shakespeare, it becomes fatiguing." Anyway, just now Paco was telling Jordi and Luis that – and I quote – "Lamb is young beef".'

'What?'

'Yes. Even the other two looked shocked. So I said: "Say it in Spanish." '

'And?'

'And he did. When the others told him he was wrong, he said – "How do I know? My mother buys it at the supermarket." '

There was a tap at the door. Paco handed Nick three pieces of paper. The teacher looked at them, then slumped forward, his chin in his hands.

'Goodbye,' said Paco.

Gannon didn't reply.

'Calamity?' the Spaniard asked, again provoking no response. Paco patted his teacher encouragingly on the shoulder, like a registrar consoling a bereaved relative, then left.

'Why,' Miller asked when they'd gone, 'do you do the Saturday Group?'

'Oh shit,' Nick replied. 'I'd almost forgotten.'

He went in to reception and picked up the receiver from one of the Bakelite telephones.

'It's locked,' said Miller.

Nick ignored him.

With a deftness born of practice, he rocked the cradle of the phone, using his index finger, like a Morse signaller, forty or fifty times.

'Sian?' Nick said. 'It's my ex,' he explained, covering the mouthpiece. 'She's in Adelaide.'

Miller went and sat outside the school entrance, in the sun. Ten minutes later Gannon appeared in the doorway, beckoning him.

'Try it,' he said. 'You just bang out the number, with a half-second pause between taps.'

'How many times for zero?'

'Ten.'

Miller tapped in Dr Norman's number. At his second attempt, to his great surprise, it rang. When the doctor answered, he hung up.

'See?' Nick said. 'I get more wrong numbers on my mobile.'

'Why doesn't Christopher change these phones?' Miller asked. Gannon laughed.

'You know what he said to me?' He reverted to his impression of Devlin. ' "It's like the names on the doors, Nicholas. It gives the place a touch of class." '

They walked to Sants station. A limbless beggar was taking his place on the corner of the Calle Numancia.

'Why,' Miller asked, 'are there so many of them here?'

'Beggars?'

'Cripples. And why are they always very old men?'

'I don't think the Civil War helped.'

They took a train down the coast to Sitges. Nick's conversation, during the twenty-minute journey, was dominated by business ideas that would bring him swift and considerable returns, and a means of release. Two years ago, he explained, he'd tried to bring a double-decker London bus over to Barcelona.

'I got it for three hundred quid,' he said. 'I was going to teach English downstairs, and have a tea shop upstairs.'

The vehicle, he explained, had been impounded at Dover because he hadn't got the right kind of driving licence.

'The other thing I thought of,' Nick said, 'was this agency... it would be like Kissagrams, but for people you don't like.'

'Why?'

'Well, you could order like... a Headbutt-o-Gram. Or a Stanleygram. I mean you wouldn't actually attack them with a Stanley knife, obviously...'

'Obviously.'

'I was going to call it Terrorgrams. Do you think that would work?'

'No.'

It was a fifteen-minute walk from Sitges station to the beach; when they arrived, Miller looked in dismay at the thousands of white plastic sun-loungers, two feet apart, most of them occupied by the glistening body of a holidaymaker.

'We're not going down there?' Miller said.

'Please yourself.'

With no other plan, Miller followed him. Nick sat on a plastic sunbed and pulled off his trousers, revealing a pair of tight nylon briefs. He took off his shirt, lay back and put on a pair of headphones.

Miller sat on the next sun-bed, still wearing his shirt and new beige trousers. Though it was early June, he found the afternoon heat oppressive. He looked down at his leather shoes. The right one still had a fine patina of silver paint from the aerosol he'd used to spray Illingworth's car. Standing in front of him was a girl of six or seven, her skin olive brown from the sun, holding an ice-cream cornet. He scanned the bodies on the beach. Many of these tourists, as he could tell from their red skin and gold-embossed novelettes, were his compatriots. He stood up and walked back to the promenade, where he bought a cheap pair of shorts, sun cream and beach shoes. He changed in a bar toilet. On his way back to the beach, he passed a newspaper stand: there were three copies of an English broadsheet, with his face on the masthead. Miller bought them all, and stuffed them into a waste bin. A policeman was standing on the corner of the street, watching him, his mouth slightly open. Miller walked away without looking back, found the *hamaca* next to Nick's, covered himself in sun cream, and fell asleep.

He was woken by Gannon pressing a cold bottle of Estrella against his stomach. The shock was followed by a wave of mournfulness, and loss. He'd been dreaming that he was back in his job, before he walked in to Bowker's Cupboard.

'I once had this plan,' Nick told him, 'for a pizza delivery service that also gives you a DVD.'

'For God's sake,' said Miller.

'Who could resist it?' Nick asked. 'The Double Chilli and a free copy of *Towering Inferno* and *Fire Down Below*? That'd work, wouldn't it?'

'No,' said Miller. He drank from the bottle. 'What were you doing before, in England?'

Nick ignored him.

'All you need to change your life for ever,' he said, 'is one really good idea.'

Miller looked out across the sea of half-naked bodies.

'That's right,' he said. 'Or one really bad one.'

Most of the sunbathers were women, but his eyes settled mainly on the men. He was worried that he might, in this number of people, find his glance falling on some British sub-editor, cleaner, or freelance writer who would recognize him. He scoured the crowd nervously for English newspapers.

'Good God,' he said, 'there's a guy in an Oldham Athletic football shirt.'

Nick looked at him.

'How many people can you see on that beach?'

'I don't know... fifteen hundred?'

'How many women?'

'Nine hundred?'

'Clothed?'

'No. Well – half-clothed'

'That makes eighteen hundred bare breasts out there,' Nick said. 'Oldham Athletic? You need fucking help you do.'

Nick looked slightly embarrassed.

'Are you gay?'

'No,' Miller snapped.

'I mean,' Nick went on, 'I don't care if you are.'

'I'm not gay. I'm...'

'Yes?'

'From Oldham. How long,' Miller asked, 'have you been here?'

'Six years.'

'Why did you come?' he asked again.

Nick sat up and took off his sunglasses. He focused on Miller with his left eye.

'Now you see – you just don't ask that.

'Why not?'

'Has anybody asked you that? Have I?'

'No.'

'Have you not noticed how everybody in this place is running away from something? And you don't ask them why. But since you ask, I had a VAT difficulty.'

'With your business?'

'I had a market stall.'

'What did you sell?'

'Books,' he said. 'Videos. Junk. Believe me, when you have Customs and Excise on your case you've got problems.'

'So I've heard.'

'They fine you,' he said, with a look of real moral indignation, 'by the hour, did you know that?'

'I didn't know they were that clever.'

'They aren't. It was their fucking computer. Without their computer – they told me this afterwards – it would have been just like they had four pieces of a very large jigsaw. It would have taken an amazing stroke of bad luck, or genius, for them to put those pieces together. But that's what computers are good at. Their fucking computer did it, in less than a second.'

Miller lit a cigarette. In the heat he could barely taste it.

'What's Christopher running away from?' he asked.

'Now there is a question,' Nick said. 'I'm not sure. I know he was a chemistry teacher in London, and he had some sort of breakdown.'

'That's his old desk then,' said Miller.
'The school shipped it over; that was his leaving present.'
'What about Jordan?'
'What about her?'
'What's Jordan running away from?'
'Jordan,' Nick said, 'keeps her distance. All I know about Jordan is she lives up on the hill, near the park, in this road full of Basques. Someone told me she used to sing with pub bands. Jordan keeps herself to herself. The only one she sees outside of work,' he added, 'is Sonia.'
'She looks...' Miller tried to find the right adjective, and couldn't.
'Hard?' Nick said.
Miller nodded.
'Yeah, you don't fuck with Jordan. But the students love her. When they're in with her she makes them feel like they're the most important thing in the world to her.'
'Are they?'
Nick laughed.
'She loathes them,' he said. 'More than any of us do. She puts on a face,' he added, 'when she goes in there.'

Miller remained troubled by the thought that somebody would recognize him, even though, with every week that passed, it was clearer how unlikely that was. He'd lost weight and he was far thinner in the face. With his shaven head, dark glasses, and the deep red of his sunburn already turned to brown, even a close friend wouldn't have known him. Even so, he did his best to avoid police officers, who, Nick had told him, would occasionally exercise the right to ask for papers.

Worse than this legitimate fear of enforced disclosure was an irrational anxiety that he would blurt out his identity by mistake. Gradually, by virtue of the simple knowledge that he could never speak it, his real name began to obsess him. He had nightmares. In one, he was back in England, standing in a court where he'd been condemned to death, but couldn't legally be executed until the judge knew what he was actually called. When Miller looked at the initials, 'ER' embossed in gold on the traditional blue velvet cloth, hanging behind the magistrate, he saw the second letter had been changed to an 'M'. The jurors, who included Andrew Norman, Illingworth, and Elizabeth, frantically attempted to reconstitute the words 'Edward Miller' from a jumble of their constituent letters, scribbling words like 'Dread', 'Dreamer', and 'Reward' on notepads, while an usher timed them, keeping his eye on an enormous wall clock, which was stopped.

'Who will reveal it?' Miller asked the court.

'Why ask me,' said the judge, 'when the answer lies with you?'

In school, he still experienced unease every time the phone rang. If he saw an English newspaper lying around, he would never open it. Periodically, the name of Edward Miller would be mentioned in the staff room: his British colleagues, he noticed, had a fascination with disgraced compatriots. One day he came in and saw Jordan in reception, reading what appeared to be a feature article on his wife. She mumbled more derogatory comments about his former life.

'Hey Will, he comes from Oldham,' Jordan called out, 'like you. Do you know him?'

Miller shook his head.

He had come to dread the whole concept of news. His sole contact with the press was with Jordi Bas, the night editor for *La Vanguardia*, who came to Oxbridge House for lessons. Bas, who spoke excellent English, sometimes attempted to initiate a discussion on journalism, at which point Miller was deliberately vague.

In its publicity brochure, Oxbridge House claimed that its courses had a business bias, though commerce was something about which its teachers knew nothing and cared less.

From time to time, however, Miller couldn't resist helping his student with the English terms for things like standfirsts and splash headlines.

'How do you know these things?' Bas asked him, one day.

'I was a text inputter,' he replied. 'At a printer's.'

Bas asked him out for a drink after work; Miller refused. Socializing with students, Nick explained, was viewed by most of the teachers as a particularly despicable form of collaboration.

'Why?'

'Because they're... they're fucking students,' he replied.

'Remember Graham Nixon?' Jordan said.

'Who?'

'Graham,' Nick interrupted, '... how shall I put this... had sex with a student, in Milton.'

'Milton?' said Miller.

'With Christopher next door,' Nick replied, 'counting his money.'

'How did he get away with that? And the student – why did she do it?'

'Well the student was a he actually,' Nick said. 'Graham, he – you know, batted for both sides. The reception was packed; they'd gone a few minutes over time. I was upstairs, having a kip in Swinburne, and I heard it. It happened just as the bell went. You could hear the groan of "Oh, yes!" from this Catalan scaffolder all round the school. At least he had the decency to climax in English.'

'Christopher came out,' Nick continued. 'I saw him knock on the door and go in. I went into the staff room. Then I heard Devlin saying something to the students waiting in reception. When the scaffolder came out, all the other clients got to their feet and applauded, then started patting him on the back. I couldn't work out what he'd said.'

'Which was?'

'He told them that Mr Candini, thanks to the tuition he'd received at Oxbridge House, had just won a scholarship to Pembroke College Oxford.'

Miller forced a smile. There were times when his melancholy stood him in good stead; he became known for his heroic ability to maintain control.

His reputation was cemented by an episode that occurred one morning, while he was sitting in reception. Nick was next to him, complaining bitterly about Señora Anglada. A company director in her thirties – at intermediate level, but with pronunciation problems – Anglada had booked herself in as an intensive student, which meant that she attended English classes for forty hours a week, for a fortnight. Each of these sessions was with Gannon.

'I mean it's not totally her fault,' he told Miller. 'It's the whole problem with these intensive courses – it's bloody awful – you have to take them for lunch, which is always at the Paris, because Christopher has an account there, and you find yourself sitting there saying things like "Where's your home town? Oh really? And are there trees there, just like there are in mine? There are? Do birds land in them? They do? And when dawn breaks – do they sing?" Coming in just now,' he added, 'I found myself hoping that she'd been run over.'

'What by?' asked Sonia.

'A truck.'

'And killed?' Sonia asked.

'Oh yes,' said Nick. The receptionist gave him a mortified look.

'No, I mean, when I say killed; I pictured it as, you know, a very clean accident,' he said. 'Very clean. Not a hideous sort of thing where she'd get all mangled up and have her body parts strewn over a wide...'

The door opened and Señora Anglada came in.

Nick sat next to her in silence, waiting for the buzzer to sound.

'What did you have for breakfast?' he asked her, in a tone which, to a native speaker, scarcely concealed his boredom.

'I ate crap,' she said.

'Really?' Nick asked her, keeping his eyes down. Miller could see that Gannon's insides were contorted but the Londoner allowed nothing to show on his face. He had the look of a boxer who is on the ropes, with his legs failing under him, but not finished.

Señora Anglada pointed up at the adjacent tower, and the flashing neon sign of the Paris.

'I ate crap,' she repeated, 'at the crappery.'

Miller kept his eyes on Nick, who had a paper clip pushed into his thumb, under the nail. In the end it was Sonia who gave way. It was the worst possible kind of laugh, beginning with a partially suppressed low snort, and building into a loud, uncontrollable explosion. She exhaled so vigorously, and for so long, in a failed attempt to keep her laughter as silent as possible, that when she eventually did breathe in, she sounded like a seal.

'What is it?' the student asked her.

For a moment, Sonia couldn't speak. When she did, it was in Spanish.

Señora Anglada nodded, and smiled. The buzzer sounded, and she went off for her class with Gannon.

'What the hell did you tell her?' Miller asked Sonia.

'I said I'm sorry,' she explained. 'Somebody told me a joke just now, and I've only just realized how funny it was.'

'Good God,' said Miller. 'You're wasted here. You're a genius.'

Sonia pushed her packet of Fortuna towards him. Miller took a cigarette and she lit it.

'Lunch?' she said.

'Where do you fancy?' Sonia asked him, as they left the school. 'The Chinese, or the crappery?'

She took him to the Chino Hoy a small, family-run restaurant on the Traversera de Las Corts.

'It's my secret place,' she said. 'You'll like it. They all speak English.'

It seemed to surprise her that he'd arrived in the country without a word of Spanish.

'Did you never come here on your holidays?'

'Holidays?' he said. 'We didn't do that. My dad had a paper shop. We had days out.'

He'd never met a woman like Sonia. She wore heavy musk, and too much jewellery. She used a fan and didn't look bizarre. She was a receptionist with the body of a diva and the self-belief of a chief executive. She drank a bottle of red by herself – he stuck to beer – and ended lunch with a cigar. Miller pierced it for her with his Swiss army knife, which, as he showed her, had an attachment specifically for the purpose.

'Hey,' she said. 'That's nifty.'

He poured her a glass of wine.

'What time's your next class?' she asked him.

'Not till five.'

She ordered them both Cointreau with ice, then fished the ice out of hers. 'I like it cold,' she said, 'but I prefer to drink it in one go.'

'We had a dog called Heathcliff,' Miller said, 'when I was a kid. We spent five years trying to teach him to eat ice-cream delicately. He understood the idea, but when it came to it, it would be just, you know…'

'Wallop,' said Sonia.

'Yes.'

'Doesn't Christopher mind you staying out three hours for lunch?'

She laughed. 'No. I mean – you know, he can be a bit of a wanker when he wants to, but as long as you get the work done, he's not too fussed about the hours.'

She was fluent in the kind of words and phrases never acquired by non-native speakers. In her impressive repertory of obscenities, especially, she reminded him of their local barman.

'Who taught you all that stuff?' he asked her.

'What stuff?'

'Nifty,' he said. 'And wallop and not fussed. And a bit of a wanker. Was it Pascual?'

She laughed. 'No. But we had the same teacher.'

'Leigh?'

'No. Another one. Sean Carroll.'

'What was he like?'

'Worse.'

'Worse than Leigh?'

He told her about the Beach Boys, the fridge-freezer and the air hostesses.

'Yes,' she said, 'but the thing is, Leigh – how can I put it – at the end of the day, he has some idea of when to stop. His wife came back to an empty bed and a new cellar door. Leigh has... strategies. Sean never gave a shit. Towards the end here, he was constantly out of it. He just kept his foot on the floor.'

'Where is he now?'

She shrugged. 'I don't know. He's not a great one for postcards.'

At four thirty she handed him another Fortuna and settled the bill.

'Let's come here next Friday, OK?' she said. 'You give me two hours of conversation in English,' she suggested, 'and I'll pay.'

'OK,' he told her. 'But I can pay too.'

She laughed.

'You forget. I see the payslips. And the duplicitous account books.'

'The duplicate account books,' he corrected.

'Believe me,' she said, 'I know what I mean.'

'Where does he keep the real books?' Miller asked.

'Now that,' she said, 'I really shouldn't tell you.'

'In the school?'

She nodded.

'Oh dear.'

'Indeed.'

When he'd first met Sonia, he remembered, his instinct was that she deserved to be sacked on the spot. Imperceptibly, some of his basic attitudes were shifting. British current affairs – even immigration policy – which used to drive him into a rage within seconds when he was living in Surrey, were an irrelevance. His underlying prejudices, he suspected, were intact: if he'd been able to go back to the Home Counties, he'd rediscover his old priorities in a matter of days. For the time being, though, he neither knew nor cared what was happening in the UK. His life in London seemed like a half-remembered dream; its politics were a soap opera he no longer appeared in, or watched.

Only six weeks earlier, the sight of his driver arriving late, or at the wrong entrance of a hotel, would have had him in a frenzy. Now, he found himself strap-hanging on a bus or travelling second class by train. To his great surprise, some aspects of life in Spain ran more efficiently than their English equivalents. There was even a part of him that sympathized with Jordan when, sitting in the staff room one day, he heard her talking about the entrepreneurs who had taken over the British railway network.

'It's such a pleasure,' she'd said, 'to see them fucking up, just when they thought they'd found another good trough to have their snout in.'

For a moment, the phrase took him back to his days as an adolescent idealist.

He took to spending a couple of hours each day watching Spanish tutorials, on DVD in a spare classroom. At the beginning he told himself the language could be a useful tool in his eventual escape into the wider world, like a British prisoner of war learning German. For that reason he chose Spanish, not the local language of business, Catalan. Gradually, he had to admit, he was almost enjoying it. Little by little, his contributions to the conversation at Pascual's, where he spent a great deal of his time, began to be delivered in faltering Castilian.

He sat and observed the *dados* players, or watched Pascual cooking. Miller especially admired the barman's technique of taking a raw red pepper and twisting it in both hands so that, with a muffled splintering sound, and one smooth action, he removed the top, and most of the seeds. Miller ate there every day except Friday, when he walked over with Sonia to the Chino Hoy. Her manner with him was easy, and increasingly open, as a woman might be, he supposed, with a homosexual man.

'Coming to a Chinese in the daytime,' he told her once, 'I always feel like I'm having an affair.'

She laughed.

'We're not,' he said, 'are we?'

'Trust me, you're not my type. No offence.'

'I was just thinking,' he said, 'I have never – ever – had a woman as a friend before.'

'Wasn't your wife your friend?'

'No,' he said. Then: 'How did you know about my wife?'

'Just a wild guess.'

'Are you with anyone?' he asked.

'No,' she replied. 'I don't do that. I have days out.'

'Like Nick. He spends half his days circling ads in the Duplex section.'

'I know.'

'I can't imagine what kind of woman would possibly want to sleep with Nick.'

She gave him a cigarette.

'Fortuna,' she said, pointing at the packet. 'It means, er... *Suerte*. Luck.'

'Thank you.' He lit it.

'I did,' she said.

'You did what?'

'Slept with him.'

'What?' he said. 'When?'

'Two years ago,' she said, 'on the Nit de Sant Joan.'

'What's that?'

'It's the Saint's Day,' she said. 'The whole town goes mental. And that year,' she added, 'so did I.'

'Christ,' said Miller.

'It had been a long evening,' she said. 'He started getting very – you know – keen. The thing is he's a bit – I shouldn't say this.'

Miller said nothing.

'Physically he's a bit... he's not very nifty. He's a bit like your dog with the ice-cream. He gave me the creeps.'

They walked back to the school, as usual, and stopped in Pascual's for a coffee.

Nick was sitting at the far end of the bar, close to Pascual's wind-up gramophone. Miller could hear George Formby, singing 'Hi-Tiddly-Hi-Ti-Island'.

'What's weird,' Sonia said, 'is that I've learned all this language and I've never set foot in England.'

'You should go,' said Pascual. 'It's not that bad.'

'Do you know London?' Miller asked him.

'I lived in London,' the barman said, 'for four years. I had a café in Maple Street. Do you know it?'

'No,' said Miller. He pointed at the Formby recording, still spinning on the turntable.

'Do you understand this?' he asked Pascual.

'Not exactly.'

'You're lucky.'

'Why did you move to London?' Sonia asked him.

'A woman,' said Pascual. 'An English woman. Called Monica.'

'Where is she now?'

'She left me.'

'Why?'

'Because I...'

'You what?'

'The usual.'

When she heard this last phrase, Sonia glared at him.

'The *usual*?' she repeated. 'That is a really terrible thing to say.'

'What?' Nick said, turning to face her. 'I never had you down as a romantic.'

'Well I am,' she said. 'And more to the point' – she waved in the direction of the barman – 'I thought he was.'

'He is,' Nick said. 'He's a compulsive gambler. That's the ultimate expression of unrequited love.'

The following day, he came to meet Nick Gannon at the school, as usual, and they took the train down to Sitges. Once the Saturday Group had left, and he'd called Adelaide, it generally took Nick about an hour to calm down. On this occasion, his agitation persisted. In the bar opposite Sitges station, he stopped and bought a half-bottle of brandy.

When they were down on the beach, side by side on their white plastic *hamacas*, Nick started using it to fortify his beer.

'What's up?' Miller asked him.

'What's up?' Nick replied. 'What do you think is up?'

'You know,' Miller replied, 'you shouldn't let them get to you so much.'

'Who?'

'Paco Calamita and his mates.'

'You know, Paco's mother brought him in the other week,' said Nick. 'She asked me how he was doing, so I told her, straight out. They're both standing in reception, which is packed, and she turns to Paco and screams: "*Hijo de puta.*'

'Son of a whore?'

'Correct.'

'I see,' said Miller. 'Is he adopted?'

'I'm afraid not. Wait here. I'm going for another.'

Getting drunker, he began to make remarks about women who walked past him on their way to the water.

'By Christ,' he said at one point, 'I'd give her one.'

'I'm sure she'd be very flattered to know that Nick,' Miller said. He took out Mr Van Thal's *Eighth Pan Book of Horror*. Gannon glared at him.

'You're spending a lot of time with Sonia,' he said.

'I've been teaching her.'

'Oh really? Teaching her what?'

'What do you think of Sonia?'

'She's OK I guess. She's a bit of a sad old slapper.'

Miller said nothing and went back to his book. Common to each of the stories was a note of gratuitous sadism – much of the kind that lurked behind newspaper reports of rape, murder or incest, except that here, in these pages, it walked with its head high. The last story he read – 'Death in Midhurst' by 'Barry Edwards', was about a demented surgeon who kidnapped two young nurses, amputated their arms and legs, and kept them alive in a dungeon, their torsos hanging side by side, held up by leather straps, for his sexual gratification, feeding his captives on fried sections of each other's limbs.

Life, it occurred to Miller, cannot have been kind to Mr Edwards. Physical abnormality had always appalled him. Something in Miller wanted the human body – like the world – to be perfect, and unsullied. He dropped the book on the sand.

'What's that like?' Nick asked, pointing at the paperback.

'It's sick.'

'Seriously?'

'Yes.'

'Can I borrow it?'

It was eleven by the time they got back to Sants station. Nick set off unsteadily for a club in the Barrio Chino. Miller walked home, alone. In the shower, just after two a.m., he thought he heard noises on the stairs. It was when he was going to bed that he noticed it – an envelope that had been stuffed under the front door of the apartment. He picked it up, and saw the name 'William Whiteside' written on it, in a neat hand he recognized as Christopher's. For some reason the formality of his full title worried him. He opened it. Inside, he found a sheet of lined paper with no address, name, telephone number or signature. The writing was less legible than the words on the envelope, as if scribbled in haste.

'Be in my office tomorrow morning at eight,' Miller read. It was signed 'Christopher.' He glanced at the back of the envelope. There, scrawled in capitals, in red felt marker, he saw the word: 'Urgent'.

Miller had a restless night. The humidity was oppressive and he was sweating heavily, even under his single sheet. He drifted in and out of sleep, troubled by foreboding. He dreamed of a street scene where he was being hunted, wearing a grey pullover he'd had at school, with a name-tag sewn in, that was scratching his neck. A lorry drove past, its tailgate bearing the name: 'Edward Miller and Sons, Est. 1966.' His nightmare ended with him carving his real initials into Christopher's desk.

'What does this mean?' Devlin asked him, pointing at the letters.

'E is a twist of silver wire,' Miller replied, with a line of Kipling's that he hadn't consciously thought of since his father read him *Just So Stories*, as a boy. 'M is a pale grey shell.'

At six o'clock, he got up. Nick, he noticed, had not returned.

Miller ran a cool bath and lay in it for half an hour or so. He could feel his pulse quickening. He was beginning to breathe too fast, and too deeply. He got out, dressed, and went into the kitchen. He found a paper bag, and blew into it to make sure it was airtight. He folded it neatly, put it in his pocket, and set off.

He took a cab to the school and arrived earlier than he needed to, just after seven thirty. As he approached the entrance, he could see that Devlin was already there, in Byron. He appeared to be talking to himself, as if rehearsing a speech. Miller went in to the principal's office without knocking, and sat down.

'Morning,' Christopher said. 'You're punctual.'

'I'm always punctual,' Miller said. 'I'm English.'

'It's true,' Devlin said, 'that timekeeping is not the Spaniard's strongest suit. Like the Pakistanis, don't you think, Mr Whiteside, and the Latin Americans and the Maoris. Rude, inconsiderate peoples, who take a pride in being deliberately late.'

There was a seriousness he'd never seen on Christopher's face before. This was it. Miller wasn't sure how – the newspaper article perhaps – but Devlin knew. He made an effort to steady his breathing.

'Possibly,' he said.

'Oh, I'm sure of it,' Christopher said. 'Would you like to know why?'

'Go on.'

'Because they learned it from us.'

Miller raised his eyebrows, waiting for the *coup de grâce*. Then Christopher reached over to his bookshelves and took down a copy of *King Solomon's Mines*.

'Right now, where is it,' he said, 'I don't read this crap every day... hang on...' He skipped through the pages.

' "The most repulsive countenance we had ever beheld; the lips were as thick as a Negro's, the nose was flat..." ' He turned to another page. " 'The lips unpleasantly thick, as in most African races." Rider's got a thing about lips, don't you find that?'

'All right,' Miller snapped. 'I think I know what you're saying. Get on with it.'

Christopher appeared not to hear him.

'Oh yes. Here we are. "It is always as well, when dealing with uncivilized people, not to be in too great a hurry. They are apt to mistake politeness for awe, or servility." '

He put the book down.

'We're both early, Will, but we're not in awe. We can't be – as you say, we're English.'

'If you don't like this stuff,' Miller asked him, 'then why do you keep it on your bookshelves?'

'I needed some books,' Christopher said. 'I got the lot for thirty quid, from a second-hand shop in Hastings. I've got three copies of *Escape* by John Galsworthy, five *Peveril of the Peak*s by Sir Walter Scott, and seven *Testament of Beauty*s by Robert Bridges. Strange, isn't it, how a man can be nationally famous, and then slide imperceptibly into obscurity. Of course in their period it took decades to be forgotten.' He looked at Miller. 'These days, it's the easiest thing in the world, to disappear.'

'Why did you come here?' Miller asked him, convinced that he had nothing left to lose.

'Because certain prevalent attitudes of my fellow countrymen disgusted me,' said Devlin. 'I am that most outmoded and derided of things – a liberal.'

'And?' Miller asked.

'And my life was a misery. I lost my job.'

'Why?' Miller asked.

Christopher cleared his throat, and returned Rider Haggard to his shelf.

'Right. Where was I? Oh yes. This is a difficult thing for me to have to say, but in the couple of months you've been here, I've come to trust you.'

Miller closed his eyes in frustration.

'That's nice,' he said, sarcastically.

'I've brought you here this morning,' he added, 'because I had a telephone call in the early hours of this morning to tell me that, er…'

'Yes?' Miller snapped.

'Nick Gannon is unwell.'

'What?' Miller's eyes shifted.

'When I say unwell… he was calling it gastric flu. He claimed to be in Casualty,' he added, 'but I could hear dance music in the background. That generally means a two-day hangover.'

Christopher cracked his knuckles.

'Your landlord has his qualities. I make certain allowances.'

'Oh.'

'The thing is…' Devlin held up a pedagogical file. 'I'd like you to take his intensive student, Mr Furata. It's full time – eight hours a day and it means you taking him for lunch. So that's every day, for the next fortnight.'

'Right,' Miller said. He reached out his hand for the file; Devlin kept hold of it.

'Has Nick ever spoken about Mr Furata?'

'No.'

'Really?'

'No. Should he have?'

'No. I asked him not to.' Christopher paused.

'Listen, Will. You remember I told you I only ever sacked one person.'

'Yes.'

'His name was Sean Carroll.'

'I know,' said Miller.

'He was a very, very good teacher and I never wanted to let him go. But then I had to sack him. He started to get...' he looked out at the bank, opposite. 'Unreasonable expectations.'

'Such as?'

'Holiday pay. Pay for hours of availability, rather than hours worked.'

'Is that why you sacked him?'

'No. I sacked him,' Devlin said, 'because he was smoking grass.'

'That doesn't seem...'

'In class. With certain students who he thought wouldn't complain. Two of whom worked for multinationals.'

'Ah.'

'After I sacked him,' Devlin said, 'I told him to work out his month's notice. And that's when he got his revenge.'

'What was his revenge?'

'Mr Furata.'

'What?'

'Kendo Furata,' Devlin said, 'is a construction engineer, from a small town in the northern island of Hokkaido. Before he came here, he'd had no contact with English culture whatsoever. He still has very little, apart from us.'

'Who does he work for?'

'He works for a Japanese systems company up in Mataró. They send him here for Spanish lessons in the week. They have no idea that he's learning English. He does that in the holidays, at his own expense.'

'Why?'

'Because he wants to go and work for their main rival, in Colorado.'

'And?'

'Last year, Sean had Furata for a month's intensive,' he said. 'It was just after I fired him; I decided to keep him with one student – I had to pay him in any case. I thought well, if he starts acting up, Furata can hardly complain to the company – they didn't know he was here in the first place.'

'And Sean started acting up?' Miller asked.

'On the contrary, Will,' he said. 'He started drinking less. He stopped smoking in school. I thought he must want his job back.'

'But he didn't?'

'Three weeks into the course,' Devlin said, 'I bumped into Mr Furata at the Paris. He was holding a print-out of a photograph he'd been emailed over the internet. He showed me the picture. It was an elderly woman. She appeared to be in some kind of day room, in a hospice. I remember I said: "Who is that?" And he said…'

Devlin took a deep breath and shut his eyes.

'Yes?'

'He said: "That is my fucking mother, in fucking Sapporo."'

'Oh,' said Miller.

'Carroll,' he went on, 'it was simple idea but brilliant, I have to grant him that, taught Mr Furata that, in English, every noun must be prefaced by, er…'

'Fucking hell,' said Miller.

'That's it.'

'What did you do then?'

'After I'd sacked Sean, again, for professional misconduct this time; he left with this smirk that I can see to this day – I had to take Furata myself, for a week, to sort of, er, de-programme him.'

'What did you tell him?'

'I told him,' Devlin said, 'that Sean Carroll was from New Brighton, which he was. And that "fucking" was a term that – while still widely used on the Wirral – is outmoded elsewhere, and would have him mocked, especially in the United States, where he is hoping to settle. I apologized. I told him that Carroll had been dismissed, and I offered him a month's free tuition.'

'With Nick.'

'That's right. Like most men with a past, he has developed a capacity to be discreet. He's taught him ever since.'

'Did it work?'

'Up to a point,' said Devlin. 'Furata still does it occasionally. Especially if he gets worked up, like when he's missing his family, or when he's doing the stuff he covered in the very early lessons with Carroll – things like numbers; basic food and drink.'

'Hasn't he... I mean he's going to find out, isn't he? Doesn't he ever watch Hollywood films?'

'Thankfully not,' he said. 'Kendo Furata is a deeply religious man. The one area of Western culture that seems to interest him is the history of the monarchy. Apart from that he spends most of his time in meditation at home or, as he told me one day –' Christopher screwed up his eyes again – 'in fucking prayer at the fucking temple.'

Miller took the file.

'Is that it?' he asked Devlin.

'Is what it?'

'Isn't there anything else you wanted to tell me?', Miller asked, still sure that Devlin suspected something.

'No,' said the principal, with a look that made it clear he didn't.

'Should there be?'

Miller shook his head, and left.

The first few days passed without incident. Miller was wondering whether the whole thing had been an elaborate joke, until one morning when he went in and noticed Furata was wearing a bandage across his forehead.

'What happened?' Miller asked.

'I'm having work done at home,' Furata replied. 'I had an accident.'

'I'm sorry,' said Miller. 'What kind of accident?'

'I was hit,' said Furata, 'by a shite.'

'By a shite?'

Furata nodded and pointed at his head.

'A shite.'

Miller stared at him.

'A shite,' Furata repeated, as if talking to an idiot.

Miller took out a packet of Ducados, and lit one.

He tore a piece of paper out of his notebook and handed it to Furata.

'Kendo?' he said.

'Yes?'

'Draw me a shite.'

The student put his pen to the paper, then stopped and looked up.

'Why?' he asked.

'Never mind,' said Miller. 'Please.'

Furata sketched out a few lines and handed the paper back to him. Miller glanced at it.

'Look,' he said, 'you can say "shite". Some people,' he added, 'still do say "shite". Especially,' he added, 'in certain regions of England.'

'Ah,' Furata said, nodding. 'New Brighton.'

'But shite,' Miller said, 'is very old-fashioned now. Very old.'

'Old,' said Furata.

'Yes,' said Miller. 'These days,' he added, 'usually, we would say something more like: "ladder".'

Furata copied the word into his notebook.

'Forget "shite" now,' said Miller. 'No more shite.'

'Olden times,' said Furata.

'Yes.'

'Queen Victoria…' Furata began, 'would have said…'

'That's right,' said Miller. 'All the time. Especially when she had the decorators in.'

There was a knock on the door. It was Jordan.

'I'm teaching Bas,' she said, not bothering to introduce herself to Furata, or to apologize. 'He says you know about newspapers.'

'A bit,' Miller said. 'I was a text inputter, at a printer's.'

'OK,' she said, 'I don't need your bloody CV. Anyway, he thinks you might know the word for…' She called down the corridor. 'What was it again?'

Bas's head appeared behind her, in the doorway.

'Free papers,' he said. 'On airlines… on trains…'

'Bulk sales,' said Miller.

On the Friday, Devlin called Miller into his office.

'How's he doing?' he asked.

'It's OK,' Miller said. 'Nothing for two days. There was just this moment on Wednesday, when we were having lunch in the Paris; he mentioned his fucking wedding to his fucking wife.'

'I thought he was divorced?' Christopher said.

'He is,' Miller replied. 'And to that extent you could argue it was correct usage.'

'But you did mention…'

'Yes. He corrected himself actually.'

'Good.' Devlin smiled. 'I think we've cracked it.'

Nick Gannon, Miller noticed, had been showing increasing signs of stress. He was off sick for three days, not two, and spent the time lying in his room with the curtains drawn, occasionally going out for tablets and mineral water. When Miller entered the school reception at lunchtime, as usual, on the last Saturday in June, he could see, through the open classroom door, that Nick, Calamita, and the rest of the group were clustered around the window. From his seat in reception, Miller could see the object of their interest: a small grass snake on the lawn outside.

'What is it doing?' Nick asked them.

'Snaking,' said Paco.

'No,' said Gannon.

Calamita pointed at the bank.

'Yes Paco,' Nick said. 'Bankers bank. Teachers teach.' He resumed his seat, with his back to the window, and noticed Miller.

'Or they try to. But snakes don't snake, not usually, and dogs don't dog, not as a rule, and ducks don't duck. Pigs, larks and squirrels are another matter,' he said, 'but they all require phrasal verbs. Which none of you bastards have a hope in hell of understanding.'

His students looked back at him blankly. Paco Calamita raised his hand.

'Yes?' Nick snapped.

'The window-cleaner,' he said, 'is here.'

Nick handed him the euros, and went into the staff room to call Adelaide. The group sat with pen and paper, observing Juan at work with his scraper.

Miller remained in reception, smoking.

Calamita came out of Milton, and approached him.

'Nick – him phone?' he whispered.

Miller nodded.

Paco pushed a piece of paper into his hand, and put his finger to his lips. Written on it were the words: '¿WHAT MEAN CAN?'

Miller took his own pen, and wrote 'can = *poder*'.

Nick came out of the staff room. He saw the paper and tore it out of Miller's hand. He screwed it up into a ball.

'Right you fuckers,' he said. 'That's it. I quit.'

He repeated the phrase in Spanish and Catalan.

The class picked up their notebooks and filed out, each member offering Gannon a handshake, which he declined.

'Why...?' Miller began, when they'd gone.

Nick took him into the classroom. There, on the board, in letters a foot high, were the words 'can = *poder*'.

'We've just done two hours on "can",' Nick said. 'Two hours, translating the whole time.'

The Londoner unfolded Paco's piece of paper and read it again. 'What mean can?' He laughed, and threw it in the bin.

'What's going to happen to them now?'

'What? Nothing. That's it.'

'Why?'

'Because no other bastard will do it.'

'I will,' said Miller.

Nick handed him the school key.

'Do you know, I've never felt like this,' he said, 'ever, in my life. I don't know how to describe it. I think I might be in a state of grace.'

The following week, Miller was summoned to a meeting with Gannon and Devlin.

'Nick', Christopher began, 'says you want to take over the Saturday Group.'

Miller nodded.

The principal looked at Miller. 'Why?'

'Money.'

'How many teachers,' Devlin asked Nick, 'have they had now?'

'I think they've been through everybody,' he replied.

'How long,' Miller asked Devlin, 'did Jordan last with them?'

'Three weeks.'
'Then what happened?' Miller asked.
'She hit Paco,' Nick said.
'Hard?'
'Well,' Nick replied, 'that all depends who you ask. Too hard for Paco and Christopher. Not hard enough for me.'
The second week of Mr Furata's intensive course passed off without incident.
'He's cured,' Miller told Christopher.
'He'll be in for a shock if he ever gets to Denver,' said the principal, 'but by then he won't be our problem.'
He shook Miller's hand.
'It's my birthday next Sunday Will,' Christopher said. 'Can you join us for dinner?'
'Where?'
'Castelldefels,' Devlin said, 'down the coast.'
Behind the director's back, Nick was nodding, vigorously.
'OK,' said Miller.
He took the Japanese businessman across for a drink at Pascual's, to celebrate. The barman came over to take their orders.
Miller ordered a beer.
'*Un té*', Furata said, in perfectly articulated Spanish.
'Certainly, sir,' Pascual replied, in English. 'Fucking cream,' he added, 'or fucking lemon?'
Miller glared at him.
Furata gave Pascual a pitying look.
'Lemon,' he said. 'Please.'
The Japanese student pointed at Pascual, as he disappeared behind the counter.
'New Brighton?' he said.
'Yes,' said Miller. 'A friend of Mr Carroll.'

When Miller arrived for his first lesson with the Saturday Group, he saw Juan, the window-cleaner, loitering by the front door. Without hesitating, he pressed ten euros into his hand. Meeting the Saturday Group was like facing a legendary heavyweight, or a chess grand master. Any source of respite, he reasoned, would be welcome.

Five minutes into the class, his instinctive reaction was that the airport maintenance technicians must have been deafened by jets, though he had to concede that they seemed able to hear in Spanish. What he found most astonishing was their absolute inability to retain information. Before the lesson even started, the Lesseps brothers – whose notes revealed that they were taking strong tranquillizers for a congenital psychiatric disorder – got lost on the way back from the toilets. Paco Calamita's file noted that his academic ability had not been enhanced by a blow he sustained to the temporal lobe after his moped collided with a petrol tanker in Badajoz.

In their company, Miller was reminded of an article his paper had run a couple of days before he left. It was an interview with a research scientist who had taught a squid how to open a screw-top jar full of bait, submerged in its tank.

'It took him thirty-eight hours the first time,' the biologist had said. 'Ten hours the second time, and after a week he could do it in thirty seconds.'

What happened, the interviewer asked, if the jar was removed for a day?

'Ah well, then,' said the scientist, 'he's back to thirty-eight hours again.'

Miller persisted with the rituals that Nick had established. He placed his own chair with its back to the window, with the students facing the view and retained the five-euro prize for the first student to spot the window-cleaner.

Their tragedy was completed, rather than diminished, by occasional moments of illumination. For his first lesson, Miller – adopting the role of a foreign aircraft technician – asked them to prime him with a handful of simple phrases they'd told him they regularly needed at work.

'Ask me if I brought the tanker,' he told Jordi Lesseps.
'You brought the tanker,' said Jordi. 'Didn't you?'
'Yes,' said Miller.
He turned to Luis.
'Ask me if I checked the water.'
'You checked the water,' said Luis. 'Didn't you?'
Miller nodded.
'Paco,' he said.
'Yes, Will.'
'Ask me if I refuelled the plane.'
Paco paused.
'You...' he said.
'Good.'
'Refuelled the plane...'
'Excellent.'
'Re-didn't you?'
Miller's head and shoulders sagged. He ran his hands through his hair.
'Calamity?' Paco said.
'No calamity Paco,' he replied. 'No calamity. Very good.'
'The window-cleaner,' Luis shouted, 'is here.'

Miller turned round and saw Juan, making his way across the lawn with his scrapers and buckets.

He handed Luis five euros. The three took out their pens and papers and, staring at the workman, began to write, Paco with his hand cupped over the paper, to prevent the Lesseps brothers copying.

Miller walked out into the staff room. He stared at the Bakelite phone. Then – on his feet, because he was too nervous to sit – he tapped in Dr Norman's number. It rang first time.

'Hallo,' said Norman, sounding cheerful. 'I was wondering when you'd call. How's the panic?'

'Better,' said Miller. 'What's happened?'

'It's fine,' said the doctor. 'It's all fine.'
'What about the house?'
'The firemen said that your house burned down by accident.'
'It did,' said Miller. 'So that's all sorted out is it?'
'Well – it was'
'Good.'
'It was… but then the police forensic people say they believe that it might have been, er, what's it called…'
'Arson?'
'Yes. They found a can of turpentine.'
'Shit,' said Miller. 'Is there a warrant?'
Norman didn't reply.
'Is there a warrant,' he repeated, 'out for my arrest?'
'Not yet.'
'But there's going to be one?'
'It looks that way, Edward, yes.'
'Oh.'
'And there is one other thing…'
'Yes?'
'It's Charles Portal – Elizabeth's father – your father-in-law.'
'Yes?'
'He's rather… he's a little bit…'
'Dead?'
'No,' said Norman. 'No, no. Not dead. It's just that he had a bit of a, er… when Elizabeth told him about what had happened – the house fire, and she reminded him how you'd abandoned her and your daughter, and everything…'
'Elizabeth left me,' said Miller.
'Yes, well anyway, when she told him all that, he had a bit of a…'
'Yes?'
'Stroke.'
'Oh fucking hell,' said Miller.
'How soon after she told him?'
'Well,' said Norman, 'it was quite, er…'
'Straight away?'

'Yes.'
'Shit.'
'Can he speak?'
'Yes,' said Norman. 'He's in a wheelchair, but he can speak. He has been speaking actually – quite a lot – he's been saying that he wants... the thing is,' said Norman, 'I mean he was really quite upset; well, more angry really. He kept going on about you having deserted, and how you'd dragged his daughter's good name into the gutter press, and he said he wanted to see you – to talk to you – and, er...'
'What?'
'Kill you.'
'Oh.'
'Or rather get some other people to kill you. I believe it's known as a...'
'I know what it's fucking known as,' said Miller.
'I mean – the thing is – he is a very, very stubborn man. In the end I managed to talk him out of it...'
'Why?' Miller interrupted.
Norman sounded hurt.
'Because I am dedicated to the preservation, not the destruction, of life,' he said. 'Even yours. He's stopped mentioning contract killers; now he's talking about lawyers.'
'Oh good,' said Miller, sarcastically. He sat down. 'Andrew?'
'Yes?'
'Where does it come from – the panic – by the way?'
'Panic? How long have you got? Attacks of the kind you were experiencing are generally regarded as a manifestation of repressed guilt. But guilt has never exactly been your thing, has it?'
'No.'
'Where are...?'
Miller hung up.

On the Sunday, they met to celebrate Christopher's birthday, in a Mexican bar attached to a restaurant in Castelldefels, a crowded resort near Barcelona airport. Miller arrived late and saw the principal sitting at a table for five, with Sonia, Nick and Jordan. The principal ordered five 'submarines' – a half-litre glass of Estrella, with a smaller glass containing a third of a pint of a clear spirit, inverted in the beer, in such a way that the contents remained separated.

He watched as Christopher sipped at his drink. When the beer was half-finished, the smaller glass tipped up, releasing its contents.

'What is it?' Miller asked him.

Devlin handed him the glass.

'Smell it,' he said.

Miller did. The drink had the scent of burnt rubber and high-octane fuel, with a subtle note of sweet decay.

'It's Mescal,' said Devlin.

'It smells like a car crash.'

'It does,' the principal replied. 'But it's the only aperitif that really breaks the ice.'

'I've never…' said Miller.

'Think of it as a learning experience,' Christopher said. 'Every learning experience is like a journey. And this one, William,' he added, 'is like London to Brighton in four minutes.'

Miller took a sip from his glass. Jordan, sitting next to him, drank hers steadily, with a look of defiance. Conversation, muted when the group had first arrived, quickly became obsessive and surreal.

They worked their way through cold starters, baked lamb and paella; Cava, white wine, and a heavy dark red from the Penedes. From the speed of consumption, Miller understood that Devlin must be paying.

The director lit a cigar and stared out at the Mediterranean.

'You know what I'm most happy to have left behind?' he said. 'It's that hideous east coast, with the wind whipping in from the North Sea, and the mean streak it breeds in the people there; that cruel, icy blast driving across the fens; the dreary stone beaches at Herne Bay and Whitstable; the shivering poverty of poor forgotten Ashington.'

'You don't have to live on the east coast,' Jordan volunteered.

'That's true,' Christopher said. 'But the thing is, wherever you are in England, you always know the east coast is there. Could you sleep at ease in an otherwise comfortable bedroom,' he asked her, 'when you knew that, on the opposite wing of the house – the east – the whole side of the building was missing, so that it was open, like a doll's house, and exposed to that bitter wind and driving rain? East,' Devlin snarled. 'I don't even like the word. It sounds as if, in some Slavic language, it must mean – I don't know – "Hold your tongue, or else".'

'Talking of which...' Sonia said.

'East,' he hissed, ignoring her. 'What has anyone ever gained from going east? East is mass graves filled with the mutilated bodies of innocent children. East is fascism, Communism... Belarus... frostbitten, famished soldiers slicing flesh from the flanks of their living horses... and east is, er...'

He looked up at the table and noticed it was transfixed in horrified, yet expectant, silence.

'East,' he added.

'As some other genius once noticed,' Jordan said.

'It was Dinah Shore,' said Christopher. 'In the theme song from *The Paleface*.'

'It was Rudyard Kipling,' said Miller.

'What?' Jordan asked.

'East is East,' Miller began, his spirits raised by his submarine, 'and West is West, and never the twain shall meet, Till Earth and Sky stand presently at God's great Judgment Seat; But there is neither East nor West, Border, nor Breed, nor Birth, When two strong men stand face to face, though they come from the ends of the earth!'

'Did he really write that?' Jordan asked him.

Miller nodded.

'I thought he was supposed to be a racist.'

'You see that?' Devlin interrupted, pointing at a brightly lit large building, up the coast.

'Do you know what that is?'

Miller shook his head.

'That,' Christopher announced, 'is the hotel where George Sanders killed himself.'

'Why would a man like that commit suicide?' asked Sonia.

'Any man can kill himself,' said Devlin. 'Possessions, at that moment, are of no more importance than a price-tag to a shoplifter. We all stand naked,' he added, 'in the moment of death, when that final salute sounds.'

Nick fired a party popper at his employer from close range; Devlin swept the thin crêpe streamers out of his hair but missed a couple of pink strands that were left dangling absurdly from his right ear. Nobody spoke.

'The question I've often asked myself,' Devlin went on, 'is – how could he have killed himself here; in a place that has such natural beauty?'

Miller looked across to the beach. In the fading light, he could still make out discarded beer bottles and ice-cream wrappers, littering the sand.

'Why the hell not?' he said.

'Ah,' said Devlin. 'You're looking in the wrong direction. You're looking east. Look west.'

He pointed up into the heavily wooded hills that rose behind the small town. Small black birds were swooping over the small forest.

'What are those?' Miller asked.

'Housemartins,' said Devlin. 'You know what they call them in Spanish? *Aviones* – aeroplanes.' He paused. 'They look so at home in the air; I'm not sure that they ever come down. Now do you see what I meant about that poem on my office wall,' he whispered to Miller. 'What the hell would a bloody bird want with a mead hall?'

'Anyhow,' he went on, 'it was this place that brought him to it. The modest town of Castelldefels. Did you know he left a note?'

Miller shook his head.

'It said: "I am leaving because I am bored. I have lived long enough." '

Miller tried to lean his elbow on the table and missed.

The waiter appeared, with a tray full of coffee cups.

'Ah,' Devlin said, 'the *carajillo*.'

'The what?' Miller asked.

'The *carajillo*. It's coffee with brandy. Literally, the name means, er...'

'It means little prick,' interrupted Jordan.
Miller smelled the coffee.
'I don't think I can do this,' he said.
'Of course you can,' Jordan said. 'It's just one of those nights.'
'One of which nights?'
'One of those nights,' she said, 'when you have to drink to stay alive.'

Just after midnight, a people carrier arrived to take them back into Barcelona. Miller sat in the back, between Nick and Sonia.
'Who do we drop off first?' Christopher asked.
'Me,' said Jordan. 'Plaza Casa Baro,' she told the driver.
'Do you remember quadraphonic?' asked Nick, trying to focus his divergent gaze on a traffic light.
'Yes,' said Miller. 'Why?'
'Because I think I'm seeing double.'
'What,' Miller asked, 'is the problem with your eyes?'
'It's called amblyopia.'
'It sounds terrible.'
'It didn't help when I was dealing with Customs and Excise,' he said. 'I think it made me look dodgy.'
Miller was about to make a remark, when Sonia kicked him on the shin.
'As a condition, it does have its advantages,' Nick said.
'Such as?'
'I don't know; it's little things really. If you get your seat at the right angle you can cheat at poker. And if you're stoned enough, you can play I-Spy by yourself.'
They stopped at Jordan's house, up towards the Parc Guell.
'You all want coffee?' she said.
'That's weird,' Christopher told Miller, as they got out.
'Why?'
'Because she's never done this before.'
'You've never seen her place?'
'None of us have,' Christopher replied. 'Except for Jordan of course – she's seen it. She has to have done... she... er... lives in it.'

They followed her in to her ground-floor flat. Its front door opened straight on to the street. At one a.m. Miller was sitting at the kitchen table with his colleagues. Nick filled a pitcher with water.

Sonia took the jug and poured herself a glass.

'I'd forgotten what this tasted like,' he said. 'It's not bad actually.'

Miller found himself listening to the CD that Jordan had put on the cheap portable system; a rumba sung in Catalan by a man with an eerie, high-pitched voice.

'What's this?' he asked Sonia.

'It's called "The Cuban War",' she said.

'Who is it?'

'His name's Jaume Sisa. A few years ago,' she added, 'he faked his own death.'

Miller sat up straighter in his chair.

'Oh, you're interested now are you Will?' Sonia laughed. 'You like that idea?'

'No,' he said. 'It's just... how did he do it?'

'He had the funeral,' she said, 'and he abandoned his car and everything.'

'Did they find him?'

'Yes,' she said. 'Eventually. It was all over the papers.'

Miller breathed in deeply. 'I'll bet.'

On the living room wall opposite him, there was a photograph of a car flying over an apartment building.

'What's that?' he asked Jordan.

'Is it San Francisco de Borja?' asked Sonia.

Jordan nodded.

'What?' Miller asked.

'It's the Jesuit college in Madrid,' said Sonia.

'Whose car is that?'

'That's Admiral de Carrero Blanco,' Christopher interrupted, 'on his last trip in his Dodge Dart. He was going to be Franco's successor. It's the one assassination that pretty well everybody in the country was pleased about. As you can see, the car was blown over the ten-storey building, there was so much explosive under it; the admiral is supposed to have ended up in the penthouse on the ninth. Even now, when you go to Madrid and ask for the Calle de Maldonado, cab drivers ask you which number, then: "Which floor?" '

'What you have to understand,' Jordan said, 'is that if they hadn't done that, Franco would still be in power, by proxy.'

'They wrote songs about it,' said Sonia. 'Coming from Britain,' she added, 'you couldn't imagine how normally decent people could be driven to such a level of hatred by a tyrant that they started to hear a kind of romantic beauty in a word like "dynamite".'

'Don't bank on it,' said their host.

Jordan got up to put a pan of water on the small stove. Then she sat down again next to Miller and – in a gesture that surprised him no less than if she had begun to spontaneously combust – she leaned her head on his shoulder, and kept it there.

Miller didn't move, but stared straight ahead of him, at the picture of the Madrid apartment block.

'Well,' said Sonia. 'I'm going to make a move.'

In five minutes the whole party was at the door, saying goodbye. Jordan ushered them out, then turned to face Miller in the hall. She took both his hands and looked into his eyes. The water still hadn't boiled.

'I... I have to leave now,' he said.

'Really?'

'Yes.'

He went out into the street and began to walk down towards the centre of town. He crossed the road, then looked back. He could see from a chink of light that she'd left the front door very slightly ajar. He thought about going back to tell her that it was dangerous, or to shut the door for her, then didn't. He walked down to the main road, the Traversera de Dalt, where he found a cab.

Miller couldn't face returning to the Calle Vic, and a scornful inquisition from Nick. Instead he went to the bottom of the Ramblas, where he got out and headed for the Pastis, a café up a side street, which stayed open till three.

He walked into the small bar. It had an oppressive, morbid atmosphere; the original owner had died young, and his wife had kept the room exactly as it had been the day he died. The walls and ceilings were stained a deep brown; bottles on the upper shelves were blackened and covered with cobwebs, their labels obscured by a coating of dust, grease and nicotine. Grotesque, tormented faces in portraits painted by the owner, who had killed himself with absinthe, looked down from the walls.

He ordered a brandy and a glass of water, and sat down. As he did so, a couple of middle-aged women, standing by the bar, tutted and hissed at him. Miller looked at them, bemused, then noticed that, on the other side of his table, were two young lovers, staring into each other's eyes. He decided to stay where he was. The couple hadn't noticed he was there. Which of them would be the first, Miller found himself thinking, to bring betrayal, distress and contempt into the innocent passion of that embrace. The girl, probably. She was held, rather than holding. She was better looking than her lover, and she had a slightly dazed, distant look about her, which Miller associated with promiscuity. There had once been a time, he reflected, when such a thought would never have occurred to him; when he had believed, and trusted. When he'd thought that nothing could be more magical than holding another living creature in your arms. The transformation in him, like a country turning to fascism, had not been sudden, so much as a succession of imperceptible steps. But disillusion, cynicism and contempt − unlike the first girl you kissed and caressed with the exhilarating flush of innocent passion − were companions that, once embraced, would stay with you for life; faithful, unswerving, and a little more seductive every day.

He walked out of the bar and up the wide central pavement of the Ramblas, crowded with pedestrians, though it was two thirty in the morning. He felt exhausted and very lonely. He stood by a traffic light by the opera house at Liceo. To his relief, a line of yellow and black cabs was making its way up the cobbled street towards him. He raised one arm.

'Plaza Casa Baro,' he said, falling into the back seat.

The driver headed north up the Paseo de Gràcia. On his left, Miller noticed a Gaudí building, designed and lit like an enchanted castle.

'*Estupendo*,' he said to the driver, pointing towards it.

'Gaudí,' he said, when the man didn't respond. '*Est...*'

'Do you mind,' said the driver, in a heavy southern accent Miller could only just understand, 'if I ask you a question?'

'No,' said Miller. 'Where are you from?'

'Cadiz,' said the man.

'A fine town,' said Miller.

'It is,' said the man. 'Have you been there?'

'No,' said Miller. 'Why?'

'Now look – let me ask you something,' the man said. 'I mean you do know; you do realize that I am not a taxi driver, and that this is not a taxi. This is my own private vehicle.'

'What?'

Miller leaned forward, looked for the meter, and couldn't see it. He wound down the window and looked along the side of the car. It was a white Peugeot.

'Oh, shit,' he said in English. Then, in Spanish: 'Why did you stop?'

'I stopped,' said the man, 'at the red traffic light. It's a sort of a custom we have here. Quite a lot of us do it. It's considered polite. I've been doing it for years.'

'I'll get out,' said Miller, deciding to abandon his impulsive journey in favour of his own room at the Calle Vic.

'I would have thrown you out back there,' said the driver, 'but then it struck me – I am probably your only chance of getting home in one piece.'

'Not home,' said Miller.

'Wherever. I live on the Traversera de Dalt. It's close.' He broke into English. '*Your lucky day*.'

He told Miller he was in charge of night security for the Caixa Bank, down by the harbour. He drove him to Jordan's front door. Miller offered him money, which he refused.

'I think – I hope,' the driver said, 'you would do the same for me.'

Miller made his way unsteadily up Jordan's path. He sat on her front step, his back to the door, and lit a cigarette. He stood up and turned round. He was about to press the bell when he noticed that the door was still very slightly ajar. He leaned against it but it didn't move. Something heavy was obstructing it. Squinting through the gap, he saw, to his horror, that the obstruction was a body.

'Jesus,' said Miller, out loud. He put his shoulder against the door and pushed, until the gap was just wide enough for him to slip through. He tore a button off his shirt as he squeezed in. When he let go of the door it slammed shut. Jordan's body, still fully dressed, fell back and lay motionless in its original position. She was stretched out on her back across the hallway, her left shoulder against the door.

He ran into the kitchen and snatched the jug of water from the table. He threw it into her face where she lay, then took hold of her shoulders and pulled her inert body into a sitting position, her back propped against the wall. He kneeled down by her.

She put her arms round his neck.

'Is it you?' she murmured, her eyes still shut.

'What?' said Miller, still in shock.

She kissed him on the mouth. Water ran down her face on to her lips.

'I'm still asleep,' she said. 'Carry me.'

He picked her up with difficulty; she put her arms round his neck, like a drowsy child. He put her on the bed and sat next to her.

'God, I'm wet,' she said. 'Who did that?'

'I did,' he said. 'I thought you were dead.'

'Oh,' she said. 'Did you?' She yawned. 'Why?'

'Why? Because you were sleeping by the door.'

'I sleep really deep,' she said.

'Why did you...'

'I lay down there,' she interrupted, 'because I knew then I'd be closer to you and then you'd come back.'

'You're mad,' he said.

'Well, you say that,' she told him. 'But who was right – you or me?'

'I went,' he began, 'because...'

'I don't care,' she told him. 'God,' she repeated, 'I'm soaking.'

He got up, and sat at the table. She came and sat on his knee.

'I'm glad you came,' she said.

'Why?'

'I've been so lonely.'
'Me too.'
'Hah,' Jordan said.
'What?'
'Well... you've got so much.'
'Pardon?'
'You've got so much. You've got many things I haven't got.'
'Like what?'
'Like... I don't know. You've got those self things, you know – self... what are they called? Self... assurance, is it? Confidence? Self, er...'
'You think so?' he said. He told her about his cab ride.
'Wow,' she said. 'Imagine that in London; some pissed-up Spaniard collapses into a Cockney banker's motor. "That's absolutely fine, sir, no charge, glad to be of service. Where to?"' She paused. 'God, you could have been killed. Anyway, I'm glad you weren't.' She gave a joking, matter-of-fact nod towards the bedroom. 'Come on then.'

Whether from fatigue, intoxication or guilt, he lay on his back, almost motionless, while she made love to him.

'God,' she told him, 'I've just remembered that self thing that you've got and I haven't.'
'What?'
'Self-control.'
She laughed. 'I hope... I didn't mean to, you know...'
'It's OK,' he said. 'You're beautiful.'
'Hey, you know what?' she said. 'You can tell that cab driver of yours he can bring you again. Will you ask him if he can do that tomorrow evening?'
'Yes,' he said.
'Really?'
'Yes.'
'Tomorrow night?'
'Yes.'
'And Tuesday?'
'Yes.'
'Anytime?'

'Anytime,' Miller said.

He felt the top of her arm. 'Where did you get those shoulders?'

'I…' She paused. 'I guess you could say that my father taught me to fight.'

'What do you mean?'

'What do you think I mean? He hit me.'

'What with?'

'A belt. A hairbrush. His fist.'

'Jesus. Why?'

'Because he hated my mother,' she replied, 'and he told me that every time he looked at me, it reminded him of her. What kind of a man would think like that, of his own daughter?'

'Well…' said Miller.

'*What*?'

'No.'

'In a strange kind of way,' she added, 'those weren't the worst days.'

'What did he do on the other days?'

She didn't reply.

'Did he…' Miller swallowed. 'Did he abuse you?'

'No.'

'What then?'

'He lived out his life,' she said, 'as though I wasn't there.' She paused. 'Will?'

'Yes?'

'Do you take women back to your place?'

'No.'

'You're a hermit,' she said, 'like Nick.'

'What about the Duplexes?'

'Well have you ever seen any of those women with him?'

'No.'

'It's another dream for him,' she said. 'Like his London bus, and his Terrorgrams, and the lottery.'

'You mean he never does it?'

'If Nick ever hired a Duplex,' she said, 'the sky would fall in. It would be like the monkeys leaving Gibraltar.'

She fell silent for a few moments, lying on her back, next to him.

'Hey Will,' she said, 'if I tell you my secret will you tell me yours?'

Miller felt an unpleasant surge of dread.

'What?'

She turned and laid her head on his chest. 'I'm going to tell you anyway, OK?' she said.

'OK.'

'Jordan,' she said, 'is not my...' She paused, and pressed her lips close to his ear. 'Real name,' she whispered.

'Your...what?'

'My real name...God your heart's beating fast,' she said, 'are you all right?'

'I'm all right,' he said. 'Go on.'

'My real name — nobody knows this, OK. Nobody. This is between us.'

'Yes,' he said.

'Promise?'

'Promise.'

'My real name...' she paused, 'is Tracey.'

She laughed.

'So why...'

'Tracey?' she said. 'Look at me. Are you kidding?'

He got up and came back with a bottle of water and a large tumbler of white wine.

'I hope that's for you,' she said, looking at the glass. She took the water bottle, and drank from it.

'It is.'

'OK,' she said. 'That's my secret. What's yours?'

Miller swallowed the wine, which was warm. It didn't help.

'I have a wife,' he said, half-heartedly.

'Oh yes?' she said. 'A good one?'

'No.'

'Is she divorcing you at all?'

'I think so.'

'You think so?'

'I mean – yes,' said Miller. 'She is.'

'Children?'

'No,' Miller lied. He held Jordan again; she smiled.

'Well that wasn't that bad,' she said. 'I like to see you sweat. I'll make you sweat again later.'

She started to sing, a tender-sounding lullaby in Spanish: '*Voló, voló... y en lo alto quedó...*'

'That's beautiful,' he said.

'In the Basque country,' she said, 'mothers sing young children to sleep with it at night. They love that song: 'He flew, he flew...'

'Is it old?' he asked.

'No,' she said.

'What's it about?' he asked. 'An angel? A bird?'

'No,' she said. 'It's about Admiral de Carrero Blanco.'

'You're joking,' he said.

'No.'

She put her head on his shoulder. Some strands of her very short brown hair were bleached blonde by the sun. He held her and stared at the ceiling, wondering whether to risk everything.

'Jordan,' he began. But she didn't reply and when he looked down at her again, she was asleep.

Miller woke at ten, and got dressed. He switched on the CD player. 'Blue and coral Kirkstall skies', a woman's voice sang. 'Timorese sunrise'. Jordan was sound asleep. He sat on the bed and watched her for a few moments. He'd tended to like women, it struck him, in inverse proportion to the resemblance they bore to his wife, and Jordan was as different from Elizabeth as anybody he'd ever met. He liked her steel and her commitment.

He found her keys, which she'd dropped in the hallway the night before, and walked down her street, with the sun on his back, to a corner shop where he bought some yellow roses. He left them on her pillow, with her keys and a note. 'The cab driver,' he wrote, 'says Anytime... Edward.'

He took a taxi back to Calle Vic, where he had a shower and changed into his work clothes. He caught the fifteen bus to the school, down Diagonal, the main artery across the city. It got held up in traffic, opposite a shop that sold wedding dresses. Miller gazed vacantly at the window display, his mind oscillating between elation, foreboding, and some other emotion he couldn't quite recognize, it was so long since he'd experienced it.

The full-length white lace dresses were precisely the sort of thing Jordan would have despised. These clothes, he decided, belonged firmly in the world of Tracey. He began to wonder what had inspired her new name – the river, perhaps, or a character he half-remembered from *The Great Gatsby*. In any case, he wouldn't have minded what Jordan was called. He repeated her names to himself – Tracey and Jordan, over and over. Then he remembered the way she'd said that phrase – 'not my real name'. He recalled how she'd pressed her lips close to his ear when she'd said 'real name', and he repeated those two words to himself. And it was then, as he said it for the third time, under his breath – 'real name' – that he realized that he'd signed his note with his.

He got off the bus by the wedding shop, which was only half-way to the school. His first thought was to get a cab back to Casa Baro. But even Jordan, he reasoned, had to be awake by now. In any case, if he went back and rang the doorbell, she'd see the note as soon as she opened her eyes. 'Edward,' he remembered her saying. 'What kind of man calls himself Edward?' And her other remark. 'Hey Will – he's from Oldham, like you.' He decided to walk the rest of the way to Oxbridge House, to give himself time to ponder his predicament. He found himself slipping back into his old way of thinking, as a devious optimist. She wouldn't necessarily jump to a dangerous conclusion straight away. He cursed the way he had disclosed the lingua franca of his old trade to Bas. But there was more than one Edward from Oldham, he told himself, who knew about print runs, and page proofs, and bulk sales. These were several pieces of a very big jigsaw.

He needed to think. Instead of going straight to the school, he stopped in Pascual's. He went down to the far end of the counter where the barman was sitting alone, reading the paper. Andres and a few other regulars were playing dominoes at a table near the entrance.

'*Buenas...* holy shit,' said the café owner, looking at Miller's bloodshot eyes and troubled expression.

'What is it? *Una resaca?*'

'It's not a hangover,' said Miller.' 'I'm in trouble. Will you call Christopher and tell him I can't go in?'

'Me?' said Pascual. 'How is that going to look?'

'I don't care how it looks,' said Miller. 'Just do it. Please.'

'I...'

'Please.'

The barman made the call. He mixed Miller a half pint of tomato juice, Tabasco and dry sherry.

'Sherry?' Miller asked.

'Drink it,' he said. 'It'll do you good.' Miller swallowed it. He ordered a *carajillo* with an extra brandy on the side, and cradled the spirit glass as he began to weigh up the danger of disclosure to Pascual; an acceptable risk, he supposed, but one that offered no likely benefit in terms of a solution.

'If you can keep your head,' he said to Pascual, in English, 'while all those around are losing theirs...'

When the barman didn't respond, he turned to his left, towards the entrance, still sitting on his stool, and saw she was there. She was standing a couple of yards from him. She was holding something – not his note, as he'd expected, but some sheets of A4 paper.

'I'll tell you another of my secrets,' she said. 'Ask me where I've been.'

He put down the brandy glass. Looking at her, he recognized the emotion that he couldn't put a name to; it was guilt.

'Jordan...'

Pascual nodded to Andres, then disappeared out to the market.

'I've been on the web – on the computer – up at the Paris.'

She put the paper on the bar, printed side up. It was an internet version of the article by Rebecca Ellis. She pointed at the picture of him crouching by the sink, with his genitals blacked out.

'You're him,' she said, 'aren't you.'

'Yes,' said Miller. He picked up the brandy again.

She stepped closer to him.

'I gave myself to you,' she said, softly. 'And you humiliated me.'

'Humiliated you? Who to?' he said, quietly.

'To me,' she said. 'To you.'

'To us,' Miller said, without thinking.

A sudden look of rage came into her eyes. He still had the brandy glass raised in his right hand; she'd taken his last remark, he realized, as a sarcastic toast. She slapped him across the face, hard. He saw a tear form in each of her eyes, and watched them roll down her cheeks almost exactly in time. He put his glass down, and gently reached out a hand to her. She drove her right fist into his face with her full force; he only stayed on his stool because his skull connected with the wall behind him. Blood was pouring from both of his nostrils and he could feel it running down his neck, from a cut to the back of his head.

She didn't move, but stood there, facing him. He was dimly aware of one of the domino players – Andres he thought – disappearing out of the bar. The other regulars looked on in silence, but did not intervene, on the grounds, he supposed, that no man should need assistance in sorting out a woman, presumably with a bigger punch. Time seemed to stand still. It occurred to him that the passive resignation of Oliver Hardy is not simply an abstract comic technique, but a real dynamic of violence. She picked up his coffee cup, and threw the hot liquid into his lap.

'*Carajillo*,' she said, very audibly. 'Little prick.'

As she left, she passed Andres, who ran back in with Pascual.

'*Hombre*,' said the barman.

He led Miller upstairs and put him in the shower.

'How's the wedding tackle?' the Spaniard shouted, through the bathroom door.

'OK,' said Miller.

'And the nose?'

'Not broken,' he said.

He came down into the café and met Nick, who'd been summoned by the owner.

'If,' Pascual said, 'you can keep your head, when all around are losing theirs…'

'Then,' Nick continued, 'you may have seriously misjudged the situation.'

Miller took two days off, and returned to find his relationship with his colleagues fractured. Jordan turned up for work but didn't speak to him. The lunches with Sonia stopped. Christopher, seeing Jordan distraught, was unhappy that one of his best teachers had been destabilized. Even Nick seemed annoyed with him, offended that he wouldn't explain what had happened. Miller did his best to avoid the staff room altogether. He gave up going to the beach, and swam at an outdoor pool, alone. He decided to save what money he could, in the hope of moving to another school in another town, should he have the opportunity, once Jordan revealed his identity, as he had no doubt that she would.

He persevered with this detached existence for a couple of weeks and then, very gradually, sensed the atmosphere beginning to ease. Jordan, to his great surprise, had clearly spoken to nobody about him.

The Saturday Group, from being a major source of stress, had come to be a welcome distraction. Sitting in the empty school facing Paco and the Lesseps brothers, his back to the window, the five-euro prize sitting in the ashtray, he felt strangely secure.

'Will!' Paco exclaimed one morning.

'Yes?'

'The window-cleaners is here.'

'The window-cleaner,' Miller corrected him.

'The window-cleaner,' Paco said, 'are here.'

Miller took a deep breath.

'What,' he asked, 'is he doing?'

'They…' Paco said.

'No. He.'

'He…'

'Good…'

'He are doing pictures.'

'He *is* cleaning windows,' said Miller.

Paco shuffled in his seat.

'No, pictures.'

As Calamita said this, Miller heard the whirr of a motor drive. He turned and, through the tinted glass, saw two men. One had a digital camera, trained on him. The other, who was much taller, was holding a large white envelope, with the words 'Edward Miller' written on it, in capitals.

Miller sprinted out of the school. The man with the envelope, seeing him, hesitated for a moment, then fled across the lawn, towards the bank. The photographer didn't notice him coming until it was too late. Miller grabbed him by the back of his hair and drove his face into the thick pane of tinted glass: the slight angle of incline made it easier for Miller to keep his victim's head pressed hard against the window. His camera fell on to the path. Miller, still holding his head with his full strength, kicked the Nikon so savagely that it shattered against the shallow brick support at the base of the window. Keeping his enemy's face pinned to the glass with his left hand, so that his features, viewed from the other side, must have been horribly distorted, Miller slammed his right fist against the back of his head with all the force he could manage. As the blow connected, he heard himself grunt like a tennis professional. The photographer's nose splintered with a sound like one of Pascual's twisted capsicums. Two rivulets of blood were running down the window.

Keeping a tight grip of the back of the man's head, Miller saw that the memory card had sprung out of the camera; he crushed it under his left heel. As he did this, he was aware that the photographer's companion was back at his side, though just for a second. Before he began to retreat, he seemed to pick Miller's pocket.

Miller glared at him. The big man halted and appeared to be about to defend his friend but then, seeing in the former editor's eyes the expression of somebody with absolutely no regard for his own safety, he backed away, then fled.

Miller pulled the cameraman's head back from the window, still holding him by the hair.

'Which paper do you work for,' he asked him, 'you cunt?'

There was no reply. Miller drove his face into the glass again and held it there. Through the window, he could see that Paco and the others were still hunched over their table, observing the scene and taking notes.

He pulled the photographer's head back again.

'I can't breathe,' spluttered the man, whose face and shirt-front were covered in blood. Drops were falling on to his shoes, from the end of what Miller recognized as a Middlesex County Cricket Club tie.

'Which paper…'

'I don't,' the man said.

Miller tightened his grip on his hair again.

'Don't,' the man yelped. 'Please.'

Miller didn't.

'I work for Furini's.'

'Who?' Miller asked.

'Daniel Furini,' he said. 'The lawyer.'

Miller let go of him.

'Who are you?' he asked.

'Nigel Bullivant.'

'Don't move.'

In his own left trouser pocket, Miller could see the white envelope, which had been roughly pushed in by the bigger man, while he was distracted.

'What's this?' he asked.

'Just some papers,' the man said, ' transferring your assets.'

'Who sent them?'

'Your wife.'

'How did you find me?'

'I think,' Bullivant said, 'that they traced a phone call.'

'My fucking doctor,' said Miller.

'It doesn't work like that.'

'What?'

'He wouldn't know they were tapping his phone.'

Miller looked at him. On the parts of Bullivant's forehead and hands that weren't soaked in blood, he could see ugly red patches; lesions from a skin disease, probably psoriasis. He noticed the man was shaking.

'Who was bugging the phone?'

'Your father-in-law,' he said. 'On behalf of his daughter.'

'Fuck,' said Miller.

He gave the man a handkerchief.

'Thank you,' said Bullivant.

'I hope they pay you well for this,' said Miller.

'No, sir,' Bullivant replied. He pressed the handkerchief to his broken nose. The cotton was already soaked through with blood. 'Most days, I'm the office courier.'

Miller bent down and picked up the film, which he put in his pocket. On the edge of the skyscraper complex, fifty yards away, he could see the tall accomplice. He was standing next to Juan, the window-cleaner.

'Who's he?' Miller asked.

'He's our security man,' said Bullivant.

'Your minder,' said Miller.

The man nodded.

'One thing,' the injured man said, through his bloodsoaked handkerchief. 'Now that they know where you are – watch yourself.'

'Why are you telling me that?' Miller asked. 'Are you threatening me?'

'I am informing you.'

'Why?'

'They want to bring you back.'

'Dead?'

Bullivant shook his head. He got down on his knees, and started to pick up bits of the shattered camera.

'I think that's a write-off,' said Miller.

'I'll have to take it back to the office,' said Bullivant. 'Or they'll blame me.'

Miller looked down at him with contempt.

'You sad little bastard,' he said.

He turned to leave and found himself face to face with Juan. Without saying a word, the window-cleaner began to wash the blood off the window. It had begun to dry in the sun, and he had to use his small scraper to dislodge the tinier spots, which had already hardened, and the coagulated edges of the three or four thick streams that ran down to a small crimson puddle on the path. Miller handed Juan fifty euros and went back inside.

'Calamity?' Paco asked, when the teacher came back into Milton.

'Calamity.'

His own shirt and trousers were splattered with Bullivant's blood.

'Bad calamity?' Paco asked.

'All calamities,' said Miller, 'are bad.'

'So… bad calamity.'

'That's right, Paco,' Miller said. 'Bad calamity.'

On the Monday, Miller phoned in sick. When he came in to work the following morning, Sonia, to his great surprise, asked him out to lunch.

'You mean on Friday?' he asked.

'I mean today.'

They sat down at their usual table in the Chino Hoy.

'What is it?' he asked her.

'Do you know what day it is?'

'It's the thirteenth of July.'

'Tuesday the thirteenth. The unluckiest date in the calendar.'

'That's Friday the thirteenth.'

'Not in Spain.'

'Ah.'

'I liked you,' she said. 'I'll miss you.'

'What?'

'I'll miss you.'

'Why?'

'Because you were OK here,' she said.

'Have been OK,' he said. 'Present perfect for something that started in the past, but continues. Simple past for a completed action.'

'I liked you,' she repeated, 'because you never came on to me.'

'No.'

'Like you came on to Jordan.'

Miller reached for one of her Fortuna cigarettes, on the table in front of him. Sonia put her hand on his wrist, to stop him, and kept it there.

'Jordan,' she said, softly, 'is a really good kid, you know that? And she's had a very, very hard time in life.'

'I think I know…' Miller began.

'I don't think you do,' Sonia said. 'Believe me. I don't think you know the half of it. To be truthful,' she said, 'I know you don't.'

'How?' he said.

'Because she told me you don't.'

'When?'

'Last night.'

'What else,' he asked her, 'did she tell you about me?'

'Nothing,' Sonia said. 'Don't think I didn't ask her. But...' she went into a reasonable approximation of Jordan's Leeds accent. 'She don't blab.'

She kept her hand on his wrist.

'Jordan,' she said, 'has been closed into herself for so long. And the last thing she needs is some other guy to fuck her around then piss off.'

He could see tears forming in her eyes.

'Will,' she said softly. 'What the bloody hell did you do to Jordan?'

Again, Miller thought for a moment about confiding everything.

'I did... the usual,' he said, as coldly as he could manage.

He looked into Sonia's eyes then and saw that her tears had gone, and the unmistakable glow of true affection had been extinguished. She picked up her cigarettes and walked out without speaking, leaving him with the bill.

When he got back to the school, Christopher beckoned him straight into Byron.

'Did she tell you?' Devlin asked.

'Yes.'

'She wanted to tell you. She likes... liked... you.'

Miller sat down.

'What is this about the fucking past tense?'

'I'm not going to ask you what happened with Jordan,' he said. 'The thing is that I don't want to lose her. She's a wonderful teacher. She teaches from the known to the unknown. She makes them feel special.'

'Even though...'

'She despises them. I know. I have noticed. Anyway one of you has to go. But that's not even the main thing. The last thing I need,' he said, 'is the London press here.'

'They've not been here,' Miller said.

'The caretaker saw you,' Devlin said, 'on Saturday, brawling with that photographer.'

'He wasn't...'

'I don't care,' Devlin said. 'I don't want to know.'

'Why not?'

'Because one thing I've noticed in life is that the less I know, the less trouble I get in. I like you Will, but you're trouble. You're out. That's it.'

'It's OK,' said Miller. 'I was going anyway.'

Devlin handed him an envelope.

'Here's your money,' he said. 'And I'm giving you the six hundred back, for the course.'

'Six hundred?' said Miller. 'Pounds?'

'Euros. Come on.'

Christopher led the way out to Pascual's café. The barman broke off from his game of poker dice with Andres and served Christopher two beers and two large brandies.

They sat down, with Miller facing the bar. Pascual put a seventy-eight on his turntable and switched it on.

The principal clinked Miller's glass.

'How did you get here?'

'I flew.'

'That's right. You flew.'

Miller swallowed his brandy and said nothing.

'Perhaps,' Christopher said, 'you've learned something while you've been here.'

'That's right,' said Miller, sarcastically. 'I've learned that there are six forms of the future.'

Devlin nodded.

'Six forms of the future,' Miller added. 'All bad.'

A delivery van arrived; the driver stacked half a dozen boxes of fresh strawberries against the bar.

Miller got up and went to the bar, where he requested a repeat of Devlin's order.

'Christopher,' he said, when he came back. 'You know you were asking me about that poem – the one about the sparrow flying though the banqueting hall.'

'Yes.'

'I think I can tell you what that's about.'

'What?'

'What happens is, he comes out of a period of suffering, and just for a very short time he's happy. It's his day in the sun'.

'Ah,' said Devlin. 'I see. I suppose it was obvious really.'

'It is now.'

'Look Will,' Christopher said. 'I'm a bit worried about, er… where are you… I can sort your flight out for you, how about that. When you know…'

'It's all right,' Miller lied. 'I know where I'm going. I've got something lined up.'

'Oh,' said Devlin. 'Good. Where?'

Miller scanned the bar for inspiration. He found it on a case of strawberries, behind Devlin's shoulder.

'I'm going to Plant City,' he said, giving the place name firmly, as Christopher had taught him.

'Where's that?'

'Florida. It's…' Miller repeated the slogan he'd read on the box, 'The Strawberry Capital of the World.'

Their conversation took place against the soundtrack of Pascual's increasingly cheerful seventy-eights: 'Jollity Farm', by Leslie Saroney, followed by George Formby singing 'When I'm Cleaning Windows'.

'That's quite a line,' Miller said, repeating one of the lyrics. 'It's not my fault that I see things I shouldn't see.'

'No wonder George Formby was Stalin's favourite entertainer,' said Devlin, sounding drunk. 'I imagine Uncle Joe could relate to that sentiment. I can.'

'Christopher,' Miller asked him. 'What in God's name brought you over here?'

'I was working at a secondary school, in Haringey. That council is a shambles, as you may know.'

'I do,' said Miller.

'Anyway, I told this girl to stop swearing,' he said, 'and she spat in my face. I talked to the head, and she told me to live with it.'

'And?'

'And I lived with it. But then I, er… broke down.'

'What happened?'

'I was writing the annual reports for my own class,' he said. 'These went straight out to the parents; I had to mail them myself actually... when I was writing them, I just started to weep.'

'They fired you for that?'

'No,' said Devlin. 'It was more... the things I wrote in the reports.'

'What were they – obscene?' Miller asked.

'No. I mean... I remember one lad... he was a wonderful kid really, hard working, just screwed up by the gang culture like all the rest of the poor sods. Apparently I wrote...'

He stopped.

'Go on,' said Miller. 'We will never meet again.'

'Apparently I wrote: "He is the fattest boy in my class." '

Miller laughed, freely, for the first time he could remember.

'Was he?'

'What?'

'The fattest?'

'Of course he was,' said Devlin. 'He was massive. If he'd been thin, I'd still be there.'

Miller listened to the opening chords of Formby's 'I Do Do Things I Do'.

'Let me give you some advice,' he said. 'Lock the photocopier, or put a meter on it. Change the telephones.'

'Why?'

'Because those phones,' he said, 'are open to abuse.'

'They're locked.'

'Yes, but – look, just do it Christopher, OK? Or get a metered bill. And put up a note to tell your staff you've done it.'

'OK.'

'Keep your real account books off the premises.'

Devlin said nothing.

'And take those names down off the doors.'

'Why?'

'Because they don't look clever,' he said. 'They just look bloody stupid.'

'And put what there?'

'Anything. Numbers. And get rid of those dodgy Oxford certificates you have pinned up in your office,' Miller went on. 'Do you really think I'm the only person who's noticed that the names on them are different but the serial number is always the same?'

'I'll change the phones,' said Devlin, 'and I'll take down the certificates. But I'm going to keep the names on the rooms.'

'Why?'

'Because,' said Christopher, 'these authors serve as an example of excellence and virtue in these lesser and decadent times.'

'Virtue?' Miller laughed. 'None of us could learn anything improving from those fuckers.'

'Even you?' said Devlin, with a hint of malice.

'All of those men – every one of them – was far worse than me.'

'Wordsworth?' asked Devlin, looking offended.

'He screwed his sister.'

'Byron?'

'So did he.'

'What?' Devlin looked mortified. 'Whose?'

'Whose what?'

'Whose sister did Byron, er… his own, or Wordsworth's?'

'Both,' said Miller, enjoying himself.

'Coleridge?'

'Drugs.'

'Swinburne?'

'Whips,' said Miller.

'Milton?'

'He starved himself in order to hallucinate.'

'Shakespeare?'

'Boys.'

Miller got a cab home at six in the evening. He got out by the English bookshop on the Paseo de Gràcia where he bought a map of the United States, then walked the rest of the way back to the Calle Vic. He retrieved his passport and credit card from their hiding place in the mattress, packed his small bag, and fell asleep. He woke up at five in the morning, dressed, and picked up his holdall. He glanced in Nick's bedroom and saw that it was empty.

As he stepped out of the flat for the last time, on to the landing, he collided with Gannon, who was coming in. The Londoner gave him a sheepish look, grunted something he didn't catch, and went into the apartment, leaving the door open. Miller was half-way down the narrow stairs that led to the street, when he passed a woman on her way up. She was young, heavily made-up, and wearing a short leather skirt. At the bottom of the staircase he met another girl, who was following her. Though she was similarly dressed, it was only when he looked at her face that he realized she was the first woman's identical twin. He watched as they made their way up to the first floor. The monkeys, Miller thought, are leaving the rock.

Miller took the six a.m. train to the airport; through El Prat, where the stench of man-made fibre from a plastics factory turned his stomach; through Castelldefels, where George Sanders had ended his life.

He glanced around him at the handful of other passengers in the air-conditioned compartment. Their luggage – unlike his own small canvas bag – was meticulously labelled with every detail of their destination. They fidgeted, afraid that they would somehow be left behind. Miller looked on, bemused. It was some time now since his own life had known any guiding purpose except flight.

His mind went back to a party he'd been to when he was eleven, and he'd drawn the name of Alison Marshall in the game of postman's knock. When he pulled out the second card – the one that allocated time (usually a matter of five or ten seconds), it showed two minutes. It seemed an unimaginable time to embrace the most desirable girl in the school. They'd put their lips together, with their friends gathered around them in a small circle. After the exhilaration of the first three seconds or so, Miller was entirely at a loss as to what to do next; he made small movements with his face, consistent with what he believed would convince his audience but not revolt his partner; inside, praying for it to be over.

His whole life, he reflected, had been getting a bit like that. He had begun to perform actions, and take critical decisions, just for the sake of it – as if his every movement was under scrutiny by somebody who feared that he might be losing his mind. He wondered if he was. Weary and purposeless, he felt compelled to keep moving, like a lost dog. Staying put would be foolhardy, now that the Portals knew he was in Barcelona. The thought of a return to Britain, which would reignite the scandal he'd escaped and precipitate a chain of events he could only imagine ending with his arrest, was worse. The more he thought about it, the better Plant City sounded. His noticing the name on the strawberry box, Miller persuaded himself, was not a random act of desperation, but a sign.

He took out his map of the United States and unfolded it on his knee.

'*Señor?*' a small boy had slipped away from his family and approached him. '*A donde vas?*'

Miller paused. Where was he going?

He didn't reply. The boy, who must have been about six, started to look confused, then distressed. He sensed irritation in the family, across the carriage.

'I am going to Plant City,' he told him, in Spanish.

'Where's that?' the boy asked, with a swallow that indicated that he had, indeed, been on the verge of tears.

'It's in Florida. In America.'

'What's it like?'

'It's ...' the family across the aisle was listening attentively. 'It's a city of flowers. It is the strawberry capital,' he added, 'of the world.'

The boy went back to his seat.

'*Suerte*,' he shouted.

'And you?' the Englishman replied. 'Where are you going?'

'London,' the boy's father said. 'Do you have friends there?'

'No,' said Miller.

At the airport, he tried to buy a ticket for Tampa, but the only direct flight was a charter to Orlando, on the east side of the state.

'You're in luck,' said the woman. 'It leaves at eleven. Eight hundred euros round trip.'

Miller invented a date for the return journey he would never make, and paid her in cash. It left him with five hundred euros. The plane was full of young families heading for Disney World. Looking in his bag, Miller found that the only book he had was Sonia's *Eighth Pan Book of Horror*. He put on the airline headphones and looked at the tiny video screen in front of him, where he recognised the opening credits from *Peter Pan*.

Miller observed Walt Disney's impression of a Bloomsbury household with a mixture of bewilderment and remorse. He'd enjoyed the film when he last saw it – probably thirty years ago – but now every scene appeared somehow surreal and tainted by loss. The dominant colour, he noticed, was a deep, melancholic blue. And yet – surrounded by shrieking children, and with Sonia's twisted story of ravaged amputees as his only other source of diversion – he turned the volume up and stayed with it. The portrayal of London – absurdly romantic as it was – made him deeply nostalgic. In the kindly if authoritarian father, he saw the parent he could have been, and never was. By the time they'd landed, and he was queuing for US entry formalities, he felt bereft. One line from *Peter Pan* kept coming back to him. 'You don't know what joy you'll find,' it went, 'when you leave the world behind.'

In the immigration booth, a young, fair-haired woman officer looked back and forth between the immaculately groomed executive in the passport photograph and the much thinner man who stood before her: shaven-headed, heavily tanned, and wearing a T-shirt and jeans.

'You might like to take your sunglasses off, sir,' she suggested.

Miller did. She asked to see more ID. He gave her his driving licence and his secret credit card.

'Purpose of visit?'

'Holiday.'

'Vacation.' She drew the word out, lingering longest on the second syllable. She sucked on her pen and met his eyes. 'In Plant City.'

She glanced across to the secondary immigration area, where suspect visitors could be grilled at greater length. The glass-walled room was already overflowing, mainly with black and Hispanic visitors. She looked back at his visa waiver form.

'And you're staying – where? It says nothing here.'

'The Holiday Inn,' Miller said, summoning some of his old power for deception and assertiveness. 'Plant City.'

'Tell me something,' the woman said. 'Who recommended Plant City to you as a destination for your vacation?'

'My ex-wife,' Miller said.

With just the slightest glimmer of a smile, she stamped his passport.

'Enjoy your trip,' she said.

'Have you been there?'

'I most certainly have, sir.'

In the airport, he changed his remaining euros into dollars: it was nowhere near enough, he realized, to get him a car. And he needed a car.

He took out his credit card and checked the expiry date: it was still valid. It hadn't worked, he remembered, on the train out of Euston. If a transaction went through now, the chances were that Charles, Elizabeth's father, had reopened the facility deliberately, in the hope that Miller would one day use it, and give a clue to his whereabouts.

He decided he had little choice in the matter. He walked up to the Hertz desk and requested a compact car for a month. The girl swiped his card; the transaction went through.

'At present you're personally liable for fire and theft,' she said. 'Do you wish to take out...'

'No,' Miller interrupted.

It was three thirty when he steered the gold Chevrolet Cavalier out of the airport car park and turned on to Interstate 4, the road that led west, towards Plant City and Tampa. Miller was heading directly into the July sunshine. The Florida light had an unpleasant white intensity, while the air coming in through his open driver's side window delivered an asphyxiating, soul-sapping level of humidity. He found his sunglasses, drew up the electric window, and turned on the air conditioning. Then he switched on the radio, which was tuned to an FM station which, as he joined it, was playing the opening chords of Bob Dylan's 'Like a Rolling Stone'. Miller had never liked the record, on the grounds that Dylan was a hippy and the lyrics were purposefully oblique. But here on Interstate 4, for the first time in his life, every word made perfect sense. When the song finished, he switched the stereo off again.

He drove steadily, at sixty, in the right-hand lane, and cursed the impulse that had brought him here. There were so many other Spanish towns he could have moved to – León, say, or Valencia – elegant, welcoming towns where he would have had a marketable skill. He still had a return air ticket. And yet, for all their charm, both of those cities had one very tangible drawback. In Valencia or León, they would find him. And once they did, it occurred to Miller, every step of his certain demise – from his arrest, to the appointment of the jury and his sentencing judge – every one of these matters could be placed in the hands of one of Charles Portal's more reliable Masonic contacts. The same would apply when it came to ensuring the lack of a conviction should his father-in-law, in defiance of Dr Norman's calming advice, persist in dispatching him by 'Route One'. Miller, as Charles had once reminded him, knew how these things worked. He eased the car up to seventy and moved into the middle lane.

There were countless advertising signs by the side of the highway. Mounted on poles, their messages were spelled out in black and red capitals that slotted into cream-coloured display boards of the kind that used to be outside British cinemas when he was a boy. Most were publicizing bars or churches – the two most attractive facilities, Miller thought, with a shudder, to a stranger who needs to make new friends fast. One of these hoardings read simply: PRAY FOR ALL TEACHERS.

Miller thought of Jordan, and felt the beginnings of remorse. What would have happened if she hadn't fallen asleep as she did, when he was about to tell her his true history? Certain of her phrases came back to him: 'I don't blab', and 'What kind of a man would think like that, of his own daughter?'

The further he drove, the more powerfully the billboards reminded him that he was alone, hungry, and very thirsty. Finally he pulled off the Interstate and followed signs for what appeared to be a regular diner. Minutes later, though, he found himself in a queue of cars heading into some kind of leisure park, containing burger bars, swimming pools and other attractions. He tried to retreat but by this time he was on a single-track approach road, with traffic behind him, and couldn't turn back. When he reached the booth, he said nothing, paid the twenty-dollar entrance fee, parked, and bought a pint of water and a hamburger from a stall. He sat on the car bonnet while he ate. The heat was unbearable; his trousers were soaked in sweat. To his right, across the parking lot, he could see a blue building with a sign over the entrance which read: 'Mermaid World'. When the door opened to admit a customer, he noticed it was pitch black inside. At least in there, Miller reasoned, it would be cool.

He went in and found he was standing in a small theatre. There were eight long rows of wooden benches that could have held around a hundred spectators, but fewer than half of the places were taken. Of these, only a dozen or so were occupied by children. Most of the spectators were unaccompanied men in their fifties, or older. In the centre of the auditorium, where the stage should have been, there was the front glass of what looked like a colossal aquarium. This panel alone must have been a thousand foot square and the expanse of water behind it extended further than he could see. This wasn't a tank, Miller guessed, but an artificial lake, stretching back into the grounds. The underwater decor wasn't tasteful – sunken galleons, treasure chests and implausible rock formations. But the theatre was air conditioned. Miller walked down to the front row, took a seat, and leaned forward so that his sweating forehead touched the glass.

Then the music started. Three young women in identical turquoise swimsuits appeared, from beneath the ocean floor, and began performing synchronized gymnastics to a techno soundtrack. The mermaids didn't actually have tails, but they were remarkable in many other respects – not least for the way that they stayed underwater throughout the twenty-minute show without once coming up for air. Each girl held a long plastic pipe, continually bubbling oxygen, from which she would inhale deeply when required. Concealing the tube was impossible but, to judge by the reaction of the more elderly male spectators, the crude logistics of the oxygen supply merely enhanced the spectacle's appeal. At one point a girl came down to the front of the tank, on the ocean floor just in front of Miller, and drank a whole Pepsi-Cola, from the bottle, without pausing, before taking a long, and no doubt uncomfortable, draw on her oxygen line.

'What does she need the pipe for, Mummy?' asked a small girl behind Miller.

'She needs the pipe,' her mother answered, 'to stay alive.'

He sat in the darkened auditorium and watched the show three times. He left when he noticed that the girl who drank the Pepsi – it was always the same swimmer – had started to stare at him through the glass.

Out in the sun, he noticed his clothes were still soaked with sweat. For the first few seconds, back in the heat, they felt like ice. When he went to buy more water from a stall, before leaving, he found that the roll of dollar bills in his pocket was so damp that the notes were sticking together. He climbed back into the car.

When he reached the exit for Plant City, he indicated right. Then a wave of panic hit him. He didn't know what he'd do, if he stopped. With his indicator clicking, he ignored the turn and stayed on the main highway, his foot on the floor, still heading west. He took the I75, heading south.

The light was beginning to fade when Miller left this main road. He turned off to the right, down a small tarmac road. The scenery was getting bleaker and more industrial. He pulled up in front of a shop with the name 'Hermosa River Auto Supplies and General Stores'. He went in and pulled out two bottles of beer, priced at a dollar fifty each, from the cold cabinet. He went to pay but had to wait, holding one of the chilled bottles in each hand, while the owner, a Mexican bodybuilder, argued with another Latino customer, in Spanish. From what Miller could gather, his fellow client had bought four yards of plastic syphon tubing which he was seeking to return, because it was the wrong gauge; the customer was now trying to negotiate a reduced price for the new length of hose the owner had just cut for him. Their conversation became more animated. In the end, Miller put the bottles down on the counter, took a five-dollar bill from his pocket and waved it in the air. Both men saw him, paused for a moment and then carried on with their argument. Miller took a book of matches from a display on the counter and put it in his trouser pocket. He picked up the bottles, left the folded bill on the counter and walked out. He was half-way to his car when the Mexican owner tore out of the shop and lunged at him. He flung Miller's back into the white-painted brick wall of the store and kept him pinned there, his arms spread out. The Englishman could feel that the bottle in his right hand had shattered, spraying his shirt with cold lager. Even so, in the Mexican's ferocious grip, he couldn't let go of the surviving shard of the neck.

'*Hijo de puta*,' the shop-owner snarled.

'*Que pasa?*'

The Mexican stood back.

Miller, suspecting the man might be armed, kept his hands where they were, wide apart and pressed against the shop wall.

The owner held up the five-dollar bill.

'*No esta bien?*' Miller asked.

Then he noticed that, behind the Mexican's back, the man with the tubing was leaving, on foot, at a speed that suggested he hadn't tendered the full retail price. Miller nodded towards the retreating figure. The owner shrugged. '*Manyana,*' he said.

He waved the five-dollar bill again.

'*No esta bien?*' Miller repeated.

'*Hombre,*' said the Mexican. 'Half a bill, like half a man' – at this last phrase he jabbed his finger in the direction of the sprinting thief – '*he worth nothing.*'

Then Miller saw that the note hadn't been folded, as he thought: it had become soaked with sweat to the point that it had torn in two when he pulled it out of his pocket. He apologized, and put the one good bottle on the ground, then found the other half of the bill, and handed it over. The Mexican took the fragment of broken glass from Miller's right hand, which was bleeding slightly. The store owner examined the cut.

'*No pasa nada,*' he said.

He beckoned Miller back into the shop and went to get him a fresh bottle of beer. Miller tripped up over the original, discarded piece of syphon hose. He picked it up, coiled it, and put it on the counter. The owner opened both bottles. Miller offered one to the Mexican and they stood by the till, drinking.

'You know what he uses this for?' the Mexican said, in English, pointing to the tubing. 'Syphoning honest men's petrol. With a sharp eye and a piece of good hose,' he added, 'you ride free, for life.'

'Except that you have to pay for the tube.'

'That,' the Mexican said, 'is what I was trying to tell him.'

'How much is it by the way?' Miller asked, pointing at the coiled tubing.

'Eight dollars. You want it?'

He nodded, and gave him the money

'I think this should be good for most automobile tanks,' said the Mexican, his voice slightly lowered. 'Juan,' he added, waving in the vague direction of his last customer, 'started doing trucks.'

Miller gave him the money, finished his beer and left. He threw the tubing in the back of his car and checked the level of gas – he still had more than half a tank left. He shifted into drive and set off once more.

He turned into a street called Atlantic Road. A small trickle of blood was still running from his deformed right index finger, where the bottle had cut it. He was heading due west, into the sun, which was right ahead of him, suspended over Tampa Bay. On either side of Atlantic Road there were small, gaily painted clapboard houses. He noticed no businesses except for a pet's beauty store and a funeral parlour. At one point, the road had an intersection with a railroad line, which was unmarked; Miller, who was tired and distracted by the sunset, failed to notice it till he'd crossed the tracks. A few yards further on, however, he realized that his journey – in this direction at least – was over.

Atlantic Road crossed Highway 41, the main road running north to south between Tampa and Sarasota, and ended in a large dirt parking lot, where Miller pulled up. Straight ahead of him were the grey waters of what a sign informed him was the Hermosa River estuary, where it met Tampa Bay. He'd stopped just a few feet from the water, still facing the sun. To his left was a run-down group of tiny wooden cabins, built around a weather-beaten sign that read 'Half Man's Camp'.

But it was the view to his right that captured his attention. A couple of hundred yards away, across the Hermosa, he saw a vast oil refinery, spewing smoke and fumes. Even now, with the light almost gone, you could see the clouds of vapour pouring up into the sky. Miller got out of the car and walked up to the perimeter fence, on his side of the river, only ten yards or so from where he'd parked. He stared through the heavy-duty mesh at the plant. It was the size of a small town. Red flashing lights, set around its ancient, colossal structure, blinked intermittently. At certain points there were chimneys belching soot and yellow flame. It looked like the gates of hell.

To his right, on the bridge that carried Highway 41 across the river, he could see a group of young fishermen with their lines in the water.

Trucks thundered by, just yards from their backs. He wondered if they were desperate enough to eat anything that existed in that water and decided that they must be. They hadn't come here for the scenery. He watched them for a while. The fishermen weren't catching anything, he noticed, probably because they spent so much time fighting over who should have which position on the road bridge. He looked on as one of the figures – a child, much smaller than the rest, but prominently involved in this argument – was struck on the head by one of his companions, so that his rod and line fell into the filthy water and drifted away. The victim ran off the road bridge, down to the riverbank and tried to retrieve the rod but couldn't. The figure turned and started walking towards the Half Man's Camp, behind him. As it approached he saw that it was not a boy but a girl; she was dark-skinned, about nine or ten, and in tears. She was going to walk past him without acknowledging he was there.

'Where's your mother?' he asked her.

'Working.'

'Your father?'

'My dad?'

She pointed in the direction she was walking, and moved on.

Up on the bridge, Miller watched one of the youths take her place. A small outbreak of spiteful laughter reached his ears. He followed her fishing rod as it floated out into Tampa Bay. He could see it quite clearly at first, a ramshackle, home-made contraption. Then he lost it and caught occasional glimpses of its metal handle until it vanished altogether. As the girl retreated into a compound of trailers, at the far end of the row of cabins behind him, he heard a wooden door open, then close. There was the sound of a slap; the small girl's sobbing came louder, then he listened as it faded away, unconsoled.

Miller went back to his car, opened his travel bag and felt for his roll of gaffer tape.

As chance would have it, the transparent tubing was very slightly wider in diameter than the exhaust, so that Miller was able to wedge the two outlets together quite firmly even before he secured the joint with the gaffer tape. When he'd done that, he folded back the last half inch of the unused tape, from habit, so that the end wouldn't get lost. He ran the hose in through the off-side back window. The rear windows weren't electric like the front ones, but operated manually. This made it easy to trap the tubing firmly, but not too tightly, between the door frame and the top of the glass. Miller checked that all the other doors and windows were closed, then got into the driver's seat and shut the door.

He noticed a board fixed to the refinery's perimeter fence: 'Dowson Petrochemicals'. Miller began to calculate the numeric value of the letters in the sign. He spoke them out loud to himself. 'Four,' Miller said. 'Fifteen. Twenty-three.' When he got to S – 'nineteen', he turned on the ignition. 'Fifteen,' he said to himself. 'Fourteen…' He looked at the cut on the maimed index finger of his right hand. Exhaust fumes, he remembered, from his days on the local paper, turned the face of the suicide bright scarlet, the colour of fresh blood. He closed his eyes and breathed in.

It was then that he became aware of a sharp tapping, close to his left ear. Miller opened his eyes and turned his head. He could see the face of a black man, directly opposite him, on the other side of the driver's window. If it hadn't been for the glass, their noses would have been touching. What was strange was that Miller couldn't see the man's shoulders, which meant he must be kneeling on the ground – or, more likely, that he was a hallucination. He shut his eyes once more.

The tapping started again, only this time it was much louder – more of a hammering – and Miller realized that the window was about to shatter. He opened his eyes. The man, his face still in the same position, had stuck a sheet of paper against the windscreen. It was held in place by the wiper. Hastily scrawled, it read: MY BROTHER NEEDS HELP.

Miller wound down the electric window. The fresh air, bizarrely, made him feel sick.

'What is it?' he hissed.

The black face nodded towards the scrap of paper on the windscreen.

'Stand up,' Miller shouted, through the open window.

The man didn't move.

'Stand up,' he repeated, more softly but insistently, 'and then go away.'

Miller wound the window up and closed his eyes once more. The hammering, to his great relief, didn't start again. He felt his mind beginning to drift.

'Why do they need the pipe?' he heard the young girl ask her mother.

'They need the pipe to live.'

He was vaguely aware of a noise. It was the passenger door opening. He heard it close again. Then he felt the pressure of a body sinking back into the seat next to him.

Miller opened his eyes. He looked across at his passenger and saw for the first time that he was a dwarf.

'Fuck off,' said Miller. 'I'm dying.'

The man didn't move.

'What does it feel like?' asked the dwarf.

'What?' said Miller.

'What does it feel like?'

'It... it's none of your fucking business. Go away.'

But his new companion only smiled. He put a hand-rolled cigarette in his mouth and fumbled with an ancient Zippo lighter. He struck the flint once; it didn't spark.

'Don't,' screamed Miller – his voice an octave higher than his normal range – unsure of whether carbon monoxide was explosive.

'Are you mad? You'll...'

The dwarf looked at him. 'Yes?'

Miller turned off the engine and threw his door open. He got out, feeling unsteady on his feet. Holding on to the car for support, he made his way round the back of the vehicle and pulled open the passenger door. The dwarf had lit his cigarette. He stayed where he was, smoking it.

'OK,' Miller shouted at him. 'You've fucked up my plan for the evening. What's yours?'

'My brother,' the dwarf said, slowly, in a Latino accent, 'needs help.'

Miller sighed.

'Where is he?' he snapped.

He leaned against the roof of the car and closed his eyes for a moment. As he did this, the dwarf slipped out, wrenched the tubing from the exhaust and threw it into the river, where it floated away to join the fishing rod.

'Come,' he said, and held out his hand.

The dwarf led him away from the car and across the dirt parking lot, towards the back of a single-storey concrete building. Miller followed him round to the front entrance, which was on Highway 41. Above the main door there was a hand-painted sign. Badly faded and surrounded by red light bulbs, mostly blown, it read 'American Show Bar'.

The dwarf stood waiting for him on the diner's front porch, holding the door open. Miller, feeling dizzy and nauseous, sat down by the side of the highway to catch his breath. He stayed there on the ground, his legs crossed and his head bowed, for a couple of minutes, as cars and trucks thundered by him on their way south to Sarasota. When he looked up again, the dwarf was in the same position, waiting patiently in the doorway. The Englishman got to his feet and headed unsteadily up a ramp to the front porch.

Inside, the Show Bar was large, much too hot, and very dark. Three dim lamps hung over a circular bar in the centre of the room. In a far corner, he could see the dining area – a few formica-topped tables surrounded by orange plastic chairs – which had an overhead strip light, and a sign reading 'Frankie's Diner'. There was a pink neon tube in the antiquated jukebox. A spotlight, suspended from the low ceiling above the zinc bar counter, was not switched on. As he followed his rescuer across the room, Miller paused to examine a crudely painted picture on a wall to his right. It showed the devil in a ringmaster's outfit; he was holding a whip and tormenting beasts and men in a sawdust arena which was shrouded in mist and illuminated by forked lightning. The title, written in fluorescent green letters on a black strip at the bottom of the canvas, was *The Great Ringmaster in the Sky*. Sitting alone, at a table immediately beneath the painting, was the fattest woman he had ever seen in his life. Her teeth were embedded in a cheeseburger. He caught her eye as he passed.

'You wondering if it's glandular, honey?' she shouted after him, with her mouth full. 'Well it isn't. It rarely is.'

The round bar had a couple of dozen stools around it, less than half of which were occupied. The dwarf hoisted himself into one of the vacant chairs, which were bound together at the base by what looked like anchor chain, presumably to discourage theft. Miller sat down next to him, on his right.

Nothing, even in the feverishly enhanced reality of his own news pages, had prepared Miller for the sight of his fellow patrons at the American Show Bar. Glancing to his left, beyond the dwarf, he saw two elderly men. Each had an oxygen cylinder, strapped to a kind of shopping trolley, which they had parked against the bar. They kept the clear plastic masks over their faces, removing them only to speak, drink, or – in the case of the nearest one – to draw on a cigar. Between them was another customer who appeared unable to talk at all. He was contributing to their conversation with improvised sign language, and by scribbling on a roll of toilet paper. Across the counter from Miller was a man in an eye patch and pale blond dreadlocks who – though clearly a Negro – was also albino.

Behind the bar he saw a lidless coffin filled with ice, which served as the cold box for bottled beer. Standing next to it was the barmaid. She was dark, Latino-looking, with striking, delicate features and a full mouth whose top lip was split and discoloured by recently clotted blood. But it wasn't her face that caught his attention, so much as her clothes: the young woman was dressed head to foot in some kind of white linen, cut into a high-necked tunic and trousers, of a kind Miller had previously seen only in photographs of old men in India. Her hands were completely covered in long gloves of the same material, bound to her forearms by white cotton ties. Once she'd served a customer, he noticed, she gravitated back towards the coffin, like a workman returning to his brazier.

'What do you want?' the dwarf asked him.

'What?'

Miller was distracted, wondering if he was witnessing a vision of hell or the real thing.

'What do you want to drink?'

The Englishman stared ahead of him, at the coffin.

'Beer.'

His accent provoked a ripple of interest among the other guests. The

Fat Lady, her hands empty, but still chewing the last mouthful of her burger, left her alcove and moved to a stool across the bar, next to the albino. The emphysema sufferers fell as silent as the mute and stared at him openly. Miller, shocked back into focusing on the external world, turned away from them, to his right. There – sitting on the customers' side of the bar but within reach of the till, in a high-backed leather stool with armrests – was a man in his late forties, surveying the premises with an unmistakably proprietorial eye. He was mainly bald; what hair he had was grey and plastered back with sweat. His short-sleeved white shirt revealed his muscular arms, twice as thick as Miller's; it was covered in grease, oil, and faint stains in various shades of yellow. Unlike his patrons, who had bottles of beer, or regular glasses, the owner was drinking from a plastic orange beaker. He waved it at the barmaid, who filled it with Maker's Mark whisky and ice, without speaking. On the landlord's immediate right, a grossly obese young man was taking delivery of a Grand Marnier and Coca-Cola.

Miller kept his eyes on the owner's face, in an attempt to distract himself from the bizarre appearance of his customers, rather in the way that a seasick passenger will try to fix their eyes on a stable point in the cabin. Then he looked down, and saw that the man had no legs. Miller stared vacantly at the place where his limbs should have been, then raised his eyes so that they met the owner's, which had an expression of deep contempt.

'What is it?' the legless man snapped. 'You never saw a freak before?'

'Yes,' said Miller. 'I mean, no.'

Behind them, the main door opened. Four youths burst in, shouting and squabbling among themselves. Miller recognized them as the boys he'd seen on the bridge. One, the biggest, who couldn't have been more than fifteen, was holding a live fish by its tail, which he'd wrapped in a handkerchief to stop it escaping. His catch, which was a foot long, was wriggling madly, though it must have been out of the water for several minutes. He presented it to the bar owner. The man nudged his fat companion, who left his stool and disappeared behind the bar for a moment. He returned with a small toolbox and what looked like a breadboard, but was twice as thick. The legless man took the fish, held it flat, against the wood, and produced a hammer. Miller watched at he drove a two-inch nail through the base of the fish's spine, where its flesh met the tail fin, pinning it to the board, which he placed on the bar counter. The fish struggled with renewed frenzy, arching its body at grotesque angles. Thin bubbles of blood formed around the nail, at the spot where it had been impaled.

Miller leaned towards the black dwarf.

'Who's he?' he asked, nodding discreetly towards the owner.

'The Half Man,' whispered the dwarf. 'The boss.'

The Englishman looked back at the fish, which was still flapping violently. He clutched at the bar, feeling faint.

'Who's this, Paul?' the barmaid asked the dwarf, pointing at Miller. She had a deep, gentle voice, and a slight Hispanic accent.

'This,' he replied, 'is my brother.'

He winked at Miller and looked at the woman as though he was hoping that she might smile. She didn't.

'What's wrong with him?'

'Don't worry darling,' the Half Man interrupted. 'This guy's fine. It's just that he's not from here. Where he comes from, there's something they don't have, that we do.'

He paused to light a Marlboro.

'Which is it?' he asked Miller.

'What?'

The Half Man drained his orange beaker and handed it back to the girl, who refilled it. Miller watched as a rivulet of sweat ran off the man's brow, down the side of his nose, and dripped off his top lip, on to his shirt-front.

'Which thing is it,' he repeated, 'that you don't have, where you come from. Manners, or cripples?'

Miller was gazing at the coffin full of ice, wondering how to respond to this when, to his great relief, the owner was distracted by another new arrival. A priest came in, very tentatively, carrying a collection box for a cancer charity. The clergyman, a frail, grey-haired man of sixty or so, wearing his preacher's robes, made his way slowly around the circle of drinkers, his tin tilted at an inviting angle. His only contribution came from the black dwarf, who dropped in a quarter. The two men breathing oxygen removed their masks momentarily, to mutter obscenities at the supplicant as he passed. The mute, presented with the collecting tin, scribbled him a note. The priest examined it, then passed on. Craning his neck to read it, Miller made out the words: 'Hit the pike.'

The clergyman didn't approach the owner but then, as he was turning to leave, he noticed the impaled fish and gave the Half Man a pitying glance. His host took his cigarette and extinguished it in the eye of the fish, which went on flapping.

'Have a drink, Father,' the Half Man said.

The priest hesitated.

'Go on,' the owner added, in an ominous tone of mock civility. 'Be my guest.'

The visitor turned to the barmaid.

'I'll have an iced tea please, Frankie.'

'Sweet?' she asked him.

He nodded.

Miller swallowed the last of his bottle of beer.

'Get the Father a wine, Hunter,' the owner said to his fat protector.

'I don't drink,' said the priest, quietly. 'As you know.'

Hunter eased his bulk off the stool once more, went behind the bar and poured a large glass of red from an unmarked gallon pitcher. He placed it in front of the priest, who didn't touch it.

'King…' The owner called to the albino, who went to stand in front of the main exit door. Immediately above it, Miller noticed, was a narrow shelf that held a handful of bottles of wines and spirits. The priest remained where he was, standing at the bar, holding his collecting tin, contemplating the glass of wine. The Half Man turned his attention back to Miller.

'Where are you from?' he asked.

'England.'

'You know – it's a funny thing,' the owner said. 'I never killed a guy from England.'

'Have you killed a lot of foreigners?' Miller asked, exasperated to the point that he allowed an undisguised sneer to enter his voice.

'Yes.'

Miller looked at the half-blind, gasping fish.

'Would you have a military background,' he asked, 'by any chance?'

'No,' the man replied. 'Not by any chance.'

The fish gave a last, terrible shudder, as though it had been plugged in to the mains, and stopped moving. The albino left his post at the door, picked up the wooden board, and put it in a fridge behind the bar. Miller shut his eyes, breathed in deeply, and sighed.

'I sense that my restaurant disappoints you in some way,' said the owner. He turned to the priest.

'You've been to Europe, Father.'

The clergyman nodded.

'I have been to Rome.'

'Is there any place in Europe,' his host asked, 'like here?'

The priest, seeing the exit unattended, didn't reply, but turned and walked towards it as fast as he could, carrying his tin box. The Half Man leaned across the counter, put his hand in the till and removed a quarter, which he threw so that it landed just behind the clergyman, halting him in his tracks, just as he reached the door. He turned around.

'Pick it up,' said the owner.

The priest stooped and collected the coin.

'Now come here.'

The man returned to the counter.

'I just asked you a question,' the Half Man said. 'Is there any town in Europe like here? Tell me, Father...' As he said this, the owner raised his hand, indicating his clients – the sick, the crippled and the congenitally malformed. 'What's the opposite of Lourdes?'

Hunter, the Fat Lady and the albino rocked with glee. The invalids took off their oxygen masks to join in. The mute smiled and raised his glass. Only the woman in white, Miller, and the black dwarf didn't laugh. The owner held out his hand for the quarter; the priest returned it; his fingers, Miller noticed, were shaking.

The Half Man whispered something to Hunter, who took the coin and put it in the jukebox. There was a pause, then the room was filled with the sound of Frank Sinatra singing 'It Had To Be You'.

'They're playing our song sweetheart,' the owner told the barmaid. Her expression didn't alter. She opened her purse, her hands still gloved, and took out a dollar bill. Before she handed it to the priest, she looked at the Half Man, who shrugged, then nodded.

'Go now,' she whispered to the clergyman.

But the legless man grasped the priest's upper arm with one large, muscular hand, preventing him from moving.

'I'm going to let you out of here,' he said. 'Because I can never say no to Frankie. Whatever she asks me for, I have to give it to her. All except for one thing. Ask me what that one thing is, Father.'

There was no reply.

The Half Man released his grip, reached over the counter and produced what – owing to its compact design and modern, silver and black finish – Miller didn't at first recognize as a gun. He pointed it at the clergyman's knees.

'What is it?' said the priest, in a level, expressionless voice.

'Mercy,' said the owner.

'May God have mercy on you, Vincent.'

'Does he have mercy on you?'

'On us all.'

'Does he protect you,' the owner continued, his gun still trained on the clergyman's knees, 'in your hour of danger?'

'That is my belief.'

The priest turned and walked towards the door. When he was one stride short of the exit, the Half Man, with no more apparent effort than a channel-hopper operating a remote control, raised his weapon and shot a bottle of Maker's Mark off the shelf above the door, drenching the clergyman in Bourbon and broken glass. The minister turned round to face the owner. Whisky was running off his nose and into his robes and his collection tin.

'Stay where you are, motherfucker,' said the Half Man, pointing the pistol at the priest's head.

His victim didn't move; Miller noticed that he had stopped shaking. The owner looked along the shelf above the door.

'You never drank your wine,' he said.

'No,' replied the priest.

'What was it – white or red?'

Drawing no response, he shattered a bottle of chardonnay, then one of shiraz. His next bullet brought down a catering-size bottle of coffee cream liqueur, leaving his visitor bathed in a viscous cocktail of alcohol. Seeing that the priest was turning to leave, the Half Man covered his eyes with his left hand and shot in his direction without looking; the bullet splintered the door frame, inches from the retreating cleric's head. The preacher disappeared into the night.

'The son of a bitch was right,' the Half Man said. 'God does protect him.'

The remark drew enthusiastic applause from his clients. From where he was sitting, the owner could see the priest through a window, as he climbed into his vehicle, in his sodden robes.

'My God,' said Hunter, 'that car's going to stink of booze.'

The Half Man watched the Father's tail lights disappear north up Highway 41 towards Tampa.

'That your car?' he asked Miller, who had to lean back in his chair to see what the owner was pointing at – his gold Cavalier, still parked on the Show Bar's dirt lot, where he'd left it.

'Yes.'

'You ever get pulled over for driving drunk?'

'No,' said Miller. 'Why?'

The owner called over the tall youth who'd brought him the fish and said something to him; the boy disappeared, with his companions.

'I asked Hunter and his friends to go call the Highway Patrol,' he announced, 'and get the reverend pulled over for a suspected DUI.'

There was more laughter. The Half Man didn't join in but frowned slightly.

'Now,' he said, turning to Miller, 'where were we, before all that?'

The man had the eerie calm of a true psychotic. The revolver was still in his hand. Miller, who, twenty minutes earlier, had been contemplating death with equanimity, felt his heartbeat begin to quicken.

'You were saying,' he said, as respectfully as he could manage, 'that you have no military background.'

'Oh, that's right.' The Half Man gave him a look of cold ferocity. 'But tell me – just help me out on this – *what would an army want with me?*'

The barmaid approached the owner, and put a hand on his shoulder. He pushed her away, hard. She retreated to her place, by the coffin.

Miller hesitated. 'I just thought you might have…'

'Yes?'

The Englishman didn't reply.

'Got my poor Southern ass shot off in Saigon, and gone crazy? You little prick.'

He drained the orange cup in his left hand, keeping the revolver in his right.

'Come here.'

Miller didn't move. Then he felt the black dwarf tapping his left elbow, urging him to comply. He glanced over at the exit. The albino was obstructing it again, standing in the pool of wine, sweet liqueur and broken glass. He winked at Miller with his one good eye.

The Englishman got up and walked towards the owner. When he was within a couple of feet of him, the legless man grabbed Miller, spun him round and pinned his left arm up his back, so viciously that he thought it would snap. He shut his eyes and gasped in pain; as he did so the Half Man, still propped on his specially adapted bar stool, behind Miller's back, rammed his pistol into his mouth, shattering his right front tooth. The barrel of the revolver, which his assailant was holding upside down, so that the trigger guard was touching Miller's upper lip, was at the back of his throat. He tried to breathe through his nose but, with the gun touching his epiglottis, he felt himself beginning to gag. The Half Man, sensing this, eased the pistol back slightly, in such a way that it scraped against the exposed root of the broken tooth. Miller thought he would pass out from the pain.

'Forgive me,' his host said, like a caring dentist. 'Is that better?'

The barrel of the weapon was pointing directly up into the Englishman's palate. He closed his eyes. He could taste blood, gun metal and a flavour of acrid carbon from the recently discharged weapon. He could smell stale sweat from the armpit of the Half Man's shirt. Pieces of tooth had lodged under his tongue. The room had gone very quiet. From the direction of Highway 41, he heard the sounds of distant lawlessness – joy-riding, shouted threats and screams.

With his eyes still shut, Miller became aware of heat and light on his face. He half-opened his eyes for a second and saw that Hunter had turned on the stage spotlight hanging over the bar, and was angling it so that it pointed directly at him. Squinting through the glare, he saw that every patron in the bar was on their feet. They were standing a few yards from him, in a tight semicircle, absorbed. The albino was shading his eye against the light with his forearm.

'I have no military experience,' said the Half Man. 'But I do know how to handle a gun. As I am now going to demonstrate,' he added, 'by pulling this trigger.'

Miller felt the Half Man's right knuckle, which was pressing against his upper lip, adjust its position as he tightened his finger.

For the second time in his adult life, he lost control of his bladder. He felt the urine flood into the thin beige trousers he'd bought for his first day at Oxbridge House. A small stream ran out of the bottom of his left trouser leg, over his shoe. The Half Man laughed, but kept his weapon steady.

'King,' he shouted, 'get a mop and pail. And fetch a sheet.'

Miller heard the footsteps of the albino, setting off.

'No – not a sheet,' the Half Man shouted after him. 'Sheets.'

The footsteps stopped.

'How many?' asked the King.

'All of them.'

'That's the King,' the owner said.

He pressed the gun much harder into the roof of Miller's mouth.

'As I was saying, I, like you, have no military experience.'

The Half Man pulled the trigger. There was a dull click.

'But in common with an able-bodied soldier, and each of my friends here tonight, I know a Khar MK40 when I see one, and I am aware that it takes five rounds, not six, of ammunition.'

He took the gun out of Miller's mouth, but kept his arm pinned up his back. The Englishman opened his eyes. Not daring to move his head, he allowed the broken fragments of tooth to fall from the side of his mouth, in a small cascade of blood and saliva which dribbled on to his shirt-front. The spotlight, he noticed, was still on him, but had been readjusted so that it was trained on his sopping groin.

'Fear,' said the Half Man, to the spectators, 'like courage, takes many forms.'

The albino appeared with a mop and bucket and began to clean the floor. Miller shifted his feet slightly.

'Stay where the fuck you are,' said the Half Man.

The one-eyed man mopped his shoes.

'When people like you,' he added, 'start asking me how I got this way, I tell them I will explain so long as they are happy to reveal the most terrible and humiliating thing that has ever happened to them in their life. That's a fair bargain isn't it…' He paused.

'What's your name?'

'Edward,' said Miller, without thinking.

'That's a fair exchange isn't it, Ed?'

Miller said nothing.

'Cigarette?'

He nodded. The Half Man put a Marlboro between his victim's lips. He released his grip on the Englishman's left arm, which fell limply against his side. With his right hand, Miller tried to feel in his pocket for his box of matches but couldn't get his hand into the cold, clinging cotton.

'Allow me,' said his host.

Miller turned round to face him, his cigarette still between his lips.

The Half Man reached behind the till and produced not a match but another revolver, identical to the first, which he pointed at the visitor's forehead.

Miller began to shake, uncontrollably.

'What are you asking yourself now, Ed?' the Half Man asked.

'I'm asking myself...'

'...whether this might be a novelty cigarette lighter?' said the Half Man.

Miller, still trembling violently, did his best to nod.

'From what you know of me, Ed, do I look like the sort of man who would carry a novelty cigarette lighter?'

'No,' he mumbled, the unlit Marlboro still between his lips.

The owner pressed the barrel of the gun against Miller's forehead. He closed his eyes. The Half Man pulled the trigger.

Feeling nothing, he opened his eyes and saw a thin butane flame coming from the top of the weapon. He was shaking too violently for his host to light his cigarette; instead the owner took it out of Miller's mouth, lit it himself, and handed it back to him.

As his trembling began to subside, the pain in his tooth seemed to increase.

'Next time you feel like coming to my place to fuck with me in front of my people,' said the Half Man, 'either think twice or else bring what you need. Bring your diapers.'

'Or my gun,' said Miller. He was still in shock and spoke without thinking. He regretted the remark the instant he'd made it, but it didn't precipitate the renewal of violence he'd anticipated.

'Or a gun,' said the Half Man, inclining his head, like a teacher acknowledging a correction from a pupil. 'At least with a gun you would die like a man. Not like a fucking weeping baby.'

'I don't weep,' said Miller. 'I have never wept.'

The spotlight was still on his thighs.

The Half Man laughed. His voice took on the resonant tone of a sideshow pitch man.

'He wets his pants and drools, ladies and gentlemen, and he trembles like a San Francisco hamster, but Eddie doesn't weep.'

'Now,' the Half Man continued, 'where was I before all this...'

'The most humiliating experience,' the albino said, enjoying himself.

'That's right,' said the Half Man. 'Thank you King. Now Ed – think hard now – what is the single most humiliating thing that has happened to you?'

Miller paused.

'Is it recent?' the owner asked, with no irony in his voice.

'Recent?' For a second, Miller, casting his mind back over the events of the past few weeks, could almost have laughed. 'Oh, it's recent. It's definitely recent.'

He saw the legless man staring at him, still waiting for a reply.

'What I mean is,' Miller said, realizing what he wanted to hear, 'it's this.'

'OK,' said the Half Man. 'It's this. Thank you for sharing that with us Ed. So I will tell you, in turn, that I was born this way in Greenville, South Carolina, to a horrified mother and a father who disowned me. The foetus – my foetus – became entangled with the umbilical cord in such a way that the blood supply was cut off to my legs, so that my body never developed below the waist. Is that enough for you Ed? No? My cock...'

'Stop,' said Miller.

'My cock,' he repeated, 'is normal. Perhaps you would like to see it?'

'No.'

'That's right boy,' said the Half Man. 'That's it. Now you're learning. Now you're settling in.'

Miller sat down on his stool, still in his wet trousers, the blood congealing against his shirt.

'Will you do something for me Ed?' the owner asked.

'Yes,' said Miller, too fast, like a bad actor.

'Little Paul needs a hand with his tow truck tomorrow, on a job he's doing for me – can you help him?'

Miller nodded.

The girl behind the bar handed him another beer. Miller began to drink it, but when the cold liquid hit his broken tooth, he winced and put it down. He looked around the room, where what passed for normal conversation had resumed. Some of the other customers were gathered round the window behind the Half Man. From outside, Miller heard a noise that sounded like a combination boiler kicking into life; there was a rousing cheer from the onlookers in the bar.

'What's that?' he asked the Half Man.

'It'll be the kids,' he said, 'torching a car. It keeps them happy.'

Miller, bruised and defeated though he was, managed a reproachful look.

'Don't you want to look?' the owner said. 'Does that kind of thing not interest you?'

Miller shook his head.

'Oh, but it should,' said the Half Man. 'This car was yours.'

Miller walked over to the window and saw the anglers from the bridge standing around the blazing shell of his rented Cavalier. One of them was urinating on the flames.

'You look shocked,' said the Half Man. 'Don't be. It is legal in the state of Florida to urinate against the driver's side of a stationary vehicle.'

There was another outbreak of coarse laughter from his entourage.

'Everything I had was in that car.'

'What do you mean,' Vincent said, 'everything?'

'My passport. My credit card. My money. Everything.'

'Think of it as a dead weight lifted.'

'What?'

'Life is much less burdensome,' added the Half Man, 'when, in the eyes of the law, you don't officially exist. It's the simplest thing in the world to disappear.' He looked at his watch.

'Hey,' he shouted. 'Hunter...'

He motioned to the Fat Boy who, with the help of the albino, lifted him into an electric wheelchair, which the Half Man drove across the room and out the front door to the ramp, without saying goodbye.

When he'd gone, the dark woman behind the bar handed Miller an empty glass and a bottle of brandy, then came out from behind the round bar and disappeared through a door next to the food counter on the far side of the room. He poured a small measure and swallowed it, then tried to hold a mouthful of the alcohol against the throbbing nerve in what was left of his front tooth.

The girl, still wearing her outfit of white cotton and gloves, came back holding a pair of navy blue shorts, made out of thin cotton, and a white T-shirt, which she handed to him. She reached under the counter and pulled out a plastic garbage bag.

'Put your other stuff in there,' she said.

Miller went to the men's room to change. There were three cubicles which, like Eton, had no doors on them. He went into the middle one, and began to struggle out of his wet trousers. He saw Paul, the black dwarf, who had followed him in, disappear into the cubicle on his right.

'Why,' Miller asked, through the toilet wall, 'did you bring me to meet that fucking madman?'

'The Half Man's not that bad,' came the reply.

'*What?*' Miller asked. 'Not that bad? Compared to who?'

'To whom,' said a deep American voice, from the other cubicle.

Miller left his cubicle and walked in to the dwarf's; he found Paul sitting on the toilet with the lid down, smoking and fully clothed. The Englishman jabbed his thumb in the direction of the unknown voice.

'Who the fuck is that?' he asked.

'That's Officer Glidden,' said Paul. 'He's our neighbourhood police officer.'

'Was he in there just now?' asked Miller. 'In the bar? When he… when I… was being… you know…'

'Yes,' said the dwarf.

Miller gave a snort.

'And he's a police officer. OK. I see. Right.'

'No – he is,' said the dwarf.

'I am,' said the voice.

'Oh Jesus,' said Miller. 'Oh Jesus Christ.'

'Welcome to Arlington,' said the dwarf.

Miller put his soiled clothes, including his shoes and socks, in the garbage bag and handed it over to the barmaid. He returned to the bar stool barefoot, in his T-shirt and borrowed shorts, which were a size too large, and continued trying to dull his toothache with brandy. After midnight the bar was crowded with new arrivals – among them jugglers, animal trainers and truck drivers – all, so far as he could tell, involved in the circus business. The Half Man's albino protector returned. The conversations around Miller grew increasingly bizarre. Paul, his rescuer, became embroiled in an angry dispute with the Fat Lady over how many people, if any, could dine off a peacock.

'A peacock,' the dwarf told her, 'is tiny. It has a heart the size of a watch battery.'

'Bull-shit,' said the Fat Lady.

'From a peacock,' the dwarf insisted, 'you couldn't get one edible meatball.'

'You could get three meatballs,' she argued. 'Big ones. You could juggle them.'

'If you can juggle them,' the dwarf said, with a look of triumph, 'then they ain't edible.'

The elderly Wurlitzer, which still cost only a quarter a song, was in constant use. It dated back to the early sixties and, unlike later models, had no mechanism to prevent a customer selecting consecutive performances of the same song; Miller counted four successive renditions of 'Take This Job and Shove It (I Ain't Working Here No More)'. This was followed by six plays of Roy Rogers 'Hold That Critter Down', which his fellow customers sang along with, led by the King.

'God I love that song,' said the albino. 'I'm going to put it on again.'

'Where are you going to stay?' the girl in white asked him, as Rogers started up for a seventh time.

'Stay?' he repeated.

He resolved to leave there and then, but with no transport, footwear or money, he quickly thought better of it.

'I don't know.'

'He could stay in Twelve,' said Paul.

'*Twelve?*' the woman replied.

'It's empty,' said the dwarf.

'It's empty,' the girl said, 'because Vincent has been using it for er...' She looked at Miller. 'How should I put it...'

'Hogs,' said Paul. 'But the hogs,' he added, 'are gone now.'

He tugged at Miller's sleeve.

'The hogs have been gone for a while. Come on. It'll do for tonight. We'll clean it up tomorrow.'

He led Miller through the kitchen area and out of the back door. In the parking lot, to their right, his car was still smouldering. Straight ahead of them there were a couple of dozen wooden cabins, not much bigger than beach chalets. The huts were arranged either side of a narrow dirt road that ran along the back of the Show Bar, parallel to 41: every one was painted white and had a tiny front porch, just large enough to accommodate a couple of chairs. And yet each of these shacks, as he gathered from the loud grinding of the air-conditioning units hanging from their back walls, served as somebody's permanent residence.

'I live there,' said the dwarf. 'In Three.'

Twelve was across the dirt road, in the middle of the row further from the bar. Its air-conditioning unit was hanging off and the door had been left open. Paul found a broom, which he rattled around in the empty cabin for a minute or so, keeping his feet outside.

'What are you looking for?' Miller asked.

'Snakes.'

Miller rested one of his bare feet on the other.

'Were there any?'

'No. Keep the door shut, you'll be OK. Warm,' the dwarf laughed, 'but OK.'

Inside, there was an old single mattress standing upright against the wall; Paul pulled it down and laid it on the floor.

'There,' he said. 'We'll fix it up properly tomorrow.'

Tomorrow, Miller thought. The word had never held so little promise. And yet this day of trauma, distress and crude aggression had not intensified his desire to die, but extinguished it altogether.

When the dwarf left, he settled down on the mattress. He could feel insects biting him on his face, shaven head and on his exposed arms and legs. His tooth ached. In the distance, he could make out the locals still singing:

'Hold that critter down... Hold him down, tan his hide...'

Fatigue overcame the discomfort caused by his injury, the mosquitoes, and the memory of the evening's events, and in a few minutes – lying on his back, with his mouth open, so as to avoid his tongue aggravating the raw nerve in his broken tooth – he fell asleep.

He woke the following morning to the rattle and hum of the air conditioning in neighbouring cabins, and the sound of running water. The humidity and the sun beating down on the roof had turned his own hut into a miniature Turkish bath. Sitting on the edge of his mattress in his borrowed shorts and T-shirt, his feet on the wooden floor, he noticed that his limbs were covered in bites. Some were from mosquitoes; others, on his legs mainly, were far larger than any he had seen before. He ran his finger over a couple of these swellings, on his right knee; they had the shape and consistency of semi-embedded scarlet cherries. He turned up one leg of his navy shorts to see if he'd been bitten under his clothes and found a flea, which he brushed away with a shudder. As he did so, he caught his tooth against his lower lip and felt the pain surge through his whole body, like electricity.

He got to his feet and opened the door. In the dust road between the two rows of cabins, Paul, the dwarf, had spread out an old bed sheet. He was kneeling on it, assembling what looked like some sort of large, hand-held sander. From where he stood, looking beyond the opposite row of cabins, Miller could see the door that led into the kitchen of the Show Bar. The sound of water was coming from a shower unit which had been built on to the outside of the building, next to this back entrance. It had brick walls, about five feet high, but no roof. He could see the shower head and, under it, the top of Frankie's head, in profile. She hadn't noticed him; he kept his eyes on her for more than a minute. In all that time she stood there, unblinking and motionless.

Miller stepped out of his cabin. When Paul saw him, he put down his oil can.

'Hey,' he said. 'What happened to you?'

'I think it was fleas,' said Miller.

'You want to use the shower?'

He nodded, and glanced in the direction of the running water.

'Not that one,' Paul said. 'That's Frankie's.'

He pointed towards an elevated standpipe, similar to the kind once used for watering steam trains. Beneath it was an improvised cubicle made from khaki sheets of canvas stretched over a three-sided wooden frame. It looked like a beaten army's latrine.

Miller went in and took off his T-shirt and shorts. He began to wash as best he could in the mean trickle of water, already lukewarm from the sun. A black hand appeared between two of the canvas sheets, holding a piece of carbolic. As Miller scrubbed himself with it, he saw two more fleas make their maddened escape from his left armpit. He trod his clothes like grapes, then turned the water off and wrung them out. He put the wet shorts back on, came out and draped the T-shirt on a bush to dry.

His mattress, he noticed, had been dumped in the dirt, outside Cabin Twelve. The dwarf was in the hut, using a spray gun.

'What's that?' Miller asked.

'Paraffin,' said Paul. 'That'll drive the bugs out. We'll burn the bed later, OK?'

He produced a pair of soiled black canvas shoes. Miller tried them on.

'Frankie sent these for you,' Paul said. 'Do they fit?'

'A bit tight.'

'They'll wear in,' said the dwarf. 'Just give them time.'

Miller glanced towards the road, thinking of escape, then remembered again that he had no transport and no money.

Paul pointed to an empty Coca-Cola bottle, standing on Miller's front porch.

'If you need water,' he said, 'you can fill that from the shower pump.'

'What time is it?' the Englishman asked.

The dwarf, who was not wearing a watch, looked at the sun. Though it was very hot already, it was low in the sky.

'Eight,' he said. 'Maybe eight fifteen.'

Miller, his back to his cabin, turned to his left and saw the wreck of his rental car near the bank of the river, opposite the oil refinery. Though the windows had cracked and the bodywork was blackened, the number plate on the back of the car was still legible.

Paul followed his gaze and gave Miller a sympathetic look.

'You wanna go fish?' he asked.

'What?'

'I only have one line,' said the dwarf. 'You can use it.'

'No, said Miller. 'It's OK. You go. You have it. I can't fish.'

Paul looked disappointed, then started to walk away. Watching him go, Miller began to contemplate his alternative diversions, including another audience with the Half Man.

'I can't fish,' he said. 'But I can watch.'

They walked past the buckled shell of the Cavalier and sat down in the dust on the edge of the Hermosa River, opposite Dowson's refinery. Across the water, the company's land was surrounded by barbed-wire fences, security cameras and incrementally threatening notices.

The dwarf opened a small tobacco tin, took out a wilting maggot and baited his hook. They were on the estuary of the Hermosa, where it entered Tampa Bay. To their right, a couple of miles further up the coast to the north, Miller could see another cluster of factory chimneys, disgorging thick smoke into the otherwise cloudless sky.

'What's that?' he asked.

'That's the power station,' the dwarf said, 'up at Big Bend.'

'Christ,' Miller said. He looked back at the fumes belching from Dowson's. 'Do people grow up around here?'

'Sure they do.'

'Did you?'

'No.'

'I...' A note of pride had entered Paul's voice, but he broke off when he noticed a fish coming towards them, on the surface of the water. It was on its side. The dwarf looked at it hopefully for a moment. It was very dead.

'Where did you grow up, Paul?'

'Mount Holly, New Jersey,' he replied. 'My dad,' he added, 'used to wash dishes at the Robin's Nest. You been there?'

'No,' said Miller.

'It's the most expensive place in Mount Holly. They get all those high-class people, you know...'

'Which high-class people?'

'High-class – you know – teachers. Office people. Bank tellers. Dinner there,' Paul said, 'costs like eight dollars – I mean that was ten, fifteen years ago – today… it must cost like fifteen, twenty dollars.'

He noticed Miller looking unamazed.

'That was for one person – not the whole table.'

'Was your father…' Miller stopped.

'My dad was normal,' said the dwarf. 'Like you.'

Miller kept his eye on the dead fish, which was floating across the bay towards Tampa. He wondered how it had died, and began to torment himself with memories of the previous evening.

'What's the most you ever spent on a dinner?' Paul asked.

'Pardon?'

'What's the most you ever spent…'

'I don't know. I can't remember.'

'Come on. You must.'

'I don't. Maybe a thousand pounds,' Miller lied, keeping the bill on the small side.

'How much is that?'

'Fifteen hundred dollars.'

The dwarf looked at him in disbelief.

'How many people?'

'Two.'

Paul stared at the point where his line met the water and slackened the tension slightly; a gesture which, Miller hoped, signalled the end of this strand of conversation.

'Where?' the dwarf asked.

'In London.'

'Fifteen hundred dollars,' he said. 'I never saw fifteen hundred dollars.'

Miller felt increasingly uncomfortable.

'What kind of fish…' He began to ask, pointing at the disappearing corpse.

'What did you eat?' the dwarf interrupted.

'I don't know… steak.'

'Steak? You mean like – regular steak? Like we have here? Meat?'

'Yes.'

'From a cow?'

'Yes. Listen...'

'What did you drink?'

'Wine,' said Miller. 'It was the wine,' he said, 'that was really expensive.'

'How much?'

'I can't remember. Three hundred pounds?' he added, again subtracting a generous discount from the real price of the Château Pétrus.

'How much is that?'

'Five hundred dollars.'

'For how much wine?'

'A bottle.'

The dwarf took his eyes off the water. As he looked up, a small fish approached the hook, nimbly stole his bait, then darted off.

'Hey,' said Miller, pointing at the water.

The dwarf ignored his line and scrutinized Miller, as if trying to detect what lasting effects such a valuable drink might have on a man. He fell silent for a few moments.

'What does it taste like?' he asked.

'Have you ever had wine?'

The dwarf nodded.

'I tried it once, in the Show Bar. I didn't like it. But the Show Bar wine is like a buck fifty a pint,' he said. 'And it's American,' he said. 'Not English.'

Miller shut his eyes.

'It wasn't English.'

'Where did it come from?' Paul asked. His eyes were on the horizon, as though he was wondering whether the price of Miller's wine could be explained by the costs of transportation from a distant solar system.

'France.'

Miller scratched one of the large round bites on his legs. It began to itch more savagely. The stump of his tooth throbbed.

'They must have some great wine there in France, huh?' Paul said.
'Yes.'
'I mean that wine – it must be – it can't just be good; it has to be real... shit, that French wine, it has to be...'
'Listen,' Miller snapped. 'Shut up about the fucking wine. How the fuck do I get out of this place?'
The dwarf returned his eyes to the water. When he looked up again, Miller noticed, he seemed hurt.
'The Half Man told me to get you to help shift the car,' he said, quietly.
'Fuck the car,' said Miller. 'I'm leaving.'
The dwarf looked at his companion's worn shoes, bitten body and damp, borrowed shorts.
'How?'
'I don't know. I'll hitch.'
'Where to?'
Paul reached into his pocket and opened another tobacco tin, identical to his maggot holder, and offered it to his companion. Miller peered in, apprehensively. It contained three hand-rolled cigarettes. He took one. The dwarf lit his own, then passed Miller his matches.
'Trust me. You don't want to leave. Not yet.'
'Why not?'
'Because the Half Man asked you to stay.'
'And?'
'And if you leave, he'll find you. And you won't like that.'
Miller lit his cigarette. A pickup arrived and stopped close to the bank of the river, twenty yards away from them. The driver, an elderly woman, climbed out and cast her own line into the water. She gave them a wave, which the dwarf returned.
'Who's that?' Miller asked.
'That's the Wolf Lady.'
'Why...' the Englishman began to ask. Then he noticed what appeared to be in the back of the truck.
'What's that?'
'It's a wolf.'

'A wolf.'
'Right.'
'What percentage wolf?'
'It's a wolf,' said Paul. 'That's a hundred, right?'
'Is it tame?' asked Miller, looking at the animal which, so far as he could see, wasn't tethered.
'No. Don't look it in the eye. Look at it sideways. If you look it in the eye, that's a challenge.'
'Paul?'
'Yes.'
'What is this place?'
'What do you mean?'
'The wolf. The Fat Lady. The Half Man. You.'
'Everyone on this part of the coast,' the dwarf replied, 'they're all carnies.'
'Carnies?'
'Sideshow people. Freaks. Ride operators. Animal trainers.'
'Why?' Miller asked.
'It's been that way in all the towns round here for fifty years,' Paul said. 'Ever since Al Tomaini built the Giants Camp, up in Gibsonton.' He pointed north, up 41.
'Did you have a car?' he asked Miller.
'What?'
'Did you have a car?'
'I had one,' the Englishman replied, 'until your mate trashed it.'
'No, I mean – in London.'
'Yes.'
'What kind?'
'A Mercedes.'
'What colour?'
'Silver. Look...'
'Yes?' said the dwarf.
'Who is Al Tomaini?'
'Al was the giant,' Paul said. 'He was married to Jeannie, the Half Lady.'

'Was she a relative of Vincent's?'

'No. Jeannie...' The dwarf lowered his voice. 'Jeannie *was* a lady.'

He impaled another maggot, which looked already dead from heatstroke, on his hook and cast his line again, further into the river this time.

'They're both dead, like the rest of the freaks. Melvin Burkhart, the Human Blockhead; Percilla, the Monkey Girl. There's just a few of us left now.'

'But you stay here.'

'Because we don't get bothered. We look out for each other. We don't have things like... the things that they have in Tampa and Orlando.'

'Like?'

'Like zoning restrictions on what animals you can keep. Like people who stare. People who beat up on us.'

They fell silent for a while. Down the river, the Wolf Lady landed a fish. She knocked it dead against her fender, and put it in a cool box. She took out a bottle of Coca-Cola, opened it, then cast her line again. Paul looked on, enviously.

'Did you have a wife?' he asked, suddenly.

'For fuck's sake,' said Miller. 'Wouldn't it be quicker if I told you what I didn't have?'

The dwarf hesitated, then gave a look of renewed curiosity.

'OK,' he said, with no hint of sarcasm or malice. 'What didn't you have?'

'I had everything,' said Miller. He closed his eyes.

'Let's shift the car,' said the dwarf.

They walked back across the parking lot and between the two rows of cabins. The rear of the Show Bar was on their left; ahead of them, beyond the huts, was a compound containing two large trailers, fenced off from the rest of the camp.

'That's the Half Man's place,' Paul said. 'You wait here. I need to get something.'

Miller picked up his T-shirt from the bush where he'd left it; he pulled it on, still damp, as he walked back to Cabin Twelve. On the front porch he found a package, neatly wrapped in clear polythene: inside were his shirt, socks and trousers, washed and pressed. Next to it were his shoes, in a brown paper bag. He looked towards the Show Bar and saw Frankie, still standing under the shower. He walked over to her.

Only her head was visible over the brick wall of the small outhouse.

'Thank you,' he said.

'What?'

'For my clothes.'

'That's OK.' Water ran down her face but she never raised her hands, as most would, to wipe the drops away from her dark eyes, which she kept half-open.

'Jesus,' she said. 'What happened to you?'

'What?'

'You look like you have chicken pox.'

'I had fleas,' he said.

'Don't worry,' she told him. 'We'll fix that. Will you do something for me?'

'Yes,' Miller replied without thinking, as had become his habit.

'Go to the kitchen,' she said. 'And get me some ice.'

He went through the open door and opened the chest freezer. It was filled with packages of ice the size of coal sacks. He carried one outside.

'Empty it in there,' she said, tilting her head to indicate a storage tank on the Show Bar's flat roof. A ladder was propped against the side of the building.

'All of it?'

'All of it.'

'Why?'

'That tank feeds the shower.'

He put his left hand on the ladder, keeping the ice clasped to his chest with his right.

'And since you're British, I don't need to tell you…'

'What?'

'Not to look, right?'

'No.'

He climbed the ladder, stood on the roof, and emptied the ice in.

'Ed?'

It was the dwarf, at the foot of the ladder, looking up at him. He was holding an extension lead and a toolbox.

'Give me a hand with this will you?'

They carried the things over to the car. Paul used a crowbar to open the bonnet, which had twisted and buckled in the flames. Then he fetched the piece of equipment he'd been cleaning earlier, on the soiled sheet.

'What's this?' Miller asked.

'It's a power grinder,' the dwarf said. He showed Miller how to pull the trigger that turned the machine on – it made a noise like a chainsaw – then pointed at a metal plate in the engine. There was a number stamped into it.

'Now grind that off,' he said.

'Why?'

'So that when we dump this,' Paul said, 'nobody knows where it comes from.'

'Oh. Why me?'

'Because the Half Man said it should be you.'

Miller took the grinder, held it against the identification plate and pulled the trigger. The vibration shook his body so violently that it made his bites itch. He turned his head to one side, trying not to inhale the rising cloud of finely powdered steel. Removing the serial number was a slow and tortuous process. The dwarf watched him for a while, then disappeared into the Half Man's compound. When he came back, he prised off the car's licence plate, then knocked the cracked glass out of the vehicle's windows, using a small hammer.

'Why are you doing that?' Miller asked, switching off his grinder for a moment.

'The safety glass can make it harder to sink,' Paul said. 'And it has the licence number stamped into it.'

The dwarf leaned into the bonnet and peered at the identification plate, then ran his finger over it.

'Right,' he said. 'That'll do. Come on.'

He took Miller round to the back of the Half Man's trailer, where there was a tow truck, a purple Tacona pick-up, and a couple of other battered cars. They climbed in to the lorry, which had been fitted with hand controls for accelerator and brake. The dwarf turned the key, which was in the ignition.

'Isn't he worried about anybody stealing it?'

'Steal the Half Man's truck?' Paul laughed.

He steered the vehicle out of the compound, down the track between the cabins, and parked it next to the Cavalier. They fixed two lines to the underside of the chassis and the dwarf winched the car so that it was tilted over, with the underside exposed. Taking turns, they ground off the chassis number.

Paul hoisted the Cavalier on to the back of the truck and motioned to Miller to get in. They drove a couple of miles up 41 to a deserted area of Tampa Bay, near the power station at Big Bend. The dwarf turned left off the highway, down a rough road, then backed the truck through an area of long grass, until the car was hanging over the water.

'Why here?' asked Miller.

'It's real deep. And nobody comes here.'

The dwarf pointed to a red button in the middle of the dashboard.

'Push that,' he said.

'What does that do?'

'It drops it.'

'Why me?'

'Like I told you, the Half Man said.'

Miller turned and looked at the car, dangling over the river. He pressed the button, releasing the grab hooks at the end of the winch. The wreck fell and sank into the grey water. They got out and watched as the last broken tail light disappeared from view.

'Shit,' said Paul.

'What?'

'Look.'

A half-melted section of foam from one of the seats had come adrift and was floating.

'Can you get that?' Paul asked. 'It's too deep for me there. And I can't swim.'

Miller, still in bare feet, didn't trouble to remove his shirt or shorts. He walked through the long grass, slipped into the water and swam a few strokes to the seat, which he retrieved. Paul threw it in the back of the truck.

'We'll torch that later,' he said. 'With your mattress.'

The Englishman, dripping with river water, got back into the passenger seat. Paul stayed by the bank for a couple of minutes, waiting to see if anything else would surface. Miller kept his eyes on the red button in the dashboard. Pressing it, he realized, had brought a new, alarming, dimension to his life. Until then, he'd imagined that his situation might in some way be retrievable; that he could ultimately return to the orthodox existence he'd left behind. It was a choice that, subconsciously at least, had seemed available, if daunting, in the same way that, in the first couple of reels of a Hitchcock film, the hero generally has the option of going to the authorities. ('How can you respect this bugger,' he remembered Elizabeth saying, in the early days of their relationship, watching Robert Donat in *The Thirty-Nine Steps*, 'when he doesn't just pick up that bloody phone and dial 999?')

Now, he reflected, he faced arrest for arson, should he return to the UK, and he had just colluded in a crime that, since the car was hired in his name, would render him of interest to the federal authorities in the US.

Paul drove them back to the Half Man's compound, stopping on the way to pick up the mattress lying outside Cabin Twelve. They dragged it to a patch of waste ground, a safe distance from Vincent's trailers and parked vehicles. The dwarf set fire to it with paraffin, throwing on the car seat once the mattress was well alight.

Miller walked back towards his cabin. To his surprise, Frankie was still under the shower.

'Hey,' she shouted. 'Go into Twelve, OK?'

'Why?' he asked.

'I'm coming out.'

He went back into his cabin. It reeked of paraffin. There was a new mattress, laid on what looked like a prison bedstead, made of iron, and a pair of sheets – ragged, but clean. His neatly laundered clothes had disappeared. The door opened.

The woman was standing there, in the same kind of linen costume she'd been wearing the previous evening. She was holding a blue towel, a roll of lint, and a large bottle of Listerine. Just for a moment, Miller forgot his predicament and was fully occupied by the beauty of her face: her high cheekbones; her large, almost impossibly dark eyes. Her split upper lip had still not healed.

'Take your shirt off,' she said.

Her voice was low, resonant and had a naturally hoarse tone he'd noticed in some women in Spain. She spoke softly, and with very little inflection, as though she was pronouncing each word, however banal, for the first time, and slightly amazed at its beauty. Each time she spoke, Miller found himself stopping what he was doing; there was some quality in her voice that seemed to connect directly with his spine.

Frankie handed him the towel and he dried his back and shoulders.

'Where's my stuff?' he asked her.

'Your what?'

'My shoes. My clothes.'

'I don't know, Ed,' she said. 'I got all those things cleaned up, then I left them right here.'

'Well, they've gone.'

Standing behind him, she removed her right glove, which she dropped on to the bed, and used the lint to apply the mouthwash to the bites on his back. Miller felt the itching begin to ease.

'Why do you use mouthwash?' he asked.

'It works,' she said. 'And it's cheaper than the other stuff.'

When she'd finished his back, she handed him the bottle and the lint.

'You can do the rest, right?'

She bent down to pick up her glove.

'Oh hang on,' she said. 'You have a tick on your ankle.'

'A what?'

Miller looked down and saw a red insect, inflated with blood to the size of a chick pea, among the half-cherries covering his legs. He went to brush it off. She grabbed his right hand with hers.

'Don't,' she said.

Miller felt her palm, against his wrist. He looked down at her hand; her skin was rough and dry, like the flaking scales of a salted fish. Towards her fingertips, the dead skin turned dark grey. When she let go, he noticed that her palm was marked not with the delicate lines and whorls he'd expected, but with coarse, red furrows.

Their eyes met but Miller said nothing.

'Don't what?' he asked her.

'Don't brush it off,' she said. 'Or the head will stay in, and then rot.'

Frankie put her glove back on.

She fetched a can of paraffin and poured a little on his leg. The parasite fell off.

'How long,' Miller asked, 'were you under that cold shower?'

'A couple of hours,' she said. 'With a break.'

'You do that most days?'

'Right.'

She looked at him, as though challenging him to pry further. He didn't.

'How's your tooth?'

He opened his mouth.

'Jesus,' she said. 'I'll get the doc to come out to you.'

'The doc?'

'Right.'

'Is he a dentist?'

'No. He's a doctor. Well – that is...'

'He isn't?' Miller suggested.

'No, he is.'

He looked at her, suspiciously.

'Well, OK – he was.'

When she'd gone, Miller daubed himself with Listerine. The dwarf appeared at the door.

'The Half Man,' he said, 'wants to see you.'

Miller pulled on his T-shirt and followed Paul into the compound. They passed the first of the Half Man's two trailers – his living quarters, the Englishman guessed, from the curtains in the windows and the washing line outside – and turned right towards his second. It was L-shaped, like the first, but far larger and surrounded by remnants of electrical wiring, old car batteries, and rusting engine parts.

He followed Paul through the door, into a welding shop. Miller noticed a bumper car, raised on a small hydraulic ramp. The Half Man was sitting in what looked like an old barber's chair, applying an oxy-acetylene cutter to the safety bar of a car from a child's ride: it was a rabbit, painted pink, with a wide, inane grin. He had a welding mask on and, what with the flame and the showers of sparks, he hadn't seen Miller come in. He was in the same sweat-stained shirt he'd been wearing the night before. Here, in his mask, surrounded by twisted machine parts and the smell of red-hot metal, bearing down with his flame on the pink rabbit, Miller thought, Vincent could never have looked more demonic. At the back of the workshop he saw Hunter, the Half Man's protector, talking to the albino with the eye patch.

Vincent noticed Miller and Paul. He turned off his blowtorch and tilted back his mask.

'Ed,' he said.

'Yes?'

'Good morning.'

On the wall behind the Half Man, there was a Hustler calendar; Miller glanced at the picture of a naked woman with her legs wide apart and a python wrapped round one ankle. Vincent caught his eye; the Englishman looked away and said nothing. The work bench, he noticed, was equipped with two soldering irons, both turned on and glowing red, supported in vertical, insulated holders. Next to them were pliers, a set of screwdrivers, the Half Man's revolver and a crudely painted figurine of Jesus Christ.

'Morning,' said Miller.

'Sleep well?'

'No.'

'The bugs got you, huh?'

'Yes.'

Vincent laughed.

'The bugs are just like us I guess. They like the scent of new blood.'

The Half Man pointed at the girl with the python.

'Do you find our artwork in poor taste?'

Miller didn't reply.

'King?'

The Half Man motioned to the albino, who removed the calendar and placed it face down on the work bench.

'Thank you King,' said Vincent.

The albino opened a cupboard across the room and returned holding another picture, which he pinned up in the calendar's place.

Miller glanced at it. Blown up to sixteen by twelve, it was a black-and-white photograph of him grinding the number off the engine mounting of his rental car, whose registration plate was still in place and clearly legible. He looked at the Half Man, in shock.

'How...'

The albino held up a telephoto lens.

'The King enjoys taking pictures,' said the Half Man. 'He has an eye for it, as the saying goes. He does his own developing. How many prints do you have of that, King?'

'Six,' replied the albino.

'It's one of his sidelines. You have a few other sidelines, don't you King?'

There was no reply.

'Do you like it?' the Half Man asked Miller, pointing to the photograph. 'I do.' He lit a Marlboro. 'I like pictures. I always have.

They're the best way for memories to be preserved.' He fixed his guest with a stare. 'Or shared.'

Miller put his face in his hands.

'I fixed your air con for you by the way,' the Half Man said.

'Thank you.'

'Will you do something for me, Ed?'

'Yes,' he replied.

The Half Man pointed to a two-gallon can of white paint, and a brush.

'Take these,' he said, 'and paint the inside of Twelve.'

'What then?'

'Then ask Paul.'

He went back to his cabin, pulled out the mattress and the table, and began painting the rough wooden boards of the walls and ceiling.

'Do the cracks good,' Paul shouted, from outside.

'What?'

'The bugs hide in the cracks.' He pointed at the tin. 'That stuff's medicated.'

'Where are my clean clothes?' he asked the dwarf.

Paul shifted uncomfortably.

'Go on,' said Miller.

'I was talking to the King just now.'

'Right.'

'And he said the Half Man had him, er…'

'Yes?'

'Throw them in the river.'

Miller put the final touches to his painting. This last piece of news left him strangely undisturbed. Just as suicides lose the will to die during wartime, so the speed and extreme nature of recent events had rekindled his determination to survive. He turned his air conditioning on. It added its own raucous note to the rasping chorus from the other cabin. Like a new boy at school, he thought, he had arrived.

Miller put down his paintbrush, came out of the hut and filled his Coca-Cola bottle from the shower pump. He walked around to investigate the light scrubland at the back of his own hut and followed a path that led to a fenced enclosure. There, under a makeshift canopy, he saw a circus banner, twelve feet long by six high. The picture – fully sketched in outline but only half-painted – showed a woman with large breasts, in what looked like a snakeskin body suit. The girl who had lost her fishing rod was sitting on top of a pair of stepladders, filling in the colours of the woman's flesh, in green and purple. Each section of the picture, even the smallest, had been shaded in around its border but not completed, rather as an adult might prepare a paint-by-numbers book for a child too young to negotiate intricate shapes. The girl was painting in the main blocks of colour that required less delicacy of touch. He approached her from behind: she was wearing a baseball hat and, like him, a white T-shirt and navy shorts. She had cropped dark hair and bare feet. She held her paintbrush in her right hand and a lighted Marlboro in her left. As he got near, he noticed the lettering that ran across the full width of the picture: 'The Amazing Lizard Woman'.

'Who's that?' he asked her, pointing at the figure.

'That's my mom,' she said.

'Who?'

'That's my mom.' She stopped painting, and looked down at him. 'That's Frankie. You're Ed, right?'

'How do you know?'

'My mom told me.'

'Does your mum really look like that?'

She laughed.

'You talk funny.'

'Does she?'

'No. Well... no. Not exactly.'

She put her cigarette in her mouth and stretched down her left hand. 'I'm Alex,' she said.

'Short for Alexandra?'

'Alexis.'

She started painting again, with her cigarette dangling from her lower lip. Miller sat on the bottom rung, watching her work. Both of the girl's feet were bandaged; what skin he could see was covered in deep, long-healed scars and more recent ugly gashes. The left one was heavily bandaged around the heel.

'How old are you Alex?' he asked her.

'Nine.'

'Don't you go to school?'

She shook her head.

'Why not?'

'My dad,' she said, 'fixed that.'

'Who's your dad?' he asked her.

'Vincent.'

He reached up and pointed to her bandaged foot.

'How did that happen?'

She indicated another pair of stepladders, propped against the wire fencing of the enclosure. They were similar to the ones she was sitting on, except that there were blades where the rungs should have been, their sharp edges tilted upwards.

'What is it?' she said. 'You never saw a sword ladder before?'

'No.'

He walked over and touched one blade, nicking his finger so that it bled.

'You walk up that?'

'Uh-huh.'

'Barefoot?'

'Right.'

'Is it possible?'

'Sure it is,' she said. 'With practice.'

'So what's that?' he asked her, pointing at the wounds on her feet.

'That?' She laughed. 'That's practice.'

'And your dad lets you do this?'

'My dad makes me do this.'

'Can I have a cigarette?' he asked her.

'Sure. Take two.'

He started to walk back up the path.

'Hey,' the girl called. 'You need a hat, right?'

She threw him her baseball cap. It was in black-and-white check and carried the slogan 'Bama 100'.

'Don't worry,' she shouted. 'We have lots.'

He adjusted the strap for size, put it on and went back to his cabin.

Inside, the dwarf was standing on the bedside table, screwing a light bulb into a fitting on the ceiling.

'I got you a clock,' he said, pointing at a cheap, battery-operated alarm, by his feet.

Paul got down, and turned the light on at the switch by the head of the bed.

'Not bad, huh?' he said.

Miller didn't reply.

'I mean – I don't have a shade. I know it's not much to a guy who drank five-hundred-dollar wine...'

'No,' said Miller. 'It's good. It's great. Thank you.'

'That's OK,' said Paul, looking pleased. 'You're welcome. I haven't fixed a lock on the door yet.'

'I don't think I need one,' said Miller, looking around at the contents of his shack.

'You do,' Paul said. 'Hey, listen,' he added, 'the Half Man...'

'Yes?' the Englishman interrupted, looking apprehensive.

'No,' said the dwarf. 'Don't worry – this is good. The Half Man wants you to help in the kitchen, with Frankie.'

'Oh,' said Miller. 'Is that good?'

'Good? It's great. It's much cooler in the kitchen. You get food,' he said, 'and cold water, maybe juice. I'd love to get to work in the kitchen.'

'But you never do.'

'No.'

'So why,' asked Miller, 'does the Half Man want me there?'

'He got the idea right after I told him about the fifteen-hundred-dollar steak,' said the dwarf, 'and the English wine.'

'French,' said Miller.

'French. Right.'
'But I can't cook.'
'If I was you,' Paul said, 'I would never tell him that.'
'But won't Frankie notice?'
'I guess.'
'And won't that matter?'
'No.'
'Why not?'
'Because Frankie's a good kid. Because Frankie's OK.'
Miller gestured in the direction of Alexis.
'And that's her daughter.'
'Right.'
'Vincent's child.'
'Yes. Keep your voice down.'
'And she walks that ladder?'
'Yes. She's a self-made freak.'
'She's a what?'
'She's a...'
Paul turned and saw the King approaching; his already alarming appearance now completed by the addition of a white Stetson. He walked over to speak to him, and then came back.
'The boss says go help Frankie,' Paul said.
The Englishman nodded but didn't move.
'Now,' shouted the King, as he disappeared into the Half Man's compound.
'What are his other sidelines?' Miller asked. 'Apart from photography.'
'Killing,' Paul said. 'That's one of them. Or it used to be.'
Miller got up, and walked over to the kitchen.

When he came in, her back was turned to him; she was dicing carrots at the sink, still in her white tunic, blue rubber gloves over her linen ones.

'Hi Ed,' she said, without turning round.

'How did you know it was me?' Miller asked her. 'Were you looking in a mirror?'

'Do you see any mirrors in here?'

'No.'

Frankie handed him a small cleaver and pointed at a large basket full of onions on a marble-topped table in the centre of the room.

'Chop those, will you?'

He sawed the top off the first onion and began to peel it, a laborious process which had got no easier since the last time he remembered attempting it, when he was trying to impress Elizabeth with a ratatouille, fifteen years earlier. In the end he made a deep cut right around the circumference and pulled off two thick white layers. Frankie watched him and said nothing.

She pointed at his hat.

'So you met Alex?'

'Right.'

He cut the onion in half. His eyes stung.

'I want to ask you something,' he said.

'Personal?'

'Yes.'

'Go ahead,' she said. 'I guess that's only fair – I mean I watched you piss your pants last night.'

He sighed.

'I used to know a guy who talked like you,' she said.

'Oh?'

'Yeah. He knew a lot.'

Miller began to struggle with another onion.

Frankie took a carrot, laid it flat on a chopping board and, rotating it, cut it deftly into small triangular pieces, which she threw into a pan.

'And he talked like me?'

'Right. He wasn't like you though.'

'Why?'

'Because he thought he knew everything.'

'How do you know I'm not like that?'

'That's easy,' she said. 'Because you have a question for me.'

'What's wrong with your hand?' he asked her.

She took off her rubber glove and held out her right arm, so that the ties that secured her cotton glove were facing him.

'Go on,' she said.

He undid the lace and pulled off her glove. The skin on the back of her hand was parched and flaking, as he'd noticed before. She turned her hand over and he looked at the thick red lines on her palm. She pulled back her shirt sleeve: her forearm was in the same condition. Miller struggled to keep the shock out of his expression, and couldn't.

'Not pretty, is it?'

'What is it?' Miller asked her.

'It's ichthyosis', she said.

'Is it curable?'

She put her knife down and turned to face him.

'Hey, you know what – I've never asked myself that,' she said. 'Maybe I should mention it to the doc next time I see him, what do you think? I never have.'

'I'm sorry,' he said.

'That's OK.'

'And Vincent exhibits you.'

'*I* exhibit,' she said. She pulled her glove back on. He tied it for her.

'Listen honey – let me tell you – you look like me and you put on a bikini, or even a skirt, and you'll get stared at anyhow, on the midway or any place else, believe me. You might as well get paid for it, huh? Don't you think?'

'No,' said Miller. 'What's the midway?'

'*Hoder*,' she said.

'Steady,' said Miller.

'OK,' she told him. 'That's two things I know about you.'

'What things?'

'You speak Spanish, and you can't cook.'

'I'm afraid not.'

'That's OK. You cut an onion like this.'

She picked up a cleaver and diced the vegetable in a couple of dozen swift, dexterous movements. Miller tried to imitate her and cut his left hand. She threw him a box of blue Band-Aids.

'Where are you from?' he asked her, in Spanish.

'I'm from Tehuantepec,' she replied, in English. 'Cut your onions. And never, ever, speak Spanish to me.'

'Why?'

'Because Vincent doesn't like it.'

'Why?'

'Because Vincent doesn't speak Spanish.'

'No?'

'No. And he doesn't like me to speak Spanish.'

'Why not?' asked Miller, his eyes streaming from the sliced onions. He struggled with his cleaver.

'Don't you know that song – "She Never Spoke Spanish to Me"?'

'No.'

'Well it's on the jukebox. He thinks that, for me, speaking Spanish has to do with love.'

'Is he right?' Miller asked.

'No. For me, it has to do with trust. And faith. And commitment.'

'Why don't your eyes run?' he asked her.

'Our tear ducts are blocked,' she said. 'Like our pores. We never cry, and we don't lose heat through our skin.'

'So Florida in mid-July is not such a great place to be.'

'Florida is about the worst place in the world to be, any time. The shower helps.'

Miller soaked a teatowel and pressed it to his eyes.

'Why did he put me in the kitchen?'

'Vincent?' I guess he thinks it's humiliating for a man. And up to a point it is,' she said. 'The way you do it.'

He raised his finger towards her cut and swollen lip.
'How did that happen?'
'I fell,' she said.
She caught his look.
'Well all right then,' she asked him. 'What would you say?'

Exhausted, Miller fell asleep in his cabin at nine that night, untroubled by the thought of his unlocked door, the noise from his air conditioning, or the dull ache in his broken front tooth. He was woken by a gentle tapping. It was still dark. He sat upright. In the distance he could hear the noise of barking dogs, racing engines and fighting. He got up, switched on his bare light bulb and pulled on his navy shorts. He opened the door slightly, keeping his shoulder braced against it.

Standing outside, in the shaft of light from the doorway, was a man of about forty, with shoulder-length grey hair and blue eyes. The first thing Miller noticed about him was that he looked extraordinarily clean. His long-sleeved white shirt had been carefully ironed. His grey chinos were spotless and neatly pressed. A pair of tortoiseshell reading glasses hung around his neck. Miller opened the door fully and stood back.

'Good morning,' said his visitor.

'What time is it?'

The man consulted a silver pocket watch, which for some reason Miller found very reassuring.

'It's just after one.'

Then he noticed that the stranger was carrying two old-fashioned metal camera cases.

'Do you take photographs?' Miller asked, with a homicidal look.

The stranger smiled, and shook his head. 'Edward Miller?'

The Englishman nodded.

'I'm John Kennedy,' the stranger said.

Miller looked blank.

'John Kennedy.' He lowered his voice. 'Dr Kennedy.'

Miller let him in, and closed the door. They sat down, side by side on the bed.

'Is this the kind of time you usually make house calls?' he asked.

'Yes,' Kennedy replied. He opened one of the cases; it was full of neatly packed medical equipment.

'Frankie tells me you've lost a tooth.'

Miller raised his top lip to reveal his jagged stump. Kennedy took out a hypodermic and a pair of small pliers. The inside of their jaws was lined with serrated rubber. He tilted his patient's head back and shifted Miller's shoulders so that his open mouth was facing the light.

'Your other front tooth's badly cracked,' he said. 'I'm going to take them both out.'

'Have you ever, er…' Miller began.

'What?'

'Have you ever done any dental work before?'

'Oh yes,' said Kennedy. 'Lots of times. Several hundred.'

'Good.'

'Only on horses so far.'

'What?'

'But I opened a fortune cookie last week, at the Chinese restaurant next to the stables and it told me that I'm ready to branch out and have a go at people now. That said…'

Miller glared at Kennedy. He noticed for the first time that he had a slight Glaswegian accent.

'You are more than welcome to consult another practitioner, though I doubt if you'll find another one who makes cabin visits free, between the hours of one and five a.m.'

His patient said nothing.

Kennedy held his hypodermic up to the light.

'Listen,' he said. 'Dentists are all failed doctors. Like me.'

Miller closed his eyes, opened his mouth again and prepared himself for the pain from the needle, but felt none.

'All right,' said Kennedy. 'That's in. We'll give it five minutes.'

He took out two cigars – Havanas, not the cheap Swisher Sweets they smoked in the Show Bar – and handed one to his patient. They stood together outside the cabin, looking towards Dowson's refinery. Thick whorls of smoke rose from their cigars, to join the dense clouds that poured incessantly from the distant chimneys. Kennedy nodded towards the complex, with its blinking red lights and security cameras.

'God damn this town,' he said.

Miller felt his top lip beginning to tingle.

'I've never seen so many car wrecks,' Kennedy said. 'And heart failure. And... how should I put it... sudden and involuntary perforation. Thankfully I'm no longer required to attend to dead bodies.'

'Why not?'

'Because I am disbarred.'

'You're Frankie's doctor.'

'Yes.'

They went back into the hut and Kennedy rested the two cigars on the edge of the bedside table. He pulled on a pair of surgical gloves and picked up the pliers.

'Can I ask you something?' said Miller.

'Sure.'

'What is it that she has?'

'Frankie?' The doctor placed the jaws of the pliers around Miller's broken tooth. He put his hand against his patient's forehead.

'Frankie has...'

He drew the teeth in two smooth, almost graceful movements, and produced a packet of Kleenex.

'... ichthyosis.'

Miller, holding the tissues, opened the door, and spat blood on to the ground.

'What is it?'

Kennedy went out to his car and returned with a large medical dictionary. While Miller stood in the doorway, spitting blood, he put on his reading glasses.

'*Ichthyosis Vulgaris*,' he read, '... onset of condition typically in early childhood... inflammation and permanent obstruction of the pores... polygonal scales, pigmented on distil extremities... tendency to chronic fever may result in seizures... distinctly worse in hot and humid climates... long-term course – lifelong... The face,' he continued, 'and the genital region, are generally spared.'

'Spared,' Kennedy repeated. 'What a terrible word, in that context.'

'What context?'

'The context,' he said, 'of what you are.'

The doctor picked up the cigars, which had burned a stain into the edge of the small table, handed Miller's to him, and re-lit it.

'Actually,' he went on, coaxing his own Havana back to life, 'it's a very rare condition. Frankie is even more unusual in that she has it fairly mildly. It can be…' he turned back to the dictionary. 'What's the word they use. Oh yes. "Malodorous". Which it isn't in her case. Her arms and lower legs are bad. When they put her in the shows, she wears a lot of make-up, so that it looks more drastic, and some sort of body suit.'

'Good God,' said Miller.

'It's interesting you should say that. When I was a medical student in Philadelphia, I remember being taken to a hospital in Baltimore to examine a dying specimen of what is known as a Harlequin. Do you know what that is?'

'No.'

'It sounds quite attractive, doesn't it?' Kennedy said. 'Harlequin Syndrome is a form of icthyosis that affects the foetus. The child is born enveloped in a hideous thick scale of membrane, covering the whole body, split by deep fissures, with these ghastly holes around the eyes, like in a terrorist's balaclava. The survival rate is mercifully poor: the patient – one of the few dignified nouns the Harlequin will ever inspire in its short life – will generally survive for no more than a few days. It was when I set eyes on that child in the Johns Hopkins Hospital,' he added, 'that I began to consider the possibility that God hates us.'

He put the syringe into a disposal bag.

'Have you seen yourself in a mirror?' he asked Miller.

'No.'

'As a visual aid, you could do the work of five men at a parasitology seminar,' he said.

'What?'

'Bed bug,' said Kennedy, pointing at the sunken cherries on Miller's legs. He looked over his other bites. 'Tick. Mosquito. Flea. By the way did you know,' he went on, 'that when a flea launches itself towards a target, its leap is the equivalent of a human jumping over an object sixteen times the height of St Paul's Cathedral?'

'I didn't.'

'The curious thing is that they have absolutely no control over the power – it's just like unleashing a coiled spring. They aim, then – once they decide to go – it's all or nothing. Which means that they often soar over their objective – the dog, or whatever – and land on the other side.' Kennedy laughed. 'They got you OK though.'

He gave Miller a tube of antiseptic cream.

'Can you cure it?'

'What – a flea bite?'

'No – icthy—'

'No. We can alleviate, and, to an extent, contain.'

'Is it contagious?'

'No. And it isn't necessarily hereditary. Why do you ask?'

'Because,' said Miller, 'I'm working with Frankie. In the kitchen.'

Kennedy frowned slightly.

'I won't ask what brought a man of your obvious education here,' he said.

Miller blew out cigar smoke, and said nothing.

'But allow me to advise you. It pays to be careful in any town,' he said. 'And in some towns, especially so. Vincent Makin is not alone in taking gratuitous pleasure in the pain of others,' he continued. 'As you will be aware if you are familiar with modern American cinema. Where he is unusual – unique, possibly, at this time, in this country – is that his circumstances allow him free rein to indulge that interest in public. I understand you've had some experience of that.'

'Yes,' said Miller.

'Try not to dwell on it,' said Kennedy. 'Last night was just one of those things.'

'What do you mean?'

'You came in on a Saturday; he had all his guys around him. If you'd come in the previous night – on Friday – you'd have been fine. Friday nights he just sits in his trailer, drinking and doing his books. Friday night the King is never here. So. You were unlucky. And he's unlikely to repeat that pattern of behaviour with you, unless you deliberately provoke him.'

'Why?'

'Why? Because now he has something on you. If it helps, he's done far worse.'

'Worse?'

'Yes.'

'Such as?'

'He especially enjoys blinding things.'

'Why?'

'Well I guess you don't need to be Sigmund Freud to work that one out, Edward. When others are blind, he is normal.'

'Blinding "things",' Miller asked. 'What things?'

'Well, you'd better ask him that,' Kennedy replied. 'Should you ever find yourself tiring of life.' He looked his patient in the eye. 'Again.'

'How do you know about that?'

'In Arlington,' Kennedy replied, 'it's hard to keep anything to oneself.' He took out another syringe.

'*Oneself?*' Miller repeated. 'What the hell are you doing here?'

'As you may have noticed, Makin rules this community through fear,' Kennedy continued, as if he hadn't heard him. 'This camp is one of the few areas in the United States where the inhabitants' constitutional right to bear arms has been suspended.'

'Except for him,' Miller said.

'Right. But guns aren't the key to his power, although they help. The key to his power,' he added, 'is that he has something on all of them.' He paused. 'On all of us. I was an outstanding medical student. When I qualified as a physician, I had every quality a doctor could wish for in the United States – a good retentive memory, interpersonal skills, a steady hand, no embarrassment at handling money and a slight Scottish accent, from my father. The Scots, in the consulting room, are like the Brazilians on a soccer field. They bring the world to heel.'

'What were you disbarred for?'

'I began my career as house physician at an institution for the criminally insane in Orlando,' said Kennedy. 'After a while it started to get to me. So I went into private practice in Sarasota, where I discovered I could charge two hundred bucks an hour. So I did. Until I indecently assaulted one of my female patients.'

Miller gave a disapproving look.

'Oh, it's very common, believe me,' said Kennedy. 'Many doctors do it. Some get caught. The problem, as with other prohibited vices, is that one develops a taste for it. The first time it happened to me, she was a fourteen-year-old Jewish girl. She didn't exactly discourage me, not that that matters... and then, again like others in my profession, I have certain...'

He tied up his own left arm and picked up the new syringe.

'What's that?' Miller asked.

'Diamorphine,' said Kennedy. 'Heroin. Which I am taking this evening, out of respect to you, in a practically homeopathic dose.'

'Why?'

'Because a reduced dosage,' Miller looked away as his visitor found a vein, and depressed the plunger, 'allows me to remain alert. It's very rare, these days, that I have the opportunity to meet a man of education. I appreciate conversation.'

Kennedy, still sitting on the mattress, eased his back against the cabin wall, like a man lowering himself into a warm bath. His eyes were half-closed. As Miller watched him, some instinct from his days as a journalist was urging him to make the most of an interviewee in a state of limited resistance.

'How many times did you sexually assault patients?' he asked.

'God knows,' said Kennedy. 'I was happily married until the first one. Then the trouble I had was that – this happened gradually – but in the end I found I could only become physically aroused by somebody who was...'

'A fourteen-year-old Jewish girl?'

'No. A patient. Any patient.'

'What?' Miller got to his feet.

Kennedy smiled. 'Female patient. In any case you don't need to worry. Malpractice is a privilege reserved for the qualified. Regular doctors can afford mistakes. When you operate illegally, in medicine as in other areas of life, your standards have to be beyond reproach.'

'Did Frankie ask you to come here tonight?'

'Yes. Frankie and me are sort of... bonded.'

'What?'

'We share a secret relating to some... treatment I gave her. Revelation of which,' Kennedy added, 'would guarantee our mutual destruction.' He opened his eyes, but didn't sit up. 'Would you like to know what it is?'

'Yes.'

'Vincent Makin is terribly keen on having another child – an heir, as you might say. He's obsessed with it. I should imagine that he prays for it, in his way.'

'An heir? To what? What about Alexis?'

'Well, he wanted Alex in the business; that's why he's got her doing the sword ladder. He told me he thinks it's the best she can do – as she is.'

'What do you mean, as she is?'

'He's always saying he'd like her to be more different.'

'Different?'

'You know – different. Not as others. Crippled. Or blind. And if Alex can't be blind, what he'd really like is another child to inherit one of the parental disorders. Or preferably both.'

'To put on show.'

'Right. And to watch, as it suffers. And yet somehow,' Kennedy continued, 'however hard he tries, it never quite seems to happen. Nor will it.'

'What?' said Miller. 'Why? Oh. Right. I see.'

'If he ever found out I'd operated on Frankie,' said the doctor, 'he'd kill us all.'

'You mean "us both".'

'I mean "all",' Kennedy said. 'Because now you know too.'

'Why is he like this?'

'He told me that his dad beat him. His dad beat his mother. His mother beat him. His mother beat his dad...'

'Has he killed people?'

'Vincent? Yes.'

'How many?'

'That's hard to say. He invited his cousin's fiancé round to his trailer, the night before their wedding, and shot him.'

'Dead?'

'Yes.'

'How did he get off?'

'He claimed that the guy attacked him because of his deformity. He's very good in court.'

'He must be,' said Miller.

'And he had a lot of witnesses,' Kennedy added, 'who were very convincing. Especially when one considers that most of them never witnessed anything. As the prosecuting attorney said, their evidence was "quite incredibly consistent". Every possible person from Arlington came to testify to his good character.'

'Even his enemies?'

'Especially his enemies.'

'Did he ask you?'

'No.'

'Why?'

'Because my name is disgraced.' Kennedy smiled. 'His talent for performing in a court of law,' he said, 'is particularly impressive in that he is a man for whom justice has absolutely no meaning. For instance,' continued the doctor, 'he is a miser, and he's fanatically jealous of Frankie. And yet he spends very large amounts of money consorting with prostitutes. But if he thought any man was so much as looking at his wife...'

'Why did she marry him?'

The doctor's eyelids drooped again.

'Who?'

'Frankie. Why did she marry Vincent?'

'For protection. You have to realize – Frankie came from a very bad place.'

'Worse than this?'

'Much worse. Frankie really has a slave history. She was sold, when she was a kid.'

'Who sold her?'

'Her father. He sold her to one of the travelling shows. And Vincent got her out of there. The other thing about the Half Man is... he's got worse. Much worse. He's become a chronic alcoholic. Now that they only do about a dozen shows a year around the country, and he spends most of his time in the workshop, he's always drunk. And when he's drunk,' Kennedy added, 'he has the capacity to be extremely violent.'

'Oh, really?' said Miller.

'But Frankie's like everyone else involved with Vincent. On some level, her relationship with him works. Or at least it used to. That's the main thing that stops people leaving.'

'So he wouldn't kill her,' Miller suggested, 'if she left.'

'Oh, he would.'

The doctor began to pack up his bags.

'When Vincent goes,' said Kennedy, 'he really goes. He has no sense of danger. It's like a switch is flicked.'

'Like the flea,' said Miller.

'Like the flea,' said the doctor. 'Exactly. As long as you're here on his land, that's worth bearing in mind.'

From the Show Bar, they could hear another drunken chorus of 'Arlington'.

'How do they live?' Miller asked.

'Who?'

'Hunter. The King. Paul.'

'He gives them like thirty dollars a week, same as he'll give you probably. Food and lodging. Four bottles of beer a night; any more they have to pay for. Vincent operates a bit like mine owners in the early twentieth century: very low wages, all of which have to be spent in the company store and nowhere else. He owns them.'

'Does he own you?' Miller asked.

'I live at Apollo Beach,' said Kennedy, 'five miles up the road. I have a couple of condos there that I rent out. But it doesn't bring in enough to, er... so I take care of the Half Man's people. And Vincent helps get me...' He hesitated again. 'What I need. Now lie on the bed,' he added.

He opened one of his camera cases again, found a new hypodermic and took Miller's wrist.

'What the hell is that?' the Englishman asked, pulling away.

'Ten milligrams of zopiclone,' said Kennedy. 'It'll put you straight to sleep. I mean it's up to you...'

'Go on,' said Miller. He felt the needle in his arm.

'Do you think he's evil?' Miller asked, suddenly.

'I have a scientific background,' Kennedy replied. 'I don't think in those terms.'

'Oh, really? Why not?'

'You know how those death-row attorneys argue that if any of us were known, like their clients, solely for the most shameful thing we have ever done, the vast majority of us would be seen as beneath contempt. Well I think those lawyers are right, on the whole. But Vincent's pattern of behaviour isn't like that. With Vincent, that sort of ritualized cruelty is routine. But he isn't predictable. He's like Stalin. It's not the pain or the killing he loves. It's the fear.'

'So he is evil.'

Kennedy paused.

'What I would say is that he is without doubt the most dangerous man I have ever met.'

'Outside of an institution,' said Miller, feeling himself overcome by drowsiness.

'Outside of an institution, yes,' said the doctor. 'That's right. Or in.'

Miller awoke the following morning feeling at ease with the world, and convinced, in his half-sedated state, that Dr Kennedy's midnight consultation had been a dream. Then, sitting up, he saw traces of cigar ash on the freshly painted boards of his cabin floor. He ran his tongue along the back of his upper teeth, and pressed it through the central gap.

He got up and walked across the dirt track towards the Show Bar. Frankie's shower, he noticed, wasn't running. He went through the back door, into the kitchen. The room was empty but filled with the smell of bacon and sausages, coming from the industrial oven. He heard a movement from behind a door leading off the room; it was slightly ajar and he could see a shaft of electric light coming through the gap.

Miller peered through the crack. What he saw wasn't a larder, as he'd expected, but a small bathroom. It was very clean and tiled, in white, from floor to ceiling. There was a washbasin and toilet but no shower. Frankie was standing with her back to him, facing a large mirror over the basin. She was fully dressed, in her white linen outfit, but she'd raised one side of her tunic by six inches or so. Reflected in the mirror, Miller could see her abdomen and lower ribs. Her dark skin – untouched, as far as he could tell, by the flaking that affected her arms and legs – was disfigured by a patch of grey, about the size of an apple, yellowing at the edges. Lifting the front of her top with her gloved left hand, Frankie was applying what looked like a thick balm to this swollen area with her right, which was uncovered. She winced as her fingers touched her stomach.

Miller, remembering his last encounter with a woman in a closet, gently shifted his weight on to his left foot, preparing to retreat. A floorboard creaked. Frankie raised her eyes in the mirror, saw him watching her, and let her tunic fall.

She turned to face him, still holding the small tub of ointment, which looked like beeswax.

'I'm sorry,' he said. 'I didn't mean to...'

'To what?'

'What's that?' he replied, flustered.

She handed him the plastic pot and picked up the lid, off the basin.

'Revive,' she read, 'Three steps to perfect skin.'

'Is that...'

He motioned towards her stomach.

'Is that what?'

'Your... icthy...'

'No.'

She raised her linen top, again by a few inches.

'That,' she said, 'is a punch. And these...' She put the lid down, turned her back on him and raised the back of her shirt, revealing four small, angry scars, in a vertical line down her lower spine '... are cigarette burns.'

Miller said nothing.

'Can you put on some of that stuff for me?'

'What?'

Miller glanced behind him, through the gap in the door, into the empty kitchen.

'OK.'

He put his finger in the tub and spread the ointment over each of the burns.

There were other, darker marks, he noticed, all over her back. One of the new scars, the last, was deeper than the others, as though the lighted cigarette had been ground in with such force that several layers of her skin had been burned away. She flinched as he applied the ointment to this injury. Miller put the pot down.

'Frankie?'

She turned to face him and he put his hands on her shoulders, very gently. She looked him straight in the eyes, but didn't move.

'We've got to get you and Alex...'

He glanced nervously at the door, which was behind her and still ajar.

'Don't stop,' she said softly, in her hypnotic monotone, without looking round. 'Go on.'

He paused.

'We have got to get you and Alex out of here...'

He looked past her again, and this time saw the face of the King, his one good eye staring through the crack in the door. Only his Stetson had prevented the albino pushing his face in further.

'I...' Miller began.

The albino's expression didn't alter. He pushed the washroom door open. Miller walked past him, into the kitchen.

'Frankie?' said the King.

She turned to face the visitor.

'Yes?'

'The boss sent me, to give you a hand with the trays.'

She put on a pair of heat-proof gloves, opened the door of the large oven and took out a large metal tray of sausages and bacon, which she placed on the marble table in the centre of the room. Frankie removed another tray, of scrambled egg, and a third of hash browns. She tossed oven gloves over to Miller and handed another pair to the King.

They carried the trays through into the dining area of the Show Bar and put them down on the long metal serving table at the back of Frankie's Diner next to a stack of plates and a large pot of coffee. A sign, scrawled in black felt marker and taped to the wall, read: 'Breakfast: $5'.

Miller looked around. Night and day were much the same in the Show Bar; though it was only nine, he noticed, by the King's watch, Hunter was already behind the bar, serving an early morning drunk a cold beer from the coffin. The diner was sparsely populated: at one table there was a group of elderly men with fishing tackle bags, drinking coffee; at another sat Officer Glidden, the patrolman who had been present the night Miller first arrived at the Show Bar. Glidden, who was reading a paperback, was sharing his table with an overweight, middle-aged man, in a white shirt and jeans. Miller found it hard to keep his eyes off the man's face, which was beautifully made up with the classic features of a clown. He was missing only the red nose which, Miller decided, must be in the leather case on the floor next to him, with the rest of his costume. His clown shoes, too big to fit in the bag, had been lashed to it with thick string.

The policeman had his book opened flat on the table; he followed the print with his finger and paused regularly to consult a pocket dictionary he held in his right hand. His progress with both books was painfully slow.

'People don't realize,' he told Miller, 'how important the precise meaning of words can be to a policeman. It doesn't matter how much you've seen, if you don't put it down like it should be.'

Miller lifted the spine of Glidden's paperback, so that he could see its title: *Double Indemnity*, by James M. Cain.

'Don't you get enough death and aggravation in your day job?'

'Yes and no,' said the officer.

'He means no,' said the man in the make-up.

'We have a book club,' said the policeman, 'over in Atlantic Road. We meet every week. I've read this one once. You want to borrow it?'

Miller took the book and joined Paul the Dwarf, who was sitting alone at a table for four.

'Who's that?' Miller asked, nodding at the clown.

'Coco,' said the dwarf. 'He's off to work.'

'No kidding.'

'You should get your eats now,' Paul said. 'Else they'll all be gone.'

The jukebox was playing Frank Sinatra singing 'It Had To Be You'. Frankie walked over to the machine, kicked the plug out of its socket, and disappeared back into the kitchen. She was followed by the King, who seemed in a hurry – no doubt eager, Miller reflected uneasily, to report his latest gossip to the Half Man, in his compound. Paul came back from the buffet with two plates heavily charged with sausage, egg, bacon and potato.

'I can't eat all that,' complained Miller.

'Have what you can,' said the dwarf. 'I'll finish the rest.'

'And,' Miller added, pointing at the five-dollar sign, 'I've got no money.'

'That's for outsiders,' Paul said.

'Outsiders?'

'The fishing guys; the truck drivers. Breakfast's free for – you know – family.'

The dwarf ate with a speed Miller had only previously observed in men who had attended British public schools, conditioned by years of limited rations, served communally. The Englishman began to cut up a sausage but paused when he noticed that the King had reappeared and was heading for his table. He was pushing a woman in a wheelchair. In her early fifties, she had straight, strawberry-blonde hair, wide blue eyes and high cheekbones that testified to what once must have been striking good looks. On her right temple, there was a purple bruise.

The King pushed her up to the table and applied the wheelchair brake, then set off for the buffet. Miller watched him, trying to gauge from his body language whether he'd already informed the Half Man about the scene he'd stumbled on a few minutes earlier. He briefly entertained the idea of explaining himself to the albino, then decided against it.

'This is Helen,' said Paul. 'The King's wife.'

The woman in the wheelchair was holding out her hand.

Miller shook it.

'Hello darling,' Helen said. 'What's that you're holding?'

He showed her the paperback.

'Officer Glidden gave it me.'

'Oh, from his club,' said Helen. 'Books are his passion you know. He just can't get enough of them.'

The King returned with two more plates of food and sat down.

'Helen is from England,' he said. 'Like you.'

'She's *what?*' said Miller. Anxiety rose in him. 'I mean…' He turned to her. 'You're from where?'

'Walsall.'

'You don't sound as if you come from Walsall.'

'I've been here since I was fifteen,' Helen said. She gave him a conspiratorial look. 'I ran away from home.'

'Oh,' said Miller. 'Right. I see. Why?'

She laughed. 'Have you ever been to Walsall?'

'Once,' he said.

He managed to swallow some sausages and eggs, though they burned the wound from his double extraction. He fetched himself some iced water.

'All I brought with me was my mother's teapot,' she said. 'I wanted to be an actress, you know. I'd had quite a few parts in England.'

'What in?' he asked.

'Local shows,' she told him, 'with Dudley rep and the Walsall Players. I loved it though. I came over as a showgirl. Then I was a dancer. And then...' She indicated her wheelchair. '... I was a trapeze artist, with Ringlings.'

Miller, more cautious than he once was about inquiring as to the cause of other people's disabilities, said nothing for a few moments, but saw that she was expecting a question.

'What happened?'

Across the bar, the door to the main entrance opened and the Half Man came in alone, riding in his electric cart. He steered it towards Miller's table and wedged himself between the King and Helen, so that the albino had to move his chair to let him in. He parked himself between the couple, on the King's left, blind side.

'Coffee,' said the Half Man. There was no politeness, only haste, in the way he pronounced the word: he might have been answering a general knowledge question about Colombia.

The King got up and fetched him a cup.

'The bars of a trapeze,' Helen told Miller, 'the aluminium ones, heat up very quickly when the sun is on the tent.'

'Especially if some asshole,' said the Half Man, 'is not doing his job.'

'They heat up,' she repeated, 'and this day – we were in Lake Charles, Louisiana. It was the afternoon show, and it was August, and it was real hot. *Real* hot. And the guy that had the job of untying the trapeze and swinging it across to me from the opposite lighting tower, he'd left the bar lashed against the front of one of the sodium lamps.'

'Jesus,' said Miller.

'So I jumped off my own tower and I caught the bar in mid-air, like I always did. I can remember, before I was really aware of feeling the pain, hearing my hands burn; they were frying,' she added, 'like pullets on a spit. I went into shock; I didn't have the momentum to get across to the far platform, so I decided to swing back to the one I'd just left.'

'How high were you?' Miller asked.

'We worked at forty foot in those days.'

'And with no nets,' added the King.

'The last thing I can remember is, I was coming up to my home platform on the back swing and I went to take my left hand off the bar to grab the guy-line but I couldn't because it was stuck fast to the metal bar. People told me afterwards the skin was white, like boiled chicken. And then I passed out.'

'And?' Miller asked.

'And I guess it can't have been stuck quite as fast as all that,' she added, 'because I landed on the edge of the ring, and I broke my back.'

One of the fishermen, Miller noticed, had gone over to try to put music on the jukebox, but found he couldn't, because Frankie had shattered the plug.

'Looking back,' Helen said, 'I think I could have got away with a busted shoulder and a broken leg, if I'd realized what was happening right away, and I hadn't panicked. Even from that height, there are ways and ways to fall. But you're taught from the start – they tell you over and over, it's ground into you…' At this point, Miller noticed, her voice took on a hint of her native Black Country. '… Whatever you do, don't let go of them bars.'

'Them bars,' the Half Man repeated, in a surprisingly accurate parody of her accent.

The King, who had been looking uncomfortable throughout this conversation, switched off the light over their table in the diner.

'What's wrong?' Miller said.

'When you only have one good eye, you have to look after it. I like it dark,' he added. 'I don't like electric light. Light dazzles.'

'The King has this trouble with his good eye,' said the Half Man.

'It's called a-stag…' the King began.

'Astigmatism,' Helen said.

'That's it,' said the King.

Miller looked his compatriot in the eyes, wondering quite what she'd seen in the King.

'You like Helen, huh?' said the Half Man. 'I think Ed's in love with you, Helen.'

Miller shifted, uncomfortably.

'Don't worry, boy,' the Half Man said. 'We all are. We're all wild for her. Even the King, and he married her. But watch yourself with Helen.' He smiled. 'She's the worst of us all.'

Miller went back to the kitchen. Frankie was at the sink, shelling hard-boiled eggs into an earthenware bowl. She motioned him towards the washroom. He went in and closed the door behind him. He turned on the light; hanging on a rail he found a clean white towel and a new white singlet, with thin shoulder-straps, like the kind of vest worn by some athletes. On the sink he found a razor, still in its packaging, a can of shaving foam, and a new toothbrush; Miller used it cautiously, avoiding the wide gap in his front teeth.

He shaved his beard, then, as had become his habit, his head. He dried himself with the towel and pulled on the singlet. He was agitated and every movement was hurried. He sensed that this was her place, and that letting him into it was an intimate gesture on her part, and one that could get them both into terrible trouble if he was found in there, even alone. But he wanted to wash his body and arms, as he hadn't done for days, in soap. He looked along a row of shelves. There were several lotions and prescription medicines; next to them he saw other, more brightly coloured bottles of cosmetics. He picked one up. The tiny bottle contained a liquid in a frighteningly intense shade of royal blue; its yellow label, which carried the name of the fragrance – 'Law Stay Away' – showed a uniformed American police officer recoiling, his handcuffs flying from his grasp – a scenario precipitated, the picture implied, by the force-field generated by the perfume. There were larger plastic bottles of liquid soaps: one was called 'Do As I Say'; another, whose label showed the Reaper, on a black horse and carrying a scythe, had the title: 'Destroy Everything'. Each of these products, Miller noticed, was made by Selene Perfumes of Miami. In the end he chose a liquid soap with the brand name of 'Deliverance' and noticed, too late, that the instructions read: 'Pour into lukewarm water while reciting the Twenty-third Psalm'.

He came out, reeking of the cheap soap. Frankie was still at the sink; he watched her take an egg and roll it gently on the rim of the bowl before pulling the shell apart in a couple of deft movements. She nodded towards a pile of carrots on the marble table; they'd been laid out on a sheet of newspaper; next to them was a small black-handled knife and a saucepan of water, for the peeled vegetables.

He picked up the first carrot and send a few clumsy orange shavings on to the newsprint, then stopped.

'What did you kick that jukebox for?' he asked her.

She kept her back to him, at the sink.

'Don't worry,' she said, 'Hunter will fix it.'

'Yes, but why did you...'

'Because I don't like that song.'

'Why?'

'I just don't.'

'Frankie...'

She turned around to face him.

'Because that's the music he beats me up to. Is that good enough for you?'

'You mean he puts that song on first – deliberately – then...'

'Right. I've kind of lost my taste for Frank Sinatra.' She paused. 'Who were you talking to in there?'

'I met Helen,' he said. 'She's with the King.'

'What did you think of her?'

'I was trying to think what she saw in him.'

'He looks out for her,' Frankie said. 'In his way.'

'That's nice,' said Miller, in a flat tone.

'I wouldn't get too generous,' she said. 'He slaps her around, too.'

'Badly?'

'Bad enough.'

'How do you know?'

'How do I know she gets slapped?'

'Yes.'

'I guess the same way you know I do.'

He went back to his carrot but cut too hard, so that the whole top shot across the floor and landed at her feet. She picked it up, and threw it in the bin.

'Never mind,' she told him. 'I'm sure we'll find something that you can do. There has to be something that you're good at, right?'

When she said this, Miller instinctively looked down at the sheet of newspaper on the table. It was a cheap rag that might have been designed by a high school student. Running across two pages was the banner headline: PRISONERS LIVE LONGER, HAVE HEALTHIER LIVES THAN GENERAL POPULATION.

Frankie, noticing him reading, glanced across at the headline.

'That's interesting,' she said. She turned away from him again and went back to her eggs. 'Healthier lives,' she said, neatly paring another. 'How do they account for that?'

Miller looked at the first couple of paragraphs.

'Less stress from irritating or abusive relatives or friends,' he began.

'That figures,' she said, her back still to him.

He looked at the small illustration, near the bottom of the page. It was a picture of an empty jail cell, and he imagined himself in it.

'I guess we've all wondered how we might cope in those circumstances,' he said.

'Yes.'

'But it's hard to believe that anyone in their right mind would seriously consider it as a route to a better life.'

'Oh, I don't know,' she said.

'You mean you have?'

She turned around again; her dark eyes looked down, then met his.

'Sure.'

'Really?' he asked her. 'Often?'

'Every day.'

'And just how do you think about arranging it?'

'I don't know. I guess there's a thousand ways.'

'You know what I think the most relaxing thing would be?' Miller said.

'No?'

'No bills.'

'No *what*?'

'No bills. No gas bills. No water bills. No...'

'Are you crazy?' she asked him. 'Of course you'd get god-damn bills.' She went back to the newspaper and brushed a couple of pieces of carrot skin off the headline.

'Oh,' she said. 'Right. I read that wrong.'

'What do you mean you read it wrong?'

'I read a word wrong. Well… just one letter actually.'

'What did you think it said?'

'I thought…' She turned away again. 'Never mind.'

'Go on.'

'I thought it said…'

She picked up an egg and cracked it against the side of the bowl. It was raw, and splattered her white tunic with yolk; albumen ran down the thick veins of her right hand.

'I thought it said: "Poisoners".'

Miller stared at her, the small knife still in his hand.

'Have you ever…' he began.

'Put some ice in the shower tank, Ed.'

He hauled a sack out of the chest freezer, carried it outside and climbed the ladder to the roof tank, holding the ice against his chest with his left hand. He kept his carrot knife clasped between his teeth. With the small blade he slit the bag open along its underside until the ice spilled into the water below. Miller thought of a report he'd once read about a military coup in Africa, where the native army had disposed of their white masters by flying them over the ocean, and slitting open their abdomens before dropping them a thousand feet into the shark-infested waters. This scene had come into his mind for years, ever since he read the news story, even if he was just cutting into a bag of organic sweetcorn in Oxted. In the past, though, he'd always wondered what it would have felt like to be a victim. This time, in his mind, he was the murderer.

With the empty bag in his hand and his knife back between his teeth, he climbed down again. When he reached the ground he turned around and saw the King at the bottom of the ladder. With the knife clenched between his own teeth, and the other man's black eye patch, Miller thought, the scene had an absurd, piratical quality. But neither he, nor the albino, was smiling.

'The Half Man,' the King said, 'wants to see you.'

Miller put the knife and the empty bag on the kitchen sink and followed the King as he turned left on to the dusty path between the cabins, passed through the mesh fence and into the Half Man's compound.

What served as the entrance hall to his residential trailer was filled with broken fridges, bicycles and more engine parts. When he followed the King into the main living room, it took Miller's eyes a few moments to adjust to the light. The brown nylon curtains were drawn, even though it was ten in the morning. The Half Man, in his soiled short-sleeved shirt, was propped in an armchair, in the middle of the room, watching television. As Miller approached, his host sent a thick whorl of cigarette smoke into the air, fortifying the already impressive fug that hung over the room. Thick though it was, the smoke didn't quite mask a fetid note that Miller associated with the clothes rails of British charity shops.

On a small table next to the Half Man's chair Miller saw an ice bucket, a bottle of Maker's Mark, a carton of Kent cigarettes, two ashtrays, both overflowing, and his gun. His orange tumbler of whisky was in his right hand; in his left, the television remote, which he was using to skip between infomercials and game shows.

When he saw Miller, he put the TV controller down, leaving the set tuned to TNT. He indicated an upturned beer crate next to his chair; there was an LP cover resting on it. Miller handed the Half Man the album sleeve – *The Greatest Hits of Frank Sinatra* – and sat down.

'I don't care what they say,' his host told him, handing the sleeve to the King. 'Nobody did it like Frank.'

On the screen in front of him, Robert Mitchum, in his role as the psychotic evangelist in *Night of the Hunter*, was running through the undergrowth, his flick knife in his hand, on the heels of two young children he was eager to kill. The Half Man, following Miller's gaze, became interested in the pursuit. He tilted his head back slightly as he watched and breathed in deeply, like a football fan appreciating a sound piece of approach play.

'How long you been with us, Ed?'

'Two weeks,' Miller said, cautiously. 'Just over.'

'The work going OK?' he asked, almost casually, his eyes still on the screen.

'Yes.'

The Half Man pointed at Mitchum, who was calling out to the infants, through the bushes.

'You seen this movie before?'

'Yes,' said Miller. 'You?'

'No,' the Half Man replied.

He began coughing and, though he didn't extinguish his cigarette, motioned the King towards the window closest to his armchair.

The albino opened it and stood back, shading his eye against the daylight.

'That's one evil bastard,' the Half Man said, pointing at Mitchum. 'He's got to be the meanest son of a bitch that's ever been on a movie screen, right?'

'I don't know,' said Miller. 'I'm not sure I quite believe in him.'

'What?'

'Because, with the truly evil…' he found he avoided making eye contact with the Half Man as he said this, but kept his eyes on the screen '… even with them… even the worst of them does one good deed.'

The Half Man pondered this for a moment.

'I don't think so,' he said. 'One good deed would make them better.'

'No,' said Miller, surprised to be debating the nature of good and evil with a psychopath. 'It makes them worse. Because it reminds you that, every day, there is a better side of their character that they reject. To be really evil,' he added, 'a man needs to do just one good deed.'

The Half Man looked at him, apparently interested.

'In the movies, or in life?'

'In the movies.'

'Just one good deed?'

'Right.'

'Not two?'

'Two,' Miller replied, 'would be one too many.'

'In the movies,' the Half Man repeated.

'Right.'

'And what about in real life?'

'In real life,' the Englishman said, 'I never met a man that didn't do one good deed.'

'You sure about that?' the Half Man laughed. 'Careful now, Ed.'

The American returned his eyes to the screen and drained his glass of whisky. A sliver of ice dribbled down his chin; he wiped his mouth with his forearm. The King came over and poured him another drink.

'You'll find that you lose us simple Southern folks with talk like that Ed,' said the Half Man. 'We don't deal in riddles here. Or in mouthfuls of words. We talk straight.'

He looked at the Englishman and his face took on just the hint of a smile.

'How's Frankie?' he asked.

'She's fine,' Miller said.

The Half Man picked up his gun and held it so that the barrel was pointing towards his guest's feet.

'Pass me that five clip,' he said.

Miller looked down and saw the ammunition, lying on the cheap beige carpet. He handed it to the Half Man, who clipped it into his hand gun, which he rested on the arm of his chair.

'Thank you, Ed.'

He reached into his breast pocket and pulled out a crumpled envelope which he handed to Miller. There were three ten-dollar bills inside it; the Englishman took it, and said nothing.

'You get your breakfast and four beers every night,' the Half Man said. 'Anything else you pay for. OK?'

'OK.'

He dismissed the King, who went off in the direction of the workshop.

'Any questions?'

'Why is the King,' Miller asked, 'called the King?'

'We have this old saying,' his host replied: 'In the kingdom of the blind...'

From the open window by the Half Man's head came what sounded like gunfire. Looking out, Miller saw it was the clown who'd been at breakfast, travelling along the dirt track leading to Highway 41 on an elderly moped, which was backfiring. His suitcase and shoes were roped to the pillion rack. The Half Man looked out, saw him, picked up his gun and fired it through the window, hitting a Con Edison Pole just as the rider was passing behind it. The clown let out a high-pitched squeal, almost lost control of his moped, then accelerated away.

'Morning, Coco,' said the Half Man, quietly, to himself.

With his wages in his hand, Miller headed back to the kitchen. Frankie was by the back door, in her shower. Alex, he could see, had left her banner painting and was sitting on the ladder he'd left propped against the wall, talking to her mother, whose face was again visible over the brick side of the showerhouse. The girl's sword ladder was close by, lying flat on the ground.

As he was going into the kitchen, Alex tapped him on the shoulder. She gave him a cigarette and lit it for him. Miller sat on the outside step and smoked it. From this position, Alex's legs were resting on a rung of the ladder slightly above his head. The bandages which covered both her feet, he noticed, were stained with dust, sweat and dried blood and were now the same colour as her dark brown skin. Around the two small toes of her right foot, there was a fresh crimson stain: the result, he supposed, of her most recent accident with the ladder.

'Alex?' he asked her.

'Yes?'

'Let me have a look at your feet.'

The nine year old giggled.

'What are you,' she asked him. 'A nurse, or a pervert?'

'A nurse,' Miller lied.

'Yeah?'

He nodded.

She came down and sat on the kitchen step. He kneeled in front of her and held her right foot in both hands, under the heel, like his father had once held his, he remembered, when he'd twisted his ankle playing football. He tried to remove the bandage but couldn't: what had been the edges of the roll of tape had become fused into one discoloured whole. He put her foot down again, went into the kitchen, and filled a plastic basin with lukewarm water.

'Put your feet in there,' he told her, 'and keep them there.'

'How long for?' Alex said, looking amused. She glanced up at her mother, who was still in the shower. Frankie said nothing, and didn't return her smile.

Miller went to Frankie's washroom. He emerged with a pair of nail scissors, his new toothbrush and towel and – finding no disinfectant – a bottle of 'Destroy Everything'. After ten minutes, the water had turned the colour of strong cocoa. Using the nail scissors, he cut the bandages off the child's feet. He cut her toenails which, in the absence of exposure to the air, had become elongated, soft and white. He ran fresh hot water into the basin and cleaned her feet using the liquid soap. The skin around her heels was hardened, like a guitarist's fingertips. As he used the toothbrush to remove ingrained dirt in the hollows formed by old scars, he watched the colour of her soles – deep brown at first, like the rest of her skin – turn a lighter pink than his own palms. The undersides of her toes were covered with cuts, the largest of which ran the full width of her left foot and was badly infected. Miller – who had delegated the physical care of his own daughter to the point that he had no memory of having changed a sticking plaster or brushed her teeth – hesitated. Then he sterilized the nail scissors in a pan on the kitchen stove, and pierced the wound. He drained the puss on to his new white towel, and rested her feet by the heels, on the step.

'Wait here,' he said. 'Don't go away, OK?'

He cleaned the washbasin for a second time and filled it with fresh, hotter water. He found a half-pound packet of salt in the kitchen, hesitated, then poured its whole contents into the basin, stirring the solution with his hands. He carried the container out and put it on the ground, in front of the young girl.

'Alex?'

'Yeah?'

'This is going to hurt, OK?'

'Right.'

She drew on her cigarette.

'A lot?'

'Yes,' he said. 'Put your right foot in first – slowly – starting with the back of your heel. If that feels too hot, or it stings too much...'

She looked straight at him and plunged both feet into the saline solution. She kept her eyes on his and they never flinched or shifted.

'How long?' she asked him.

'Five minutes.'

'OK.'

Miller got to his feet and turned to the girl's mother, who was still standing in the brick-walled shower, water running down over her forehead and open eyes.

'Frankie,' he asked her, 'will you call Kennedy?'

'What time is it?' she asked.

'Ten thirty.'

'You call him,' she said. 'His number's on the cell phone, on the kitchen table.'

'Which number in the memory?'

'Number one. You might just catch him.'

'What do you mean?'

'He sleeps most of the day,' Frankie said.

'Like Count Dracula,' Alex added.

When Kennedy arrived, carrying his camera cases, Frankie was out of the shower and Alex was still sitting on the step, her feet on Miller's white towel. The doctor saw the empty packet of salt by the basin; he put his finger into the hot water and allowed a drop of it to fall on to his tongue.

'You're gross,' said Alex.

Kennedy examined the girl's injuries. He looked up at Miller.

'Congratulations,' he said. 'But you overdid the saline a bit.'

Kennedy dried the child's feet in sterile towels, dusted them in white powder, then applied a couple of smaller bandages. Miller knelt and watched. A shadow was cast over him from behind; he turned and saw the figure of the King.

'Don't you need to disinfect those cuts?' Miller asked Kennedy.

'Trust me professor,' the doctor replied, pointing at the salt water, 'nothing could live in that.'

'Tell her to keep her feet up when she can,' Kennedy told Frankie. 'Get her some clean cotton socks for when she's outside. Change the socks every day. No showers for a week,' he added. 'And no sword ladder.'

'The Half Man,' said the King, 'ain't going to like that.'

'I'll talk to Vincent,' said Kennedy. The King turned and set off for the Half Man's trailer, evidently determined to get there first. Frankie disappeared into the kitchen. The doctor handed Miller a polythene bag containing clean bandages, adhesive tape and a box of the white powder.

'Change those dressings every two days for the first week,' he said. 'Every three for the second.'

'What if they get infected?'

'Call me. But they won't.'

'What are you going to tell the Half Man?'

'Don't worry,' said Kennedy. 'I'll tell him she had acute septicaemia. Another few days and she might have done. I have to see him today, in any case.'

'Why?'

'Because he has to give me what I need.'

Miller collected up the old bandages, and put them in the trash.

'And,' Kennedy added, 'because he's sick.'

'What?'

'Or – to be exact – he might be sick.'

The Englishman overturned the basin and watched the salted water soaking into the parched earth. A beetle, noticing the imminent deluge, sprinted from its shelter, behind a clump of dry grass.

Miller stepped on it.

'Badly?' he asked.

'Could be,' said Kennedy. 'He came to me with chest pains and a persistent cough; just recently he's started coughing blood. According to the report he brought out of the Emergency Room, he appears to have a shadow on his lung. I got him to persuade his regular doctor to book him in to Arthur James's; he's going in a couple of weeks, for a biopsy.'

'What's Arthur James's?'

'Arthur James's,' Kennedy replied, 'is the cancer hospital in Tampa.'

'Has he got lung cancer?'

'What do you reckon?' the doctor asked.

'What do you mean, what do I reckon?'

'I mean that your guess is as good as mine, given that you, like me, don't have an x-ray unit and an operating theatre in your cabin. My guess, for what it's worth, is that he hasn't.'

Kennedy left for the Half Man's compound.

'If you have any trouble,' he said, as he was leaving, 'call me.'

Miller got Paul to drive him up to the store at Big Bend, where he bought a cotton handkerchief, cigarettes and a Hershey bar. Back at the camp, he handed his bag of purchases to Alex. She smiled and gave him back the handkerchief.

'I'm not gonna need that,' she said.

'Keep it,' he told her. 'You're bound to, one day.'

Miller worked all afternoon in the kitchen, scrubbing surfaces and cleaning the large oven. Public hygiene regulations, he gathered, were one area of the law the Half Man's empire was obliged to respect. He thought of asking Frankie about her husband's state of health, then didn't: she seemed anxious and resentful, as though she felt that Miller had done something she might pay for.

'Did you mind,' he asked her, 'that I cleaned Alex's feet?'

'No,' she said. 'They were bad. I could see that.'

'Then why the hell,' Miller asked her, 'didn't you look at them before?'

'You have to go through pain when you're learning the sword ladder,' she said. 'And then there's the matter of consent.'

'She's only nine for Christ's sake.'

Frankie nodded towards the fenced compound.

'It's not *her* consent I was worried about. Do you think I don't...' she stopped.

He walked round to face her but didn't touch her.

'Have you never left him?'

'Yes.'

'What happened?'

'I took Alex, and Little Paul drove us to the bus, and we got on it, and we went to Phoenix.'

'And?'

'And he busted Little Paul's jaw, and then he came to Phoenix, with the King, and he found us. I'm not hard to find.'

'Were you working in carnival?'

'I have to live.'

'Why did you come back?'

'He made me promises.'

'Has he kept them?'

'Some.'

'Like?'

'Like he built the shower, and he put in the washroom. Like he stopped hitting Alex. He lets me see Kennedy any time I need to now.'

'Which promises didn't he keep?'

'He said we'd move.'

'Where to?'

'Some place cold.'

'And he didn't stop beating you.'

'For a while he did.'

'Then he started again.'

'Right.'

'I just can't begin to understand,' Miller went on, 'how you can possibly live with...'

'Can we talk about something else now?'

'Why?'

'Because you make me feel like I'm stupid.'

'I don't think you're stupid,' Miller said. 'I think you're numb, and I think you're desperate, and I think you're trapped.'

'And you can begin to understand how that feels, right?'

'Right.'

In Frankie's bathroom, at the end of the day, he washed in the disappointingly mild lather of 'Total Domination', then walked across to the Show Bar. Hunter was behind the bar, drinking a pint of Grand Marnier and Coke, his pendulous breasts drooping outside the thin top of his orange singlet and down towards the counter. The Half Man was sitting in his high leather chair on the customers' side, talking to Helen, the King's wife, who was playing a video blackjack machine which had been reduced to half its usual height.

Miller went across to the dining area, where Paul the Dwarf was sitting alone at a table, with a beer and a plate of egg mayonnaise sandwiches.

'You want some food?' Paul asked.

'No.'

'You got to eat.'

Miller swallowed a couple of the egg sandwiches. On the other side of the diner, he noticed Coco, who'd removed his greasepaint, eating a steak sandwich and a plate of fries.

'Why don't you have steak?' he asked Paul.

'Steak is ten bucks,' said the dwarf. 'Sandwiches is two bucks, for as many as you can eat.'

'How does he afford steak?'

'Coco makes good money,' Paul said. 'Especially now, in the school vacation. He does children's parties; he even does some TV shows.'

'TV? So what the hell's he doing here?'

'He works for the Half Man,' the dwarf said. 'He gives him a percentage.'

Miller went to the bar and ordered two Coors, which Hunter marked off with crosses against his name, on a pad he kept under the counter. While he was waiting to be served, Kennedy came in and started talking to the Half Man. Miller said nothing to the doctor, worried that any exchange might precipitate a conversation with the owner.

He returned with the bottles and handed one to Paul. Once they'd finished their night's allocation of beers, Miller started buying drinks with the money the Half Man had given him.

'You want to go sit at the bar?' Paul asked.

'No.'

From their table in the corner of the diner, they looked on as the Show Bar lurched towards its usual anarchy. Hunter fixed a new plug on the jukebox; Kennedy went over to it with a handful of quarters and stacked it up with old Beatles songs. The Half Man, Miller noticed, could be sporadically affable, almost urbane: when his fellow drunks at the bar sang along with 'Yesterday', they fell silent, mid-chorus, as they had clearly done countless times before, to allow Vincent to deliver, in a raucous baritone, the line 'I'm not half the man I used to be'. As his fellow drinkers joined in on the next phrase, 'There's a shadow hanging over me,' Miller noticed the Half Man glance towards Kennedy, who appeared to shake his head, in reassurance.

After more than a month in Arlington, Miller could still be disturbed by the atmosphere in the Show Bar but in other ways felt oddly at home. It was true that he had almost no money and that, as he'd lost weight, his flimsy shorts were now held up with a length of Paul's old fishing twine. But there were occasional moments in his new life that reminded him of his existence with Elizabeth; they had to do with familiarity, indifference and surrender.

The dwarf got to his feet.

'Come round to my cabin in five minutes, OK?' he said.

'Why not now?'

'I have a surprise for you.'

'I don't want a surprise,' said Miller. 'I've had surprises, and I don't like them.'

'You'll like this one.'

A few minutes later, with most of his week's wages spent, Miller walked unsteadily out of the Show Bar. As he approached the dwarf's cabin, he noticed that its wooden shutters were open. Protruding from the window was what looked like a small bazooka.

He opened the door and found Paul's cabin in darkness, except for a flashlight that cast a dim glow around the floor. What he'd taken for a weapon was a telescope, on a tripod. The instrument was bound in dark leather and had immaculately polished silver retaining rings for its lenses. Even in this poor light, Miller could see it was probably the most valuable object in the Half Man's camp.

'Take a look,' said Paul.

He shifted his specially lowered stool out from under the telescope. Miller had to sit on the floor to get his eye low enough to meet the lens. He made out a blurred shape that was just about recognizable as a planet.

'Mars,' said the dwarf.

Miller got up, and sat on Paul's bed.

'What do you think?' the dwarf said.

'It's amazing,' Miller replied. 'It's beautiful.'

'Yes. And it's thirty-five million miles away.'

'I meant the telescope. Where did you get it?'

'It was my dad's,' said Paul. 'And before that, it was my grandpa's. He was in the merchant marine. I've still got the box that it came with, that has all the cleaning stuff. You know where he bought it?'

'No.'

'He bought it in Anchorage. Anchorage, Alaska. Isn't that a beautiful name for a seaport town, Anchorage?'

'It's very beautiful,' Miller said.

The dwarf opened a small case made out of walnut wood. It had compartments lined with green felt, containing tins of leather conditioner, soft sections of old chamois leather, tissues and metal polish.

'And you keep it here?'

'The Half Man won't let me take it in the Show Bar,' he said. 'He told me it ruins the atmosphere.'

Paul began to clean the telescope's eyepiece, then stopped and looked up.

'How can it do?' he asked.

'How can it do what?'

'Ruin the atmosphere.'

'Don't ask me,' said Miller.

'Try it again now.'

The Englishman got down on the floor again. This time he adjusted the lens, bringing the red planet perfectly into focus.

'You know,' he heard the dwarf say at his shoulder, 'the King has been talking about you to the Half Man.'

'Oh?' said Miller, his eyes still on the distant star.

'Yes. He's been talking about you and Frankie. And you and Alex.'

Miller didn't move. 'I guess that isn't good,' he said.

'It isn't, Ed, no. It isn't good.'

Miller got up and sat on the dwarf's bed again. He looked up at the night sky, through the open window. Even to the naked eye, the stars looked clearer, brighter and more imposing than they ever had in Surrey. He brought his eyes down to the horizon, and glanced nervously across to the Half Man's compound.

'Don't worry,' said Paul. 'We'll think of something.'

The dwarf switched on a table lamp. Paul's cabin, Miller noticed, had a kind of faded delicacy: matching gingham shades over the lamp and the overhead light; a ripped chintz curtain half-drawn across the two shelves where the dwarf kept his few, very crumpled, clothes. Neatly stowed behind the door, there was an ironing board; it was covered in a thick layer of dust.

'Who did all this?' Miller asked, pointing at the gingham lampshades.

'My wife.'

'Your wife?'

'She died last year.'

'How?'

'She had an aneurism. You know what that is?'

'Yes.'

'I'd never heard that word before.'

'Your wife .. was she...'

'She was a dwarf, like I am. But she was white,' he said, 'like you are.'

Miller gazed out of the window again, up at the stars.

'How did you get here?'
'Vincent bought me.'
'*What?*'
'I was sold,' he said. 'Lots of us were. I was.'
'How old were you?'
'I was six,' he said. 'We'd only just moved to Mount Holly. My dad sold me to Frank Levene's Freak Show.'
'When was this?'
'In the fifties.'
'Frank Levene owned you?'
'That's how it worked. The Half Man bought me out. He brought me here. He looked out for me. When my dad died and left me the telescope,' he added, 'he had it sent to Frank, and he handed it on to Vincent, and he gave it to me.'
He said this with a degree of pride, as though flattered that anybody thought enough of him to pass his inheritance on.
'So you weren't born in New Jersey?'
'I was born in Clarksdale, Mississippi.'
'Do you remember it?'
'Sure I do.'
'Have you ever been out of the United States?'
Paul laughed. 'I've been to Mississippi.'
'I don't know what you mean.'
'Go there,' Paul said, 'and you will.'
'How long do you spend with the telescope?'
'Since Ruth died?' Paul asked. 'Two hours; maybe three.'
'Every week?'
'Every night.'
'Are you always looking at Mars?'
'Mars? No. I look everywhere.'
He shone the flashlight under the bed. Miller kneeled down and saw little piles of cuttings from astronomy magazines and newspapers.
'Three hours a day?'
'Right.'
'Why?'

'Ruth asked me that. I told her maybe I was looking for some place where I could blend in. Or shine.'

'What did she say?'

'She said – you don't need that thing...'

The dwarf fell silent. Miller looked down at him and noticed there were tears in his eyes.

'Never mind,' he said. 'Tell me tomorrow.'

'She said: you don't need that thing,' Paul continued. 'You shine here.'

The following morning Miller was woken by a dream. He was back in London, looking into the face of the small Asian girl who was clinging on to his car at the traffic lights. As she started to cry, the outline of the passenger window changed into the frame of a tank and the top of the glass, slowly rising, became a line of water, which threatened to drown her. But Miller, indifferent to the girl's distress, kept his finger on the button that forced the water level upwards, until finally there was no air left. The girl, wholly submerged, scraped and pummelled at the window, trying to reach him, then went limp and drifted away. As he watched her body recede in the water, her skin had become white, her hair straight and blonde, and her face had taken on the familiar features of his daughter. When he awoke he was sitting up and drenched in sweat; his mouth was wide open, emitting a noiseless scream.

At eleven he was in the kitchen, cleaning work surfaces after breakfast, when the King arrived. He came in quietly, without knocking, and he was carrying a small parcel wrapped in brown paper. He handed it to Miller who – sensing instinctively that this was a community where no gift, especially from the King, was likely to bring him any benefit, put it down gently on the table, and stepped back as though he thought it might explode.

'It's not for you,' the King said. 'It's for Coco.'

'Coco?'

'Right,' said the King. 'The Half Man says to take it to him. Now.'

'I don't know where he lives,' Miller said.

Standing on the back step, the King pointed over the two lines of cabins, past the roughly erected tarpaulin that covered Alex's painted banner. Fifty yards beyond that, half-concealed by a clump of pine trees, Miller made out a red trailer.

On his way to the clown's cabin he passed Alex, who was sitting on her painting ladders, her brush in her hand. The banner was two-thirds completed; the Amazing Lizard Woman – now in purple, green and silver – was lying in a lascivious position against a jungle background. Alex was putting the finishing touches to a baby cobra that was coiled round the woman's left calf.

'Whose idea was that?' he asked, pointing at the snake. 'Your dad's?'
'Yes,' she said. 'How did you know?'
'How do your feet feel?' Miller asked her.
'Good,' she said.
'Was your dad annoyed?'
'He went crazy at first,' she replied. 'Because he said the skin would need another eight weeks to toughen up again. Then the doc told him I would've lost my toes, and if that happened I couldn't climb nothing.'
'But they're OK now though – they're not itching, or throbbing at all?'
'No.'
'Right.'
Miller started to walk away, towards the clown's trailer.
'Ed?'
She beckoned him back.
'Yes?'
He was standing next to her stepladder. She leaned down and put her lips next to his ear.
'What do you think of my mom?'
He stood back to get a better view of the picture.
'Not that, you fucking idiot,' she said. 'My *mom*. What do you think of Frankie?'
'I think she's OK.'
'Just OK?'
'Yes.'
'Does she seem happy to you?'
Miller glanced around the small clearing, and saw nobody.
'No,' he said.
He showed her his parcel.
'I have to take this to...'
'Why do you think that is?' Alex interrupted.
'What?'
'What makes you think that my mom isn't happy?'

'I don't know,' he said. 'I've never seen her smile.'
'Me neither.'
'What – never?'
'No. You know what she told me once?'
'No.'
Alex whispered in his ear again. 'She told me once that she only ever smiles when she's in love. That's weird, huh?'
'Very,' said Miller. He set off again, out of the clearing.
'When do I change my dressing?' Alex called out.
'Tomorrow,' he shouted back.
'Will you do it?'
'Yes.'

He walked across a stretch of scrubland and through the trees that surrounded the clown's trailer. It was large, neatly painted and, unlike any of the other local dwellings, had an upper level. A low picket fence protected an area of garden. There were cactus plants in terracotta pots next to the flight of wooden steps leading up to the front door, which was open.

'Hallo?' Miller shouted, through the door. There was no reply. A swarm of black flies was circling his head; he felt one bite into his bare skull. Irritated, he hammered firmly on the side of the cabin.

A couple of seconds later, a youth of about thirteen sprang out of a window in the upper floor of the trailer, landed in a clump of bushes, then sprinted away from the Half Man's camp, towards the stretch of the Hermosa on Dowson company land. By the time Miller had thought about giving chase, the boy had scaled Dowson's perimeter fence, and plunged into the water.

'Hey...' Miller shouted. He went up the steps and into the trailer's main lounge. It was comfortably furnished, with an armchair, two sofas and an upright piano. All around the room there were glass showcases, housing replicas of the showgrounds of the United States, most of which had long since disappeared. On the walls, Miller saw posters and showbills advertising the great performers: Melvin Burkhart, the first Human Blockhead, hammering a nail up his nose; Percilla the Monkey Girl; the Amazing Prince Rai.

'What is it?'

Coco came down the stairs from the upstairs bedroom, wearing a clean white shirt and khaki shorts, but no shoes or socks.

'I just saw this kid jump out of your back window,' Miller said. 'Didn't you hear him?'

'I heard something,' said Coco. 'Did he get away?'

'Yes. Did he steal anything?'

'I don't think so; not so far as I can see.'

'Do you want me to call Officer Glidden?' Miller asked.

'This boy – was he carrying anything?'

'No. He dived in the river.'

'Never mind then,' said Coco. 'Leave it. It's OK.'

Miller handed him the package from the Half Man, and sat down on the sofa. He'd assumed the clown must have been expecting the delivery but as he opened the parcel, Coco's face lit up with surprise.

He took out four shot glasses, each one decorated with a clown's face.

'They're great,' said Coco.

Miller nodded.

'I think we should christen them,' the clown replied.

He poured two shots of Teacher's and handed one to Miller.

'Cheers,' said the Englishman.

'Cheers,' Coco sat down next to Miller on the sofa and put his hand on his upper thigh.

Miller leapt to his feet and took a step backwards, dropping his drink and knocking over a matchstick model of the Cyclone roller coaster. 'What the fuck do you think you're doing?' he shouted.

'Ed…' Coco said.

'Yes?'

'Just relax for a moment.'

'Relax?'

'Don't you think it's time that you and me…'

'That you and me what?'

'Being, er…' The clown reached up and put his own glass on the closed keyboard of the piano, then picked up Miller's, and refilled it.

'You don't need to worry. I know all about your...'
'You know all about my what?'
Coco smiled, good-naturedly.
'You're so English,' he said. 'You're so coy.'
'Coy?'
'About the obvious truth,' the clown said, 'that you are gay.'
'Gay?' Miller barked. Keeping an eye on Coco, he darted across to the piano, recovered his novelty glass, and drained it.
'Who told you that?'
'The Half Man.'
'What?'
'The Half Man told me,' Coco repeated, 'that you...'
'I heard what you said. Was he joking?'
'The Half Man doesn't joke about such things, believe me. But listen, if I'm not your...'
'It isn't you,' said Miller. 'It's just that I'm not – you know. I'm not a fucking poof. I'm not gay; I mean... I'm sorry.'
Coco smiled. 'Me too. But why did you bring me the glasses?'
'I didn't. The Half Man sent me over with them.'
Miller refilled his own shot glass without asking, and emptied it. 'Why the hell would the Half Man say that I was gay?'
'I don't know. He said that you told Little Paul.'
'*Paul?*'
Miller, furious, went to the dwarf's hut, which was empty. Then he saw the small black figure standing between two parked cars, with his back to the camp, bending down at the edge of the river, opposite the grotesque façade of the petrochemical plant. As Miller got closer, he saw that Paul was rinsing out paintbrushes in a metal bucket.
'What the fuck got into you?' Miller shouted, stooping so as to shout into the dwarf's ear.
'What?'
'I saw Coco just now.'
'Coco? Oh. Right. Yes.'
'He said...' Miller had to pause for a couple of seconds to catch his breath, 'that you told the Half Man I was a faggot.'

'Well,' Paul said, 'not in those words. By the way,' he added, 'you should never lean down to a dwarf.'

'Why the fuck not?'

'Because it brings you bad luck. And because we don't like it. It's not considered polite. It makes us feel like children.'

Miller picked him up by his armpits, so that the bucket and brushes were scattered on to the bank. He slammed his back into the side of the white Dodge parked next to them and held him there, so that Paul's face was on a level with his own.

'Is this better?'

'Put me down,' said the dwarf.

'Why?'

'Because if the Half Man sees you,' he said, 'he'll kill you.'

Miller put him down.

Paul picked up the brushes, and put them back in the bucket.

'It was for your own good,' he said, quietly.

'What?'

'It was for your own good, because the Half Man has noticed that Frankie likes you. A lot.'

'So?' Miller said.

'So,' said Paul. 'The Half Man came to see me last night, right after you left.'

'He came to you?'

'Yes. He called on me. Personally. Which never happens.'

The dwarf opened his tobacco tin. There were two hand-rolled cigarettes left; he gave one to Miller. Paul lit both. The dwarf looked around for bystanders and, finding none, lowered his voice.

'He came with his pistol. And he told me that, at the time of his choosing, he was going to kill you – personally, himself, which...' the dwarf took a long draw on the cigarette, 'also never happens. Or hardly ever. I had to think fast.'

'Oh,' said Miller. He sat down and stared at the water. Paul sat next to him.

'Did he mean it, do you think?'

'Why do you think the King lost his eye?'

'I don't know.'
'Because the Half Man noticed him looking at the wrong thing.'
'What thing?'
'Frankie.'
'Oh.'
'And a few days later, he had an accident, I believe with a soldering iron.'
They fell silent for a moment.
'Was Frankie looking back?' Miller asked.
'At the King?' Paul laughed. 'No.'
'So what do I do now?' asked the Englishman.
'Nothing. This way Vincent will leave you alone. He hates gays.'
'But he seems good to Coco.'
'He's good to him, but he's blackmailing him as well. He takes more than half of all his money.'
'Why does he let him?'
'Because Coco – he's gay – but he also has a thing for boys. And he's working children's parties in Tampa and he does a Saturday Club for a burger bar in Saint Pete and Baptist Church functions. If the Half Man told them half of what he knows, Coco would never work again.'
'Or breathe again,' said Miller.
'Right. Same with Glidden.'
'*Officer Glidden's gay?*' said Miller, forgetting to whisper.
'Keep your voice down for Christ's sake. Yes. It's only ever men with Glidden, not boys. But he's gay, in a very macho world.'
'Who does Glidden, er...'
'His friends in Atlantic Road. At the club.'
'So they don't read any books?'
'Well I heard they do,' said Paul. 'But that's not all that they do. I mean,' he lowered his voice further, 'I never knew guys could do stuff to each other like that.'
'Like what?'
Miller followed Paul as he carried the clean brushes back to the Half Man's workshop. The dwarf unlocked the door and led the way in, then stood still for a few seconds, listening for approaching footsteps.

Hearing none, he opened the cupboard containing the King's photographs, and showed Miller a black-and-white picture.

On a double bed in a room decorated with a poster for *The Sound of Music*, Miller saw three men in the kind of adventurous sexual pose that he had only previously seen in pictures he'd been offered by paparazzi, but had been unable to print in a mass circulation newspaper. Glidden, who had a pivotal role in the tableau, was staring into the lens with a look of mortification.

'Like I say,' said Paul, 'they ain't always reading each other their stories.'

Miller went over to the cupboard and saw several copies of the picture of him grinding the serial number off his rental car.

'Doesn't the Half Man keep these locked away?' he said.

'Why should he?' said Paul. 'The King makes dozens of these prints. This is just like the Half Man's showcase. There's more in the King's cabin; there's another lot in the…'

'Where are the negatives?' interrupted Miller.

The dwarf shrugged.

'We've been here too long,' he said. 'Let's go.'

The two men walked back along the line of cabins.

'Does the Half Man take half of Glidden's money?' Miller asked.

'No,' said Paul. 'As a police officer, Glidden's contribution takes a different form.'

'I'll bet,' Miller replied. 'So why did the Half Man send me over to Coco?'

'Because now that is another thing he's got on both of you. I've saved your life,' the dwarf said. 'Again.'

'Oh good,' said Miller. 'Thanks a bunch.'

'And now you can go on working with Frankie and seeing Alex and…'

'Yes?'

'And stay alive.'

'And shag Coco.'

'No. I'll talk to Coco. Coco's OK. Trust me. He hates the Half Man. And even if he wasn't OK, he would never say anything.'

'Why not?'

'Because now you know his secret too.'

'This young lad dived out of his window when I arrived,' Miller said.

'Right,' said Paul. 'He meets them at the Baptist tea parties, then invites them back to look at his miniatures.'

'Bloody hell,' said Miller.

'You know Coco once said to me: it's hard when your love is...'

'Is what?'

'Forbidden.'

'You make him sound like Oscar Fucking Wilde.'

'Who?'

'Never mind.'

Miller went back into the kitchen. Frankie was at the table, finishing a tortilla.

'Hi,' he said.

She didn't reply.

'Vincent told me you went to see Coco just now.'

Miller looked at her. She kept her eyes on the tortilla pan, which was three times the size of a normal frying pan. She was working an oiled knife around its inside edge so that the mixture wouldn't stick when she turned it out.

'Well, did you?' she asked.

'Did I what?'

'Did you... *see* him.'

'Yes.'

'Do you like him?'

She completed her circuit with the knife and put it down. She was looking at him now all right, with her black Spaniel eyes. Miller said nothing. He began weighing up the dangers of disclosure.

'Yes,' he said. 'I like him.'

'A lot?'

'Yes.'

She gave him a look of contemptuous disbelief, turned over the pan and slammed it down on the table so that the tortilla came out – perfectly in one piece – and lay on the marble top, steaming, in between them.

'Really,' she said, with no hint of a question in her voice.

If there was one thing that surprised him more than any other about Arlington, it was how quickly word got around. He wasn't looked down on as a homosexual – if anything the reverse was true: difference, not conformity, was what kept the community bonded. He was very rarely mocked, even by the Half Man, but he did notice an immediate change in his relationship with everyone he knew. The King, for instance, became positively friendly; a symptom, Miller guessed, of the albino's lingering affection for Frankie. Helen, the King's wife, previously largely indifferent to Miller, began to mother him. His day job with Frankie continued as before, though she began to snap at him over nothing and no longer shared confidences about her life with Vincent. She remained – the very application of the adjective to anything connected with the Half Man's Camp should have told him that their relationship, as currently defined, was mad and unsustainable – civil.

For appearance's sake, Miller was obliged to go and visit Coco for an hour or so, once or twice a week, during which time the clown would serve him sherry or tea and talk about circus history.

One afternoon, a couple of weeks after his first alarming encounter with Coco, he was returning from the clown's trailer when he was stopped by Alex, as he passed her clearing. She was holding the clear plastic bag containing her dressings.

She followed Miller back to the kitchen; he sat her on the step and went into the washroom for his towel, hot water, scissors and soap. Frankie was sitting at the marble table; she watched him as he washed his hands at the sink, but said nothing.

He put Alex's feet on the towel, and removed the old bandages. He began to apply a little of the antiseptic powder to the deep lateral cut on her left foot, which was still weeping slightly.

'My mom says you're having a thing with Coco,' Alex said.

Miller looked at Frankie, who was still sitting within earshot, at the kitchen table.

'Yes.'
'My dad says you're a fucking faggot.'
'Oh.'
'Are you?'
'Yes.'
'He told me what you do,' Alex continued.
'I'm sorry?'
'He told me what it is,' she continued, 'that you faggots do.'
'Well he shouldn't have.'
'Why not?'
'Because...'
Miller fastened the last new bandage and stood up, holding the old dressings. Alex pulled on her socks.
'Why not?' she asked him. 'Because you think it's really gross?'
'No.'
'Do you think it's gross?'
'No.'
'It sounds gross.'
'Alex...'
She took her first few steps with her new bandages, then began to walk back to her painting. As she left, she turned and asked him, in a voice that reminded him, as he often tended to forget, that she was only nine years old.
'Does it hurt?'
'What?'
'When you do – you know – that... does it hurt?'
Miller could see that she wasn't going to leave without an answer.
'Yes.'
'But you still like it, right?'
'Yes.'
'Does it hurt a lot?'
'Yes.'
She walked back and squeezed his hand, and whispered so that her mother wouldn't hear.
'I'm sorry.'

Miller came to enjoy his occasional visits to the clown's trailer; on a superficial level he got on well with Coco, who was fascinated by England, though he had never been there and forgave his guest for being unable to answer questions about British circus tradition and other, more general, cultural inquiries concerning the many European countries Miller had never troubled to visit.

Looking through Coco's old pictures of the local circus community, Miller noticed, Dowson's refinery was little more than a group of shacks, all belching smoke. The name of the town, painted in capitals on the perimeter fence, was different.

'Darlington?' Miller asked.

'That's what George Dowson called the place when he settled here,' said Coco. 'It was where his father was from, in England. He'd never been there himself.'

'So why did he change it?'

'He went to England. He went to Darlington. And he didn't like it.'

'Darlington's not that bad,' said Miller.

'Well what he told the papers was that his father Ernest had hung a picture over George's bed when he was a boy – it was all, you know, college spires and people in punts with striped blazers and cricket pants, drinking cocktails through straws; I think it was…'

'Oxford?' Miller volunteered.

'Right. But he told George it was Darlington. So when he saw the real one he came back and changed the name of this place to…'

Coco went through the pile of photographs, and pulled another out.

'D'Arlington?' Miller read. 'Why?'

'He thought D'Arlington looked real distinguished. But then someone told him it sounded like one of the Three Musketeers, so he just dropped the D.'

They were having lunch together one day in the Show Bar, when the Englishman went over to the jukebox, and put on 'She Never Spoke Spanish to Me'. It was a slow, almost mournful country song. Miller listened to the chorus:

'Favourite poets all agree, Spanish is the loving tongue. But she never spoke Spanish to me.'

'You speak Spanish?' Coco said, a look of eternal hope in his eye.
'Yes.'
'But you only ever went to Spain?'
'And Switzerland,' Miller said. 'And France.'
'But you never went to Naples, or Sicily?'
'No.'
'Or Florence? Or Rome?'
'No.'
'Or Athens?'
'No.'
The clown looked appalled.
'But it's so close,' he said. 'And Greece is where civilization was invented.'
'Right,' said Miller. 'Among other things.'
Coco jokingly put his arm round Miller's shoulder.
'Why not try it dear?' he said. 'You never know – you might like it.'
Seeing this gesture of apparent intimacy, the Half Man, who was sitting at the bar, talking to Frankie, Hunter and the King, made some remark that made the men burst out laughing. The Englishman waited until their attention was distracted again and removed Coco's arm.
'You must never forget, Edward,' said Coco, 'that I am your life assurance.'
'I won't,' Miller whispered to him. 'So long as you and those Baptist communion boys always remember I'm yours.'

On a Friday morning in the first week of September, Miller watched the Half Man struggling into his purple Tacoma, ready for the drive to Arthur James's Hospital, and wondered whether, once Vincent had left, his kingdom would disintegrate like some fairytale castle in the absence of its ogre. Kennedy had told him that the Half Man would be away for three days, perhaps longer. If ever there'd been a time to flee, Miller thought, this would be it. And yet, try as he might, he couldn't think of any scenario that didn't end in further hardship, disgrace and possibly prison. At least here – in Little Paul, Coco, and even, these days, the King – he had company, even if the last two couldn't quite be called friends. And if the Half Man's prognosis was bad, he reasoned, running away now would make no sense at all.

But as soon as the King returned to the camp, alone at the wheel of the distinctive pickup, it became obvious that little would alter while the Half Man was out of town. His great talent – for spreading dread and paranoia by proxy – didn't depend on his physical presence. When he wasn't there, Miller told Coco, over a sherry in the clown's trailer, it was almost worse, because of the fear of what someone might accuse you of having done in his absence.

'That's right,' Coco said. 'He loves the thought that people will be most terrified of getting a beating for something they haven't done. He'll get his guys to kick the crap out of someone from time to time without any warning, just so as the others know it happens. Or he'll get a guy in a position where he thinks that he's finished, and then back off.'

But only that night there was a hiccup in the camp's routine. It occurred when the King went drinking in the Skirts and Spurs – a frightening barn of a place across Highway 41 – and didn't come back. The bar, where the King had friends, but which Miller had been warned never to enter, had a big orange banner across the front reading 'Bikers Welcome'.

Helen rolled her wheelchair up to Miller in the Show Bar, at around nine, and asked him to go and retrieve her husband.

'From the Skirts and Spurs?'
'Just don't open your mouth when you're in there,' she said.
'Why not?'
'Because you're foreign. They don't like foreign.'
'Remember when that French guy went in there,' Paul said.
Helen shook her head.
'Don't tell him about the French guy,' she hissed.
'Can't you go?' Miller asked Paul.
The dwarf laughed.
'Now how can I put this,' he said. 'The people in the S and S don't seem to like my kind.'
'What about Hunter?'
'Hunter's working here. And Hunter'll tell Vincent the King went AWOL and he'll go crazy.'
'Please,' said Helen. There was a small plug of what looked like solidified blood, Miller noticed, in her left ear.
She pointed down at her manual wheelchair.
'What can I do?'
'OK,' said Miller. 'How do you know he'll come back?'
'Just give him this,' she said.
She scribbled a message on a coaster, put it in an envelope Paul found, under the bar, and handed it to Miller.
He crossed 41, and walked the half-mile to the Skirts and Spurs. He saw the purple Tacoma on the parking lot surrounded by Harley-Davidsons. Inside the bar it was very dark. There was no music playing and at first sight the S and S seemed more civilized than he'd expected. There were a few middle-aged Hell's Angels playing pool on two tables in the centre of the room and a group of younger bikers smoking grass at the counter. There were, Miller noticed, no women anywhere in the bar. He saw the King, who was wearing his white Stetson, with a beer in his hand, sitting with a weasel-faced man, at a table at the far end of the room.
Adopting a purposeful stride and avoiding eye contact with the patrons, he was half-way across the floor, level with the pool players, when his note was snatched out of his hand by the tallest, and most

muscular, of the Hell's Angels. The man was in his forties, with a thick black beard which half-concealed a Maltese cross tattooed on his cheek. His denim jacket, discoloured by filth and engine oil, was sleeveless, revealing forearms as thick as some men's thighs.

'Give me that,' Miller said.

Hearing his accent, his aggressor stared at him and put down his pool cue. He reached in to the breast pocket of his jacket and produced a pair of reading glasses. Miller couldn't have been more surprised if the Hell's Angel had pulled out a lighted votary candle, or a rabbit: it seemed impossible that a man of such appearance would know what spectacles were, let alone use them. But he put them on, opened the envelope, and placed the coaster underneath the central light over the green baize. Then, rapping his cue on the edge of the table, he brought the room to silence, and started to read.

'Come home right now my angel...' he began. He cleared his throat. '... my angel... and make love to me with the light on...' At this he paused and, peering over his reading glasses, gave Miller a look that was almost more quizzical than hostile, before delivering the last phrase: 'Like you always used to do'. He put the coaster back in the envelope.

'Now which of these boys,' he asked, are you inviting to party?'

A wave of coarse laughter went round the bar.

'You're not from this part of Florida,' the pool player added, 'are you boy?'

The King sprinted across the room.

'It's OK Hollis,' he said, 'he's with me.'

'Well, why the fuck didn't you say so?' said the Hell's Angel.

'I didn't see him.'

'Drink?' said Hollis, apologetically, to Miller, who hesitated.

'No,' said the King.

'Is this yours?' the biker asked the albino, holding out the coaster.

The King nodded.

'From Helen?'

'I guess.'

'See you tomorrow then.'

Miller and the King left the bar together and crossed the Highway on foot.

'What about the Half Man's car?' the Englishman asked, looking back at the monstrous purple vehicle.

'I'll get it tomorrow.'

'Why?'

'Because I don't want a DUI.'

They began the short walk back to the Show Bar.

'What did they do to the French guy?' Miller asked him.

'The French guy? Oh – right, yeah, the businessman. He got on the TV news.'

'What did they do?'

'It wasn't that bad really, it was just – the guys knocked him about a bit; I think Hollis broke his nose' – the King looked at Miller – 'I mean, he *was* French...'

'Right.'

'And then they made him eat his tie.'

'What? And he did?'

'Yeah, well by that stage he sort of had to. He'd stopped in for a sandwich there and he kept complaining that the bread was all the wrong shape, not like in Paris, France, and he said as how it was sugared and it shouldn't have been, because bread was never sugared in Paris and he asked them why couldn't he get a... what's it called... that long white French thing...'

'A baguette?'

'Right. So the boys went out and got him one, from the store. Hollis served his tie up real nice for him, in thin slices, with lettuce and mayo and everything.'

'What does Hollis do?' Miller asked.

'What do you mean, "do"?'

'For work.'

'Hollis's work,' the King replied, 'has to do with my sideline.'

'What's that?' Miller asked.

'Contracts.'

'What?'

'Hits.'

'What?'

'Hollis kills people, Ed.'

'Oh.'

'For money. Just like I used to.'

'Is he your best friend?'

'I never thought about that,' said the albino. 'I guess he must be.'

They drew closer to the outline of the oil refinery. Miller remembered how appalled he'd been when he first saw the Dowson plant after dark. Now, somehow, it had become almost reassuring.

'Used to?'

'Yeah well, I'm kind of retired now.'

The King took his Stetson off as they entered the Show Bar and explained what had happened, to Helen, who roared with laughter.

'God knows,' she said, 'what Hollis would have done to you. You never know,' she added, winking at her compatriot, 'you might have quite enjoyed it.'

Miller forced a smile.

Helen went over to talk to Alex, in the diner.

'How did that business work, then?' Miller asked the King.

'What business?'

'Your business with Hollis. Your sideline.'

'Now you know you really don't ask those sorts of questions.'

'It's just a world I know nothing about.'

'Well how it works is, an envelope appears in your letter box with a thousand dollars in it, that's basically how it works, and the next day…'

Miller saw Helen, wheeling herself silently towards her husband. He tried to warn the King, but the albino didn't notice him.

'And the next day,' Helen continued, from behind the King's back, 'you get another letter, with the name of the victim.'

'A thousand dollars?' Miller asked.

'Right.'

'As a first payment?'

The King looked puzzled.

'No.'

'A thousand dollars for a life?'

'Right.'

'What about two men?'

'That business has two rules,' Helen said. 'There are no refunds, once the wheels are in motion, and there are no two-for-one offers. Two men – two thousand.'

'And so on,' Miller ventured.

'That's right,' she said, and smiled. 'It's all quite straightforward, really. When you get right down to it, it's just like buying bananas.'

Miller's respite from confrontation was to prove short-lived. On the following night, a Saturday, he came over to the Show Bar with Little Paul; the dwarf was carrying his telescope, which Frankie had told him he could set up on a window table in the bar.

As they crossed the car park, a black Pontiac van with Alabama state plates pulled up on the dirt lot by the River Hermosa, opposite the petrochemical plant. Six women climbed out. In their late twenties and early thirties, they were dressed almost identically, in very short black skirts, diaphanous black tops and too much make-up. A second, similar truck drew up, heavy metal blaring from its open windows; it discharged five men, some wearing Lynyrd Skynyrd T-shirts, all in jeans with large belt buckles and lizard-skin boots. When the strangers came into the Show Bar, on the heels of Miller and Paul, Miller noticed how they immediately set up a ripple of unease: Hunter, the King, Frankie and Coco, he sensed, were reading signs he didn't recognize.

The men and women, though they were clearly together, didn't mingle in the bar but stayed in two separate groups, drinking heavily. From the way they remained segregated, the women's clothes, and the occasional outburst of crude innuendo, Miller gathered that this was some sort of chaperoned hen party.

'Don't go near those guys,' Little Paul advised him.

'Why?'

'They have out-of-state plates; they look loaded... I just don't like the feel of them.'

'And stay away from the women,' the dwarf added.

'Why?'

'I didn't like the way... didn't you see how they just parked right across from the refinery, belching out all that fire, and sulphur, and shit and stuff – I mean hell, none of that seemed to bother them at all. They barely gave it a second glance.'

'We,' Miller replied, 'barely give it a second glance.'

'Yeah, but we're guys,' said the dwarf. 'And we see the Dowson plant every day. We're used to it. They're not from here. And they're ladies. Except they ain't no ladies,' he added. 'Trust me.'

The atmosphere elsewhere in the Show Bar, in the absence of the Half Man, was one of uneasy release. Paul had his telescope pointed out of the window. Everyone had just been paid; Frankie doubled the workers' allocation of free beers to eight.

By ten in the evening the visitors were very drunk. One of the men was slumped against the jukebox, reading off song titles, when he noticed a single called 'Woman Is the Nigger of the World'.

'I don't know about that too well,' he said. 'Way I've always seen it, *niggers* is the niggers of the world.'

Frankie walked over to the jukebox, put in a quarter, and made a selection.

The first line of the song began: 'Last night I saw Lester Maddox on a TV show, with some smart-ass New York Jew...'

'Oh, shit,' said Paul.

These first few bars of the record silenced the visitors for a moment and drew poisonous looks, especially from the men. Miller understood why when the song reached its chorus: 'We're rednecks, and we don't know our ass from a hole in the ground...'

'I don't think they appreciated that,' Paul said.

'Why not?'

'Because that song is what they are. I think we should go now.'

But it was the visitors who left – the men at least – to set up a barbecue in the parking lot, next to their trucks. The women stayed in the bar, getting more drunk, on boilermakers and sweet liqueurs. Once the men had gone, they started putting country songs on the jukebox. They all took off their shoes and started dancing.

'What do you reckon?' the King asked Frankie, looking at the barbecue in the parking lot, the empty seats in the Show Bar's diner, and the makeshift dance floor.

'With what these girls are spending on liquor,' she said, 'I don't think we need to worry where they eat. The last thing we want at this stage is to provoke them.'

Miller sat at the bar with Frankie and the King. Kennedy arrived and Frankie handed him a small package. The mood outside seemed to be turning uglier. The men had stopped coming in for their drinks. Sitting around their barbecue, they'd produced their own cool boxes full of beer and a crate of Wild Turkey, which they were drinking from the bottle.

Inside, the women stared openly at Frankie's white tunic, trousers and fine cotton gloves.

'How much do you charge,' one shouted, 'to haunt a house?'

Frankie looked at her.

'That would depend,' she replied, 'on how many rooms it had.'

The woman giggled, then looked away.

'You girls staying in Arlington tonight?' Frankie asked her.

'We're headed down to Sarasota,' she said. 'Unless we get lucky.'

In the end it was Miller who started it. Drunk and bored, he sat by the till, trying to read a motto tattooed on the neck of a blonde woman, in her mid-thirties and obese, who was waiting to be served. He'd just made out the words 'Strangers Have the Best Candy' when her companion prodded him in the chest.

'Are you looking at Maria's tits?' she asked him.

'No,' said Miller. 'I was just reading…'

'You fucking were.'

'I wasn't.'

The King stepped over.

'What's your name?' he asked the woman who was complaining.

'Andy.'

'It's all right Andy,' he said. 'He isn't that sort of a boy, if you see what I mean.'

Maria, who was very unsteady on her feet, gave the King a puzzled look.

She turned to Miller.

'Is he saying you're a fucking homo?'

Miller nodded.

She picked up her two boilermakers and made to walk away, then turned back.

'Are you?'

'Yes,' he told her.

'Is he?' she asked Frankie.

'What you see here,' Frankie said, 'is 100 per cent prime English faggot.'

The two women left in a fit of laughter and went back to dancing with their friends. A few minutes later Miller slipped off his bar stool to go to the men's room. As he passed through the alcove decorated with the painting of *The Great Ringmaster in the Sky*, an area screened from the main bar, two of the women stepped out of the shadows and pinned Miller to the wall, holding him firmly, but not violently, taking one arm each. He recognized Andy, who introduced him to her friend Nicole – a redhead; younger, taller, and better-looking than her girlfriends.

Maria appeared, and stood in front of him. She was wearing a sheer black nylon blouse, pulled back off her thick shoulders, a black lace bra which, from where he was standing, concealed almost nothing of her large breasts, and a short black skirt revealing her ample thighs, in black stockings and suspenders. Maria began to lean into him, pressing her breasts into his chest. She smelled of corner-store perfume and cheap tequila. From this distance, Miller noted, her tattoo was all too legible and her blonde hair was clearly a wig.

Andy and Nicole still had hold of his arms.

He made to pull himself free but they held him there.

'Don't fight us now,' Andy said, 'or I'll scream, then tell the guys out there that you tried to touch us up.'

Maria lifted the front of her short skirt, angled her torso back slightly and began rotating her heavy thighs against his thin navy shorts. She closed her eyes. Miller wondered if she was going to be sick.

'I had a bet with Nicole and the other girls,' Andy said. 'I bet them that Maria can turn any guy on.'

'What?'

'Any guy,' she repeated. 'Even you.'

They remained, unnoticed by the rest of the room, locked in this peculiar position for a minute or so. Miller at first assumed that his shock, intoxication and the sheer bulk of his seducer would rule out any risk of his becoming physically aroused. But it was clear, almost immediately, that Andy's bet had been spectacularly well placed.

Andy slipped her hand inside his shorts, and kept it there for a moment or two.

'Girls!' she screamed.

Her remaining companions arrived from the jukebox, in a charge.

Maria stepped away from him, but Andy and Nicole kept hold of Miller, whose flimsy shorts revealed the full, galvanic effect of his first physical contact with a woman since he'd left Barcelona.

The bar staff, sensing trouble, followed the women around into the alcove. As on the night of his first humiliation, they were standing in front of him in a semicircle, a group which included Frankie, Coco, Dr Kennedy and the King. He felt Frankie's eyes on him, but couldn't look back.

'If there were more English faggots like this one,' Andy slurred, 'there'd be a lot less miserable women in the state of Alabama.'

When Miller did finally look at Frankie, he saw that she was staring not at him, but Coco, with a look that had turned from bewilderment to accusation.

'Er – good Lord,' said the clown, looking at Miller's shorts.

Andy turned to Nicole.

'You owe me ten dollars.'

It was then that Miller heard one of the male barbecue party, which had returned to the bar, shout: 'That's my wife.'

Two of the men advanced towards Miller, who retreated backwards across the bar, both hands clasped in front of his awkwardly distended shorts, until he reached the far row of tables, where Paul was sitting.

The men stopped.

'You know what?' one of the visitors said. 'The sun, as my grandpa used to say, never set on a nigger in our town...' He cast a look at Frankie and then, apparently deciding her skin was not quite dark enough, turned back to Paul. 'I think we should take both of these boys for a ride.'

Miller looked behind the bar for the King. He wasn't there.

'Who's coming first – the nigger, or the phoney faggot?'

One of the men grabbed Paul and held him up, with his feet off the ground. Another snapped the dwarf's telescope across his knee, then crushed it into small pieces, by stamping on it with both feet.

In the car park, one of the men was fixing a tow-rope to the back of the Pontiac.

Two of the men had hold of Paul and began to drag him towards the door. Miller smashed his Coors bottle over the head of the bigger one. It split the stranger's head open but the bottle didn't break. The man sank to his knees. His companion – a tall, fair-haired figure in a lumberjack shirt, with a build that suggested first-hand knowledge of the trade – picked up a bottle of Budweiser and broke it against the bar. It was a very different movement to Miller's awkward lunge: smooth, practised, almost graceful, shattering the glass as his arm swung upwards, not down, showering the Englishman in beer and broken glass. He began advancing, holding up the jagged edge, with a slow swagger.

Miller took a few steps backwards but felt bodies blocking his path. A hand gripped his shoulder. He turned and saw Hunter and the King. Behind them was Hollis, flanked by what looked like the entire population of the Skirts and Spurs; grizzled veterans for the most part, armed with pool cues, baseball bats, bicycle chains and shotguns. The albino in the Stetson looked almost the least threatening member of the delegation.

It went very quiet.

Miller's attacker dropped his broken bottle. Behind him, the women began trying to help the injured man to his feet. Nicole, the young redhead, slipped and cut her knee slightly as she headed for the exit.

'Would you like me to take a look at that leg?' Kennedy asked her, stepping over the body of the semi-conscious man. 'I think it needs immediate attention. I am a qualified doctor.'

The King held Kennedy back.

'Pack up your vans,' he said. 'And get out of here – all of you. And don't ever come back.'

Miller sat at the bar with Little Paul.

The King gave them both a brandy.

The dwarf looked out of the window into the night sky, which had become overcast.

'What did that feel like?' Paul asked Miller.

'Terrible,' said Miller.

'In what way?'

'It felt like total humiliation. I can still see those faces, staring at me, and laughing.'

'The guys from Alabama you mean.'

'Right.' Miller paused. 'Are you saying there were some people who weren't laughing?'

'Right.'

'Like who?'

'Like me. Like Frankie.'

'Why not?'

'Because being stared at is our living.'

'I'm sorry about your telescope,' Miller said.

'It wouldn't have been no good anyhow,' the dwarf said, looking at the clouds. 'Not on a night like this.'

Miller helped Paul gather up the fragments of his instrument; he offered to help carry the pieces to his cabin.

'No,' said Paul. 'I'll keep the case. The telescope's no use now. You have to know when the game's up. Talking of which, Ed,' he added, 'I think you've really done it this time.'

Miller went back to his cabin and fell asleep without undressing. That night he had a recurrence of his dream of the Asian girl at the traffic lights; he woke up, as he had the first time, watching his daughter's body float away from him, and found himself sitting, soaked in sweat and trying to scream. As he recognized that it had been a nightmare, his breathing came more easily. Miller had begun to calm himself when he heard a noise from the foot of the bed and, for a moment, had the impression that he was staring down the barrel of a gun. He rubbed his eyes, turned his light on, and saw that the weapon was really there.

It was only a small one: a delicate silver pistol, pointing at his forehead, and held in a thin white glove. He looked at Frankie, who was in a long-sleeved linen nightgown, sitting next to him, on his bed.

'I thought there was only one gun in the Half Man's Camp.'
'There are two,' she said. 'Except when he's away'.
'What is that?' He nodded at the pistol.
'It's a Derringer two-shot. That's a lady's gun. It carries two bullets. One each.' She paused. 'Just kidding.'
She kept the weapon pointed at him.
'Anyhow,' she said, 'what did I come to ask you... Oh yes. Are you gay?'
'No.'
'Bisexual?'
'No.'
'Thank you. I didn't think you were.'
'Why not?'
'Because on the way here, I called in and talked to Paul.'
She lay down on her back, on his cabin floor.
'Where would you like to be?' he asked her.
'In a cold country,' she said. 'In a little house, with a back yard. Where do you want to be?'
'There.'
'And in the yard,' she went on, 'there's a dog. Did you ever have a dog?'
'Yes,' he said.
'What was his name?'
'Heathcliff.'
'Like the gypsy in that movie...'
'You saw that film, then.'
'I saw that movie ten times.'
'When my mum took him for walks and called him, other people would shout back "Cathy". '
'God I like you,' she said.
'Me too.'
'That's... OK then. That's... better.' She got up. As she opened the door, on her way out, she pointed up at the sky.
'Looks like a storm, hey.'
'Yes,' said Miller.
She looked at him fondly, and smiled.

The next morning he walked across to the kitchen, as usual. The clouds were still there, thick and black, hunched over Tampa Bay, but they seemed to be drifting west. It hadn't rained.

Once they'd made the coffee, fired up the oven and loaded it with the trays of sausage, potato and eggs, he sat on a chair by the kitchen table, reading *Double Indemnity*.

'I never saw you so mad,' she said.

'No.'

'Have you ever been so mad?'

There was a new tone in her voice; new life. She sounded like a little girl.

'No,' he replied.

'They would have killed you, you do realize that?'

'Yes.'

'So why did you try to defend Little Paul?'

'I don't know. Because they were picking on him. Because he saved my life. And because they were… I don't know… they were…' he stopped.

'Racist redneck scum,' she said.

'What?'

'Racist redneck scum,' she said.

Miller pondered this phrase.

'Yes,' he said. 'Right.'

'The world,' she added, 'would be a better place without them. Other people's lives would be better if they weren't there.'

'When's the Half Man back?' he asked her.

'Tomorrow.'

'Has he been in the hospital a lot?'

'Yeah.'

'What with?'

'Gunshot wounds, a couple of times. And he's diabetic.'

'Kennedy told me that he shot his cousin's fiancé the night before his wedding.'

'Yeah – Jerry. Except that time, Vincent didn't go to the hospital. Jerry did. They took him to the hospital, then they took him straight to the mortuary.'

'Did Jerry threaten him?'
'Jerry?' She laughed. 'Jerry was a real nice, simple guy.'
'Why did he kill him?'
'I think Vincent had a thing for Louise.'
'Jerry's fiancée?'
'Right.'
'His own cousin.'
'Yes.'
Miller still had the paperback open on his lap. He was at the end of a chapter; he closed the book, and folded over the top corner of the next page.
'So when was the last time the Half Man was in hospital?'
'The last time before this?' She stopped to think. 'It was when he slipped... Oh no. No it wasn't.'
'Go on.'
'You really want to know?'
He nodded.
She turned to face him.
'The last time Vincent was in hospital was when he got beaten up by a pimp, after he wouldn't pay the hooker he'd just fucked in the back of his Tacoma, in Saint Pete. That was the last time, if you want to know.'
'Jesus.'
'He got a terrible beating that night.' She paused. 'And he caught syphilis from the girl.'
'Oh.'
'And then he wouldn't go to the hospital until Kennedy forced him to. He wouldn't go of his own... what's the word...'
'Of his own volition.'
'Right. Because he said going to the STD clinic would be degrading. And even when he did go, and they told him what he had, he refused to go back for the last shot. Because it's a course of shots. John – Dr Kennedy – got hold of the stuff and brought it out here.'
'When he had syphilis,' he began, 'did you...'
'No.'

She was by the sink, looking out of the window. Miller stood up, but turned away from her.

'Do you sleep with him?'

'No,' she said. 'Well... not – how can I put this? Not of my own volition.'

'You know it's little things of this kind,' he said, 'that tell you that your marriage is in trouble.'

She turned to face him.

'You know we're travelling to Connecticut next week, to the state fair, did you know that?'

'No.'

'With the banner, and the trailer, and me in this body suit, on a revolving stage.'

'I can't believe that still goes on.'

'Well, it does,' she said. 'Just. There's another twisted son of a bitch that still shows deformed foetuses at two dollars a time in a tent at Coney Island.'

'I thought you said you didn't mind the shows?'

'I don't mind the midway so much,' she said. 'But Vincent... he arranges these... what would you call them... private viewings.'

'What of?'

'Me.'

'Who for?'

'For sick fucking perverts,' she said. 'But even that isn't what really matters.'

She wasn't crying, he noticed, though her voice sounded as though she must be in tears.

She put her head on his shoulder and he held her for a few moments.

'What's that?' he asked her.

'What really matters,' she said, 'is that I don't trust him around my daughter. You know, Alex needs a father, Ed.'

'Alex has a father.'

'She needs a different kind of a father. Someone like you.'

Miller, surprised, glanced at her face, looking for some sign that she was joking, and found none.

Frankie stepped away from him. She picked up *Double Indemnity* and looked at the opening paragraph of the page with the corner folded over.

'I don't know when,' she read, out loud, 'I decided to kill Phyllis.'

'Why did you leave it folded over at that page?' she asked him. 'Were you hoping that I'd pick it up?'

'No,' he said. 'I folded it over because that's where I was up to. I hadn't even read that page. Why do you ask?'

'No reason.'

'Death – or rather thoughts of death,' he said suddenly, 'have been seeming to dog me just lately.'

'Don't let it invite you on to it,' she said. 'Death can call you on to itself.'

'Do you believe that?'

'Sure I do. I think that, to die, some small part of you has to give consent to leave. Once you do that, it's like you've bought your airplane ticket. Once you've done that, it can happen any time.'

'Not like murder,' he said.

'Well murder, that would be small consent in some other person's heart. There's not much you can do about that.'

'So what about Vincent?' he asked. 'Has he had his results?'

'I don't know,' she said.

'Is he going to be OK?'

'Vincent?'

She opened the oven door to check that nothing had burned, then let it slam shut.

'The King had a cancer, you know,' she replied. 'You get a cancer affecting an organism, you cut it out, and the whole body is better afterwards. It thrives. The misery is gone. The operation,' she said, 'is just a difficult moment to go through. It's like pulling a bad tooth. You take the risk, and the evil's gone.'

'I remember reading something like that in a play by Shakespeare.'

'Oh, really?'

'Except that he wasn't actually talking about cancer.'

'No?'

'Will the Half Man ask me to come,' Miller asked, 'to Connecticut?'
'No,' she said.
'How do you know?'
'Because Vincent's not going to Connecticut. Nobody is.'
'But you just said...'
'Sick or well,' she said, 'Vincent's sitting in Departures.'
'What?' said Miller.
'After we spoke last night, in your cabin, I... I arranged it.'
'You what?'
'I fixed it.'
'What do you mean, "fixed it"? Who with? Somebody local?'
'Kind of.'
'Well fucking unarrange it,' said Miller. 'You'll get us all killed.'
'You can't unarrange these things,' she said. 'Anyhow, how do you think he'll react when he gets back and finds out all about you and your frigging Alabama girlfriend?'
Miller said nothing.
'It's in hand,' she said. 'In three days he'll be gone.'
'You might as well tell me,' he said. 'Who is it — Hollis?'
She shook her head.
'Who, then?'
'It isn't Hollis,' she told him. 'It's Coco.'
Miller laughed. 'And they say Americans have no sense of humour.'
'I'm not American,' she said. 'And it is Coco.'
'*Coco?*' Miller repeated. Though the word murder, in principle, no longer seemed to disturb him, the sound of these other two syllables made him feel physically sick.
'Coco,' he told her, 'as his name suggests, is not a trained assassin. Coco is a fucking clown.'
'That's right,' she said. 'He's a clown with a motive, fury in his heart, supporters all around him and, as of last night, a loaded gun. So back off.'
She threw him his pair of oven gloves.
'OK,' she said. 'It's ready.'

They took the three trays out of the oven and laid them on the marble table. There was a knock at the back door, which was open. Standing in the entrance was the King. Frankie gave the albino his gloves, and he led the way to the diner.

As they crossed the bar, Frankie dropped back from the King slightly.

'That's funny,' she whispered to Miller.

'What is?'

'That's the first time in seven years that he's ever knocked before he came in.'

They put the trays down on the metal serving table in Frankie's Diner. It was fuller than usual – the result, Miller guessed, of the Half Man's absence and his employees' desire to gossip about the events of the previous evening. His most recent conversations with Frankie had put the Alabama incident quite out of his mind. Once he set foot in the diner, though, he was aware of attracting more attention than usual. Helen, the King's wife, broke the tension by initiating a small round of applause. Miller forced a smile.

He saw Coco, who was sitting alone, wearing his full clown outfit – bald wig, checked suit and red nose. On the table in front of him was a cup of coffee, his brass klaxon and his squirting ball. Looking at him, Miller's heart sank.

Little Paul was already on his feet, reaching for an empty plate.

'I think I'll sit down for a coffee,' said Frankie.

The King looked at her.

'You want to sit with Ed?' he asked, with a leer worthy of his employer.

'No,' she said, with what looked like conviction. 'As a matter of fact, I wanted to talk to Paul.'

She took her drink and went to join the dwarf. Even as she moved over to Paul's table, Miller felt himself missing her. He loved the way she walked across the floor.

The King served Helen, from the buffet.

The Englishman, who didn't feel like eating, poured himself a coffee and sat down with Coco. There was a moment of awkward silence.

'Where are you off to,' Miller asked him. 'Holy Communion?'

'I'm doing a spot on the kids' show, on Tampa TV,' said the clown. The King left his wife's table and sat down with them, uninvited.

'Why are you already in costume?' Miller asked the clown.

'They film it in a school,' he explained. 'There's no dressing rooms. The crew send a car,' he added, 'to pick me up.'

'How very wise of them,' said the King.

'You know what?' Coco said. 'That's the first time I ever saw Frankie come in and stay for breakfast.'

'Not breakfast,' said Miller. 'Just a coffee.'

'Yeah, well that's only understandable,' said the King.

'Why?' asked Miller.

'Because, you know, I think Frankie probably needs a coffee. When you spend half the night trudging round the camp, from cabin to cabin – it's thirsty work.'

Coco gave the King a look that, even from behind his thick greasepaint, exuded guilt and fear.

'What?'

'Even when it's cool, you know – walking all that distance – I mean it's a long way to your trailer, Coco, you know that. You do it every day.'

'You mean you followed her?' said the clown.

Miller kicked him under the table but Coco took no notice. The clown gave a desperate look towards Frankie, who was deep in conversation with Paul.

'What did you hear?' the clown hissed, to the albino.

'I heard it all,' said the King.

Coco took his car horn and his squirting ball, got up and, with the most speed his huge rubber shoes would allow him, headed for the kitchen exit.

'What was that all about?' Miller said, rather half-heartedly, to the King.

'I followed her last night,' said the albino. 'I sat on the steps of his trailer and I heard them talking there, in his lounge.'

'And?'

The King gave a broad, unpleasant smile. 'Believe me,' he said, 'you really don't want to know.'

Miller, forcing himself not to appear flustered, finished his coffee, and rolled a cigarette. He said goodbye to the King then, without looking at Frankie, went back to the kitchen, which was empty. He sat at the table with his head in his hands.

A couple of minutes later, she joined him.

'What is it?' she asked.

'The King was following you last night,' Miller said.

'What? When last night?'

'He followed you to Coco's trailer.'

'Oh, Jesus.'

'Correct. I did tell you...'

'Never mind that now,' she said. 'Does Coco know?'

'Yes.'

'Where is he?'

'I don't know – he just took off.'

'Which way?'

'He left through here, I think.'

'Go over to his trailer and... no – hang on – have you used this?'

She picked a cell phone out of the empty sink.

'No.'

Frankie picked it up and pressed its recall button.

'Oh my God.'

She sat down, as though at the end of her strength.

'Who's he rung?' Miller asked. 'The Half Man?'

'No,' she said. 'It's worse than that.'

'Worse?' Miller repeated.

'Much worse. He's dialled 911.'

Miller lit the cigarette he'd just rolled and smoked it hard, as if it was going to be his last.

'Why?' he asked Frankie. 'Why would he do that?'

'I guess he thinks he's better off in a prison cell than with Vincent on his case.'

'Which station will answer a 911 call?'

'Arlington or Big Bend I guess.'

'How many officers are there?'

'Big Bend, I don't know,' she said. 'Arlington, maybe half a dozen.'

'Why the hell didn't he just call Glidden?'

'Because Glidden wouldn't lock him up.'

'Call Glidden on his cell phone,' he told her.

'Why?'

'Why not? Isn't that what he's for?'

'Glidden's very bonded to Vincent...' she began.

'Bonded?' said Miller, 'by what? By loyalty, duty and respect? Or by that sixteen by twelve in the King's picture cupboard?' He felt driven by a vigorous determination he hadn't experienced since he was sitting behind his desk at the paper. 'Call him.'

Frankie rang the policeman. The first time, his cell phone cut out. When she got through again, he said he was on 41, heading north to Big Bend police station.

'Tell him,' Miller said.

'Tell him what?'

'Tell him everything.'

'Dan...' She began, then stopped.

'He's telling me he can't talk now.'

'Why the fuck not?'

'Because he's driving, and he has a civilian in the car, under arrest.'

'Shit,' said Miller.

He drew on his cigarette again.

'Frankie...'

'What?'
'Ask him if it's a clown.'
'What?'
He dropped the cigarette end on the kitchen floor.
'Ask Glidden if his prisoner is a clown.'
'He said: "Affirmative",' she replied.
'Tell him to pull over,' Miller said, 'and talk to you from outside the car.'
'He wants to know why.'
'Tell him it's a matter of life and death.'
Glidden stopped the car.
Frankie handed Miller the phone.
'Glidden?' he said.
'Hi, Ed. How are you?'
'Have you spoken to Coco yet?'
'No, we're just headed down to the interview room. He called 911 and he said he wanted to make a statement about a homicide. I picked him up on 41, outside the S and S. He seems real upset. He just handed me a gun. And he... oh, shit.'

There was scuffling and cursing in the background, and the sound of a car door opening.

'What is it?' Miller asked.
'He just got sick out the car.'
'Bring him back here.'
'I can't do that, Ed.'
'Why not?'
'Because he phoned 911 talking about homicide. The calls are all logged. He has to be interviewed.'
'Can you interview him yourself?'
'Sure,' Glidden said. 'Sunday morning at Big Bend, there ain't no one else there to do it.'

He paused. There was the sound of muffled retching.

'Are you OK, Ed?' Glidden asked.
'Listen,' said Miller. 'Get Coco to make a full statement and tell him that, should he require it, he will be given twenty-four-hour police protection.'

'Against what?' Glidden interrupted. 'Anyhow, I can't do that.'

'Then when he's made the statement, tell him you will press no charges, and then lose the fucking interview tape. Log him as a crazy.'

'We don't have no int…'

'Never mind. Then let me talk to him; I'm coming down.'

'I'm not sure I…'

'Listen Dan,' said Miller. 'I have seen *The Sound of Music*.'

There was a pause.

'Everybody,' Glidden replied, his voice tremulous and uncertain, 'has seen *The Sound of Music*.'

'Yes,' Miller replied, 'but I've seen the other version – the one without the nuns and Julie Andrews.'

'*What?*' Glidden shouted. 'You've seen it?'

'I haven't just seen it,' Miller lied, 'I have a copy.'

'How?'

'I stole it.'

'Give it me,' said Glidden, defeated.

'I'll give it you,' said Miller. 'When you've done what I told you. Because if you don't, Dan, we're all finished. And so are you.'

Miller hung up.

Frankie looked at him.

'I'm sorry Ed,' she said.

'Never mind,' he said. 'Drive me down there.'

'Where?'

'To Big Bend.'

They drove the five miles north. Frankie dropped him on the corner, opposite the small police station. Big Bend was a sub-station, little more than a concrete box, with one cell and an interview room; it was locked up when no officer was present.

Miller walked round the side of the building, away from the road, and crouched behind a bush. Through a window covered with a thick grille, he could see the clown talking to Officer Glidden. Coco was sobbing. His horn was on the table in front of him. He was nervously toying with his empty squirting ball, twisting it like a set of worry beads.

Miller tried the armoured front door of the station, which was open. He waited in the tiny reception area, on a bench.

After twenty minutes, Glidden came out. He handed Miller an envelope, containing Frankie's gun and his handwritten version of Coco's statement.

Miller went into the interview room and closed the door behind him. He sat down and put the package between his feet.

The clown's rubber shoes were stained with vomit. He looked desolate. His make-up was smeared around the eyes, but the wide arc of his lipstick grin had somehow survived intact.

'Sorry, Ed.'

'It's OK.'

'He'll kill me.'

'He won't. Listen to me,' said Miller. 'I used to be a very important man.'

Coco put down his squirting ball and reached into his pocket. He took out a red and white handkerchief, two feet square, and used it to dry his eyes.

'Oh, right. That's why you scrub out another guy's kitchen every morning, in borrowed soccer shorts.'

'I was important, once.'

'In what?'

'In newspapers.'

'So how come you never went to Rome?'

'I just didn't. I never wanted to, when I was important. I do now. But when I was important,' Miller added, 'I learned to understand people. I noticed how a person can choose to listen to their voice of logic,' he said, 'or their voice of fear. And you,' he added, 'are listening to your voice of fear. Listen to your voice of logic. What does it say?'

The clown put his handkerchief down, and looked up at him.

'My voice of logic?'

'Yes.'

'What does it say?'

'Right.'

'It says that the Half Man,' Coco replied, 'is going to come home from hospital, talk to the King, get loaded on Maker's Mark, beat the crap out of me and then shoot me dead, like a rat.' He stared out of the barred window. 'If I'm lucky.'

'Why would he do that?'

'Why wouldn't he? The King said he heard everything.'

For a moment, Miller's resolve failed him.

'Would you say,' he asked Coco, 'that the King was a truthful man?'

'Well…'

'Where were you when you were talking to Frankie?'

'In my trailer.'

'Yes, but which room?'

'Oh. Upstairs. In the bedroom.'

'With the door shut?'

'Of course.'

'And the windows closed?'

'Yes.'

'Well then, you're OK.'

'You think so?'

'Trust me Coco… what's your real name?'

'Richard.'

'Trust me, Richard. The King told me he was sitting on your front step, and that he heard you talking in the lounge. He didn't hear anything. I'm sure of it.'

'I've missed the TV show,' Coco said.

Miller got him a drink of water from the cooler.

'Never mind,' he said. 'I'll call them. I'll tell them you were sick.'

'I was,' Coco said. 'I threw up on my handcuffs.'

'I won't tell them about the handcuffs.'

'Better not.' He took a sip from the paper cup. 'The trouble is,' the clown said, with new despair in his voice, 'I just told Daniel everything.'

'Glidden won't talk to anyone.'

'But he wrote it all down. You can't turn time back.'

'Just this once,' Miller said, 'you can.'

He handed Coco the envelope. The clown gave him back the Derringer, and tore his statement into small shreds.

Miller swept the tiny pieces into the envelope.

'What about the gun?'

'I'll give it back to Frankie,' the Englishman said.

Glidden drove them back down 41 and dropped them ten minutes' walk from the Half Man's Camp. Miller threw the envelope into a trash can at a picnic area, and set fire to it.

Coco walked back to his trailer to change. Miller found Paul in his cabin.

'Listen,' he said, 'can you get me one of those prints of Glidden?'

'At the book club? Jesus – why?'

Miller told him.

'I think I can get it,' said the dwarf, 'but what if they miss it?'

'How often does the Half Man count those pictures?' Miller asked.

'Every day? Every week?'

'I guess not,' said Paul.

Later that afternoon, in Miller's trailer, the dwarf handed over the print, which he'd smuggled under his shirt.

'It's a bit crumpled,' Paul said.

'That's OK.'

Miller tore the picture into pieces, which he tied up in an old carrier bag. That night, in the bar, he handed it over to Glidden, who disappeared with the package without finishing his drink.

Coco was sitting at the bar, his spirits restored.

'I never wanted to do it,' the clown whispered to the Englishman. 'It's just that – he's made her so unhappy. Every minute she spends with him, she's in hell.'

'I've noticed,' said Miller. 'I know.'

The following evening, the King drove the Half Man back from the hospital. He came straight into the bar, where Miller was sitting at the counter, watching Frankie hanging clean wine glasses in their rack, upside down by their stems. Her greeting to her husband was to hand him a whisky, in silence.

'Give one to the King,' Vincent said. He turned to Frankie. 'Since you ask,' he told her, 'that biopsy hurt like hell.'

Nobody spoke.

'But it was worth it,' he added. 'It was benign. The guy told me I'll live to be eighty.'

The Half Man kept the whisky bottle on the counter, and he and the King started drinking heavily. Vincent showed little effect from the alcohol, but the albino, who had kept his Stetson on, began looking very drunk and started boasting about how he had ejected the party from Alabama.

'And Ed,' he said, 'hit the biggest guy over the head, with a bottle of Bud.'

'Coors,' said Miller.

'Whatever,' said the King, 'he didn't like it.' He roared with laughter. 'He didn't enjoy that at all.'

Miller looked at the Half Man; he wasn't laughing.

'The King,' he said, 'Tells me you're more of a man than we thought.'

The bar fell silent.

'Come see me tomorrow,' he told Miller. 'We'll have a talk.'

In the kitchen, the next morning, while Miller washed up, Frankie was refilling the salt cellars from a large tub. Her gloves were off and he noticed her hand was trembling.

'Are you cold?' he asked her.

'It isn't cold,' she said. 'I'm never cold.'

'What is it?'

'I'm scared.'

'Did he hit you last night?'

'No,' she said. 'He was real quiet. He was practically courteous.'

'And?'

'And that's why I'm scared.'

She stood up and turned to face him. He put his hands on her shoulders. It wasn't just her fingers: her whole body was trembling. For a moment, with his eye on the door, he held her close to him. He put his hand on the back of her neck. The shaking stopped.

She took a step back from him.

'How did you do that?'

'I don't know.'

'Would you do it again for me some time?'

'Any time,' Miller said.

She went to put her gloves back on. Miller took her right hand and pulled back her sleeve, to reveal her forearm, which was covered in scale-like membrane, with red patches, and intermittent dots of a much darker red. Here and there, he could see heavy white flakes of skin which hadn't yet dropped off.

'Don't,' she said. 'I know it's hideous.'

'How do you know?'

'Because I have someone who tells me that,' she said, 'every day.'

He took her arm and pressed it to his face.

'Well it isn't hideous to me,' he said.

She shook her head but she didn't move.

'I think you should leave,' she told him.

'What?'
'I think you should run. Now.'
'Where to?'
'Anywhere.'
'Why?'
'Because I think he's going to kill you.'

He was in his cabin after lunch, when Little Paul came in without knocking.

'Come on,' he said. 'Get your things.'

'Things?' Miller said. 'What things? I haven't got any things.'

'I got the keys to the truck,' Paul said. 'I'll take you up to the Greyhound station at Tampa.'

'Then what?' said Miller.

Paul put his hand in his pocket and took out a clear plastic bag; he pressed it into Miller's hand. There were six ten-dollar bills and a pile of loose change.

'This is all I have,' he said.

Miller took it. He looked out through the open door, across to where the Half Man's trucks were parked, in his compound. The King was in the yard, watching him. He gave Miller a wave, which the Englishman did not return.

'How the fuck do you think you can get a lorry out of there without the Half Man or the King seeing you?'

'I can't. You'll have to walk up the highway and I'll pick you up.'

'What did he do to you after you gave Alex and Frankie a ride?'

'He hit me,' Paul said.

'You told me,' Miller continued, 'that wherever I ran, he'd find me. Were you joking?'

'No.'

'Well, then.'

'Well, you might be lucky.'

'I'm not lucky,' said Miller. 'Do I seem lucky to you? And – before you ask – you aren't lucky either. And even if I did manage to get away, do you think he wouldn't work out who took me?'

The dwarf stared at the floor.

Miller bent down. 'I'll go alone,' he said. 'Tonight.'

Paul took a breath, as though he was going to speak, then didn't.

'Go on,' said Miller. 'What were you going to say?'

'Never lean down to a dwarf, OK?'

Miller spent the rest of the afternoon helping Paul in the yard. In the evening, he sat in his cabin alone, nauseous. Just after ten, hearing no noise except the distant cries from the bar, he opened his cabin door as quietly as he could, and stepped out. The King was sitting in the dirt pathway, on a deckchair, holding a flashlight which he turned on, then shone in Miller's face.

'You know,' said the albino, 'you could always sneak out the other way, through your back window. That way you can have a little talk with Hunter.'

Miller looked behind his hut and saw a bulky figure, standing in the undergrowth. He went back into his cabin, and lay on the bed, trembling, waiting for a knock that never came. Frightened and exhausted, he fell into a fitful sleep. He woke up just after midnight, and immediately sensed that he was not alone.

'Frankie?' Miller said, when he saw the figure standing in the shadows of his cabin.

'No, sir,' said a familiar voice.

Miller switched his light on and saw the King. He was holding his Stetson in his right hand, with his arms crossed against his chest, as if he was already in mourning. He was swaying slightly.

'Come on,' he said. 'They're ready for you now.'

'They?' Miller asked.

They walked down the dirt road between the cabins. The King led him into the Half Man's compound, then took him not to the living trailer, as he'd expected, but to the workshop. Miller paused on the steps. He could hear music from inside. It was Frank Sinatra, singing 'It Had To Be You'.

'After you,' said the King.

The room was lit by work lamps and candles. The Half Man was sitting at his welding bench in the middle of the room, on his old barber's chair. Frankie was standing against the wall, to Miller's left, next to Hunter, who was holding her gun. On the opposite side of the room was Alex. She was in her pyjamas, and she was wearing a blindfold.

'Evening, Ed,' the Half Man said.

'Ed's here,' he said to Alex. 'Now we can start.'

'Hi, Ed,' said the girl, apparently unconcerned.

Miller looked back towards the door, and saw the figure of the King standing across it.

'We're playing a party game, Ed,' said the Half Man.

Miller said nothing. Behind the work bench, he noticed the two soldering irons in their holders, both switched on, their elements glowing red.

'It's called Blind Man's Buff.'

'Alex is going to find me,' the Half Man said, 'aren't you Alex?'

She nodded.

He picked up the soldering irons and held them out at the height of the girl's eyes.

'OK, darling,' he said. 'Come on.'

She began walking towards him, her arms extended in front of her.

'Drop your arms, Alex,' the Half Man said.

The girl did.

Hunter had the gun pointed at Frankie's head.

Miller watched the girl advance until she was within a couple of yards of the irons.

'How am I doing, Dad?' she asked.

'You're doing good,' said the Half Man. 'You're getting warm. When you're real close,' he told her, 'I've asked your mom to give a funny kind of a scream. When you hear that funny scream,' he added, 'walk faster.'

'Don't move, Alex,' Miller said.

She giggled, and kept coming forward.

He stepped between the girl and her father, so that he was facing the Half Man.

'Stay where you are,' he shouted, over his shoulder, in an instantly commanding tone he didn't know he still possessed. Alex stopped.

'Mom?' she said.

'It's OK darling,' said Frankie. 'But stop walking OK?'

Miller was so close to the Half Man that the irons were marking his singlet with two brown circles.

'Do you want them instead of her, Ed?' The Half Man smiled, and nodded at the soldering irons. 'Well, take them.'

Miller reached his hands out and took both irons, by the red-hot elements.

The Half Man kept hold of the insulated handles for what seemed like an eternity. Miller felt his flesh burn, and thought he would pass out. The Half Man let go. Miller opened his mouth to scream, but found himself breathing air in, not out. His gaze fell on the cheap figurine of Jesus, on the Half Man's bench. There was what felt like a flash of light in his head, and a strange, queasy shiver that ran down his arms, through his legs, to the flesh in his heels.

'Drop them!' Frankie screamed.

'You just have to hold on to them bars,' he heard the Half Man say, in his English voice.

Miller dropped the soldering irons on the ground; they touched, and the power shorted.

Miller fell to his knees. He looked down at his hands, where weals and blisters were already forming. The pain of the burns, numbed at first through shock, became more intense. His teeth were clenched and his mouth went into a strange rictus. He had his hands out, palms uppermost, in front of him, like a beggar, and he felt sick.

'What's that smell?' Alex asked.

Frankie ran up to her, and swept her out of the room, still in her blindfold.

'Like I told you before,' the Half Man said, 'we don't talk in riddles down here.'

'So?' Miller asked him, through his teeth.

'So you're fired,' he added.

'From the camp?'

The Half Man shook his head.

'On the contrary,' he replied. 'You mustn't leave here on my account. Or on anyone else's. But I find something for everybody. That's the kind of guy I am. I find something for everybody. And I'll find something for you. But I don't want to see your face in the bar again.'

Miller turned to leave.

'Wait,' said the Half Man. 'Come here.'

The Englishman edged to within a few feet of him.

'Closer.'

Miller stood next to the Half Man, who reached for the statuette of Jesus and unscrewed its resin base. Half a dozen small plastic wraps of white powder fell out. The Half Man stuffed them into the pocket of Miller's shorts.

'If by any chance you should see Kennedy tonight,' he said, 'give him these.'

Miller walked back to his hut alone, his hands still opened in front of him, sweating and grimacing with the pain, which had built to a maddening intensity. He was sitting on his bed, his eyes shut and his teeth gritted, when Little Paul arrived.

'Get some ice,' Miller gasped.

Paul ran into the bar and came back with a sack of ice. Miller plunged his hands into it.

'Is this what you're supposed to do?' Paul asked.

'I don't care,' Miller gasped. 'It helps.'

Kennedy appeared, with his camera cases.

'That was fast,' Miller said. 'Did he call you in advance?'

The doctor shook his head.

'I was in the bar.'

He took Miller's wrists, and lifted his hands out of the ice.

'That's not quite the worst thing you could have done,' Kennedy said, 'but it's not far off. All you'll end up with is ice burns on top of your real burns.'

He looked at Miller's hands. Running across each was an ugly purple furrow, already covered with a frankfurter-shaped blister. Another line of blisters ran across the underside of both sets of fingers.

'I think I recognize the implement,' he said.

He opened one of his cases.

'Are you in pain?' he asked.

Miller managed a glare.

'Am I what?'

'Are you in pain?'

'Now that you come to mention it,' the Englishman replied, through gritted teeth, 'I think I might be.'

'Is it severe?'

Miller nodded.

'Right,' said the doctor. 'That's good.'

'Oh really? Why?'

'Because it means that you haven't burned through the nerves in your hand.'

He gave Miller an injection in each wrist and the agony began to ease.

Kennedy handed Paul ten dollars.

'Fetch two large brandies.' the doctor told the dwarf, 'then go to the kitchen.'

Paul lingered on the threshold as he left, with a hopeful look in his eye.

'OK, three brandies. But get a move on.'

The dwarf met them in the kitchen. He held up a tumbler of brandy to Miller's lips, and he drained it.

'Go and watch my cases,' Kennedy told Paul, 'in his cabin.'

The doctor ran the cold tap.

'Put your hands under there,' he said to Miller.

'How long for?'

'We'll give it forty minutes,' he said. 'How long do you think you were holding those damn things?'

'It seemed like an hour,' said Miller.

'I'd say under ten seconds,' the doctor told him. 'In spite of which, you should be in the hospital.'

'Well, take me there,' said Miller.

'As your personal medical adviser,' Kennedy said, 'it is my duty to inform you that every treatment plan should be tailored to the needs of the individual, and in your case I don't actually recommend the hospital. In fact I think the hospital is a very bad idea. They're going to start asking how you inflicted this injury on yourself; then it will be the police – by which I mean the real police, not Officer Glidden – and then...'

'OK,' said Miller.

'I can treat you here at the camp,' he said, 'but those burns will have to be dressed daily. I need to come up and do that.'

'Can you?'

'Sure.'

They went back to the cabin, where Paul watched as Kennedy dressed his patient's hands in sterile bandages.

'Shouldn't you puncture the blisters?' Miller asked.

The doctor shook his head.

'Would he have blinded her?'

'Yes.'

'Why didn't he kill me?'

'It's like I told you,' Kennedy said, 'he's like Stalin. It's not the killing he loves – it's the fear.'

When he'd finished, the doctor sat back and lit a cigar. Little Paul gave Miller a cigarette, which he managed to hold between the tips of his bandaged fingers.

'Before I left England,' Miller told Kennedy, 'I always used to think I was ill, when I wasn't. I seem to be cured of that problem.'

'Because,' Kennedy replied, 'you've got something to worry about.'

'Is that it, do you think?' Miller asked.

'Is what it?'

'I mean, will he be back?'

'I doubt it,' Kennedy said. 'I'd have thought this will keep him going for a while.'

'How could the King stand by and watch,' Miller asked, 'when he's had that done to him? Why does he stay with the Half Man?'

'The King? Because, like I say, Vincent has too much on him. The King is basically an assassin. He keeps saying that he's retired, but when an opportunity presents itself, he just can't resist it.'

'Regardless of the victim?' Miller asked.

'Pretty much. The King has murdered four men that I know of.'

'Can the King... *like* the Half Man?'

'One would have thought not,' Kennedy said. 'Aside from anything else, Vincent keeps making passes at Helen. I would imagine that privately, the King loathes him with a vengeance. But there are some thoughts that are better not given voice,' he said. 'Even by us.'

He rummaged in one of his cases.

'I'm going to leave some painkillers with Paul,' he said, 'which he will give you with water, at six a.m., not before.'

'What if I'm not awake?' Miller asked.

'You'll be awake.'

'Oh. Right.'

'I'm going to give you a shot to put you out now.'

'Wait,' said Miller. 'There's some stuff for you, in my pocket.'

Kennedy took out the heroin.

'Why did he send it with me?' the Englishman asked.

'I guess that technically – legally – you're no longer a bystander,' the doctor replied, 'so much as a dealer.'

He gave Miller another injection, in the forearm.

'By the way, Ed...'

The doctor looked at his watch, waiting for his patient to lose consciousness.

'Yes?'

'Watch yourself.'

'Right,' said Miller. 'OK. Yes.' And then – just as Kennedy was closing the door, and he was drifting off – 'How?'

He spent the next day in bed, then went to sit on a chair, under the porch, at Coco's trailer.

'What had you done?' the clown asked him, pointing at his hands.

'Nothing,' Miller said.

'That's what I heard.'

'He did that to you for nothing,' Coco said. 'Just think what he would have done to someone he thought deserved punishing. And I do deserve punishing.'

'As far as me and Glidden are concerned,' Miller said, 'none of that business with the gun ever happened.'

'It wasn't the business with the gun I was thinking about.' He fetched his guest a root beer, with a straw. 'Do you think a person can change?' the clown asked.

'Sure they can.'

'The habits of a lifetime?'

'Yes.'

'The essence of what they are?'

Miller nodded.

'How do you know?'

'I just do.'

Miller sat back and stared at the Dowson refinery, then fell asleep. After Kennedy's visits, just before midnight, he slept badly, if at all, so that he'd often find himself dozing fitfully in the daytime. One morning he dreamed of his daughter's floating body, and this time awoke with a real scream that fetched Paul, who had been given Miller's job in the kitchen, across to the cabin.

'What is it?' the dwarf asked.

'Nothing,' said Miller. 'I lay on my hand.'

Paul brought him drinks, and sandwiches cut into pieces.

'How are you getting on with the cooking?' the Englishman asked him.

'It's really great,' the dwarf said. 'It's just fantastic. I love it.' A look of guilt entered his expression. 'What I mean is – it's quite good. It's all right, I suppose.'

'Don't worry,' said Miller. 'I'm glad you like it. Look after her, OK?'

When he sat outside his cabin, Miller could see Frankie, working in the kitchen, or standing in the shower.

On the second day after he was burned, she risked coming over to bring him an iced tea.

'Don't go,' he said.

She glanced back into the yard.

'I have to,' she said. 'But if ever you really need me,' she said, 'just call.'

'You're doing OK,' said Kennedy, on the second night. 'There's no infection, that's the main thing. I talked to the Half Man just now...'

Miller looked at him apprehensively.

'He said tomorrow you can come up to my place, at Apollo Beach.'

'How?'

'Paul'll drive you.'

They left at eight in the evening, the dwarf at the wheel of the Half Man's purple Tacoma. Apollo Beach was five miles north up 41, towards Tampa. A left turn off the highway took them on to a small road, heading due west. The sun was straight ahead of them, low on the horizon, like a huge red ball.

'Have you seen that sunset?' Miller said.

'It's the same every night.'

'What's at the end of this road?'

'Tampa Bay,' Paul said.

'What does it look like?'

'There's a beautiful white hotel, with a swimming pool; it has free coffee in the lobby, and a Hawaiian bar, and everything. For one night, it costs like, three weeks' wages.'

'How far is it?'

'It's a ten-minute drive,' said the dwarf.

'Have you stayed there?'

Paul laughed and shook his head.

'Me and Coco did a show there once.'

'Can we go see it?'

Paul looked doubtful and glanced in his rear-view mirror. Miller looked back. The road behind them was empty.

'Better not,' he said.

The doctor's apartment was above a sports bar called Sidelines, just a couple of hundred yards down the side road.

When he took the dressings off, Miller saw his blisters had subsided slightly.

'How long do I keep these on?' Miller asked.

'At least another week,' said Kennedy. 'And if you think they're infected, call me – it doesn't matter how unsociable a time it is.'

'Even nine to five,' said Miller.

'Right.'

'They're still fucking painful,' he said.

'Like I told you,' Kennedy said, 'that's good.'

He handed his patient two white tablets.

'Take one of these now,' he said, 'and you'll fall asleep as soon as you get in. Take the other if you wake up.'

Miller swallowed both.

'As you like,' said Kennedy.

'Make sure he gets to bed OK,' the doctor said to Paul. 'That's twenty mill of diazepam he's just swallowed.'

'Is that a lot?' asked the dwarf.

'Yes,' said the doctor. 'Unless you're, you know…'

'What?' Miller interrupted.

'Addicted. Or a horse.'

They got back at eleven. Paul steered the truck into the Half Man's compound. Miller, light-headed and overcome with fatigue, got down awkwardly from the cab, and saw a figure in a Stetson waiting for him.

'I need to talk to you,' the King said.

'Oh?' said Miller, recognising the fearlessness he'd experienced just before he stood up in assembly and began his speech at Mauldeth Hall.

'I need to ask you something. Hunter and me found some guys nosing around the camp this evening, while you were gone.'
'What kind of guys?'
'Weird guys,' the albino said. 'Two weird guys, in weird clothes.'
'Weird?'
'They were wearing dark suits and ties,' said the King. 'And they were soaked through with sweat. There was one very big one, and a small one. The little one had these patches of red skin all over his face.'
Miller yawned and struggled to concentrate.
'They said they were tourists,' the King added. 'They didn't look like tourists. They had bags like tourists,' he added, 'but they didn't have tourist things in them.'
'What did they have in them?'
'Cameras,' said the King. 'And papers.'
'How do you know?'
'I had a talk with them.'
'Then what happened?'
'I belted the small one a couple of times,' said the King. 'And then the big one ran off.'
'And then?'
'And then they both left.'
'So why are you telling me?'
'Oh yes,' said the King. 'That's what I was forgetting. There was something else really weird about them.'
'Yes?'
'They were English.'
'What?'
'They were English. Do you know who they were?'
'No.' Miller yawned again. 'Look, Kennedy gave me some drugs.'
'Oh, really?' said the King.
'Medicine. To put me to sleep.'
'Right.'
'Can we talk about this tomorrow?'
The albino shrugged.

'If you ever bring the police in here,' he said, 'even English police, you're dead.'

Miller felt unsteady on his feet. Paul helped him back to his cabin. He felt his way to his bed, lay down and fell asleep. The dwarf closed the door for him.

When he woke up, it was nine in the morning. He was looking at his borrowed alarm clock, in surprise, when he noticed something else, next to it, on his small bedside table. It was a silver picture frame. When he looked at the face inside it, for a moment he stopped breathing.

He screamed Frankie's name.

She ran across from the kitchen.

'Are you OK? What the hell is wrong with you?'

He pointed at the picture.

'So?'

'What do you mean – so?'

'So, it's a photograph of a dog. You called me over right under their noses to tell me you got a picture of a black dog?'

'Yes,' Miller said, 'but I didn't put it there.'

'So somebody brought you a picture of a black dog.'

'Yes,' Miller said. 'But who?'

'I don't know.'

'Neither do I.'

'Does it matter?'

He pointed at the picture with his bandaged right hand.

'That is not a black dog,' he said.

'It is.'

'Well, OK, it is.'

'So what's your problem?'

'My problem,' he told her, 'is that that's Heathcliff.'

Frankie picked up the picture frame.

'Hey, he's all right,' she said.

'*Was* all right,' said Miller. 'He's been dead for twenty years.'

'There's a card under it,' she told him.

She picked it up.

'Wow, this is really beautiful,' she said, looking at the fine bonded, cream-coloured paper. 'It has the address kind of stamped down into it.'

'What does it say?'

'Elizabeth Portal,' she said, 'Glastonbury, Oxted, Surrey. RH8...'

'Oh, shit,' said Miller. 'Oh, fucking hell.'

'It says...'

The King burst in through the door, and snatched the card from her hand.

Behind him, Miller could see the Half Man, in his electric cart, a couple of feet from his cabin door.

'Meet me at 12.30 tomorrow,' the albino continued, 'at the Grand Carnatic Café, 1301 Carnatic Road, Orlando 30810 FLA.'

'The Grand Carnatic Café?' Miller asked. 'What's the Grand Carnatic Café?'

'I know what the Grand Carnatic is,' said the King. 'Who's Elizabeth Portal?'

'That's my wife,' Miller said.

'Your wife?' said Frankie.

'My ex-wife. Throw it in the bin,' he said to the albino.

But the King handed the letter to his employer, who inspected it.

'In your opinion,' the Half Man said to Miller, through the door, 'would Elizabeth Portal have sent those goons around here yesterday?'

'Yes,' said Miller.

The Half Man tilted his head to one side and said nothing for a few moments.

'If you see her,' he asked, 'can you get those limey cops off our case?'

'Yes,' said Miller, as confidently as he could manage.

'Well you'd better go, then.'

'Right,' the Englishman agreed.

'How will we know,' the King said, with a sly look, 'that he won't just try to run to the cops, once he's out of here?'

The Half Man thought again.

'Can you go with him?'

'Sure,' said the albino.

'Yeah,' said the King, 'but once he's in the Grand Carnatic, he could still run, whoever was with him. It's crawling with security.'

Nobody spoke.

'OK,' said the Half Man to Miller. 'Go tomorrow. Take the Half Man's Tacoma. Fuck us over and I'll kill you. You understand?'

Miller nodded.

'On my own?'

'No,' said the Half Man, with a malicious smile. 'Not on your own. Take Alex.'

'Alex?' Miller asked. 'Why Alex?'

'Because that'll draw less attention to you. And because then I know you'll come back.'

'Right.'

The Half Man drove his cart back towards his compound. The albino turned to leave.

'King?' Miller called out.

'Yes?'

'What is it?'

'What's what?'

'The Grand Carnatic.'

'The Grand Carnatic?' replied the King, as he left. 'It's a hotel. Just outside Disneyland.'

'Disney World,' Frankie corrected, as she got up to go.

'Have you been there?' he asked her.

She shook her head, leaned down and whispered to him: '*No nos dejes, vale?*'

'No,' said Miller.

He was behind the wheel of the Half Man's purple pickup, the following morning, with Alex at his side, by the time he realized that he hadn't thought about the practicalities of driving. The car had been adapted, so that the accelerator and brake were operated by handles coming off the steering column. Just touching them with his palms was painful.

'Does this work with foot controls, too?' he asked Alex.

'Sure,' she said and pulled down a lever on the dashboard. He pressed the accelerator, and heard the engine pick up. He could manage the steering wheel using his lower palms and fingertips but he had to ask the girl to shift the automatic into gear for him.

'Hey,' she said, as they set off. 'This is fun. Can you drive?'

He took the small roads up to Interstate 4, the main highway running east to Orlando. Outside the camp, he began to brood on the Half Man's hold over him, and to entertain vague thoughts as to how he might break it. 'The King,' he remembered Dr Kennedy saying, 'is a born killer. When the opportunity arises, he just can't help himself.'

It was only on the Interstate, with other cars around him, some driven by men with pressed suits hanging up against the back window, that his mind turned to his wife – how she'd tracked him down to Florida, and what she could possibly want. He became conscious of his clothes – the thin navy shorts, unwashed since his hands had been burned, four days ago, and his white singlet, covered with sweat marks, its front still soiled with the two round stains left by the Half Man's soldering irons.

While they were queuing on the approach road to the hotel, he looked at himself in the driver's mirror. He was bald; his scalp was burned a deep brown by the sun, and there were five days' stubble on his face and head. He opened his mouth, and examined the gap left by his missing front teeth. Looking down, he noticed how his split and discoloured nails protruded from his bandages. His black canvas shoes were torn, and covered in dust. Alex had come out, as the Half Man ordered her to, without any shoes; her right foot was still in a dressing. He turned on the radio, which was tuned to an FM station. For all his difficulties, Miller found he was immediately distracted by the music;

a brooding, hypnotic song that seemed to capture and intensify his uncomfortable sense of impending doom.

'I was staying at the Marriott,' it began, 'with Jesus and John Wayne; I was waiting for a chariot, they were waiting for a train…'

He'd lost all awareness of his surroundings by the time it reached its chorus: 'My ride's here…' A horn sounded behind him. Miller moved forward to close the gap that had opened up between him and the car in front.

They parked, and joined the trail of customers – families with young children – heading into reception, on foot.

'Hey,' said Alex. 'I bet you never thought my dad would let *you* bring me here, huh?'

In front of him, heads began to look around then, seeing Miller's face, turned back.

'Listen,' he whispered to her, 'Alex, just for today, call me Dad, OK?'

'OK,' she said. 'Right. Dad.' She paused. 'Why?'

'Because there are weird guys who kidnap small girls and I really don't want these people to think that I'm one of them.'

'Do you have any children, Dad?' she asked.

Heads turned again.

'Yes,' he replied.

The Grand Carnatic was a large, air-conditioned development, built in the style of a Victorian grand hotel, designed to attract the overspill from Disney World. As Miller and Alex came in, the security staff, noticing the Englishman's appearance, asked him why he was there. His accent appeared to reassure them and they directed him to the dining room. He took the young girl up to the second-floor restrooms to get a drink of water. Miller went into the men's room and plunged his head into a bowl of cold water.

When he came out, he found Alex standing on a balcony above the restaurant, next to a plastic grandfather clock, showing quarter to one. He looked down into the Grand Café. There was a raised ornamental fish pool in the centre of the room and a white grand piano with nobody sitting at it. A chamber orchestra was playing in one corner.

He saw his wife. She was sitting next to Ellie, his daughter, and looking impatiently at her watch. Elizabeth was wearing a pale cream and lemon floral dress and, despite the heat outside, matching tights. Her face and arms were lobster-pink.

'Is that her?' Alex asked, pointing. 'She's a real English lady, right?'

'Yes.'

They took the elevator down to the lobby. Miller held Alex by the arm and led her across the dining room. When Elizabeth noticed them approaching her table, she physically recoiled, as he'd seen her do from vagrants.

Then, recognizing Miller, she got to her feet, and attempted a smile. He came to the table, still holding Alex by the arm. Ellie got up and stared at him. His daughter was wearing jeans and a sweatshirt and she'd grown more than he'd expected: she was six inches taller than Alex, who was almost the same age. On the table in front of Elizabeth was a Berlitz Spanish phrase book. She looked at Miller as if he was a criminal and said nothing. The four of them sat down together.

'Mummy?' Ellie said.

'Yes?'

'Who's that?'

'Who's who, darling?'

'That black girl.'

Elizabeth turned to Miller.

'Who is she, dear?'

Ellie added, a little louder than was necessary: 'She smells.'

Miller, who had been struggling with a combination of guilt, dread and anxiety, found these reactions instantly extinguished in a wave of anger.

'We all smell,' he said.

'Daddy,' said Alex.

'Yes?' said Miller, ignoring the looks from his wife and daughter.

'I want to leave. I don't like it here. I wish we'd never come to this diner.'

'*Daddy?*' said his daughter. She sniggered, and met her mother's eyes.

'You shut the fuck up,' Alex told her.

'Darling,' Elizabeth said to her daughter, 'isn't it time for your riding lesson?'

A young woman of Scandinavian appearance, sitting alone at the next table, got up and took the girl's hand.

'Dad?' Ellie asked him.

'Yes?'

'I came top in Latin.'

As she walked away, he thought he saw her take a handkerchief out of her pocket.

'Dad?' Alex said.

'Yes Alex.'

'What's Latin?'

'It's... look,' he said to his wife. 'Why am I here? Who's that?' He gestured towards the retreating figure of the Swede.

'That's Anneka,' she said. 'Ellie's nanny.'

'Oh.'

'And you're here,' she said, 'because I need something from you.'

'What?'

'I need you to sign some papers.'

'With a view to what?'

'With a view,' she said, 'to making everything over to me.'

'I already have.'

'You haven't,' she said. 'Not in law.'

She leaned down, put her hand into a straw basket by her feet, and took out a small pile of papers. Each page had boxes, neatly highlighted, in yellow or peach-coloured felt marker.

'This gives me full right to dispose of your share options, will, and investments, premium bonds, pension...'

'Pension? How much of it?'

'All of it. Yellow for signing,' she said, 'pale pink for initials.'

She handed him a fountain pen, so thick that Miller could barely hold it.

'I don't know if I can write,' he said.

'Do your best,' she said. 'We have a witness.'

He looked across to the next table where Nigel Bullivant, the legal courier with psoriasis, had taken Anneka's place. He was wearing a grey suit and the same cricket tie Miller had last seen when he drove Bullivant's face into the windows of Oxbridge House. His right arm was in a sling; he had a badly swollen upper lip and two black eyes. In his left hand there was a small digital camera.

Miller, holding the pen as best he could, with the tips of his fingers, put it to the paper. Bullivant's flash went off.

He put the pen down.

'What possible reason do I have for doing this?' he said. He looked at Alex. She was staring at the floor.

'Why should I,' he insisted, 'when you already have everything?'

Elizabeth reached into her basket and took out a new, pale yellow folder.

'I don't think you realize,' she said, 'quite how much I have done for you already.'

'Such as?'

'Such as I stopped Simon pressing charges on the Mercedes.'

'Simon?' he asked her. 'Mercedes? What Mercedes?'

'The Mercedes that you sprayed with...'

'I see,' Miller interrupted. 'Right.'

She opened the yellow folder and took out a receipt.

'Avis car rental company,' she read. 'Twelve thousand eight hundred and seventy three pounds...'

'What for?'

'One...' She screwed up her eyes to read the printing. 'Chevrolet Cavalier subcompact 1.4 litre gold automatic transmission...'

'Ah.'

'Where is it?' she asked him.

'It's at the bottom of Tampa Bay,' he said. 'It got torched.'

'How unfortunate. Well, I paid for it.'

'How...' he began.

'The credit card company came back to the billing address – to me.'

'Right.'

'But that's not the best thing I've done for you.'

'No?'

'No. The best thing I have done for you is to find you first.'

'First?'

'Before Daddy did.'

'How is he?' Miller asked.

'He's out of his wheelchair,' she said. 'And he's not paralysed any more. But he's still livid.'

'How did you find me?'

'When the car rental papers came through,' she said, 'Furini hired this private detective in Orlando; he is very well connected,' she added, 'with the criminal fraternity of Florida.'

'But your man from Orlando didn't come down to Arlington himself?'

'No,' said Elizabeth. 'He didn't seem to like that idea.'

Alex wandered off and sat on the edge of the ornamental pool, looking at the goldfish.

'Who's she, Edward?' Elizabeth asked.

He looked at the yellow and peach shaded boxes on the paper in front of him, and ignored her.

'Oh, don't misunderstand me, dear,' she said. 'I, above all people, appreciate the benefits of a child calling another man father.'

Miller picked up the pen. Alex cupped her hands and cooled her face in the water of the pool.

'I'll do it if...'

Elizabeth laughed and tilted her head back slightly. She crossed her legs and clasped her hands across one knee.

'If?'

'Can you get us a drink,' he said. 'One for me and one for her. And an ice-cream for Alex.'

As he put the pen to the top sheet of paper, he felt something prod his shoulder, and looked up. It was a man dressed as Pluto.

'Fuck off,' Miller said.

'Darling,' Elizabeth said. It was a word he'd only ever heard her use with contempt. 'He's the waiter.'

'Oh,' he said. 'Right. An ice-cream,' he said.

'What flavour?' the waiter asked.

'Any flavour.'
'Dad,' Alex shouted.
'Yes?'
'Can I get a beer?'
'Not in here,' Miller told her.
'Or at any other licensed bar,' said the dog, 'in the state of Florida.'
'And two sodas.'
'What...'
'Any flavour.'
'There is no *if*,' Elizabeth went on. 'You are in absolutely no position to dictate to me.'
'I want – I need – something from you,' he said.
'What is it, Edward?' she asked, with mock compassion.
'Money.'
'Money? I'm surprised to hear that. Is it a lot?'
'Yes,' said Miller.
'A lot of money... but what could it possibly be for, dear? Orthodontic work? The launderette?' She looked over at Alex. 'Barbie dolls? Condoms?'
'Please,' he said.
'How much?'
'I need a thousand dollars,' he said.
Elizabeth opened her handbag and took out a platinum credit card. She handed it to Bullivant, who got up and left.
'Where's he going?' Miller asked.
'To the cash dispenser, in the lobby.'
'Can you get a thousand dollars, just like that?'
'Yes. So could you, once.'
'I guess I could.'
'Edward,' his wife said, 'what in God's name has happened to you?'
Miller began work on the papers; his signature was clumsy, but recognizable.
'And I need a passport,' he said.
'Well go to the consulate,' she snapped, 'and get one.'
'How can I?'

'Why not?'

'They're looking for me,' he said. 'What about the warrant?'

'There is no warrant.'

'But what about the fire?'

Elizabeth searched through the new folder and produced a letter from the chief constable to her father. It stated, with deep and unconcealed regret, that forensic tests had found the fire at Miller's house not to have been started deliberately.

'What did you do with your passport?'

'It was in the car we dumped in the bay. But I can't tell them that at the consulate. What can I say?'

'Tell them that you screwed a girl in a cupboard... that's lovely, thank you.'

The man in the Pluto suit was back, with the ice-cream and drinks.

'And then ran like a whipped dog, abandoning your wife and family,' Elizabeth continued. 'If that doesn't work, you could make something up. You always had a lively imagination.'

Alex came back to the table and started eating very loudly, with her mouth open, licking droplets of ice-cream off her nicotine-stained fingers.

She picked up the phrase book that Miller's daughter had left on the table. It was open at the page: 'In the Restaurant – Lunch.'

'So many of the staff at this hotel are Hispanic,' Elizabeth said. 'They do appreciate it when one makes the effort to address them in their own language.'

'How can you tell?' Miller asked.

'Because they say things back in Spanish, like, er...'

'*Que se vaya, esta puta de mierda,*' said Alex.

'What does that mean?' said Elizabeth.

'That one won't be in your book,' Miller said. 'It's not really a lunchtime remark. It's more of an after-dinner phrase.'

He kept on signing.

'Can you give me fifty dollars?' he asked his wife. 'I'd like to take Alex on some of the rides.'

She opened her purse, and gave him thirty.

Bullivant came back with an envelope. He held it out towards Miller with his body leaning back and his arm fully extended, as though he was feeding a potato crisp to a crocodile. Miller took it, opened it with his teeth, and tipped out the hundred-dollar bills.

'Count them,' he told Alex.

Elizabeth produced a small plastic folder, containing a slightly charred piece of paper. It was his birth certificate.

'Where was this?'

'I found it in the cellar,' she said, 'with Heathcliff.'

Miller paused with his pen over the last paper, which signed away a share of any further assets he might be bequeathed, or win in a lottery.

'I forgot,' he told Elizabeth. 'I need another four hundred.'

His wife gave him a look of immeasurable contempt. She handed the credit card back to Bullivant, and nodded.

Miller initialled the last document.

Her companion came back with the money. Alex counted it, and put it with the rest.

'Tell me, darling,' Elizabeth said: 'I don't expect we'll ever meet again, so this is my last chance to ask you such a sensitive question.'

'Go on.'

'What was that last four hundred dollars for?'

'This is another phrase you won't find in your Berlitz book,' he said. 'I have to buy a dwarf a telescope.'

Miller walked out of the luxury hotel in silence, with Alex at his side. There was no pocket in his shorts and he was holding the envelope containing the money with both bandaged hands, pressed against his stomach.

'Give it to me,' Alex said.

He handed it over.

As they walked towards the truck, she lagged behind him slightly, looking into the distance at Disney World, with its colourful spires and roller coasters.

'Do you want to go in there, and go on some rides?' Miller asked her. 'We have time.'

'No,' Alex said. 'Not with her money. Anyway it's a waste, right? Let's keep it.'

'Right,' Miller said.

On the way back, Miller stopped at a diner and ordered grouper sandwiches and sweet iced tea. The other customers were mainly truck drivers; the bill came to nine dollars. He bought cigarettes and two cans of beer, then set off again. Alex had her feet up on the dashboard, a Marlboro in one hand and a Coors Lite in the other. The envelope containing the money was on a shelf under the dashboard in front of him.

Just after six in the evening, when they were twenty miles north of Arlington on 41, Miller pulled up at a general store.

'Do you want anything?' he asked Alex.

'Can I have another ice-cream?' she asked him, as though she thought he would refuse.

'Sure,' he said.

'What are you buying?'

'I need an envelope.'

'You have an envelope.'

'I need a different envelope.'

'What's wrong with this one?'
'Never mind. Stay here.'
He went into the shop clasping Elizabeth's thirty dollars, and found the ice-cream, a postcard of Tampa Bay, a packet of envelopes, a pen and a roll of gaffer tape.
'Anything else?' the woman asked him.
'Yes,' he replied. 'Do you know where I can buy a telescope?'
'Right here,' she said.
'What?' Miller asked her.
She pointed at a Sears catalogue on the counter. Miller picked one up and, on a single page between the sections on camping and sports equipment, found a small selection of binoculars and telescopes. He circled one, the Vixen 80M at four hundred dollars, tore out the page and put it in a blue carrier bag with his other purchases.

They drove for another five minutes,
'Dad?' Alex asked him. 'What *is* Latin?'
'It's...' Miller kept his eyes on the road ahead, '... it's something that she learns. It's something that she does at school.'
'And she's saying that she's good at it?'
Miller nodded.
'She's very good at Latin,' Alex repeated
'Yes.'
'The best of any of them.'
'Right.'
'So why did that make her cry?'
Miller was about to reply, when he was surprised by a wave of emotion that seemed to have its source at the back of his throat. He could feel the beginning of tears in his eyes. If he managed to speak at all, he realized, it would not be in his usual voice. So he swallowed, instead, inhaled deeply, and pulled off the road, on to a piece of waste land. He crossed his hands on the steering wheel in front of him, rested his head against his forearms, and wept.

After a minute or so Miller felt a small hand tap him on the shoulder. He sat up again and turned to face the nine year old, who he couldn't see properly through his tears. She was holding something out to him;

he wiped his eyes with the back of his bandaged hands, and saw that it was the handkerchief he'd given her; it was clean and unused.

'I told you you'd need it one day,' he said.

Miller pressed his face into the white cotton.

'Get out now,' he said softly, to Alex.

They stood together by the roadside. Miller took his singlet off and put the hundred-dollar bills into his bag of purchases. He threw away all of the envelopes except one, then removed the roll of gaffer tape. He stood facing Alex, the car shielding them from traffic on the highway.

'Will you do something for me?' he asked her.

'Yes.'

'Can you keep a secret?'

'Sure.'

'Will you tape this bag to me?'

She laughed.

'Why?'

'Because I'm not supposed to have this much money in the camp. You know that.'

He held the plastic bag to his side and the girl walked around him as though circling a maypole, taping the bag to the side of his ribs.

'Is that too tight?'

'That's OK,' he said. 'Tight is good.'

As they approached Arlington, Alex was asleep, her head resting on his shoulder, keeping his arm pressed against the small but uncomfortable bulge on his right side.

He turned into the rough road leading back to the Half Man's camp.

'That was a great day, Dad,' she said, still half-asleep.

He looked at her and smiled.

'Don't call me Dad any more, OK?'

'OK.'

He took the truck into the Half Man's compound and switched off the engine. Before Miller had opened the driver's door, his employer had appeared in his cart, at his front door.

'Did you fix that, then?' the Half Man asked him.

'Yes,' Miller said.
'Sure?'
'Yes.'
'Come here, Alex.'
The girl's head went down as she walked past her father, into the house.
'Leave the truck there,' he told Miller, 'with the keys in the ignition. Then get back to your hut and stay there.'

Miller walked back to Cabin Twelve. He closed the door then, with difficulty, unwound the several yards of brown tape. He took a thousand dollars and put them in his new, unmarked envelope then put the four remaining hundred-dollar bills back in the plastic bag and hid it under the mattress. Leaning over his small bedside table, he picked up the biro and held it over the postcard of Tampa Bay. He steadied the top of the pen with his lips and guided it with the fingers of both hands. Slowly and deliberately, in child-like capitals, he wrote: 'Vincent Makin – The Half Man'. He put the card in with the money, and sealed the flap. He waited until it was properly dark then, clutching the envelope against his chest, he slipped out, closing his cabin door quietly behind him.

Miller walked along the row of cabins until he came to number two, home of the King. The hut was in darkness. From the bar to his right, he could hear the regulars singing along with 'Galveston'.

He came to the door of the King's cabin, which was in darkness. Kneeling down, he began to feed the envelope under the narrow gap at the bottom of the door. 'When you get right down to it,' he remembered Helen saying, 'it's just like buying bananas.'

He'd got it half-way through and had just paused to rest his fingers, when the door opened and the main light came on. Miller found himself on his knees, looking down at a large pair of dirty training shoes.

He raised his eyes.

'Good evening,' said the King. He bent down and snatched up the letter. 'For me?' he asked.

Miller said nothing.

'Come in,' said the albino.

He followed the King across the threshold. The cabin was about fifteen foot square, larger than his own. Helen was sitting in her chair, heating a saucepan on a camping stove. The King turned the main light off again. The room was lit by two small candles.

'What are you doing sitting in the dark?' the Englishman asked.

'You know I don't like light,' said the albino. 'Light dazzles.'

Miller sat on the bed next to the King.

'I've just made tea,' Helen said. 'You want some?'

Miller nodded.

The King handed his wife the envelope.

She turned on a table light, looked at it, and saw it was not addressed.

'Is this yours?' she asked.

'Yes,' said Miller and held out his hand.

'He was posting it to us,' said the King. 'Shall I go get Vincent?'

Helen opened it, took out the money, and read the name on the card. She switched off the electric light.

'No,' she replied.

She poured Miller tea, from a large flowered pot.

'My mother's,' she said. 'It's my little bit of England.'

Miller said nothing.

'You really haven't got the hang of this at all, have you, Ed?' Helen said.

'What?'

'It's the name first, and then the money. Or – at the very worst – the money first, and then the name, although that option has certain disadvantages, as you can imagine. But never, never...'

She looked at his card, and the brand new hundred-dollar bills, and spread both out on a small side table. 'The name and the money together.'

'Are you going to tell him?' Miller asked her.

'The Half Man?' she said. 'Well, that depends.'

She looked at his bandages.

'How are your hands, dear? I know how that must feel.'

'It depends?' Miller asked her. 'What does it depend on?'

'Him,' she said. She pointed at her husband.

'I know how that must feel,' she repeated, pointing at Miller's bandages. But I don't know how *that*...' – she pointed at the albino's eye patch – '… must feel. I can't imagine how that would feel at all.'

She picked up the thousand dollars, and held it, gently folded, in her right hand. The King looked at Helen, then looked at the money. He seemed to be on the point of speaking, but didn't.

'Tell him what Vincent did to me,' she said.

'What?' the albino asked her.

'Tell him what the Half Man tried to do to me,' she repeated, a harshness entering her voice, 'last week.'

'Oh.' The King picked up the empty envelope and began to fidget like a child.

'He tried to – you know – do it with her.'

'Christ,' said Miller.

'But he didn't manage,' the albino added.

'Now tell him what Vincent said to me yesterday,' she told him.

'He said…'

The King paused.

'He said: "I'll have you when he's gone,"' Helen recalled. 'That's what Vincent told me. *I'll have you when he's gone*. Didn't he?'

The King nodded.

'And I said: "You'll be waiting a while for that then,"' she continued 'And then he looked at his watch and said: "Oh, I wouldn't be so sure."'

'Were you there?' Miller asked the albino.

'What?'

'Were you there, when the Half Man said that?'

'Oh, yes,' said Helen. 'He was there. My husband was there. And he just sat there, like he's sitting there now…'

Her voice had reverted to the accent of her native Black Country. 'And he said bugger all.'

She handed Miller his tea.

'Bugger all,' she repeated. 'And yet he'll punch a woman in a wheelchair. And he calls himself a man.'

The King, sitting next to Miller, picked up the envelope, and twisted it around in his fingers.

'Tea, dear?' she asked him.

'I'll do it,' said the King.

They met again, in the King's cabin, at ten o'clock following night.

Helen handed Miller his Tampa Bay postcard.

'You'd better get rid of that,' she said. 'Even though it's a pretty little view. I do like the way you put his surname on it. Like there are two Half Men in Arlington, called Vincent…'

'This is how it's going to work,' the King interrupted.

'Should I know this?' Miller asked.

'Yes,' said Helen.

'At eight o'clock tomorrow night,' the albino said, 'the Half Man will be in his trailer, alone.'

'How do you know?'

'Because he always is, every Friday. He goes through his dope money and he gets the next payment ready for his man, so he can refill his statue of Jesus. I have to go round there at eight, to pick up the money to take up to Tampa.'

'Do you go round to the trailer at that time every week?' Miller asked.

The King nodded.

'Well then, isn't that going to look just a little bit suspicious?'

Helen shook her head.

'When Frankie finds the body, the King will be having coffee with two solid alibis in Saint Pete.'

'What do you mean, solid?'

'They're police officers,' the King said.

'And what do you mean, "When Frankie finds the body"?'

'Frankie,' Helen said, 'has to find the body.'

'Why?'

'Because she would. Because that would be normal. And we like normal. She goes over to take him his food at nine. Believe me, Frankie has far worse nightmares than finding Vincent Makin's body.'

'What about Alex?'

'Alex will be with Frankie in the bar. I'll keep her there, when Frankie leaves.'

'How?'

'Trust me dear, I will.'

'So what you need to do,' the King told Miller.

'Me?'

'What you need to do, is just sit in the bar until eight, and make sure nobody leaves there for the compound.'

'Who could come over?'

He shrugged.

'Nobody could, I guess, except maybe Kennedy. But he's never here that early anyhow. So you sit there till seven...'

'Eight,' Helen corrected.

'Oh yeah, eight,' said the King.

'Oh, Jesus,' said Miller.

'Listen,' said Helen, 'you do want this done, don't you?'

'No,' said Miller. 'I don't. I don't want it done. Give me my money back, now.'

'I'm afraid it's too late for that, dear,' Helen said.

'Who says?'

'I say,' she told him. 'I'm his banker.'

'You can keep the money.'

She shook her head, and smiled.

'It's like I told you – you can't uncommission these things. The wheels are in motion. And I don't think you'd like the alternative.'

'What's that?'

'Me and the King would be obliged to tell the Half Man everything.'

Miller put his head in his hands.

'Why?'

'Because we couldn't risk him finding out. Don't worry, dear,' said Helen. 'We've done this lots of times before.'

'And at ten past eight,' the King said, 'you'll see me pull out on to 41 in the Tacoma.'

'And what do I do then?'

'Nothing,' Helen said. 'You just wait.'

'Till Frankie finds the body.'

'Till whoever finds the body. In this sort of job dear,' she told Miller, 'I'm afraid you'll find there always is a body.'

'Won't we hear the shot?'

The King laughed. 'In the Show Bar?'

He reached under his mattress and took out a pistol with a large silencer screwed on to the barrel.

'Not with this girl,' he said. 'She just sounds like a blowpipe. She sounds like a tiny gust of summer wind. Sometimes I think it must almost be a pleasure to be…'

'Anyhow,' interrupted Helen.

'Anyhow,' the King continued, 'then I'll take the pickup out the compound, like I'm supposed to, and drive up to Tampa. Except I'll drop this in the Bay on my way. Are you OK with that?'

'No,' said Miller.

'Why not?'

'Because something always goes wrong.'

'That's only in books, dear,' said Helen. 'You've read far too many of them. And the King has never read a book, have you King?'

Just after seven the following evening, he took his place at the Show Bar counter, choosing the seat next to the video blackjack game, which offered a clear view of the highway. Frankie and Hunter were serving. The Half Man's wife, who seemed worried that Miller had come back to the bar after his exclusion, gave him a look, but said nothing. He ordered a large brandy and a beer.

Little Paul came over and sat next to him.

'Are you OK?' the dwarf said.

'What?'

'You look very nervous. You seem on edge – as if you're really, really worried about something... what's the word – agitated, tense...'

'Keep your voice down.'

'Why?'

'You know that I'm not allowed in here any more.'

Miller saw Alex eating a burger, sitting at a table with Helen. After eight, he kept his eyes on the highway and clumsily fed dollar bills into the blackjack machine.

When nothing had happened by ten past eight, he felt himself beginning to relax. Then he saw the purple Tacoma on the 41, heading north.

He kept his eyes on the video screen. At five to nine, he watched Frankie preparing to leave the bar.

'Can Alex stay with me?' Helen asked her. 'I just promised her an ice-cream.'

'Sure,' Frankie said.

Five minutes later, she was back. She looked businesslike, more than distressed.

'Call the cops,' she told Hunter.

'You mean Dan Glidden?'

'No,' she said. 'The cops. The real ones.'

'You want me to call the cops?' he said. 'Here?'

'To the trailer,' she said.

'Why?'

'Because I just found a dead body in there.'

Hunter was about to protest again.

'Just do it,' she said. 'Now.'

He made the call.

She leaned over the counter, towards Miller.

'God, I feel sick,' she said.

'Was he shot?' the Englishman asked her.

'How do you know it's a he?' Frankie asked. 'How do you know it was murder?'

He didn't reply.

'Yes,' she said. 'I found him shot, in the living room. Once, through the head.'

'What are you saying?' Helen arrived in her wheelchair, with a feigned surprise worthy of her years in amateur dramatics. 'The Half Man has been shot?'

Frankie sat down next to her.

'It isn't the Half Man,' she said. 'It's the King.'

A set of headlights came down the dirt road off the highway and a car pulled up in the parking lot, opposite the Dowson plant.

'That'll be the cops,' said Little Paul.

Miller looked out. It was the purple Tacoma. The truck remained beside the water, with its tailgate facing the refinery plant and its motor running. Everybody in the bar, including Alex, was lined up against the windows, looking down at the vehicle. For a couple of moments, everything was silent. Then a pistol appeared through the driver's window of the car and two bullets struck the top of the bar windows, shattering the panes and showering the onlookers in broken glass. As they stepped back, picking shards out of their hair and clothes and reassuring themselves that nobody had been hurt, there was a third report, which had no visible consequences in the bar.

Frankie ran out of the back door. Miller followed her.

When she opened the driver's door, the body of the Half Man fell on to the dirt lot. On the floor of the cab, under the accelerator pedal, was his hand gun.

She turned to look at Miller, her face devoid of expression.

The onlookers had returned to the blown-out windows of the Show Bar, above.

'Go in,' she said. 'Tell them to keep Alex inside.'

Five minutes later, two police cars arrived; Glidden was at the wheel of one.

Seeing four officers and a detective approaching the bar, Miller slipped out by the back door and returned to his cabin.

At intervals throughout the night, he heard vehicles come and go, their blue flashing lights just discernible through the gap in his door. Miller lay awake, on his back, trying to make out the stern male voices that drifted towards him. They were loudest on his right, where forensic officers were going over the Half Man's compound, but he could also hear activity from the other side of the camp, where Vincent had parked the Tacoma. He waited for the police to come and question him, or for Kennedy to look in and bring news, but no visitor arrived.

Just after dawn, Miller fell asleep. When he woke up, it was ten thirty. He walked across to the kitchen, where Paul was clearing up breakfast, alone.

'Have they interviewed you?' Miller asked.

The dwarf shook his head.

'When are they coming back?'

'The cops? Glidden says they're not.'

'What?'

The dwarf shrugged.

'They say that the Half Man shot the King... so there's no point in talking to him,' he said, 'because he's dead.'

'Right.'

'And then the Half Man shot himself.'

'Why would he do that? Where's Frankie?'

'She stayed at the station last night.'

'Are the police still here?'

'Dan's over in the diner.'

Miller walked through to the Show Bar. He could see Glidden, who was clearly enjoying being questioned by a group of admiring customers, including Hunter and Coco.

'What happened?' Miller asked him.

'Like I've just told everybody,' Glidden replied, 'my sergeant said this is basically a case of ballistics and DNA. The Half Man's MK40 matches both incidents. His prints are the only ones on the gun. We have three fishermen who witnessed the Half Man's suicide.'

'Where's Frankie?'

'She was down at the station just now,' he said. 'The detectives told me they're making no further inquiries because they consider both cases closed. They said the inquest will be a formality: murder and suicide.'

'That was quick,' Miller said.

'Yes,' the policeman said. 'There was one weird thing, though. You know Hollis?'

'Hollis from the S and S?'

'Right. Well, one of the fishing guys saw Hollis hanging around the Half Man's trailer last night just before seven,' Glidden said. 'Hollis has a reputation as a hit man. When we went around to his trailer last night, we found he had an unlicensed firearm and a thousand dollars in cash.'

'What denomination,' Miller inquired, 'were the banknotes?'

Glidden gave him a vacant look.

'What's that about the banknotes?'

'Were they fifties? Miller asked, impatiently. 'Or twenties? Or a mixture?'

'Why?'

'I'm just trying to picture it,' said the Englishman. 'I never saw that much money before.'

'Oh that didn't shock me,' Glidden said. 'Not at all. I mean – I've seen lots more money than that. Lots more. Mountains of it. I've seen, oh, I don't know, like...'

'So what were they?' Miller interrupted.

'They were hundreds. New notes. There were ten of them.'

'So somebody hired Hollis...'

'It looked that way.'

'But he didn't kill anyone.'

'No.'

'Has he been charged?'

'He's been charged with possession of an unlicensed firearm. That's like a two-hundred-dollar fine.'

Miller felt a hand on his shoulder, and looked up.

Frankie was next to him. She looked exhausted.

'Hi, Dan,' she said.

She tapped Miller gently on the shoulder. 'I need to talk to you.'

They went down to Miller's cabin; he closed the door.

'Where did you sleep?' he asked her.

'I didn't sleep. I was up all night at the station. Then I had to go see the body.'

'That can't have been good.'

'It wasn't. He blew the top of his head off. He was very good with guns.'
'Where's Alex?'
'Alex is here; she came back earlier, with Helen. I guess she's asleep in her cabin.'
'I didn't know Helen had room.'
'Helen has room,' Frankie said. 'She has room now.'
'The police,' she added, 'have been everywhere.'
'What did you do with the, er... you know...' Miller glanced towards the door, 'with Jesus?'
'Oh, right before I called them, I threw Jesus in the river.'
She sat down on the bed, next to him.
'Why did he kill himself?' Miller asked her.
'Kennedy was down at the station in Tampa,' she told him. 'He said that Vincent drove up to his place last night, at half past eight, and parked the Tacoma outside the sports bar downstairs. Then he kept sounding his horn; people were screaming at him, but he wouldn't stop until Kennedy came down. When he did come, Vincent made him hand over a load of painkillers and barbiturates. Then he sat in the car waving his gun around, and sent Kennedy into the bar, for a half bottle of Wild Turkey to wash them down.'
'How did Kennedy get picked up?'
'Well you know what, Ed – a packed bar with ten outside tables, a legless gunman behind the wheel of a purple pickup, with his fist on the horn for five minutes, shovelling down pills and drinking whisky from the bottle before he set off – I guess somebody must have noticed them.'
'Bang goes his practice,' said Miller.
'I'm afraid so.'
'What was the Half Man taking all this stuff for?'
'Because he was dying.'
'What? He said he was OK.'
'Vincent said a lot of things.'
'Did you believe he was OK?'
'Sure I did.'
'Did Kennedy know about this?'

'He said Vincent only told him the truth last night. The hospital had said he had maybe three months.'
She gently took hold of his bandaged fingers.
'How was it with your wife?'
'It was OK.'
'She doesn't want you back, then?'
'Apparently not.'
'Alex told me that she's really beautiful.'
He lit a cigarette, and said nothing.
'And she told me about your daughter.'
'Oh?'
'She said that she's very good at Latin.'
'Right.'
'And she said that you had her in tears, is that right?'
'Yes.'
'How old is she?'
'Who?' Miller asked, hoping to change the subject.
'Your daughter. What's her name by the way?'
'Ellie.'
'How old is she?'
'Eight.'
'She's eight,' Frankie said, 'and you made her cry.'
Miller didn't reply.
'Haven't you missed her while you've been out here?'
'No,' he said.
'Have you ever missed her?'
'No.'
'I don't believe you.'
'It's true.'
'You never missed your own daughter?'
'Because she wasn't part of my life. Because she belonged to my wife. Because...' He remembered the phrase Elizabeth had used to him. 'We didn't connect.'
'Alex said that when she tried to talk to you about it afterwards, you went all weird.'

'All weird?' Miller looked at her. Her dark eyes were on him, and he turned his head away.

'That's what Alex said. "All weird". She said you were driving the truck, and you put your head down on the wheel and you started to cry. Did you go all weird?'

Miller cleared his throat. 'Yes,' he told her.

'Did you cry?'

He nodded.

'Why was that, then?'

'I think I might be missing her now.'

'Alex told me something else, as well.'

'Oh yes?'

'She told me that you came into some money.'

'Did she tell you how much?'

'She said fourteen hundred dollars. She said she counted it herself.'

'She did. She counted it perfectly. You see…' He held out his bandaged fingers. '… I can't count.'

'No,' said Frankie. She looked around the cabin. 'But I can. Can I count it, too?'

He took the plastic bag from under the mattress. Frankie counted out the four hundred-dollar bills.

She put both arms round him.

'I don't care what you did,' she said. 'It's over.'

They walked down to Cabin Two. Helen was sitting on her bed, alone, with a handkerchief in her hand.

'Alex is asleep in Paul's place,' she said. 'We put her there because it was quieter.'

Frankie left for the dwarf's cabin.

'Come and see us later,' she told Miller.

'In a minute,' he said.

He sat down in the easy chair, opposite Helen.

'Tea?' she said.

Miller shook his head.

'Can I get you something else?'

'I'd like my thousand dollars.'

'Now you know very well it doesn't work like that,' she said, as if speaking to a child. 'No two for ones, no refunds.'

'Let me see it, then,' he said. 'Count it for me.'

'I can't do that,' she said. 'I don't have it, dear.'

'Where is it?'

'I gave it to somebody.'

'You gave it to Hollis,' Miller said.

'Look, there's no point getting yourself worked up about this, Ed...'

'Why did you give a thousand dollars to Hollis?'

'Because you can't get two for one,' she said.

'So after we told the King to kill the Half Man...' Miller said, 'you paid Hollis to wait outside afterwards, then kill the King. Except that he didn't.'

'No. Because Vincent screwed it up by shooting my husband.'

'How did that happen?'

'The King bought that pistol off some friend of the bartender at the Skirts and Spurs,' she said. 'Right after you gave him the money, he spent a couple of hours in the Skirts and Spurs, getting drunk and talking big to his buddies about what kind of things he might like to do with it. I told him at the time that was real stupid.'

'So the Half Man was ready for him?' Miller asked.

'Right,' she replied. 'Vincent was a guy... how can I put this – for a very unpopular man, he had a lot of friends.'

That evening, Frankie knocked on his door. She was holding a large carrier bag, stuffed with clean clothes and bottles of medication. Alex was standing behind her, barefoot. Her last bandage, Miller noticed, had been removed.

'We can't stay in the camp tonight,' Frankie said. 'Let's go.'
'Where to?' he asked her.
'Where you like.'
'What in?'
She pointed to the compound.
'There's only the trucks.'
'Do you have any money?'
She nodded.
'Hang on,' Miller said. 'There's something I have to do first.'

He took the four hundred dollars and the page from the Sears catalogue, and walked with Frankie down to Cabin Three.

Paul was sitting on his bed when they came in, and gave them a muted greeting.

The dwarf seemed confused and disoriented by the previous night's events: like a goldfish, Miller thought, that has spent miserable years trapped in a small tank, and now sees the water level falling and a net poised over the water. Whatever else the Half Man had done, he'd offered Little Paul a kind of security.

'This is for you,' Miller said, and handed him the money.
'For me?' The dwarf looked at the four hundred, and hesitated.
'What's wrong,' said Miller. 'Did nobody ever give you money before?'
'Nobody ever gave me nothing before.'
The Englishman unfolded the page of the catalogue.
'Will this do?'
'Do?' Paul said. 'Look – achromatic lenses, convex crown glass and concave flint glass elements. All air-to-glass surfaces are multi-coated to maximize light transmission.'

'Of course it won't be as nice as your old one. And it will never be from Alaska.'

'No,' said Paul, 'but I bet my old one wasn't multi-coated to maximize light transmission, don't you?'

'I'm sure of it.'

'And that's the great thing – this one will be new. And then it will get old, and they'll say this telescope, it came all the way from Arlington, Florida. It'll be the just same, but better.'

'Right.'

'And then I can leave it to someone else, and it'll be old to them, when I, er…' Paul stopped. 'Frankie?' he asked.

'Yes?'

'What's going to happen to me here?'

'Nothing,' she replied. 'Like you say, it'll be just the same, but better.'

'Who's going to be in charge?' Paul asked.

'You are,' she said.

The dwarf laughed at the absurdity of this idea.

Miller helped Frankie and Alex into the cab of the Half Man's white breakdown truck, and they pulled out on to the 41, heading north. Driving, he noticed, was less painful than it had been. Five miles up the highway, he turned left on to the road down to Apollo Beach. The sun was a fierce red ball, straight ahead of them, hanging over the water, in the west.

They came round a bend and saw Little Paul's beautiful white hotel. It was a concrete, two-storey Ramada Inn. As they drove towards it, a black snake twisted across the tarmac in front of them.

'I didn't know they could move that fast,' Miller said.

'That's called a racer,' Frankie told him.

'Is it poisonous?'

'A racer?' said Alex. 'No. A racer means luck.'

He let Frankie book the rooms – two of the most expensive, on the first floor, with a balcony looking right over the tiny beach and a view across Tampa Bay. Miller, who'd lost track of the date, noticed the calendar behind reception was showing September 30.

'Do you have any luggage?' the desk clerk said.

Frankie showed her the carrier bag.

'Credit card?' he heard the woman ask.

'Cash.'

'In advance,' the woman told her.

'Sure.'

Miller walked over.

'Do you have bath robes?' he asked her.

'Bath robes?' the woman looked him up and down. 'Bath robes is eighteen dollars extra.'

'Get three,' he told Frankie.

Miller went into his room. The view from its full balcony window, otherwise idyllic, took in by the power station at Big Bend. He took the bandages off his hands. The palms were scarred and tender but the blisters had subsided. He stepped into the shower. The warm water had a curious, metallic odour . It was the first time he'd washed in hot water, he realized, since he left Barcelona more than two months ago.

He put on the white bath robe, then knocked on the door of Frankie's room. The three of them went and sat on a small wooden jetty in front of the hotel. Miller felt as if he had struggled ashore from a protracted and arduous shipwreck. Alex had changed into a clean T-shirt and shorts; she dangled her scarred feet in the water. Frankie was still in her white linen tunic and gloves. A couple of truck drivers were sitting at the hotel's Hawaiian bar, on a raised platform, fifty yards to their right. The sun was sinking over Tampa and Saint Petersburg, across the water; the bottom of the red globe, which infused the whole sky with gentler shades of orange and pink, was beginning to disappear below the horizon.

An elderly man was taking photographs of the sunset.

'It's beautiful,' Frankie said.

'Paul says it's the same every night,' Miller told her.

'Well it isn't,' the stranger interrupted.

'How often do you take pictures of it?' Frankie asked him.

'Every night.'

'Why?'

'Because it isn't the same.'
Frankie, who didn't trust hotels, had brought her plastic bag out with her.
Miller pointed at it and smiled.
'What is it?' Frankie asked.
'When the receptionist asked: "Do you have any luggage?", and she gave you that look, and then asked you for cash,' he said. 'I was just thinking – if only she knew what I own.'
'What do you own?'
'I own my birth certificate,' he said, 'and a framed photograph of a dead dog.'
Alex lit two Marlboros, and passed one to him.
'I used to spend four hundred dollars a week on laundry,' he added.
'We have money now,' said Frankie.
'You do?'
'We do.'
In the shallow water he could see a shoal of striped fish, like large tiger barbs, of a kind he'd never seen before.
'I'd like a dog,' Alex said. 'A girl dog. Can I have a dog?'
'Yes,' said Frankie. 'We'll call her...'
'Cathy,' said Miller.

Frankie put her daughter to bed, then came and sat next to him on the decking by the sea. Quietly, he told her about the progression of the previous evening's events and the conversation he'd had with Helen.
'That witch,' Frankie said. 'Vincent always said she'd be the death of somebody.'
'Do you think she was?' Miller asked her.
'Of course she was; what do you mean?'
'I mean was it her, or was it me?'
'I don't believe it was you,' she said. 'Vincent had weeks to live. The King, by the sound of the threats Vincent was making to him, possibly less.'
'Has Alex talked about her father?' Miller asked her.
She shook her head.

'I told her that he killed himself. But she knew that. She was in the bar.'

'What did she say?'

'Nothing. She hasn't spoken to me about her father for the past two years.'

'What – never?'

'No.'

'Is she going to be upset?'

Frankie looked at him.

'I think she's anticipated his death in the way that we all have,' she said.

'Which is?'

'Like a shadow lifting off the land. Like lifting up a stone, and all the bugs creeping out, and the light and the air coming in.'

'What does she want to be?' Miller asked.

'Alex? I don't think she's ever thought about that. You know what Vincent used to say to her?'

He shook his head.

'He used to say: "You're a waste of food." '

'What did you want to be?' she asked him.

'I think I wanted to be a hero,' he said. 'What did you want to be?'

'Invisible,' she said.

She took his fingers in her gloved hand.

'My hands are getting better,' he told her.

'Right,' she said. 'A good trick if you can do it.'

Miller took her glove off and held her hand. He looked at the flaking skin and the coarse red lines running across her palm.

'I never needed a gypsy to tell me what those lines meant,' she said.

'What?'

'Misery.'

'You're reading your past,' he said. 'Not your future.'

He walked over to the Hawaiian bar, where a morose-looking barman in a suit, a pink paper garland hanging feebly round his neck, served him two iced teas. Miller took them, and went back to Frankie. She put her head on his shoulder.

'I know what you own,' she said. 'But what do you want?'

'This,' he told her. 'What do you want?'

'I want that small house, with the yard, and the dog, up in the hills, in a cold country,' she said. 'Somewhere where I don't have to wear all this stuff. Is it cold,' she added, 'in England?'

'It's cold,' he said, 'but I can't go back to live there.'

'You can't go back to England?'

'I can't go back,' he told her, 'to what I was.'

'What's colder than England?'

'Scotland,' he said. 'Norway. Iceland.'

'Iceland sounds OK.'

'I might have to think about Iceland,' he said.

'I want some town that sounds quiet and peaceful,' she said, 'and has one of those names…'

'What names?'

'One of those names like a poem. I want some place that makes you think of falling snow. Some place where it sounds like you could really settle.'

'Anchorage,' he suggested. 'Anchorage, Alaska.'

'OK,' she said. 'How are we going to get there? Drive, or fly?'

'We're going to fly,' he said.

'Is it direct?'

'Not for us,' Miller told her.

'Why not?'

'Because there's somebody I have to see on the way, in London.'

'Is she very good at Latin?'

Miller swallowed.

'Yes.'

She put her hand on the back of his neck, like he had once done in the Half Man's kitchen, when she was trembling.

Tentatively, like a young girl, she kissed him.

'There you go,' she said. 'Like I said, I always knew that we'd find something you were good at.'

'How are we going to live?' he asked her.

'Vincent left a lot a money.'

'Oh, yes?' he replied, with apprehension in his voice.

'A lot. Apart from the illegal stuff – that was all in cash; the cops took all that – he had real estate, and fairground rides, and concessions.'

'What are you going to do with that – sell it?'

'Sure.'

'What about the camp?'

'I think we'll leave Little Paul the camp, don't you?'

'Did Vincent make a will?'

'No. In Florida law it goes to me. I think if he'd had more time to think, he wouldn't have left me anything. Oh – by the way…'

She reached into her carrier bag, and pulled out an envelope. The back of it was stained with what he took to be strong coffee. Looking more closely, he saw that it was blood.

'What's that?"

'He left a suicide note,' she said.

'What? Why didn't you give it to the police?'

'Because I was frightened what it might say.'

'What does it say?'

'I don't know.'

'What do you mean, you don't know? Why don't you know?'

'I don't know,' she said, 'because I haven't opened it. It wasn't addressed to me.'

She handed the envelope to him, and he turned it over.

In the top left corner, he saw the single word: 'Ed.'

He looked at it, in horror.

'Open it, then.'

'I haven't had a lot of luck with envelopes just lately,' he said. 'Is this a joke?'

'Do I look like I'm joking?'

He tore it open. Inside was a piece of cheap lined paper that looked as if it had been torn out of an account book.

He spread it out on his knee. He had to tilt the paper up slightly, to read it by the light of the setting sun. The message had been written in block capitals, in felt marker. Even so, it took Miller a moment to make out the words.

'To Ed,' it said. 'My one good deed.'